SUBTOTAL RECALL

Cassidy was surprised to find her pulse rate steady as she struggled to convince herself that she had heard her friend correctly.

"Rowena, don't you see? You're the only other person I've met here that once knew they came from somewhere else. Maybe you don't remember it anymore, but at least you realize that you don't remember. Since I got here, all I've had is a vague feeling that I belonged somewhere else. Then I started to remember things, and to see that there are things *missing* here—things that should be here, but aren't."

"I know what you mean about feeling that things are *weird* here," Rowena said, her voice oddly flat. "But I'm not sure that I have that feeling anymore."

Cassidy gave Rowena a gentle shake. "You do still have that feeling—you have it right now, don't you. You know what it means to *remember*."

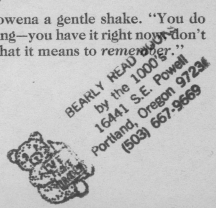

By Karen Ripley
Published by Ballantine Books:

PRISONER OF DREAMS
THE TENTH CLASS

The Slow World:
Book One: THE PERSISTENCE OF MEMORY

THE PERSISTENCE OF MEMORY

Book One of *The Slow World*

Karen Ripley

A Del Rey Book

BALLANTINE BOOKS • NEW YORK

A Del Rey Book
Published by Ballantine Books

Library of Congress Catalog Card Number: 93-90514

ISBN 0-345-38120-3

Manufactured in the United States of America

First Edition: Novemeber 1993

To my mother, who always wanted me to write "something with horses and without so much sex." Mom, this is probably as close as I'll ever come to that!

PART ONE ◀‖‖‖

Chapter 1 ◀||||

Suddenly she was just *there*: crouched over the pumping withers of the galloping horse, with its bare back hot and slippery between her clenched knees and its powerful muscles surging beneath her thighs. A light froth of lather whipped back past her legs as the rush of wind brought stinging tears to her eyes and the insistent slap and tug of dangling vines and branches threatened to unseat her. And although her only anchor and her only means of control was the hold of her fingers, tightly wound in the steel-gray horse's long, flying mane, she felt amazingly little fear. Even when she heard the shouts and the sound of crashing in the brush and the thud of hoofbeats behind her, and even when the horse beneath her thrust forward faster through the clawing vegetation, and adrenaline burst like a firecracker in her veins, what she felt was more a sense of pure exhilaration than fright. It was only when the adrenaline's buzz had spread, ripplelike, through her limbs that she realized there was something that did frighten her. For when she took the split second to think about it, she discovered that not only did she not have the faintest idea where she was, or why, or even how the hell she'd come to be there: She did not know *who* she was.

Beneath her, the horse's body suddenly seemed to drop away, so precipitously that for a moment she felt the abrupt coolness of the passing air on the exposed wet fabric that covered her inner thighs. Then her body automatically rejoined the horse's, and they were sliding pell-mell down a long gravelly slope. There the heavy growth of trees and brush had thinned, but damp iron-colored strands of the horse's mane still beat like whips against the bare skin of her forearms, and a gathering shower of small rocks and clods of earth, plowed up by the horse's hooves, rained down from behind upon her, pelting her head and shoulders. Balancing herself over the steeply pitched withers, she dug her fingers even more deeply into the thick, foam-flecked mass of the horse's mane and blinked furiously to try to clear her vision.

At the bottom of the rocky hill, the horse crashed through a chest-high hedge of gnarled and thorny canes. The barbs snatched at the legs of her denim jeans, pocking the already well-worn fabric with fresh tufts of white. Beyond the sloping sprawl of briars, the land dipped and flattened, spreading out into a marshy plain that was studded with the blackened stumps of dead trees and hammerhead-shaped tuffets, limned with brilliant green moss. Light, flat and clear, from a sun directly overhead, reflected sharply off the opaque and oily surface of the water, shimmering in the heat and glittering with insects. Reflexively she straightened slightly on the horse's back, as if by this totally instinctive movement she could bring the animal's haunches up under it and brake its heedless speed. But the gray horse never hesitated, never slowed. It hit the swampy ground at a full-out gallop, great slurping jets of muddy water shooting out like brown wings from beneath its pounding hooves.

It was crazy; a horse couldn't—or wouldn't—run in muck like that. But this horse could and did. Wincing helplessly as they shot past the rotted spearpoints of dead trees and the anvillike protrusions of root-laced mud, she nearly had to close her eyes in a desperate attempt at self-preservation. Something, however, made her not only keep her eyes open, but risk a glance behind her. Above the roiling, sucking sound of her mount plowing across the marsh, she heard the wild rattle of loose gravel and the excited shouts of several voices. Her pursuers had reached the slope.

There were at least three of them; she could count that many riders as they slid down the loose shale of the hillside. The two in the lead were mounted on chestnut horses, with a third close behind on a blood bay. There could have been still more riders beyond the lip of the slope, but she didn't look back again to make sure. She didn't think that their exact number mattered much anyway, because the ones she had seen were all mounted on big, long-legged, powerfully built horses; horses that, like hers, looked as if little things like thorny bushes or deep bogs weren't going to slow them down any.

An unpleasant mixture of perspiration and splattered swamp water glued her short-sleeved knit shirt to her chest; beneath it, her heart was thudding like a drum. And for the first time she was certain, grimly and absolutely, that it all wasn't just some kind of race or game. The riders were really chasing her—and she didn't want to be caught.

Flying gobbets of mud and fetid water continued to spatter her face and body, making the gray horse's back and sides grow even more slippery. Squinting against an eyeful of the foul liquid, she could see that she was already nearing the far margin of the marsh. Cattails, with their flattened and leathery leaves cutting like green saw blades, whipped at her boots and pants legs as the horse heaved itself up out of the sucking muck. Then they were on solid ground again, plunging through a dense copse of low willow and red dogwood, before the thicker growth of trees abruptly resumed.

There was no trail—or at least there was no trail that she could see. How the hell did the horse know where it was going? The gray was like a jackrabbit, leaping and dodging around the trees. She had never known a horse with such a feckless disregard for its own neck. Or had she? Hunching more tightly over the bounding muscles of the horse's neck, trying to duck the branches slapping at her, she was again forced to admit to herself that she wasn't sure what she knew. Was this even her horse? It put a whole new perspective on her pursuers. Maybe there was a good reason they were chasing her: Maybe she was a horse thief.

For just an instant she felt the hot, sweat-soaked body beneath her hesitate, almost as if the horse had read the moment of indecision in her mind. Forcing her head up, she quickly realized why the gray's furious pace had slackened slightly. They had reached the crest of a long, serpentine moraine of land. Its slopes, like the hill they had just climbed, were thickly wooded; but the spine of the crest was sharply eroded and relatively clear of growth, although calling it a trail would have been stretching the limits of the definition. The options were obvious: Go down the next slope and hit the trees again, or strike out across the rocky crest. For the first time during that crazy ride, she felt as if the choice were entirely hers.

On the incline below them, she could hear the other riders crashing inexorably closer through the brush. Within seconds they would be in sight again. *Shit!* she thought. Why was she suddenly in control *now*? She felt a little spasm go through her limbs, a volatile mixture of excitement and fear. *The crest*, something told her: *Take the crest*. There wouldn't be any cover, but at least the gray would be able to make better time without the hindrance of the trees. And then, as soon as the decision about their course formed in her mind, the big horse altered its direction. The surging body beneath her pivoted, the gray's bunched haunches propelling them forward again with a rattling shower of loose gravel and dirt.

Although the spine of the moraine was free of brush and trees, the ground was uneven, steeply graded, and covered with sharp scales of shaley rock. The horse's hooves slid and slipped, throwing up a clatter of shardlike pebbles. On the hillcrest the sunshine was unfiltered, and on the brightly lit trail the air that rushed through her hair and whistled in her ears was warm and muggy. Flakes and clods of drying mud and random bits of amputated vegetation that had caught on her skin and clothing were being shed in a wake of debris. But with the big gray's sudden surge of renewed speed, she once again felt some of the same exhilaration she had felt when she had first found herself on the galloping horse's back. Clenching the whipping salt-and-pepper mane more tightly in her fingers, she gave the great curved neck a giddy squeeze of encouragement.

"There! On the hill!"

The shout was so loud and the words were so distinct, even over the sound of the horse's hooves and the rattle of the rocks, that she half expected to turn her head and see the other riders were right behind her. But when she did turn, she saw that a good hundred yards still separated them. That was still too close, and her pursuers' horses looked fresh and able. There definitely were three of them, and they were closing fast.

Her own horse was still running flat out, or as flat out as any horse could have run on those damned rocks. But the heat that was seeping through her wet jeans legs had grown more intense, and she noticed that the horse's sweat, once a frothy lather, had grown stickier and less profuse. The ribs between her spread knees still moved in and out in a steady rhythm, without distress; but the rate had increased. The gray wasn't in trouble yet, but it was tiring. If it had all been in fun, they were already long past the time when she would have called a halt.

Okay, she thought, if she couldn't outrun these assholes then she would just have to outwit them. A good strategy, but with one glaring flaw: She didn't know who these assholes were. And other than the fact that they'd demonstrated a fierce determination to catch her and a wild disregard for her and their own safety, she found she had no idea what their motives were. She also had no idea just what they were capable of.

That thought caused her head to snap around again, and made her blink and strain to try to make out some detail on the mounted figures riding crouched on the trio of big horses that thundered right behind her. But in the heat of the moment, she still couldn't see them clearly: a splash of bright clothing, a whip of hair, the sudden glint of metal in the sunlight. And in spite of the gray's impressive speed, they were steadily gaining on her. Soon they'd be near enough for a more detailed inspection, she concluded ironically.

On either side of her, the shaley ground was broadening slightly, the hillcrest beginning to flatten. Cautiously encouraged, she peered ahead to where the widening concourse steepened perceptibly. She was coming to some kind of plateau or mound, a scree-littered incline that was almost clear of vegetation. As the gray's big body tilted, its surging rear legs gathering beneath it for the climb, she found herself fervently hoping that the top of the crest would provide them with some miraculous means of escape.

Suddenly she felt a sharp, stinging pain in the middle of her back; then, before she could even twist around, another biting *ping* nipped the bare skin of her arm. What the hell—rocks? She risked diverting her attention from the gray's course just long enough to glance behind her again at the ragged line of her pursuers. She could see now for certain that at least one of the riders, one of those mounted on one of the chestnuts, was a man. He was brandishing a device of wood and leather that looked like some kind of sling. More projectiles whizzed past her, all harmlessly off target. But these sons of bitches meant business! Nearly to the top of the steep mound then, she again hunched more closely over her horse's back, willing it speed.

Beneath her the gray's muscles tensed and bunched, its head dropping, as if it were going to—what? Take wing and fly? The whimsical notion took on a certain desperate appeal as she suddenly realized just exactly what they were galloping straight into. Before them—seemingly directly ahead, as seen framed in the notch formed by the gray's two wet, slate-colored ears—the land ended abruptly in a rocky promontory, a breathtakingly sheer cliff that jutted out into thin air over a tree-glutted chasm, with no discernible bottom.

"Oh, God!" she exclaimed. Her fingers, still twined deeply in the horse's long mane, clenched so tightly that she felt the strands of coarse hair cut into her skin. Then the gray's rump dropped out from beneath her, and the big horse sat down and slid. Its braced legs plowed furrows in the loose shale, sending up a shattering wave of pebbles and earth. When they came to a halt, the horse was still crouched in an awkward squat, its nose just inches from the lip of the precipice.

So shaky that an actual tremor seized her arms, she sat gaping numbly at the yawning space before her. Behind her, someone laughed: a sound of triumph amid the rattle of rocks and the clatter of hoofbeats. In desperation she glanced from the rapidly closing trio of riders to the stunning drop-off before her. There wasn't even the saving grace of a river at the bottom of the chasm, just more rocks and brush and the tops of trees, sticking up like thick green lances.

"*Shit!*" she spat, despairing. It was like some kind of cosmic bad joke: So long, Butch Cassidy; so long, Sundance—

It took a few seconds, but when the realization hit her she nearly fell off the horse. Beneath her, the gray had suddenly swung around, its long neck whipping like a serpent's, pivoting on its rear legs a full 180 degrees. Automatically, without conscious consideration, she hung with the horse. But there was only one thought in her mind, something momentarily even more important than the vital business of saving her own neck. *Butch Cassidy and the Sundance Kid.* They were names, and there was an image that went with them: two desperate men pursued by relentless riders, helplessly poised on the edge of a lofty precipice. She had a point of reference, and suddenly the world was altered.

This was no dream; she was already sure of that. She'd never had a dream in which her wet legs actually chafed from a horse's sweaty bare back, or in which her back and arm still smarted from the blows of a couple of well-lobbed rocks. Still, there was a certain nightmarish quality to the sight that greeted her as the gray horse swapped directions and inexplicably charged directly back into the path of their pursuers. There wasn't enough room on the narrow summit to avoid the other riders; her horse didn't seem interested in even trying evasive maneuvers. As the gray charged, she had the fleeting impression of three very surprised faces. Momentarily startled, the other horses reflexively shied back, creating a ragged hole in their ranks. The gray dodged through the imperfect opening, slipping past so closely that she felt her knee brush the shoulder of one of the chestnut horses.

For a few seconds, with the rocky trail suddenly clear ahead of her, she almost thought they had pulled it off. But her sense of elation was short-lived. As she gathered herself again over the horse's withers and leaned down over the flying mane, she felt a jolting blow strike the back of her neck. An inch or two higher and the rock would have knocked her out, maybe even killed her; as it was, the force of the impact made her lose her balance. As she slid sideways over the gray's left shoulder, feeling the strands of mane being torn from her fingers, she found herself wishing she would lose consciousness, so it wouldn't hurt so much when she landed on that damned shale. But that didn't happen.

Chapter 2 ◀▥

Getting caught at all was bad enough; falling off her horse in the process was even worse. She had nearly fallen in front of the gray, but it agilely sidestepped her, the big hooves passing within inches of her shoulder. She tried to roll, but instead she hit the ground in an awkward three-point landing, on both knees and one arm, and felt the litter of scree cut right through the fabric of her jeans and bite into the bare skin of her forearm. The only thing she could have called luck was that she didn't get the wind knocked out of her, as well; once she had landed she was able to twist around immediately and face her antagonists. It was not a reassuring sight.

Two of the riders, those who had been on the chestnuts, were already off their horses and pounding toward her. They both were young men. One of them was black, muscularly built, with dark hair cropped in a crown of short ringlets. He had been the sharpshooter; as he ran, he swung his sling. The second man was smaller and more wiry, with long light-brown hair pulled back tightly in a ponytail at the nape of his neck. Both of them were shouting loudly.

"I got her! She's mine!"

"Yours? I saw her first!"

Flinching, she pulled up her knees and locked her arms around them, ducking her head in a universal posture of defense. Things were just getting worse and worse. First she'd been chased, pelted by rocks, and knocked off her horse, and it looked like she was about to be assaulted by those two homicidal rowdies. Grimly clutching her knees, she vowed to herself that they would not get by without one hell of a fight.

But to her astonishment, the two young men ran right past her. The gray horse—it was a mare, she could see from her

10

vantage point on the ground—snorted loudly and shied back as the two men both pushed and shoved at each other in their eagerness to try to catch hold of the exhausted animal.

"She's *mine*!" the black shouted, bumping his companion so hard that the other man nearly fell.

"Like hell! It was my rock you used!"

Stumbling and cursing they both tried to grab for the mare. Exhaling noisily, the gray sidestepped even farther, nearly lunging into the brush at the edge of the trail. The horse's big liquid-brown eyes rolled, showing a shiny rim of white.

Surprisingly, the two men began to pummel each other with their fists, screaming and yelping like a couple of children. But now that she could see them more clearly, she realized that was practically what they were; teenagers perhaps, with the pony-tailed white boy two or three inches shorter and a good twenty pounds lighter than his black companion. The black made another futile grab for the gray's sweat-streaked mane before the mare wheeled around and again easily evaded them. Then the two men merely redevoted themselves to attacking each other.

"Cut it out! Hey!—that's enough!"

She hadn't even been aware that the third rider had approached until the loud female voice had bellowed, nearly in her ear. Before she could turn to face this new threat, a sharp whine cut through the air between her and the squabbling boys and the ground exploded at their feet, peppering their legs with a shower of broken shale.

"I said *that's enough*!"

A woman sat astride the big bay horse, a gelding whose ruddy coat was still darkened in patches with sweat. In her hand she held a long tapered switch of wood, to which had been fastened a thin popper of leather. She flicked the whip again, slightly less emphatically, sending up another little scatter of pebbles.

The two boys hesitated, then took a reluctant step apart. The ponytailed boy's hands were still clenched into fists, but both of them turned obediently toward the mounted woman, breathing heavily.

"That's better," the woman said. With a deft movement that was almost too fast to follow, she flipped up the leather popper of her whip and caught it in her hand. She looked maybe ten or fifteen years older than either of the boys, and a good deal smaller, but she was clearly the boss. Sitting easily upon the bay horse, she was dressed in faded dungarees and a loose leather vest with no shirt beneath it. Her dusky skin was deeply tanned, even down the cleavage between her half-exposed breasts, and her dark hair was cut short to fit her head like a cap. Sunglasses, the reflective kind with lenses like mirrors, covered her eyes, and when she looked down upon their captive on the ground, her expression was calm and commanding.

"Get up," she told her.

With scarcely time to bemoan the woman's impersonal lack of concern, she scrambled stiffly to her feet. Her knees stung fiercely, and a fine coating of grit clung to the heel of her hand and the underside of her forearm, where blood had oozed from a mottling of tiny abrasions. Her head throbbed mercilessly. Trying to block out the pain and summon up what little dignity she could under the less-than-ideal circumstances, she deliberately ignored the two panting young men and turned to face the mounted woman with the whip.

"Who are you?" the dark-haired woman demanded.

That was the last question she had expected, and her surprise was transparent on her face as she gaped up stupidly at her captor. "You mean—*you* don't know?" she blurted out in amazement.

The mounted woman's expression changed then, the calm confidence dissolving into an exasperated air of annoyance. "Oh, great," she muttered, the whip drooping. "You just got here . . . "

She heard what the woman said, but it didn't really register with her as anything that was useful or that made any particular sense. Rather, she grappled futilely for the answer to the woman's question. Who *was* she? Staring up at the mounted woman, she could see herself as they must see her, her image reflected in the wide lenses of the mirrored sunglasses: a totally unremarkable young woman with straight, shoulder-length brown hair and stunned brown eyes, covered with filth and sweat. But when she reached inside of herself, deep within to where her sense of self should be, there was nothing—a chasm as empty and dangerous as the one into which she and the gray mare had nearly plunged.

Looking up at the woman responsible for her capture, she was suddenly consumed with a righteous sense of indignation. "If you don't even know who I am, then why the hell were you chasing me?" she demanded. Automatically she brushed with her good hand over the dirt and gravel embedded in her other arm. "Why were you attacking me—damn it, you could have *killed* me!'' she concluded, throwing a baleful glare at the two boys who still stood between her and the weary gray horse.

"I doubt it," the woman on the bay responded. She shook her head in apparent annoyance. Then, in answer to the original question, she added, "We wanted the horse."

"She's *my* horse," Cassidy immediately insisted; although she realized even as she said it that the ownership of the gray mare was among the many things she was unable to remember. But if the reception she'd just been given was any indication of the way horse thieves were treated around there, it didn't seem prudent to admit to the possibility that the horse wasn't hers.

"Oh, yeah?" the black teen retorted. "If you just got here, how could she be your horse? How could you even be a Horseman?"

From his inflection, she automatically heard the term as a proper noun, although the only context in which she understood the word was the obvious one: a person skilled in the handling of horses. And once again, she didn't have the faintest idea how to answer the question, since basic things like her own name, and just where the hell she was, were still eluding her. She was saved from having to fabricate some sort of answer only by the dark-haired woman's timely intervention.

"She could have brought the horse with her, Rafe; I've heard of it happening."

But the young man just shook his head and scowled. Now that she looked more closely at him, she could see that he wore an earring, a small gold hoop in his right ear, and as he shook his head the ornament winked in the sunlight. Beneath the tight, sweat-dampened fabric of the red tank top he wore, his muscles were still bunched tautly. "Sure!" he said skeptically.

The boy with the ponytail was eyeing her warily. If he seemed a little less aggressive, it was not because he believed her. To her surprise, she suddenly noticed that he was odd-eyed: his left eye was hazel and the right was a pale, pellucid shade of blue. He wiped his sweaty hands on the front of his ragged tan T-shirt. "If she is your horse," he said, "let's see you Call her."

Once again, the vocal inflection weighted the word, and once again, she understood the word only in its most literal definition. Too confused by then to continue to feign indignation effectively, she looked helplessly back to the woman who seemed to be in charge. To her chagrin, the woman on the bay horse appeared to agree with the boy's idea; she was nodding thoughtfully. "It'd prove your claim," she told her. "If you're a

Horseman, and she is your horse, then you're the only one who'd
know her true name.''

True name? First Horsemen, then Calling, and now true
name; the exchange was definitely becoming more and more
baffling. She didn't even know her *own* name—how the hell was
she supposed to know the name of the gray mare, a horse whose
actual ownership was still a complete mystery to her? Stalling
for time, she temporized, ''But if I called her by her true name,
then I wouldn't be the only one who knew it anymore, would
I?''

Obviously the literal approach had been the wrong one to
take. The two boys hooted derisively, and even the dark-haired
woman seemed visibly annoyed. ''Don't get smart with me,''
she said, giving her long whip an impatient little twitch. Beneath
the loosely laced edges of the leather vest, her shadowy breasts
bobbed slightly. ''Just Call her.''

''*If* she really is your horse,'' the black boy taunted.

''She's mine! I already told you—''

The woman on the bay horse had obviously reached the effective limits of her patience. ''Just Call her!'' she commanded
brusquely, tightening her grip on the haft of her whip.

True name or not, she understood by then that this Calling
was not an audible summons. She squeezed her eyes half shut,
trying to concentrate; but her headache bloomed afresh, as if
her brain were ballooning within her skull. Perspiration wept
from her pores.

From across the narrow, broken path of scattered shale, the
big gray mare was quietly watching her, with head low and
flanks moving slowly but deeply. The horse's thick forelock,
like a tangled crown of salt-and-pepper hair, nearly obscured the
gray's dark, wide-set eyes. But the horse was watching her, she
realized then; not just looking in her direction, but really *watching* her, as if she were waiting for something. Maybe the horse
really *was* hers, she thought desperately. She certainly felt an
extraordinary link to the animal. She remembered how twice
during the chase the mare seemed to have anticipated what she
was thinking: once in the trees, when she had momentarily fal-
tered because she wondered if she had stolen the horse; and then
again when they had climbed the moraine, and she'd had to
choose between brushy slope or the barren crest. She also viv-
idly recalled the surge of excitement she had felt on the galloping
horse's back, the rush of exhilaration, the feeling of power.

Searching the mare's watchful expression, she wondered, *Are you my horse?*

A spatter of gravel exploded at her feet, kicked up by the long leather popper on the dark-haired woman's whip, startling her back to the immediate situation. "Call her," the woman repeated impatiently.

They had said the horse had a "true name," a name only she, a Horseman, would know. Also implicit was that only the horse would hear her if she Called it by that name. As she helplessly studied the gray mare's big, calm eyes, she seized upon the only word that she could pull out of that aching chasm in her mind. Like the sudden, disjointed gestalt of Butch Cassidy and the Sundance Kid, the word caught in her head: *Dragonfly.*

The mare's short, curved ears swiveled, pointing forward as if at some secret sound. Then the horse nickered and stepped forward to come to her, the long-legged body swaying with a casual grace, the calm and unhurried way a grazing horse would move from place to place in a pasture. And as the gray reached her, she lifted her arms and the mare moved into them, putting her finely chiseled head over her shoulder. Stunned and relieved, she just hugged the horse's neck, burying her dirty face in the warm, sweet musk of the horse's damp mane.

Grumbling their disappointment, the two young men exchanged a look. The black stooped to retrieve his sling from where it had fallen during his squabble with his companion; then the two of them backtracked up the trail to where their mounts stood, munching on twigs from the bushes. The dark-haired woman seemed unaffected, as if the outcome of the whole demonstration had not mattered much to her one way or the other. But she did coil up her whip again, wrapping the lash around its wooden stock. When she looked down at the woman with the gray mare again, she said, "You'll need a name then, I guess. We can give you one if you don't remember yours."

She lifted her face from the gray's neck. "I don't think I—"

The two teens had already remounted, vaulting up onto their chestnut horses' bare backs with a familiar ease. "Are we taking her with us?" the ponytailed boy interrupted, visibly unenthused about the idea.

The woman on the bay gelding threw both boys a sardonic look. "A few minutes ago, you two could hardly wait to get your hands on that horse," she reminded them acerbically.

"Yeah, but we only wanted the horse," the black explained tactlessly. "Why do we have to take her?"

"Because she's a Horseman," the woman replied.

"Some Horseman," the black boy muttered, shoving the wooden shaft of his sling into the waistband of his pants. "If she's a Horseman, how come she fell off?"

She couldn't restrain herself any longer. She had Called the horse, and she was irked to think that the brash young man would deny her the title that she so desperately embraced even though she didn't fully understand it. The nagging ache in her head didn't act as a deterrent; if anything, it only served to goad her on. Glaring over at him, she snapped, "I fell off because you pegged me in the head with a damned *rock*, you stupid nigger!"

The epithet did have an effect, if not exactly the one she felt it should have. The black hesitated, staring at her suspiciously as if he were uncertain just what she'd called him. He shot a glance at his ponytailed friend, but the other young man seemed equally baffled. Even the dark-haired woman appeared unperturbed by the outburst, and simply continued as if the exchange hadn't taken place.

"Well, do you remember your name?" she asked her.

"Uh, Cassidy—my name is Cassidy," she blurted out, using the first of the few secret scraps of memory she had managed to pull from the vacuum.

As the two boys urged their chestnut horses past her on the rocky trail, the black threw her a reproachful look. "Cassidy." He snorted, tossing his head contemptuously—although whether at her personally, or at her choice of name, Cassidy wasn't sure.

"I'm Yolanda," the dark-haired woman offered, gesturing with the stock of her whip. "The lout with the big mouth is Raphael, and the charming fellow with the ponytail is Kevin."

As she was speaking, Yolanda's bay horse had begun to move forward, following the two chestnuts up the shaley trail. "Now let's go," she concluded. "We've lost enough time here already."

"Wait!" Cassidy called after her, turning so abruptly that she caused the gray mare to jerk back her head. "Where are you going?"

Yolanda's horse paused, but just barely; it was as if the dark-haired woman's impatience was being directly transferred to the big gelding, and he fidgeted at the delay. "First back to our camp," Yolanda replied. "Then, eventually, to the Warden."

The boys on the chestnut mares were already disappearing around a bend in the crest of the rocky moraine. Even the gray mare shifted restlessly now, eager to follow. "Wait a minute!" Cassidy protested. "Who is this Warden? Where did you come from—and where the hell are we now?"

"I'd just come along if I were you," Yolanda said, not even turning. "This isn't a good place to travel alone."

Unable to argue with that, Cassidy realized she really had very little choice in the matter at that point. Yolanda had let the bay horse spring forward again, practically forcing Cassidy to hop back up onto her mare or be left behind. Vaulting onto the horse was a lot easier than it looked; she realized she must have done it plenty of times before. Settling onto the horse's still-sticky back, she let the gray jog to catch up to the bay. But before she could repeat her protest, Yolanda just cut her off by saying "You're a Horseman, and you ride with a Horseman's camp now."

Ahead of them, the two young men were attempting to ride abreast on the narrow trail, playfully jousting for position, trying to bump each other's horse off the edge of the slippery scree and into the brush. Their previous flirtation with mayhem seemed forgotten.

"Yolanda, wait," Cassidy persisted, urging the gray up right behind the bay gelding. "Listen, if you won't tell me where you came from and where we're going, will you at least tell me where *I* came from?"

Without slowing or looking back, Yolanda replied, "I don't know that."

"What do you mean, you don't—" Cassidy had to break off to urge the gray forward as the bay surged ahead of them. The mare's shoulders moved up alongside Yolanda's horse's haunches, struggling to keep aside him on the broken, winding path.

"Yolanda," she said plaintively, "will you at least tell me what the hell I'm doing here?"

The dark-haired woman glanced back this time, briefly and impassively; but her response was just as terse and useless. "I don't know that, either," she said.

Chapter 3 ◀IIII

Cassidy had no idea how long Yolanda and the two boys had been chasing her, or how far they had come, but it took the rest of the day to return to their camp. On the trip back they skirted around some of the hazardous areas, like the bog, which originally they had all so blithely blundered through; and they more or less followed trails, rather than just crashing their way through the trees and brush. Cassidy was relieved to find that the chase did not appear to be typical of their usual style of riding. Gradually the sweat dried on the gray mare's back, leaving the fork of Cassidy's jeans just slightly sticky. The high, bright sunlight felt pleasant on the back of her knit shirt, and the horse's smooth and rolling gait was strangely soothing, lulling her with its timeless rhythm. If it hadn't been for the niggling ache in her knees and forearm—and the fact that she still had utterly no idea just what the hell was going on, and even thinking about it gave her a headache—she would almost have enjoyed herself.

As soon as they had traveled beyond the area Cassidy could remember, the place where she had sprung into consciousness on the galloping horse's back, the terrain became completely unfamiliar to her. Most of the land was forested, but the woods were crisscrossed with narrow trails and numerous creeks. Eventually the steep hills of the moraines gave way to longer, gentler slopes, most covered with thick brush and old-growth trees. And gradually the heavier vegetation thinned out, leaving small grassy clearings that then became larger and more confluent, until finally, by the time the sun had sunk low in the sky, the meadows predominated and the trees were confined to groves and patches.

Raphael and Kevin kept the lead on their chestnuts, with Yolanda riding right behind them. The long switch of her whip was

18

propped casually over one shoulder, its leather popper bobbing
in time to her gelding's gait. Cassidy could have ridden alongside
her once the land had become grassy and the trails had grown
broad, but there didn't seem to be much point to it. Although
the dark-haired woman had defended her from the two boys'
aggression, her response to Cassidy's last question still chilled
the younger woman and discouraged her from asking anything
more. Whether Yolanda was being truthful or just curtly face-
tious, her words had pretty much precluded further inquiries.
And beyond that, even attempting to probe the margins of that
appalling gap that lay where her memory belonged stimulated
an immediate pounding in Cassidy's head.

Long shadows from the occasional lone tree or bush snaked
darkly across the grassy trail. Her clothing had dried and the
breeze was beginning to feel chilly on Cassidy's bare arms. But
none of the others seemed to notice the falling temperature.
Raphael had even pulled off his tank top and hung it like a flag
from the wooden shaft of his sling, which protruded from the
waistband of his pants. And Yolanda was nearly shirtless as
well, her unbuttoned leather vest swinging loosely over her
browned breasts.

Cassidy gently squeezed the thick crest of the gray mare's
neck with her fingers, and one of the horse's scimitar-shaped
ears instantly curved back in acknowledgment. *Dragonfly* . . .
The horse was hers, of that much she was certain. The mare
was hers, and she was obviously a better-than-average rider.
Apparently that made her what Yolanda and the boys had called
a Horseman; but Cassidy couldn't help suspecting that there was
more to it than that. And why didn't she know where she was—
or even *who* she was, and how she'd come to be there? Worse
still, why was it that every time her thoughts even skated near
the edges of these terribly basic questions, her brain felt like it
was going to drop out from beneath her like loose rocks in a
landslide? The three people who had found her seemed alarmingly undisturbed by her incredible ignorance. Did Yolanda truly
not know the answers to Cassidy's questions—or were the three
of them so unperturbed because they actually were a part of
whatever bizarre misfortune had brought Cassidy there?

Throughout the afternoon, as she had followed Yolanda and
the two teens, Cassidy came to realize that she had been so
consumed with the magnitude of what she *didn't* know that she
hadn't given much attention to the things she *did* know. Beyond
the obvious—like how to verbally communicate and how to

ride—and even beyond the unexpected—like the image of Butch and Sundance, and the command of at least one racial slur—Cassidy discovered that she had a veritable wealth of unexamined, automatic knowledge. She knew, for example, that the tall coarse-stemmed plant with the delicate sky-blue flowers, growing scattered over the meadows through which they rode, was chicory. She knew that the small animals that occasionally erupted from the grass and scurried across the dirt trail were striped ground squirrels. And she knew which evergreens were spruce and which were firs and which were white pine. She knew approximately how long it would take the sun to set, and she knew from the kind of feathery, attenuated clouds that streamed across the deepening sky that there would be a change in the weather in the next day or two. She found that she knew so many basic physical facts about everything else she observed that she could not imagine how she still knew so little about herself. It deeply troubled her that she could not somehow extrapolate from all that external knowledge, and apply the same sense of recognition to the things that were . . . *missing*.

Throughout the long warm afternoon, Cassidy had had plenty of time to think about several specific things that especially bothered her. When Yolanda had found out that Cassidy didn't know who she was, Yolanda had said Cassidy had just gotten there. And although Yolanda had seemed annoyed, she didn't seem to have been surprised. It was as if Cassidy's confusion were of no importance to Yolanda. And yet there was nothing that Yolanda or the two boys had said that would suggest any of them had ever been through a similar disorienting experience.

Another thing that still confused Cassidy was the matter of names, "true" or otherwise. They had expected Cassidy, as the gray mare's owner, to know her true name; and yet when Cassidy had confessed that she didn't even know her own name, Yolanda seemed unperturbed. Her simple remedy for that deficit was to offer Cassidy a name, as if her former identity and the glaring fact that she couldn't even recall it were of no significance.

The last thing, which had at first seemed sort of trivial, nonetheless still deeply troubled Cassidy. Perhaps that was because it seemed so symptomatic of the bizarre sense of slightly skewed reality that she continued to feel about that place. When she'd grown angry with Raphael for his constant denigration of her abilities, she'd called him a "stupid nigger." The term had come to her in a single and discrete little burst of knowledge, the same way Butch and Sundance and Dragonfly had, but Cassidy had immediately known exactly what it meant. And yet Raphael hadn't. None of them had. Cassidy had been able to tell from his expression that Raphael suspected he was being specifically insulted—but he hadn't known what the word meant. Wherever and whatever she had gotten herself into, Raphael was one black person who had apparently never heard anyone called a nigger.

Cassidy tried, quite fruitlessly, to try to put all of the troublesome little things together and make out of them some larger, more meaningful whole. She found that if she edged around the question of her own past, she could keep the staggering headache at bay. Was it possible, even likely, that all three of these people had always lived there? That would help to explain some of what Cassidy was beginning to think of as gross cultural discrepancies. But nothing, at least nothing she could think of, explained the basic inconsistency that still dogged her thoughts: How could they so casually accept her total memory loss and even her presence there, when she herself was so profoundly disturbed by both—unless they knew what was responsible?

The sun had already set when they reached the Horsemen's camp. Cassidy had watched as the sky went from rose to gold to ruddy mauve and finally to a deep indigo blue, still brushstroked with the paler wisps of the feathery clouds. She had begun to worry that they were never going to stop—that they might just keep on riding right into the night. Although the horses were sure-footed and their night vision was more than adequate, Cassidy was becoming increasingly sore and tired. Her abraded and bruised forearm and knees ached stiffly, she was cold, and she really had to pee. Just when she was seriously considering asking Yolanda to at least call a temporary halt so that she could relieve herself, she heard Kevin call back something from the dimness ahead of them.

The trail had been gradually descending for some time, winding randomly along between some old-growth oak and poplars. The sound of night insects had become a steady drone, but Cassidy had only recently noted the ratcheting accompaniment of peeper frogs. A waning moon, still large but somewhat lopsided, had begun its climb in the sky. Cassidy peered ahead in the thin efflux of its faint yellowish light, searching the shadowy depths beneath the huge trees for some sign of habitation.

"You two circle around first," Yolanda directed the boys. "Make sure it's clear."

Raphael and Kevin disappeared between the dark boles of the trees, and Yolanda's bay gelding moved off the trail in the same direction. Cassidy was confused, but she didn't have to urge the gray mare to follow the bay; the horse automatically kept up with the big gelding. They slipped between the black columns of the trunks of a couple of huge, gnarly rooted oaks and out onto a long, moon-silvered spit of sandy beach. To her surprise, Cassidy realized that the trail had been paralleling a river. Now she could see the water clearly, sliding darkly past, its surface smooth and almost rippleless. The channel was narrow enough that she could see the silhouette of the tree line on the other side, backlit by the slightly lighter backdrop of the night sky.

With sinuous ease, Yolanda slid from the bay gelding's back, dismissing the horse with a fond pat. She stood, slowly scanning the shadowy trees and brush around them, holding onto the slender shaft of her whip like a staff. "Well, here we are," she said, to no one in particular.

Glancing around, Cassidy felt perplexment and disappointment in equal measure. "What do you mean, here we are?" she asked Yolanda. "This is *it*—this is your *camp*?"

Yolanda turned and gave her a funny look. The older woman had finally removed her mirrored sunglasses, but now it was too dark to really be able to see her eyes clearly anyway. "Yeah, this is it," she replied, as if Cassidy's disillusionment had been both inexplicable and unreasonable.

"But—there's no one here!" Cassidy blurted out, unable to conceal her dismay.

"What do you mean, there's no one here?" Raphael's voice came from right behind her, making Cassidy jump involuntarily. The black boy's chestnut mare stopped right alongside the gray. He grinned over at her, both his earring and his neat white teeth gleaming in the moonlight. "We're here, aren't we?"

Cassidy looked from Raphael to Yolanda; then she shook her head in frustration. "But—but I thought there'd be other people here," she explained insistently.

"We're lucky there aren't," Kevin remarked. His chestnut mare, silently materializing like a wraith from the shadowy ranks of the slender reeds that lined the riverbank, stepped daintily out onto the sandy beach. "Perimeter's clear," he reported to Yolanda as he slipped off the horse's back.

"Okay, let's get the stuff," Yolanda said.

As Raphael dismounted, the two chestnut horses heaved twin snorts of exaggerated relief. Yolanda's bay was already a short distance away on the little peninsula, down on his knees in the sand, rhythmically rubbing his long neck in the coarse grains. Within moments, the chestnuts had joined him and then all three of them were rolling and squirming and kicking, sending little sprays of sand sailing out across the beach.

Cassidy had been so engrossed in her own disappointment that she had almost forgotten about the mare beneath her. The gray shifted restlessly, pricking her ears eagerly at the other frolicking horses. Cassidy tried to ease herself down gently, but the soft ground still jolted her from the soles of her feet all the way up her aching legs to her spine and the fragile-feeling base of her skull. The minute Cassidy was off her, the gray hurried to join the other horses in an orgy of grunting and rolling. For a moment Cassidy half wished she could join them as well; she felt filthy, exhausted, and sore.

"Looks like everything's okay," Yolanda said. She and Raphael were tugging on the edges of what appeared to be some kind of tarp or canvas that had been shallowly buried at the edge of the beach, while Kevin helped brush loose the last of the sandy earth that had covered their cache. "Rafe, you get the ground covers. Kev and I'll get the fires going."

Cautiously Cassidy approached them. They were all busily bent over the canvas-wrapped bundles and none of them appeared to even notice her. "Uh—do you have anything to eat?" she asked hopefully.

Yolanda looked up from where she was kneeling in the sand, several small sacklike containers in her hands. In the faint moonlight, Cassidy couldn't tell what the pouches were made of, much less what they contained. Even Yolanda's face was just a shadowy outline, framed by the blunt line of her short hair. "We will," she replied, "as soon as we get a fire going."

Cassidy hesitated, glancing from the kneeling woman to where the two boys were already separating and sorting other items from the cache. "Is there anything I can do to help?" she asked warily.

She fully expected some kind of wise-ass remark from one or both of the teens, but they remained silently engrossed in their tasks. Yolanda merely shrugged and said, "No, not right now."

Cassidy looked across the shadow-pocked stretch of sand to the shoulder-high band of reeds that hemmed the river's edge. "I'll just go down by the water for a few minutes then," she told Yolanda. "I need to, uh, clean up a little."

Yolanda didn't even glance up that time, but her tone immediately commanded Cassidy's attention. "Be careful," she said.

Raphael's head lifted; his wide-set brown eyes were liquid in the moonlight, and he gave Cassidy a long look. "Yeah, don't go in the water," he elaborated.

Staring at them in mild confusion, Cassidy said, "It's not that deep—not right along the edge anyway." Actually, given the relatively narrow width of the river and the character of the water flow, Cassidy was reasonably certain the water couldn't be over her head, even in the middle of the stream.

Kevin looked up from where he crouched bent over the sandy ground tarp; his oddly colored eyes regarded her with a solemn blend of tolerance and caution. "It's deep enough," he said enigmatically.

Yolanda was still sorting the various sacks and bundles; she didn't look up again. "Just be careful," she repeated, "and stay out of the river."

Still puzzled, Cassidy turned and crossed the cool dark sand. The yielding surface felt gratifyingly soft beneath her feet. As she approached the river, she walked right by the four horses. They had grown tired of wriggling around on their broad backs and had all fallen to feeding, greedily cropping the tender whip-like shoots of willow that grew in profusion from the bases of several ancient broken stumps near the water. If there was anything around to be careful of, Cassidy thought the horses seemed particularly unimpressed. Did Yolanda and the boys think she'd drown? Hell, she wasn't that stupid, even if she didn't happen to remember who she was. As she pushed her way into the thick mass of bobbing reeds, automatically feeling in the dark for the water's edge with the toe of her boot, Cassidy thought that it would have been far more helpful if they had shown some of that same concern for her health and welfare when they had been chasing her across hill and swamp earlier—especially when they had started to pelt her with those damned rocks.

It was a little awkward squatting down in the reeds, but her sense of relief at being able to empty her bladder made the clumsy maneuver well worth the trouble. Once Cassidy had pulled her jeans up again, she carefully waded a little farther through the tall fronds, testing ahead of her with one foot. The ground was spongy, but the water hadn't soaked through her boots yet. She thought if she could just get a little closer to the open water, she'd be able to wash some of the sweat and grit off her hands and arms and face. A more thorough cleanup may have been indicated, but she was too exhausted to plan anything more complicated.

The hum of insects seemed loudest there at the water's edge; the smell of damp, peaty earth swam in her nostrils, and the sweet cloying odor of decaying vegetation. Flattening down the reeds, Cassidy squatted again, cupping her hands toward the rippled, moon-brushed surface of the river. Just an instant before her fingers touched the water, something leapt up from between her forked legs, startling her so badly that she actually sat back on her rump in the wet cattails. Heart racing wildly, for a few seconds she was literally paralyzed with fear. Then, feeling stunned but foolish, she stared down at the gleaming, fist-size frog that stared back up at her, goggle-eyed, from the shallow water.

"Brrraaacht!" the bullfrog twanged.

"Shit!" Cassidy muttered softly, lifting her rump from the ground.

Swiftly, so gracefully that it almost seemed suspended upon the silvery plane of the calm surface of the river, the frog glided away from the bank. The rhythmic movements of its legs left a thin tracery of ripples across the water. Letting out her breath in a long, ragged sigh, Cassidy once again bent over the edge of the river and quickly dipped her cupped hands into the water. In a way she was glad that it was too dark for her to see exactly how clean the water was; if she was washing herself with pond scum, she would just as soon not have known about it. At least the water smelled fresh and it felt cool; the effect on her dirty face and sticky arms was wonderful. She scooped up more water, exhaling through her nose as she let the water sluice across her face to drip from her elbows and chin. Finally, when she glanced out again over the river, what she saw there made it, for a few moments, quite impossible for her even to draw another breath.

The night air was still calm and cool, abuzz with the manic chorus of insect sounds. The rising moon, an asymmetrical circle of electrically silver light, still poured its ghostly luminescence over the surface of the water. And across that surface, perhaps midway between the two banks of the river, a huge, dark sinuous shape rose from the water. It was slick and gleaming, a featureless coil with no discernible beginning or end, propelling itself forward with a screwlike motion, undulating so smoothly that its passage scarcely raised a ripple.

Cassidy could not move, but she could react. *Ohmygod!* she thought. *Ohmy—*

And then the thing was gone. It was as if she had blinked, and it had disappeared.

Only she hadn't blinked.

Gasping for breath, Cassidy straightened herself with a jerk, abruptly pulling back from the water's edge. She sat back against one of the wet, fibrous tuffets at the base of the reeds, staring open-mouthed at the now-empty moonlit surface of the river.

Nothing.

The dark water slipped silently by, smooth and ordinary, leaving her suddenly to wonder if she had seen anything after all.

Getting stiffly and clumsily to her feet, Cassidy took one last long look at the quiet surface of the water. *That was no fish!* she told herself vehemently. What else could there be in a stream that size? Fish and snakes and maybe the occasional irate snapping turtle—but nothing like *that*. Taking a step backward into the thick net of cattails, Cassidy heard the soft snort of one of the horses, only a few yards behind her. She tried valiantly to pull herself back to reality—or to whatever the hell was passing for reality around there these days . . . Maybe it was a log?

That was no log! she countermanded promptly.

Only one real possibility occurred to her then: She was losing her mind. First she didn't know who she was, or where she was, or why she was there. Next she was beginning to hallucinate. No wonder these people didn't seem sympathetic to her plight; she was *crazy*. Could that be why she had been brought there— was the place a refuge for lunatics?

Turning from the river, Cassidy pushed her way through the stand of cattails. The four horses were pretty much where they'd been when she'd passed them before. They were feeding less greedily and more leisurely, selectively nipping off leaves and twigs from the willow shoots, their facile lips deftly sorting through the whiplike branches. Only the gray mare looked up, giving Cassidy a friendly nicker as she walked back across the sand.

Yolanda and the two teens had been busy while Cassidy had been off getting the shit scared out of her. Four small fires burned brightly on the beach, each one forming a corner of a rough square about twenty feet across. Yolanda was sitting cross-legged before one of the little blazes, tending something cooking over a metal grill. Whatever it was, the smell instantly made Cassidy's mouth water. As she felt her stomach cramp hopefully, she realized she had no idea how long it had been since she'd last eaten.

Winding her way past the other fires, Cassidy gave both Raphael and Kevin a curious glance. Both of them were sitting on the rolled-up ground tarp, tinkering with some kind of pot or pitcher standing at the edge of the third fire. Then a totally familiar and utterly welcome aroma reached her nostrils: coffee.

"God, that smells good!" she exclaimed.

"Almost ready," Yolanda told her, looking up from her cooking. She still wore the mirrored sunglasses perched on the crown of her head; the reflective surface of the lenses caught the flickering firelight like a tiara of flames. As Cassidy stepped closer to her, she could see that the mouth-watering aroma from the grill was coming from a phalanx of sausage links, sizzling and spitting over the fire.

Raphael poured dark liquid from the metal pot he and Kevin had been tending into a big, double-handled mug. As he handed it to Cassidy, he eyed her with a certain sardonic amusement. "How was the water?" he asked her, his mouth pulled into a smirk, his big dark eyes subtly mocking her.

Dropping down onto the sand beside Yolanda, Cassidy shrugged. "It was fine," she replied with deliberately affected nonchalance. Already the raw immediacy of what had happened at the river's edge seemed to be fading; and with that waning went much of the certainty that it had even taken place at all. She was exhausted, confused, in a dark and unfamiliar place. What she had seen—what she *thought* she had seen—seemed less and less plausible with every passing minute. And she was damned if she was going to give the black youth the satisfaction of hearing her admit that she was losing her mind.

The firelight fluttered over the pockmarked surface of the sand, throwing the irregular contours of the ground into sharp relief. The quivering glow painted all four of them with a strangely harsh and intermittent light. Over the rim of her mug, Cassidy studied the quadrangular arrangement of the fires again, puzzled by the seemingly needless redundancy.

"Why do we need so many fires?" she asked Yolanda, wrapping her hands around the warmth of the heavy mug.

Raphael, the lower half of his face covered by his own mug, made a rude snorting sound. Ignoring him, Yolanda replied, "Watch fires."

"Four of them?" Cassidy said quizzically. "What the hell are we watching for?"

Apparently relegating that remark to the domain of rhetorical questions, Yolanda merely concluded, "This way there's one for each of us."

Cassidy decided not to pursue it. She had already learned that around here, even a direct question did not always garner an answer; and that was assuming you knew which questions to ask in the first place. She was just too tired and hungry to waste any more energy on the subject.

Kevin unwrapped a greasy-looking paper parcel that contained a blocky loaf of some kind of bread. Using a long thin knife, which appeared to be made of a single piece of metal, he pared off several thick slices and passed them to Yolanda. She used each slice like a mitt, slapping it over one of the sausage links and lifting it off the hot grill.

Cassidy was not especially interested in trying to figure out just what kind of meat the sausages might contain. They were smoky and somewhat greasy, but she wolfed down her share without hesitation. Noting her enthusiasm for food, Yolanda silently offered her more. The coffee was hot and strong, with a burned and slightly bitter aftertaste that seemed vaguely familiar.

By the time she'd finished eating, Cassidy could hardly keep her eyes open. Yawning widely, she stretched out on the soft sand. She was dimly aware of the others moving around her, their shadows flickering crazily in the light from the four fires. Empty coffee mugs clinked; Yolanda murmured something to Kevin; Raphael gave a soft hoot of laughter. Then someone threw a cover over her. From the stiff texture and the somewhat musty smell, Cassidy recognized it as the ground tarp. Still fully clothed, she snuggled into it, her hip and shoulder pressing into the yielding sand, fatigue weighing her like an anchor.

The last thing she remembered thinking about before she fell asleep was important enough to temporarily jerk her back to the edge of consciousness. With everything else that had happened, she had almost forgotten about it; but as she lay there she realized that she had done it—she had extrapolated. At the river's edge, when she had seen or not seen that thing, she may not have known what the hell it was; but she had known what it wasn't. And she had been able to think of all the things that could or would be in the water, things like fish and snakes and turtles—even though she had not seen any of them there.

It was a small thing, and the subject matter seemed discouragingly trivial, but that was not the crucial part. What was significant was that for the first time since this freakish experience had begun, she had been able to anticipate and visualize things that she had not already seen there.

She had . . . *remembered*.

Dragonfly was a good horse, one of the best horses she had ever trained. She had always had a weakness for gray horses; but even beyond that, this mare was special.

They were galloping, the gray mare's gait so smooth that it was like flying, the wind whipping through her hair and the horse's long mane. The ground was rough and thickly wooded, but she was not afraid—not on Dragonfly. She could not see what was ahead of them, but the ride was so exciting, so exhilarating, that it didn't matter.

There was someone behind them, following them, chasing them. She wanted to turn her head, to look and see who it was, but she couldn't. But that was all right, too, because on Dragonfly she was safe. And so she leaned down to hug the mare, to squeeze her neck in encouragement. But as her arms went down around the long gray neck, she suddenly realized that it wasn't Dragonfly she was embracing. It was something dark and glistening and sinuous, something that writhed beneath her like a huge snake and—

Cassidy awoke with a start, choking and sputtering, her heart hammering in her chest as she struggled to spit out the rigid object that was jammed into her mouth.

"Okay—it's okay! She's coming out of it," she heard Yolanda say.

Someone was holding her head in a viselike grip; but as she blindly strove to free herself, she felt the offending object slip from between her teeth. Still confused and groggy from sleep, for a moment Cassidy had only the dimmest idea of what was going on around her.

"Shit—she nearly bit my finger off!"

The indignant voice was Raphael's. Blinking rapidly, Cassidy could then determine that the hand gripping her chin had been his as well. To her surprise, she found herself looking up directly into the boy's smooth dark face. He was sitting behind her with her head and shoulders pulled up onto his jackknifed knees. Frantically casting around, Cassidy's eyes caught on Yolanda's concerned face, bent frowning over her own.

"You're okay now," the older woman reassured Cassidy. "You just had a fit."

Cassidy glanced quickly from Yolanda to Raphael to Kevin. She was a little bewildered to find the ponytailed boy straddling her ankles. "A *fit*?" she croaked hoarsely.

"Yeah, a fit," Raphael repeated. His tone had quickly reverted to its customary sarcasm now that the crisis appeared to be over, and his expression was swiftly transformed from worry to aggrieved annoyance. Cassidy could see then that the object he had thrust between her teeth was the polished wooden handle of his sling; her bite marks were clearly visible on its surface.

"Can you sit up?" Yolanda asked her.

Kevin scurried off her feet as Cassidy wobbily pushed herself up. She felt an irrational flash of anger. "I didn't have a fit," she said.

Yolanda was still studying her with a clinical sort of concern. "It's no big thing," she told Cassidy. "Lots of people have them, even when they're sleeping."

Cassidy had been gingerly feeling the side of her mouth, where Raphael's sling had probably left a visible bruise. "I told you, I wasn't having a fit," she reiterated peevishly. "It was just a nightmare."

Kevin and Yolanda and Raphael all looked blankly at her.

"A what?" Raphael asked skeptically.

"A nightmare," Cassidy repeated, rubbing her sore lip. Rapidly assessing their expressions of continuing incomprehension, she added irately, "You know—a bad dream."

Cassidy's elaboration had no discernible effect on their confusion. The three of them exchanged puzzled glances; then Yolanda, with total seriousness, asked her, "What's a 'bad dream'?"

For a moment Cassidy just gaped at the trio of perplexed and expectant faces. *This!* she thought. *This is a bad dream!* The implication of their ignorance so stunned her that she found it difficult to find the words. "You mean," she said slowly and carefully, "that you don't know what a dream is?"

"If we knew, would we be asking you?" Raphael shot back querulously.

But a thoughtful, strangely abstracted expression had come over Yolanda's face. She stared at Cassidy as if she had suddenly seen something totally unexpected there. In a tone almost of wonderment, she said softly, "You have the Memories."

Further perplexed by Yolanda's abrupt change in demeanor, Cassidy returned the scrutiny, quickly correcting "Dreams aren't memories, they're just—'' She groped in frustration for a term. ''—images; things your brain makes up in your sleep.''

''That's crazy,'' Raphael retorted, pulling back from her. In the dim light from the banked fires, his gold earring winked faintly as he stubbornly shook his head. ''Nobody thinks in their sleep!''

''I've heard of such a thing,'' Yolanda said quietly. Sitting back on her heels, she regarded Cassidy with a candid intensity.

''Well, I never have,'' Kevin put in, sleepily rubbing his eyes. ''So can we just forget about this,'' he added plaintively, ''and get back to sleep?''

''Good idea.'' Raphael grunted, pushing himself to his feet. ''I do enough thinking during the day,'' he muttered as he moved away. ''Sleep is for sleeping!''

To Cassidy's surprise, Yolanda reached out and gently laid one hand on Cassidy's bare arm. ''Tomorrow,'' she said. ''I want you to tell me what you saw in your sleep.''

Involuntarily Cassidy found herself yawning hugely. ''Sure,'' she murmured, dropping back down onto the musty ground tarp. *If I can remember!*

In a few minutes the camp was silent again, the others once more rolled in their ground covers. But Cassidy, for all her grogginess, could not fall back to sleep so easily. She could think of only one thing, something so astounding and yet so alien that it filled her with despair: These people did not dream. Incredibly, they didn't even seem to know what a dream was. Her suspicions that Yolanda and the boys must have known something about her own appearance there seemed contradicted by that bizarre realization, and it did nothing to explain how she had gotten there. But if they didn't dream, if they thought that a person having a nightmare was suffering from some sort of seizure, and if they thought that dreams were ''Memories,'' then perhaps they all were as crazy as she herself seemed to be.

Chapter 4 ◀▮▮▮▮

The first thing Cassidy heard when she awoke the next morning was the angry hiss of two voices arguing, but the first and only thing she thought about as she regained awareness had nothing to do with that discordant sound. She lay there with her eyes clenched shut and automatically and desperately reached for the knowledge of who she was. But the events of the previous day had not been just some bad dream, and nothing she could remember predated the breakneck chase astride the gray mare. And in the place of the information for which she reached there was nothing—or worse than nothing, for a stabbing pain began to shoot from her temples to her eye sockets at the mere attempt to remember.

Opening her eyes just a slit, she tried to make some assessment of the situation before she revealed that she was awake. She recognized the voices as Yolanda's and Raphael's, but they were sitting far enough away from her, squatting together by the far side of one of the watch fires, that she could not understand their loud whispers. They seemed so engrossed in their disagreement, however, that she didn't think they'd notice if she moved. Rolling over, she slid out from between the musty folds of the ground tarp and lurched awkwardly to her feet.

On the horizon, the sun wasn't quite visible yet above the tree line, but the sky was filled with the ethereal lemon and rose colors of predawn light. The air was still cool enough to raise gooseflesh on her bare arms as she started limping stiffly across the sandy strand. She felt stupendously sore; her knees burned where the shredded fabric of her torn jeans had stuck to her abraded skin, and her scraped right arm throbbed. She was sure there must be a bruise the size of her fist on the back of her head where that damned rock had smacked her. Most discouraging of all, her buttocks and inner thighs were a cacophonous riot of aches and strains from the day's ride. The thought of climbing—dragging herself—back up on the gray mare's back again made her wince.

Glancing around, she noted Yolanda and Raphael still huddled by the fire, joined in audible discord. A quick look up and down the little spit of beach revealed no trace of Kevin, or of any of the four horses. As if by some subconscious decision, Cassidy avoided the path she had forged through the reeds the night before and hobbled a bit farther upstream instead. Birds, twittering excitedly, exploded out of the thick brush along the edge of the sand as she passed. As Cassidy began to wedge her way through the waist-high wall of cattails, she saw the first molten glow of the sunrise spill into the sky.

The boggy ground near the river's edge, which had been difficult enough to negotiate in the dark the night before, presented a continuing challenge even in the daylight because of her stiff and clumsy gait. Making her way cautiously through the uneven clumps of reeds, Cassidy did not even look up until she was almost at the edge of the water. When she did look out over the river, she jumped back with an inarticulate little cry of surprise. Out in the stream, his head barely breaking the surface of the placid water, Kevin was leisurely swimming toward her. The slow, sure movements of his arms and legs hardly even raised a wake.

For a moment, Cassidy could only stare stupidly at him. Then, as she watched, he neared the shallow water near the bank. Pulling his legs under him and straightening up, he pushed himself up out of the river. He was, of course, completely naked.

Stepping up onto the patch of reeds beside her, Kevin shook back his long, unbound hair; water flew from his head in a sun-glittered spray and dripped in runnels from his arms and legs. In the curiously gilding quality of the sunlight, his lean body was unexpectedly well proportioned and cleanly sculpted with long, hard muscle. Cassidy realized that in his ragtag clothing, Kevin had appeared more lanky and scrawny, especially when compared to Raphael; but now she could see that he was fit and athletic looking. As he stood on the riverbank his stance was casual and entirely unaffected. The fine wet hair on his arms and legs and belly glistened copper in the oblique light. Casually, with a graceless sort of shrug, he shook back his dripping hair again. Then he looked over at Cassidy, his odd-colored eyes luminous in his tanned face, and his brows arched quizzically.

"What's the matter—do I have duckweed in my hair?" he asked her.

Suddenly she was aware that she had been staring—and just what she had been staring at, as well. She was equally surprised to note that Kevin was also judiciously endowed in that regard. "Uh, yeah!" she said, jerking her eyes away. "Duckweed—just a little."

Kevin tossed his head again, shaking his hair. "Thanks," he said.

"I thought you said not to go in the water!" Cassidy blurted out.

Kevin's expression remained mildly puzzled, his eyes glinting golden green and blue in the growing light. "Only at night," he replied, carding his fingers back through the honey-brown strands of his thick wet hair. "It's okay now."

For a moment longer Cassidy stared, temporarily unable to form another coherent comment. But Kevin seemed unperturbed. With another bemused little shake of his dripping head, he started to step back through the stand of reeds, away from the riverbank. As he moved away, Cassidy had to resist the surprisingly strong temptation to turn and surreptitiously watch his long lean legs and that tight rear end as he walked away from her.

Somehow disturbed by the impulse, Cassidy dropped down into a knee-wrenching crouch and cupped her hands into the river. Splashing her face and arms with the cool water, she tried to dispel the jarring impression of strange familiarity that Kevin's nonchalant nudity had sparked in her. For some reason the interest that his casually innocent display had aroused in her was all the more distressing in light of that vast vacuum that still existed where Cassidy's memory should have been. Besides, he was just a boy—practically a child, she admonished herself, although she wasn't exactly sure just where that censure fit in, since she wasn't certain why he had made her uncomfortable in the first place.

When Cassidy returned to the campsite, the argument between Yolanda and Raphael still raged unabated. If anything, the dispute between them seemed only to have intensified: They were standing squared off and not bothering to confine themselves to harsh whispers anymore. Raphael may have been a good head taller than the dark-haired woman, but Yolanda's stance and demeanor were every bit as pugnacious as his. With the morning sunlight glinting brightly off the harshly reflective surface of her sunglasses, her dusky face held a strange air of menace.

Kevin had dressed again in his jeans and T-shirt, his damp hair pulled back into a ponytail. He sat by the farthest watch fire, putting together something to eat and pointedly staying out of the ongoing disagreement between Yolanda and Raphael. When he saw Cassidy approaching, he gestured to her with the thick slab of coarse brown bread he held in his hand.

"I still don't see any reason why we have to change our plans," Raphael was insisting loudly, jerking up his ground cover and shaking the sand out of it with sharp, irritated snaps of his wrists.

"Because this is more important," Yolanda argued, firmly but impatiently. It was obvious to Cassidy that the two had been covering and re-covering the same ground for some time, and the dark-haired woman's aplomb was suffering from the mileage.

Raphael made a snorting sound of disapproval. "What's more important—her?" he asked, throwing an overtly disdainful glance in Cassidy's direction.

Kevin was holding up two slabs of bread to Cassidy, each generously slathered with what appeared to be some kind of thick fruit jam. "Here," he told her quietly. "May as well eat while you can."

Kevin's comment made Cassidy notice that despite the rigors of their disagreement, Yolanda and Raphael did seem to be in the midst of dismantling the little camp. Raphael bent to fold his ground cover, as Yolanda deliberately and methodically tossed utensils, containers, and other small objects into the folds of her own rolled tarp. But their actions seemed guided by rote, as most of their energy remained devoted to their argument. Taking the food Kevin offered, Cassidy continued to watch the pair warily.

"We have to take her to the Warden," Yolanda resumed, tugging briskly on a leather strap.

"So? I'm not saying we won't take her," Raphael countered. "Just *after* we get the horses."

"But that could take too long," Yolanda insisted. She used one of her feet as a lever to compress the folds of her ground cover to where she could stretch the straps into the buckle. The rough manner in which she did it made Cassidy think Yolanda was probably wishing it was Raphael's neck and not the tarp beneath her heel. "It could take us as long as a week to catch up with them."

"Two days, tops," Raphael corrected. He lifted his folded ground cover, which now resembled a crude backpack, by its straps. "Would have taken even less," he couldn't refrain from reminding the older woman, "if we hadn't already wasted one whole day chasing her."

Yolanda shook her head impatiently, the sunlight shooting off the mirrored surface of her glasses' lenses. "And if we hadn't followed her, we wouldn't have found out," she persisted.

"Found out what?" Raphael shot back. "We haven't found out anything! She doesn't *know* anything—she just got here!"

Despite her uneasiness, Cassidy had begun to eat one of the pieces of bread. It really was quite good, sweet and chewy. But at Raphael's loud assertion, she swallowed hard, gulping down a big lump of it as her body tensed. She was leery of the black boy's belligerence, but he had captured her attention with his reference to her origins. Perhaps those people knew more about her than they were admitting.

Beside her, Kevin lithely got to his feet, a folded slice of bread held casually in one hand. With his other hand he lightly touched Cassidy on the shoulder. "Come on," he said evenly, "let's go find the horses."

Cassidy wasn't sure if Kevin just wanted to stay clear of his two companions' display of temper or if he was actually interested in getting the horses. The third possibility, that he might somehow be concerned about her own feelings being upset, occurred to her only belatedly. Whatever his reason, she found Kevin's gesture unexpectedly touching, and when he started off across the sand toward the tree-lined trail, she quickly followed him.

As she moved away from the little clearing, taking another bit of bread and jam as she walked, she could hear Yolanda responding to Raphael's most recent outburst.

"Rafe, what if she has the Memories?" Yolanda said resolutely. "Don't you realize what that could mean?"

Raphael's reply was loud enough that Cassidy had no trouble hearing him, even though she and Kevin had already walked far enough away that she could no longer see the campsite through the screen of trees.

"And what if she doesn't have them?" Raphael demanded of Yolanda. "Right now she's got *nothing*. And what chance would we have if we showed up before the Warden with nothing but some crazy woman—and no horses?"

After that they were too far away from the camp for Cassidy

to be able to hear Yolanda's response. All she could think about was that Raphael had actually said it: She was a crazy woman. Whatever the Memories were, and whether or not she had them, they wanted to take her to some authority—the Warden, they called him. Did that mean that she was in fact a prisoner of the Horsemen? She looked ahead to Kevin's back, where his damp brown ponytail bobbed against his shoulders as he led her through a narrow strip of brush and out into the broad meadow beyond it. Wolfing down the last of her makeshift breakfast, Cassidy hurried to catch up to him.

As she drew alongside him, Kevin noted with a little gesture, "Lots of good grazing." He glanced around. "Let's hope they didn't wander off too far; all we'd need on top of everything else is a late start."

Cassidy gave him a sidelong glance and frowned. "Why can't we just, uh, 'Call' them?" she asked him.

Kevin slowed, his head jerking around. He grinned at her as if he were certain she was making a joke; and for a long moment Cassidy was too struck by the sunny purity of the expression to recognize his assumption. Then, as he began to realize that Cassidy was deadly serious, the grin quickly faded. He seemed torn between perplexity and annoyance at her ignorance. "That might work for you, but it won't do me any good," he commented, with the slightest trace of irritation in his voice.

Cassidy realized that somehow, however unwittingly, she had insulted Kevin. Apparently not all Horsemen could Call their horses, or had she missed some other, more subtle distinction between the brown-haired boy and herself? Confused, she simply shrugged. For every discovery she had made, for everything she thought she had figured out, there were always a dozen more contradictions thrown up in her face.

The young man suddenly paused then, turning to face her. He studied her for a moment with a plain and forthright interest. "How can you be a Horseman, and be able to Call your horse, and not know that?" he asked her bluntly.

Again Cassidy shrugged, slightly averting her face as if to somehow deny the baffling contradiction. "I don't know," she said.

Cassidy thought he would simply resume walking again, but Kevin still hesitated. She knew he was still scrutinizing her; finally she looked up, straight into those oddly dissimilar eyes. In addition to their contrasting colors, she further noticed that they were widely spaced, set off by a thick fringe of chestnut-colored lashes. But they were also unfathomable, as lost to her as everything else in that foreign place.

"Last night," he asked her, "did you mean it when you said you could see things in your sleep?"

Cassidy sensed that it was more than just curiosity that prompted his question, but she wasn't certain just what it was that Kevin sought from her. She didn't have an adequate basis on which to judge any of these people; she didn't understand their standards of conduct and she could barely remember her own. But Kevin provoked a different reaction from her than did Yolanda, with her arbitrary abstruseness, or Raphael, with his mocking contempt. It wasn't precisely that she trusted the pony-tailed boy, it was just that she didn't distrust him.

"Yeah," she said, "I had a dream."

His eyes narrowed. "What did you see?"

Cassidy made a vague gesture. "I dreamed about horses, about my horse," she said guardedly.

Kevin's head cocked slightly. "But you said it was a 'bad' dream," he reminded her.

"Yeah, well, I dreamed about you guys chasing me," she temporized. No way in hell was she going to try to explain what had really happened in the nightmare. They already thought she was a crazy woman; God knew what they would do if they knew she was a crazy woman who also hallucinated that there were giant creatures in the river.

The answer seemed to satisfy Kevin, but just barely. He eyed her intently for a moment longer, then pointed to the grassy sward just ahead of them. In the cool dawn air, a pungent aroma rose from an olive-colored pile of horse manure. "Fresh," he said. "Looks like they're close."

The land ahead of them rose abruptly in a long hummock, rippling with thick grass and dotted with summer wildflowers: tansy, goldenrod, feverfew, Queen Anne's lace. Trees and clumps of brush were scattered across the slope. The topography looked naggingly familiar to Cassidy, but she wasn't sure if that was just because they'd ridden through a lot of similar landscape the day before. Her boots soaked from the dew-drenched grass, she climbed the steep slope behind Kevin. At the crest of the moraine he halted, holding out one arm as if to keep her back. In another moment, Cassidy saw why.

Below them spread a long prairie valley. The four horses were there, grazing industriously, their long tails flicking lazily as they cropped the grass. And spread out among the horses, their big scoop-shaped ears constantly swiveling, were a half-dozen white-tailed deer. The sight of the graceful animals was oddly comforting to Cassidy; it was almost as if they were some kind of omen, creatures both familiar and benign. She shot a sideways look at Kevin, strangely pleased to see that he was smiling.

"They're beautiful," she whispered softly. "They never seem to be afraid of horses, do they? It's almost as if they—"

Cassidy broke off, suddenly confused. Kevin blinked at her. "As if what?" he prompted.

But Cassidy couldn't remember what she had been going to say. And the deer, their antennalike ears all flipping toward the direction of the moraine, were suddenly alerted to the human presence on the hill. Almost as one, their long wedge-shaped heads jerked up. Then they were off, bounding with nearly comic springiness in huge leaps across the sun-flooded meadow.

Kevin's blaze-faced chestnut mare looked up, scanning the moraine. Then she whinnied loudly. To Cassidy's surprise, Kevin put two fingers to his mouth and blew a sharp, piercing whistle. The other three horses' heads snapped up as well. Led by the white-faced chestnut, all four of them came trotting up the slope to where Cassidy and Kevin stood.

The gray mare came directly to Cassidy, burying her aquiline forehead against her shirtfront and blowing an inelegant snort of grass-stained slobber into the fabric. Despite the sloppiness of the greeting, Cassidy was embarrassingly happy to see the big mare again. She fondled the curving ears and ruffled the heavy mane. The horse might well be, Cassidy realized with a pang of despair, the only link to her past that she had.

Kevin sprang easily onto his mare, slapping the chestnut's neck and scratching playfully around the base of her withers. Cassidy was only dimly beginning to understand the depth of the bond between a Horseman and his mount. Looking down at Cassidy, Kevin remarked, "We better get them back to camp; Yolanda's probably itching to get going."

Hopping up onto the gray's back was an automatic movement; only the painful pull of her sore muscles was a jarring and unwelcome reminder to Cassidy of yesterday's ordeal. As she shifted gingerly on the broad back, Kevin gave her an astute little laugh. "You'll ride out of it," he assured her, starting the chestnut back down the other side of the slope.

The other chestnut mare and Yolanda's bay gelding obediently followed them as they retraced their path to the camp. It was a short distance, and Cassidy knew that on the horses it would only take a few minutes. Suddenly she realized that there still were several things she wanted to ask Kevin. Although the ponytailed boy hadn't yet provided her with much information, Cassidy sensed that unlike Yolanda or Raphael, this shortcoming had not been due to his being deliberately obtuse. She knew she just hadn't asked him the right questions yet.

Urging the gray mare up alongside Kevin's white-faced mare, Cassidy said, "Are there a lot of deer around here?"

Kevin leaned forward, easily sweeping an annoying fly off his horse's neck. "Some," he replied simply. After a moment, he further volunteered, "We don't always see too many of them, though; they're kind of spooky around people." He shrugged lightly, his lean shoulders shifting beneath the thin fabric of his T-shirt. "Guess because the Riders hunt them."

"Are there other kinds of animals around here, Kevin? Bigger ones?"

Kevin glanced over at her, frowning briefly. His head was backlit by the sun and stray wisps of his drying hair, which had escaped from his ponytail, fluttered like strands of gold. "You mean bigger than deer?" he asked.

Pulling in a long breath, Cassidy sought to keep her voice casual. "Yeah, bigger than deer—bigger than the horses, even."

Kevin was silent for so long that Cassidy began to regret having asked the question. Perhaps it had been a mistake to have asked him something like that so soon. But so far he had seemed like her only willing source of useful information, and his friendly manner had raised her hopes. Just when she was about to speak again, to try to clarify or restate her query, Kevin finally responded.

"Bears," he said quietly, the hazel and blue eyes widening. "I've never seen one, but I've seen the tracks."

Cassidy hesitated, debating the wisdom of pursuing the subject. But they were nearly back to the sand-beach camp; it might be a long time before she had another chance to speak to Kevin alone. "Anything bigger than bears?" she asked him, almost holding her breath.

He shot her another look, this time one of patent cynicism. "There isn't any animal bigger than bears," he asserted.

"What about in the water?" she persisted.

Again Kevin frowned. "Animals don't live in the water," he stated simply.

"Frogs do," Cassidy reminded him. "And turtles and fish and—"

"Little stuff," Kevin interjected, seemingly growing either bored or irritated by the conversation. He urged his mare into a trot. "Come on; Yolanda's probably still pissed."

As they rode back through the line of trees and onto the stretch of beach, Cassidy was surprised to see that not only were Yolanda and Raphael no longer arguing, but other than the small pile of packed equipment stacked beside them, they had already completely obliterated all signs of their camp. She couldn't even tell where the four watch fires had been. There wasn't a trace of ash and the sand lay smoothed out, the entire strand unmarked. It was as if no one had been there at all.

Yolanda looked up at Cassidy and Kevin as they rode in, but she said nothing. When Kevin stopped his mare beside her, she bent and lifted one of the folded packs, passing it to him. While he settled it behind him and fastened the straps, she finally spoke. "We're going to keep going after the Riders."

"Yeah!" Raphael echoed emphatically, making a triumphant gesture with his fist raised. As Cassidy watched with grudging admiration, he agilely hopped onto his mare, his action seemingly without effort, even though he was carrying one of the packs.

Yolanda looked sharply at Raphael, then she bent to retrieve the third pack. "But only for two days," she continued firmly. "Then, whether or not we catch up to them, we're going to start for the Warden's."

Raphael's only response was a scowl. But Yolanda ignored him and passed her pack to Kevin to hold while she mounted her gelding. When she was astride the bay, Kevin handed it back to her. Cassidy marveled at the economic dimensions of the folded packs, and at the simple way the mounted Horsemen carried them. With the straps fastened low around the waist, they were more like fanny packs than backpacks; once in position they rested on the horses' backs, right behind their riders' hips. Yolanda completed her preparations by sticking the shaft of her whip through one of the pack's straps, so that the leather lash dangled down around her shoulders.

As they had the day before, Kevin and Raphael led out, with Yolanda and Cassidy following. Cassidy considered offering to carry something, but there didn't seem to be any need. In fact, the group traveled so lightly that she had to wonder how long they could have been on this journey. They seemed to be out in the middle of nowhere, and yet they could hardly be carrying enough food to sustain a long trip. Then again, that little mystery seemed so inconsequential compared to some of the other questions Cassidy had that she didn't even bother to ask about it. She had two days at most before the Horsemen would resume their course toward the Warden. It didn't appear that she was to be given a choice as to whether or not she wanted to accompany them. What she desperately needed to determine was if going to him would be a danger to her—or if he could be the solution to her baffling exile.

It turned out that Kevin was only partially right about Cassidy "riding out of" her soreness. The initial stinging ache caused by first refitting herself to the gray mare's body did indeed pass, and after riding for a while, she even began to feel a comfortable rhythm with the horse again. But as the morning progressed and the summer air grew warmer, a light film of sweat began to soak through the legs and seat of her jeans, and the damp fabric began to chafe her skin. After several hours of continuous riding, the long muscles in Cassidy's calves and thighs started to complain again, and she felt as if she were gradually losing her sense of centered balance on the mare's back. Instead of being a part of the horse, she was fast becoming a piece of freight.

None of her three companions seemed similarly affected. All morning they continued to follow the dirt trail along the river. Cassidy actually saw very little of the stream, however, as it was usually hidden by the row of big trees and brush along the path. Raphael and Kevin kept the lead, mostly riding abreast, often jockeying playfully for position and engaging in obscure but friendly contests of riding skill. They each sat their chestnut mare easily, their canvas packs bobbing rhythmically behind them on the horses' broad backs. Yolanda's demeanor was perhaps a bit more businesslike, but her posture was no less casual. She rode right ahead of Cassidy, the sun glinting off her mirrored glasses as she evenly but constantly scanned the passing landscape. As her big bay gelding strode calmly along, the wooden haft of her long whip swung slowly from side to side, the thin leather popper brushing hypnotically back and forth across her shoulders.

It was a thoroughly pleasant summer day, and the countryside they rode through was beautiful and unspoiled. If it hadn't been for the nagging ache in her legs and the growing numbness in her butt, Cassidy would have been in a better position to enjoy the ride. As it was, she soon found herself beginning to concentrate on other things to try to forget the unrelenting soreness she felt developing. And after all, she thought with a certain rueful fatalism, it wasn't as if she didn't have anything more important than her aching ass to worry about. The terrifying gap where her memory should be would do for starters; not to mention the hellacious headache that swelled whenever she blundered too close to the edges of that empty chasm.

Temporarily setting aside the issue of just who these people were, and how and why they were so different from her, Cassidy tried to concentrate instead on what little information she had been able to come up with. Even if it wasn't information about herself, then it was at least about the world and how things should be. She realized that in addition to knowing what things were once she saw them, and in addition to the little flash of extrapolation she'd had the night before about what animals were appropriate to a river, she'd done something else that morning that was significant. On the ride back to camp with the horses, when Kevin had mentioned bears she had known exactly what bears were, even without a physical example. When he said the word, she could have closed her eyes and *seen* bears—what they looked like, how they behaved, how they fit into the scheme of things. If only she could find some way to unlock the words for the rest of the things she had yet to see. Over the course of the morning, riding placidly along the winding trail beneath the sheltering sweep of those ancient trees, Cassidy had nursed a slowly building but undeniable feeling that there were a hell of a lot of things that were *missing*.

Looking at her companions, Cassidy silently marveled at just how quickly she had accepted what she had found there. *Then again, what choice did I have?* she reminded herself. Even beyond that, she still realized that there was something strangely different about these three people, something that went beyond their peculiar nonchalance about her unexplained origins. And that persistent sense of alienation from them depressed Cassidy nearly as much as did her inability to remember; because at least for the moment, these three people were the only friends she had.

Just when Cassidy had begun seriously to consider the horrible possibility that perhaps they were just going to ride straight through the day without stopping to rest, Yolanda finally signaled a halt. They had reached a fork in the trail, a confluence where a smaller stream joined the river and the dirt path split. One arm of it forded the new intersecting creek and continued along the river, and the other arm branched off to travel parallel to the smaller tributary.

"We'll stop here to eat," Yolanda announced. "Rafe, you cross this ford and check out the main trail. Kev, I want you to go up the side path. See if you find any signs."

Although Cassidy could hardly wait to slide down off the gray mare, neither Raphael nor Kevin seemed particularly put out at being sent on Yolanda's errands before being allowed to dismount. As the two boys split up and rode off, Yolanda guided the bay gelding around in a circle in the low grass beside the trail. Not waiting for her to set a precedent, Cassidy gingerly eased herself down off the gray's back. As her feet hit the sod, her legs felt so wobbly that for a moment she had to cling to the horse's mane just to keep her balance. Then she saw that Yolanda had hopped down off the bay and was regarding her with thinly veiled amusement. Straightening herself with deliberate dignity, Cassidy stiffly stepped away from the mare and dismissed the horse with a little slap.

"Pretty thin-skinned for a Horseman" was all Yolanda said, but Cassidy detected no real malice in the mildly mocking tone. Then the dark-haired woman dropped down cross-legged in the grass and began to dig in the folds of her pack.

Slowly and carefully Cassidy eased herself down near Yolanda, wincing as her rump connected with the grassy ground. She eyed the pack hopefully, her stomach rumbling in anticipation. She didn't care what Yolanda was serving up; she was hungry enough to eat almost anything, and discouragingly grateful for the chance to get down off her horse. Some Horseman; how was she ever going to keep up with these people? They must have butts like boot leather, she thought.

By the time Raphael and his mare came splashing back across the shallow ford of the smaller stream, Yolanda was busily slicing cold sausages onto cut slabs of the coarse brown bread. Raphael dropped down off the chestnut mare nearly at Yolanda's feet, deftly helping himself to a newly made sandwich the moment he hit the ground. Yolanda took a halfhearted swat at him, but he scampered out of range, shooing his just-freed horse ahead of him.

"See anything?" Yolanda asked him, cutting more sausage.

Chewing heartily, his mouth full of bread and sausage, Raphael shook his head. When he had swallowed, he elaborated. "More of the same; no sign of Riders."

Cassidy still hadn't figured out just who the Riders were, except that they obviously had horses—horses that the Horsemen seemed to want. And from the way they had been stalking the Riders, she had the distinct feeling that any encounter between the two groups would not be a mutually desired thing.

Instead of sitting down beside them, he continued to walk away, taking another huge bite of his sandwich as he went. Cassidy was puzzled for a moment; then she saw where he was heading. As Raphael strolled off, casually unfastening the fly of his pants as he went, she quickly averted her eyes. The need to relieve herself had also occurred to Cassidy, but she had been far too hungry to give it precedence. Raphael had neatly solved that problem by doing two things at once, she realized with a grudging admiration.

Cassidy had finished one sandwich and was well into a second before Kevin returned. His blaze-faced mare seemed impatient; but whether it was impatience to be free of her rider or to be able to start grazing, or both, Cassidy couldn't tell. Kevin was holding her to a walk, but she stepped along quickly, her long tail switching in irritation. She stood for him to dismount, but the moment he was off her back the horse scurried off after her fellows without waiting for any gesture of dismissal. Kevin paused a moment to stretch his arms up over his head; then he slapped at his damp jeans over the backs of his thighs and gave his whole body a little shake, as if to rearrange all of his clothing.

Yolanda silently passed Kevin a sandwich, which he took with an appreciative little smile. He had, Cassidy had noticed, particularly nice teeth, very white and even. Without conscious intention or warning, her mind jumped back to sunrise that morning and to the indelible image of the boy with the brown ponytail casually stepping, dripping and naked, from the river. She had total and vivid recall of every detail of that sun-speckled body: the rounded lines of his shoulders and hips, the flat planes of his back and belly, the—

Jerking herself back to the present, Cassidy took another fierce bite of bread, just as Raphael rejoined them.

"What did you find?" Raphael asked Kevin immediately.

Kevin, who'd been munching at his cold sandwich, just shrugged. "Not much," he reported. "No tracks; a few piles of horseshit, but they were all dried up. They could be weeks old."

But Raphael still seemed enthused by Kevin's discovery. "If you found horseshit, then there's got to be Riders in this area," he insisted. He threw Yolanda a pointed look. "We could catch up with them anytime now."

The mirrored lenses tilted slightly as Yolanda cocked her head at him. "Two days, Rafe," she reminded him. "Then we're on our way, horses or no horses."

Cassidy could think of several relevant questions, but she wasn't sure if it was a good time to bring them up. Yolanda's increasing determination to get to the Warden was making her uneasy, but the idea of some kind of hostile encounter with the group they called the Riders also held little appeal. But in a moment she was glad that she had kept her silence, since Raphael seemed determined to reopen his and Yolanda's earlier argument.

"If we don't find them in two days," Raphael said, "then why don't you go ahead and take her to the Warden, and let me and Kevin go on after the Riders?"

Yolanda had been using the blade of her short knife to shave off thin slices of the cold sausage, which she would then fold over and pop directly into her mouth. She didn't even look up at Raphael's proposal; but Cassidy noticed that the sharp edge of the knife suddenly bit deeply into the dry husk of the sausage with an emphatic little jerk. "No," she said simply.

"Why not?" Raphael persisted, obviously warming to his argument. He tossed his head, the sun glinting off his gold earring. "We could take the—"

Yolanda's voice was even but implacable. "I said *no*," she repeated.

Kevin had moved a few steps away from them but still hadn't sat down. He nipped delicately at his sandwich, his eyes darting back and forth between Yolanda and Raphael. He didn't seem comfortable with their continuing confrontation.

Scuffing his boot in the sod, Raphael began again, "But why—"

The movement was both unexpected and amazingly swift— so unexpected that it made Cassidy jump and so swift that she literally did not see how Yolanda had gotten to her feet. With one pouncing stride the dark-haired woman was face to face with Raphael, her blunt and stained fingers tightly clenched in double handsful of the front of his tank top, her elbows locked so that the glaring surface of her sunglasses was just inches from his chin. "Because *I said no*!" she hissed fiercely at him. "Because this is dangerous territory for us—hell, we aren't even safe traveling like this, much less in pairs!" She gave him a little shake—not roughly, but testily, as if to be sure he was paying absolute attention to her. "And because in spite of what you may think, you two aren't full-fledged Horsemen yet; until you've taken horses you're just apprentices—*my* apprentices—and if you screw this up there's no way under the heavens that any of us will ever get accepted as Troopers by the Warden!"

Slowly, deliberately, Yolanda released her grip on Raphael's shirt and took a half step back from him. "This is too important to take stupid chances, Rafe," she concluded.

Cassidy and Kevin had watched the entire performance in wide-eyed silence. Even Raphael seemed momentarily speechless. Chastised, but only begrudgingly, he briefly lowered his big brown eyes. "But if we don't get the horses—" he started to say.

"The horses aren't everything," Yolanda reminded him quietly.

But Raphael just grunted, throwing Cassidy an openly skeptical glower.

The rest of the simple meal was eaten in silence, but Cassidy hardly noticed. Conversation, whether at mealtime or otherwise, had never seemed to be a plentiful commodity around there anyway. She was much too busy thinking to notice the glaring lack of small talk. For in one sudden stroke of temper, Yolanda's outburst had supplied Cassidy with more answers than she had been able to garner from this maddeningly taciturn woman with any of her questions.

Whoever or whatever Horsemen were, apparently the title was something that had to be earned. Yolanda had called Raphael and Kevin her "apprentices," and that implied that she was responsible for their training. And whoever the Warden was, it was obvious that he commanded their respect, since belonging to his "Troopers" seemed to be their common goal. If just the threat of failing to achieve this acceptance was enough to shut up the hot-headed Raphael, Cassidy thought wryly, then it must be a desirable position indeed! And that explained the original reason for their journey: They were going to the Warden to try to become members of his Troop.

Cassidy was less certain what part the elusive Riders and their horses played in all of it. It seemed that Riders were something less than Horsemen, but for some reason it was necessary to deal with them to obtain horses. Unfortunately, she was beginning to suspect that the Horsemen's methods for obtaining those horses were not necessarily legitimate; she suspected in fact that she was riding with nothing more than a glorified band of thieves. Slowly chewing on the rind of her sandwich, Cassidy frowned. There was another thing, something that she preferred not to think about but could not avoid considering. Yolanda had said that this was dangerous territory, that even the four of them were not safe traveling there. But just exactly what was the danger? Cassidy wondered. The Riders? Or something even less defined . . . something hidden in the darkness and warded off with watch fires?

After she'd finished eating, Cassidy barely had time to slip off into the bushes to relieve herself before the others began to mount up again. Both the seat of her pants and the gray mare's back had dried off during the break, and to Cassidy's surprise and relief, she felt slightly less sore when she hopped up on the horse again. Raphael and Kevin led off down the new path at a brisk trot, putting some distance between themselves and Yolanda; the older woman seemed content to let her gelding walk. There was a lot of heavy brush and young saplings along the banks of the smaller stream, and the narrow trail wound among them. The two boys were quickly out of sight ahead of them. The trail was also more uneven than the river path, but the slower pace suited Cassidy fine.

After they had been riding again for a while, and the river had long since disappeared behind them, Cassidy began to try to think of a productive way to broach a conversation with Yolanda. The smaller woman had been riding along in her typically efficient manner, her face fairly expressionless behind the reflective sunglasses. The path wasn't quite wide enough to make riding abreast either casual or convenient, so Cassidy had been letting the gray mare follow the bay gelding, an arrangement that also made conversation awkward. Just when Cassidy was about to do something to get Yolanda's attention, Yolanda solved the problem for her.

The bay gelding slowed slightly, edging off to one side of the trail. Yolanda glanced back at Cassidy, then made a small gesture. Cassidy let the gray mare move up so that the two horses were walking side by side, so close that her and Yolanda's knees were nearly touching.

"I want to talk to you about what happened last night," Yolanda said without preamble.

For some reason it took Cassidy a few seconds to realize just what aspect of last night it was that Yolanda wanted to discuss. For one weirdly disjointed moment, the first thought that occurred to her was the almost-forgotten image of that dark and sinuous form, gliding effortlessly through the river's moon-silvered water. Then, jerking her mind past that, Cassidy seized upon a more plausible subject. "Oh—you mean my *dream*," she blurted out.

Yolanda nodded, smoothly flicking her fingers at a pesky fly that had landed on the bay's shoulder. "Yeah, the dream," she said. "The images that you said came in your sleep." She looked directly at Cassidy, and once again Cassidy could see the distorted echoes of her twin reflections in the lenses of the mirrored sunglasses. "What did you see?" Yolanda asked her.

Cassidy hesitated a moment. Her experience trying to explain the dream to Kevin had made her somewhat cautious about just how specific she was willing to be. If those people didn't dream, then they might attach an entirely different significance than did Cassidy to the subject and nature of dreams. "My horse," she said finally. "I just dreamed that I was riding my horse."

No less astute than the ponytailed boy had been, Yolanda immediately asked her, "Then why did you say it was a 'bad' dream? And that fit you had; you acted like you were scared or something."

Seeing no reason to deviate from a proven formula, Cassidy responded, "It was a bad dream because I dreamed about you guys chasing me—and I was about to go over that damned cliff!"

Yolanda seemed to consider that for a few moments. Cassidy wished she could see those shrewd eyes behind the impenetrable sunglasses. She couldn't tell if Yolanda was actually satisfied with her answer or just unwilling to waste more time on what appeared to be an unproductive line of questioning. Either way, Yolanda moved on.

"What do you remember from before you came here?" she asked Cassidy bluntly.

The question was like an unexpected jolt of adrenaline; Cassidy felt her heart race. Given the woman's previous indifference to Cassidy's initial confusion, she had not expected this forthright ackowledgment of her previous life, her unremembered existence. She shook her head helplessly. "Nothing," she said. That was not precisely true, but how could she explain the other things—the image of Butch Cassidy and the Sundance Kid leaping from the cliff, training the gray mare, and her knowledge of frogs and fish and bears—to a woman who didn't even know what a dream was?

"But you knew how to Call your horse," Yolanda countered

immediately, "so you remembered something, you remembered her true name."

Cassidy didn't know how to manufacture a lie that would cover that one, even if a lie had seemed prudent. "I don't know how I did that," she confessed. "I just know that she's my horse—my horse from before, I mean—and I guess that subconsciously I—I remembered something about her."

Yolanda seized upon that revelation with as much zeal as she had seized hold of Raphael's tank top. "Then you *do* remember something," she insisted.

Cassidy tried to extricate herself from the tangling web of Yolanda's suppositions and wishful thinking. "I remember that she's my horse, yes, but that's all." Her earnestness was entirely genuine. "Listen, I wish I *did* remember more—anything more. I wish to hell I even just knew who I was!"

But Yolanda just studied her calmly, unruffled by Cassidy's heartfelt outburst. "If you do remember anything, anything at all, I want you to tell me right away," she said. Then the bay gelding moved away from Cassidy, effectively ending the conversation.

Cassidy urged the gray mare forward, trying to catch up with Yolanda again. "Yolanda, wait!" she called out. But for all practical purposes she was blocked on the narrow path by the bay's big rump.

"What?" Yolanda responded, without turning around or even slowing her horse.

Leaning forward, almost shouting, Cassidy continued, "This morning, by the river with Raphael, you said that I might have the Memories—"

The word captured Yolanda's attention, even if Cassidy's entreaty had not. Her gelding came to a halt, so abruptly that the gray mare nearly slammed into him. Yolanda turned, twisting on the horse's back so that she was facing Cassidy. The mirrored sunglasses were like two relentless eyes, interrogatory and demanding, but her voice was soft and level. "What do you know about the Memories?" she asked Cassidy. "Where did you hear that word?"

"I heard it from you," Cassidy said, with a touch of exasperation, "when you were arguing with Raphael. Hell, you were yelling loud enough that *anyone* could have heard it!" Assuming there actually were any other people in that miserable place, Cassidy added dourly to herself. "What the hell are these Memories, anyway?" Cassidy added in a more civil tone of voice,

"Why are they so important, and what makes you think I might have them?"

Yolanda reached up and slowly slipped the sunglasses from her face, pushing them up onto the crown of her head. She blinked in the bright afternoon sunlight, regarding Cassidy in silence for a few moments, her expression a strange mixture of doubt and hope. Then she said, "They say that there have been people who have come here, people like you, who could remember things from before."

"Before what?" Cassidy asked, puzzled.

Yolanda made an irritated little gesture. "Before they came here," she explained impatiently. Without waiting to see if Cassidy understood her, she went on. "Most of them are gone now, of course, but they say there still are some of them at the Warden's."

"Is that why you're in such a hurry to take me there?" Cassidy asked, her brow knotted in a frown. "I want to know who I am and how the hell I got here, and why—but why would that be so important to anyone else?"

But Yolanda shook her head, as if she was annoyed at Cassidy's ignorance. "You're not important, but the Memories are," she said. "Almost everything that we have has come from the Memories."

Cassidy's mind flailed frantically, trying to absorb the full implication of what Yolanda had just said. If there were other people like herself there, then they must know how they'd gotten there. For the first time since that nightmare began, Cassidy felt some small stirring of hope of finding her way back. Eager for more information then, she leaned forward over the gray's withers, as if proximity to Yolanda could somehow persuade the woman to answer her. "But what if—" she began.

It wasn't Yolanda who interrupted Cassidy, it was a wild whoop from farther up the trail. Startled, she looked up to see both Kevin and Raphael galloping back down the path, the two chestnuts head to tail on the narrow, brush-choked track.

"Riders!" Raphael shouted, his mare sliding to a rough halt practically under the bay gelding's nose. "We found fresh tracks!"

With one smooth, automatic motion, Yolanda slipped the sunglasses back down onto her nose. "How many?" she asked calmly. "How far ahead?"

"Just a couple of minutes up the trail," Raphael assured her, his wide eyes bright with triumph and excitement.

"At least two dozen horses," Kevin supplied, keeping his mare behind Raphael's. "The tracks can't be more than a day old."

Raphael gave a sharp, spontaneous little hoot of victory. "I told you they were close!" he crowed, slapping his mare's neck.

"We haven't caught up with them yet," Yolanda reminded him dryly. But Cassidy could see that the dark-haired woman was nearly as excited as were her two apprentices.

"Well, let's go," Raphael enthused, making his horse pivot neatly in an exuberant little spin.

"Single file," Yolanda ordered sternly, "and no faster than a trot—this trail is too rough for galloping." But she ended up giving the last part of her admonition to the two boys' departing backs as, whooping and shouting eagerly, they urged their mares back up the rutted path at a less-than-prudent speed. Muttering a curse, Yolanda let the gelding bound off after them, far faster than the cautious trot she had dictated, leaving Cassidy no choice but to follow suit.

Chapter 5 ◀IIII

Loping along the winding trail behind Yolanda's bay gelding, Cassidy once again realized that most of the deductions and discoveries that she had made since she had found herself there had been made only in retrospect, or by default. It had been more a process of inference than one of remembering, which made the results particularly frustrating and inefficient. Still, she doggedly kept on, skirting around the edges of that gaping hole in her mind, trying to piece together information. As the long summer afternoon wore on, her body slowly surrendered again to the insidious assault of a stupendous collection of muscle aches and joint pains, while the gray mare traveled tirelessly along behind the other three horses. The steadily mounting roll call of physical discomforts grew to occupy most of Cassidy's attention, until finally questions such as just who the Riders were, and why it was so important to catch up with them, just blurred into the background and all she cared about was getting down off her horse again and hopefully staying off for a long time. And that was why it had taken Cassidy so long to notice that the weather was subtly changing, and longer still to realize that she had already known the day before that the change was coming.

The previous afternoon as they had ridden along the meadow trail, one of the many things Cassidy had noted without even having to think about it was the significance of those feathery "horsetail" clouds that had streamed across the western sky. She had known that they presaged a change in the weather, obviously a change from fair to foul. Cassidy began to see the evidence of that coming meteorological shift.

The sun was still high on the horizon, but beneath it, the western sky was clotted with a deepening mass of dark, turbulent clouds. The sky above the sun was murky with a swirling haze that bled a ruddy color and cast an eerie light that distorted the normal green hues of the grass and trees. The air had grown heavy and still, so thick that its metallic tang could almost be tasted. *Storm weather*, Cassidy thought. Things were getting ready to blow.

Raphael, Kevin, and Yolanda seemed completely oblivious to the approaching disturbance. In fact, for the better part of the afternoon they had seemed completely oblivious to anything but following the fresh hoof prints that littered the narrow and winding dirt track along the creek. In places the path was so pinched that brush encroached on either side, slapping Cassidy's knees and whipping her bare arms as her mare trotted along. Many times she couldn't even see the bay gelding, even though he was only a few lengths ahead of her. Eventually Cassidy stopped thinking about the rigor of the pace or the roughness of the trail. All she could think about was how sore her legs were and how much her butt ached. Thinking about the deteriorating weather was still a diversion, but increasingly it was a temporary diversion at best.

As badly as Cassidy wanted to stop, she didn't dare. Even if she'd only gotten down off the mare for a few minutes, she could have lost the others, and as callous and obsessed as their behavior may have seemed, she knew she still needed them to survive. A couple of times she had shouted at Yolanda, but the woman on the bay gelding either didn't hear her or had chosen not to pay attention. As the afternoon finally began to wane and the sun slipped completely into the ominous quagmire of swollen clouds that choked the western sky, Cassidy realized that she soon would have no choice. She would either have to get down off her horse and rest, or she would fall off.

Coming around a sharp bend in the rough and partially overgrown track, the gray mare suddenly dropped down to a walk. Just ahead of them on the path, Yolanda and the two boys had come to a halt. Like the gray mare, their horses were breathing deeply and spotted with patches of sweat. Kevin's blaze-faced mare snorted loudly and rubbed her head against the side of Raphael's chestnut's neck. But none of them was paying attention to the horses; they were all intently studying the ground and the surrounding brush.

"Three horses left the trail here," Kevin said, gesturing at the thick scrub of bushes that crowded the narrow path. "But the rest stayed on this track."

Thunder rumbled in the distance, a faint but disquieting sound. Cassidy glanced uneasily overhead at the bloated clouds, but the others seemed unconcerned about the approaching storm.

"We stick with the main bunch," Yolanda said. She barely glanced back at Cassidy as she joined them. Instead, she scrutinized the uneven wall of vegetation on the creek's side of the path and announced, "We'd better break for water now."

Almost giddy with relief, Cassidy let the gray mare follow the other three horses as they shouldered their way through the dense growth and down a short rocky grade into the shallow waters of the creek. The stream came only to the horses' knees, but the creekbed was much broader than Cassidy had expected. The bottom was gravelly but level, and the water was so crystal clear that she could see every tiny pebble in perfect detail.

Cassidy felt a tug of caution as the horses splashed greedily into the water. Hot horses and cold water were a dangerous mix; you didn't have to be a Horseman to know that. Yolanda's bay plowed his dark muzzle through the water, sending up a spray that splattered on both sides of him in a wide arc. Kevin's chestnut pawed furiously with first one forefoot and then the other, liberally dousing herself and Kevin's legs with water. Yet despite all the theatrics, Cassidy noticed that none of the horses did any more than just sip at the surface of the creek, drinking perhaps a few swallows in the first several minutes.

After a few minutes of allowing their horses to amuse themselves, both Raphael and Kevin dropped down off their backs and into the creek. Fully clothed and holding their canvas packs up out of the water, the two boys plopped themselves down on their rumps and immersed themselves as far as the shallow creek allowed. Yolanda slid down off her gelding but she remained standing, with her pack and whip still fastened at her waist. She seemed content simply to bend and splash herself with the cool water. Cassidy longed to join them, but she had a very real doubt that she'd ever be able to get back up on the gray mare if she got off.

Raphael looked up at her from the creekbed, easily reading her doubt, and admonished her, "Come on—get off and give that horse a break."

Yolanda's look was a little more sympathetic. "Go ahead," she told Cassidy, "I'll give you a leg-up if you need help."

Whether or not Cassidy had intended to sit down in the water, it turned out that she didn't have much choice in the matter. As she slung her leg back over the mare's rump and slipped over her side, she realized that she had virtually no strength left in her cramped and weary legs. Gracelessly crumpling, she landed in the water with a soaking splash. Luckily, Raphael and Kevin were both already well drenched and didn't object to the additional dousing.

The water was more than cool, it was outright cold but the icy soaking was invigorating and entirely welcome. The gray mare lowered her head, peering solemnly at Cassidy for a moment. Then, snorting in commiseration, the horse pawed at the water, soaking them all again.

Cassidy felt as if she could have happily sat in that creek for the rest of the day; but the repetition of a distant yet distinct sound jerked her thoughts back to more practical matters. The low grumble of remote thunder grated again in the heavy air. Cassidy looked up, scanning the increasingly gray and turbulent sky. The storm was catching up with them.

Yolanda had also been watching the clouds. "Come on," she said, reluctantly but firmly, "we'd better get moving again."

Raphael and Kevin stood, water streaming off their arms and legs. Their saturated clothing clung to them like second skins. With an easy agility that left Cassidy wide-eyed with incredulous envy, both hopped back up on their wet horses, canvas packs and all.

"Wait," Cassidy said, having to struggle clumsily just to get to her feet again. "Don't you think we should start looking for some kind of cover? There's going to be one hell of a storm."

Yolanda threw her a brief look. "We can't stop yet," she said. "We've still got some daylight left, and once it rains we'll lose those tracks."

Cassidy quickly scanned the expanse of darkening sky, where the color of the light had changed from its former eerie greenish glow to a malevolent shade of bile, and the thickening clouds boiled like smoke. The wind was rising, rattling the leaves and chilling her through her wet clothing. "But it's not safe to ride in this kind of weather," she insisted doggedly, staggering a step through the water. "What about lightning?"

Yolanda just tossed her head impatiently, much like one of the horses tossing off a fly or some other nuisance, and stepped toward Cassidy, her hands cupped. "Mount up," she instructed briskly. "We have to get moving again."

Despite her apprehension, Cassidy complied. She was reluctant to ride in the thunderstorm, but she also had the presence of mind to realize that if she didn't accept Yolanda's offer of help, she'd probably never make it back up on the gray mare by herself; and if she didn't go with them then, she might never find her way out of that place. *Anything to get to this Warden*, she reminded herself. And for the first time she permitted herself the luxury of hope: *Anything to get back home*.

Cassidy's legs ached in fresh protest as Yolanda boosted her back up on her horse, and her butt stung as she landed on the mare's broad back. But there wasn't any time to reconsider. The moment Yolanda sprang back up onto her gelding, all four horses sloshed rapidly out of the creek and back onto its brush-choked bank. Once they reached the narrow dirt path they began to jog again, their wet tails streaming out behind them in the rising wind.

Cassidy's clothing hadn't even begun to dry yet when the first raindrops hit. Fat and warm, the splotting missiles seemed deceptively harmless at first, as they melted into her already saturated clothing. But the low reverberation of thunder was growing steadily closer, and intermittent flashes of distant lightning skipped like diffuse explosions across the slate-colored horizon.

Beyond the point where they'd stopped to water the horses, the terrain had begun to change again. The surrounding land was still heavily wooded, and the crude trail—scarcely more than a deer path, Cassidy thought depreciatingly—still wound haphazardly through a thick tangle of secondary growth. But it was becoming more hilly, and the dirt trail was choppy with broken rock. As the hills became steeper, the track deviated more and more from the edge of the creek, feinting and twisting in a series of cutbacks to climb the more formidable slopes. The horses slowed to a jog-trot, forced to search for their footing amid the rubble of loose stones.

The rain, which at first fell in fits and starts, assumed a fairly steady patter, which only made navigating the trail more difficult. Cassidy couldn't quite believe that either Kevin or Raphael could still be seeing any tracks in that mess. As her wet hair began to slap irritatingly against her cheeks and neck, Cassidy realized that a soaked horse's hide wasn't exactly the most stable of surfaces on which to keep a grip, especially in wet jeans. And the more she tightened her knees around the gray mare's barrel, the more slippery the horse's back seemed to become. To add to her discomfort, the thunder had become nerve-wrackingly close, the bursts of lightning illuminating the whole vast expanse of the darkening sky.

Coming up over the crumbling crest of one steep hill, the gray slowed so precipitously that Cassidy nearly went off forward over her shoulder. Ahead of them the other three horses had been forced to break down to a walk. Runnels of muddy water were snaking down the rough surface of the sharply angled path, turning the trail into a small river. The other horses were already fetlock deep in a whirling slurry of mud and suspended bits of shale.

"This is crazy!" Cassidy shouted, not caring anymore if she sounded ungracious. "This storm is only going to get worse—we've got to find some kind of shelter!"

Raphael, his once-curly hair beaten into a lank mop of wet friz, gestured impatiently at the trail ahead of them. The musculature of his chest and the tiny points of his nipples were clearly visible through the soaked fabric of his tank top. "If we stop now, we'll lose their trail!" he insisted.

"What trail?" Cassidy shot back at him, warming to her cause. Not giving him time to make a reply, she furiously shook back the dripping strands of hair that kept dangling in her face and proclaimed loudly, "If we keep on going, we're going to break our damned necks!"

Angrily the black boy jeered Cassidy with the most fitting insult he could imagine. "Not if you really know how to ride, you stupid nigger!"

Stunned speechless, Cassidy nearly lost control and burst into hysterically inappropriate laughter. But she was saved from that spectacle by the storm itself. A near-deafening boom of thunder detonated almost directly overhead, accompanied by a seemingly simultaneous flash of lightning. Painfully brilliant light exploded all around them, and Cassidy heard a peculiar high-pitched ripping sound, like that of tough fabric being torn. Then the air was filled with the choking metallic odor of an electrical discharge.

"Look out!" Kevin shouted. His blaze-faced mare leapt forward, bowling into the gray and Yolanda's bay.

Cassidy had to clutch the mare's mane to keep from falling as the horse slewed sideways on the slippery trail, nearly losing her footing from the impact. Then they all were being peppered with a stinging shower of leaves, wood chips, and shredded bits of bark. Cassidy squinted up into the pelting rain, astonished to see that one of the huge oak trees that had stood alongside the path was now nothing more than a shattered stump, its truncated stub smoking and steaming in the sheeting downpour.

"*Shit!*" Cassidy breathed. "That's *it*—I'm getting the hell out of here!"

"She's right," Yolanda agreed, albeit reluctantly and belatedly. She spun her gelding around on the muddy trail. "Come on, we'd better head for the ledges."

Her horse veered off the trail and plunged obediently into the chest-high tangle of wet brush.

"But the Riders' tracks—" Raphael started to protest.

Yolanda cut him off without a backward look. "The Riders won't be going anywhere in this weather, either," she offered pragmatically. "We'll just have to start over again after the storm blows over."

Kevin automatically swung his horse around after Yolanda's bay and the gray mare, but his rain-streaked face was creased with an anxious frown. Cassidy had observed that the ponytailed boy was well practiced at avoiding the ongoing friction between Raphael and Yolanda; but she had also noticed that he was tough and uncomplaining about following orders. Thus she was surprised to see him hesitate.

"We can't stop in the rain," he said to Yolanda. "It'll be dark soon—and it's going to be too wet to light fires."

Just what constituted "dark" seemed to Cassidy a moot point. The storm had already created an artificial ending to the day's light, and it didn't look as if the weather was anywhere near easing up yet.

"We can find shelter under some of the ledges," Yolanda assured Kevin. "Don't worry, we'll be able to light watch fires there."

Cassidy shivered as the rain began to pound down even harder. She blindly let the gray mare follow the bay, not bothering to try to direct her. She couldn't imagine why Kevin was so concerned about being able to make a damned fire, considering they'd just nearly been ignited by lightning. Obviously the most important thing right then was just getting the hell out from under all those organic lightning rods and out of the drenching downpour. Other creature comforts, such as warmth, dry clothing, and hot food, could easily wait as far as she was concerned.

Yet even Raphael, who was visibly sulking at having been overruled about following the Riders, seemed uncharacteristically concerned about where they would be able to find shelter. Impatiently he urged his mare forward. "What if we can't find enough dry wood?'' he demanded of Yolanda as his horse skidded up behind Cassidy's gray.

"Once we find a cave, we'll have a fire!'' the dark-haired woman snapped back at him, the lash of her whip flapping around her face as she encouraged her horse on. The bay scrambled agilely down a slippery, brush-filled slope, leading the way back toward the creek.

Thunder boomed deafeningly again, and across the sky the churning clouds strobed with a crackling blue light. In the sudden garish glow, Cassidy could see that the shallow creek had been changing along with the rest of the terrain. The horses slid on their haunches down a steep, muddy slope toward a watercourse that had split into several smaller but deeper streams that dodged around huge outcroppings of stone and roiled busily around roots and boulders. They were at the foot of a cliff; not nearly as high a cliff as the one Cassidy and the gray had almost plunged off of the day before, but high enough to have created an impressive series of waterfalls. Over time, the erosion by the swiftly flowing creek had carved out deep cutbacks into the stone, and frothing pools churned at the cliff's base. On the far side of the water, eaten back into the rocky face of the steep wall, were a series of crudely overhung stone ledges, like shallow caves.

Yolanda led the way across the uneven and surprisingly deep tributaries of the creek, past the silvery waterfalls that poured into the turbulent pools, and up into the shelter of one of the larger outcroppings. Repeated volleys of thunder echoed through the canyonlike valley; lightning painted bright gilding on the tumbling water and dripping stone. The storm was all the incentive the horses and their riders needed to press themselves together in the shallow indentation in the rough rock face of the cliffside. It wasn't much of a cave, Cassidy noted; not even deep enough to get the horses completely in out of the rain. But their circumstances tended to magnify the shelter's virtues.

"Get the packs off,'' Yolanda said, dropping down off her rain-soaked bay gelding. "We can spread the ground covers by the back wall and use the horses as a windbreak.''

Raphael slid down, but Kevin remained on his mare. He looked rapidly around the meager dimensions of the narrow, crescent-shaped niche, his odd-colored eyes appearing particularly wild in the lightning's pulsing flashes. "There's no wood here!'' he exclaimed, shooting Yolanda a look of both accusation and dismay. "How can we make fires—there's no wood here!"

"Just get down and give me your pack," Yolanda said calmly. "We'll get wood."

Still not completely mollified, Kevin nevertheless slipped down from the blaze-faced mare's steaming back. Fumbling to unstrap his pack, he regarded Yolanda testily, as if she were guilty of some sort of trickery or betrayal. "It'll all be wet," he reminded her tersely.

"It'll dry out enough to burn," Yolanda insisted sharply. She had already shaken out the heavy tarp; then she set the other packs on it. "Rafe, you and Cassidy see how many branches you can pick up out there." She beckoned to Kevin and continued, "We'll set things up in here."

Cassidy used her mare's thick mane as an anchor to blunt her descent as she clumsily slid down off the broad wet back. Since she was already completely soaked, she didn't really object to briefly going back out into the downpour to gather firewood. Even the proximity of the frequent and brilliant strikes of lightning seemed less threatening away from the biggest of the trees and with the rocky wall of the cliff face as a backdrop. The thing that still troubled her most was Kevin's reaction to their having to seek shelter there and his almost frantic insistence on getting some fires lit. Just why was he so worried?

Out in the rain, along the bank of the creek, Raphael worked quickly and efficiently, scooping up broken branches and bits of old wood with a practiced and methodical rhythm. He paused once or twice to shake back his dripping hair; otherwise he gave no indication that the storm was any inconvenience to him at all. Cassidy tried to copy his businesslike technique for gleaning wood; but the storm distracted her, and her weary stiffness made bending to lift and carry the sticks difficult. And she found herself throwing frequent glances back to the outcropping of rock, where the wet rumps of the horses were lined up fanning outward like four stolid boulders. What was Kevin afraid of? she wondered. For it was fear that Cassidy had recognized in the boy's gleaming eyes, and that emotion was something she had not seen there before.

When Raphael broke and headed back for the cave, his arms filled with branches, Cassidy followed him, even though she had barely gathered a third as much wood as he had. All of it was thoroughly soaked, and she wondered just how Yolanda intended to get it to burn, unless she was planning on letting it dry overnight and making a fire in the morning. But as she slipped back between the gray mare's and bay gelding's big slick and steaming bodies, she saw the way Kevin's bright eyes were watching her and Raphael, and Cassidy realized that tomorrow morning would not be adequate for Kevin. He needed the fire right now.

While Raphael and Cassidy had been gathering wood, Yolanda had laid out the group's simple gear and spread out the ground covers to dry. There had been a small amount of dry debris in the shallow cave, a detritus of old leaves and twigs that had blown in over the course of time and had lodged against the far wall, protected there from the rain. Yolanda had formed a neat little pile of brittle tinder. Then she used the wet branches that they had found to shape the rest of her stack. When she had the wood arranged to her satisfaction, she reached into one of the pockets in her water-darkened loose leather vest and drew out something.

Cassidy had not been there the night before to notice how Yolanda had started the fires; she had been down at the river—hallucinating that she was seeing a giant creature. Truth be told, how Yolanda made fire would have been one of the last things Cassidy would have thought about anyway, given the bizarre circumstances in which she found herself and her troubled state of mind. But now she stared in utter fascination at the small object the dark-haired woman held over the neat pile of wet sticks. She gaped not only because she recognized what it was, but also because it was a clue—a link to that vast and shuttered chamber of memory, the barely accessible storehouse of what Cassidy had already come to think of as the *missing* things: things that should exist, but seemed to be weirdly absent from that place. She gaped because the object in Yolanda's hand was a cigarette lighter.

Automatically, without thinking, Cassidy's hand shot out to grasp the small metal-and-plastic device. Yolanda was surprised by the sudden movement and her grip reflexively tightened. She jerked her hand back, holding the lighter to her chest and staring at Cassidy with shocked reprovement.

"Where did you get that?" Cassidy asked, her voice sounding unsteady even to her own ears.

Yolanda grew more puzzled than alarmed, once she could see that Cassidy was not likely to actually battle her for possession of the lighter. She held up the little rectangular object and shrugged. "Kevin found it," she replied.

"What do you mean, 'found' it?" Cassidy persisted. She threw a sideways glance at the ponytailed boy, who still sat huddled warily against the back wall of the cave. "*Where* did he find it?"

Yolanda turned to Kevin, and he was the one who responded to Cassidy's interrogation. As usual, his answer was candid, if not particularly enlightening. "I found it when we were out riding one time," he said. "I don't remember exactly where we were." He shrugged, a little tug of his lean shoulders that seemed half a shudder. "I found her sunglasses, too." He darted an anxious glance at Yolanda. "Can you just hurry up and light the fire?" he asked her plaintively.

With one last little lift of her eyebrows at Cassidy, Yolanda again bent over the stack of wet wood and thumbed the metal wheel on the lighter. An instant flame, fat and bluish, sprang from its top. She touched it to the dry tinder at the base of the stack and the crumpled leaves quickly caught fire.

Although Cassidy was still staring fixedly at the stack of wood, she was no longer really seeing it, any more than she was cognizant of the grumbling thunder or the erratic flashes of lightning that still continued outside the cave. All she could think of was the startling thought that had leapt into her mind the moment Yolanda had pulled out that cigarette lighter from her vest pocket: It was not matches, which was what she somehow *expected*, even without having previously seen them there; but instead a cheap disposable lighter, the kind with the clear plastic reservoir so you could always see just how much lighter fluid you had left—

The single object seemed to open some small floodgate in her otherwise dammed-up mind, loosing a little gush of images that streaked so rapidly that she could not even begin to inspect or sort them, so rapidly that the anticipated stab of headache was reduced to only a modest twinge. Her gaze moved again to Kevin, whose own odd-colored eyes were firmly fixed on the smoking bits of tinder. How could Kevin have just *found* the damn thing? It was only a disposable lighter, but it didn't fit in with anything else in that place—

Which meant that maybe it didn't belong there, no more than Cassidy herself did. Which meant that someone had to have brought it there, just as she had been brought.

"It's not burning!"

Kevin's panicky exclamation jolted Cassidy back to the situation at hand. In the guttering illumination of another burst of lightning, she saw that the last of the dead leaves and small twigs were indeed burning themselves out, without having ignited the main stack of wet wood. A thin curl of white smoke, wavering eerily in the drafty cave, coiled its way up toward the top of the rocky outcropping. Then even that was gone.

"Rafe, scrape up some more of those dry leaves from back there," Yolanda said briskly, pushing apart the pile of sticks. It was dark by then, nearly as dark as night, and Cassidy found that she could barely see Raphael against the rock wall as he scuttled along the back of the shallow cave. He knelt on the edge of the ground tarp and offered Yolanda a double handful of leafy debris, which she quickly arranged in the gap she'd created in the stack of branches.

"What if it won't burn?" Kevin said, his voice strangely breathless. "What if we don't have a fire and they—"

"Shut up!" Yolanda snapped. Then she seemed to catch herself, and she let out her breath in one long, patient sigh. "It'll burn, Kevin," she said, as she meticulously repositioned the little pyramid of sticks over the fresh tinder. "I promise you it'll burn."

Cassidy could see that Kevin wanted to believe her; but his terror had eroded his trust. "But what if—"

That time it was Raphael who interrupted Kevin, his hand shooting out and closing over the slighter boy's forearm with an almost bruising force. Raphael didn't speak, but the little shake that he gave Kevin's arm said all that needed to be said. And for the first time, catching the half-moon gleam of the whites of his dark eyes in the storm's erratic light, Cassidy realized that Raphael, too, was very frightened. She just didn't know why.

Calmly, almost clinically, Yolanda shifted her grip on the cigarette lighter and used both hands to decapitate it neatly. As she cracked the metal top free of the plastic reservoir, lighter fluid spilled out, sprinkling like a benediction over the stack of branches. A sharp smell, pungent and oddly familiar, filled the little cave. After she'd emptied the reservoir, Yolanda tossed it aside and flipped the lighter's metal wheel again. A series of sparks sprang up, several of them flying uselessly over her fingers. But at least one spark struck the fluid-soaked wood, and a sudden blue-and-gold flame licked up, dancing along the top of the stack. The glow brightened, flickering eerily over Yolanda's face. The flames spread, eating their way up over the side of the pyramid of branches.

Yolanda sat back, tucking the flint wheel from the lighter back into her vest pocket. Her half-exposed breasts were painted in firelight. "See?" she said, her voice steady and self-satisfied. "I told you."

Kevin grinned in sheepish relief as Raphael, grunting deprecatingly, punched him in the arm. The two of them eased away from the back wall of the cave and gathered closer around the now briskly crackling fire. Even the horses leaned in a little closer, their wet and steaming necks bent toward the warmth of the flames.

"Rafe, get out the kettle," Yolanda said, poking at the fire with a stick. "We'll have some hot food and then get our clothes and stuff dried out."

"What about the Riders?" Kevin asked her. Cassidy saw that although the fire had considerably eased his fear, he still seemed anxious.

"They're hunkered down somewhere by now, too," the dark-haired woman said, tossing another large stick onto the fire, where the wet wood promptly popped and sputtered. "We'll go after them again in the morning."

Raphael paused long enough in the act of passing utensils to Yolanda to cast a disparaging look out at the storm. "Damned rain," he muttered darkly. "Now there won't *be* any tracks."

But Yolanda seemed unperturbed. "There'll be tracks again tomorrow," she reminded him. "Fresh tracks—when they start to move again. So for now just shut up and give me my knife."

As Cassidy sat cross-legged on the cave's stony floor, watching the lively play of firelight over her companions' crouched, wet bodies, she tried to make some sense of the little drama she had just witnessed. Surreptitiously studying Kevin as he unpacked one of the canvas parcels, she remembered the way he had warned her the night before about going into the river. Had he known what she would see there?

That thought was profoundly disturbing to Cassidy, for it suggested one of two things to her. If what she thought she had seen in the river had been just a hallucination, had Kevin seen similar illusions? If he had, that opened up the possibility that the odd-eyed boy had come from a similar background as Cassidy, and might very well be here for the same reason she was. The other possibility suggested by Kevin's reactions, however, was even more disconcerting. What if the reason Kevin was so afraid of the darkness was because the creature Cassidy had seen had been no hallucination? What if it had been *real*?

* * *

When Cassidy awoke, she had no idea how long she'd been sleeping. She hadn't been dreaming, but she was jolted out of a sound slumber by a disturbing sense of dread that was not dissimilar to a nightmare's toxic hangover. Like the others, she'd been sleeping rolled up, fully dressed in her still-damp clothing, in an equally damp ground cover, as close to the edge of the smoky little fire as she could comfortably lay. She blinked in the gloom. Her mouth felt tacky and sour with the lingering aftertaste of the heavy spicy stew Yolanda had cooked up for their supper. Every muscle and joint in her body felt exquisitely stiff, and a hank of her hair, limp and reeking of smoke and sweat, was twisted uncomfortably around her neck.

Lifting her head slightly from a cowllike fold of the ground cover, Cassidy quickly scanned the shallow cave. Yolanda and the two boys still slept, three indistinct lumps in the dimness of the cavern, motionless but for their breathing. The fire had burned down considerably, but it still glowed with a glittering bed of red and gray embers. The rain, which had settled down into a steady shower by the time they had finished eating, was still streaming from the black sky. The odor of wet horsehide and smoke filled her nostrils. The horses had crowded in as close as they could under the overhang, but dripping courselets of water kept pelting down on their wide rumps and running in rivulets from their long tails.

Then Cassidy realized that it was the horses that had awakened her. The gray mare nickered low in her throat; it was an anxious sound, not necessarily a friendly one, and was echoed by Raphael's mare. Yolanda's bay gelding stood with his ears swept back against his skull, his big umber eyes rolling nervously.

Something is out there, Cassidy thought, feeling her heart begin to thump in her chest. And then: *Shit! What if it's a bear?*

It was, she realized with a small twinge of self-congratulation, a suprisingly logical and cogent thought for someone who had just been booted out of sleep—especially someone who couldn't even come up with her own name. Bears lived in caves, didn't they? Maybe the bear had been caught out in the woods when the storm started to kick up, and now that things had quieted down a little and the worst of the thunder and lightning were over with, it was—

But that wasn't it, Cassidy had to interrupt herself, no matter how neatly appropriate the theory may have sounded to her amnesia-ridden little brain. Which was a pity, she had to add to herself, since she'd been able to come up with damned few such convincing-sounding reasons for anything else since she'd found herself in this mess. No, forget the bear—that wasn't it. Once again, it was something . . . *missing*.

Pulling herself up into a sitting position, ignoring the protest of her muscles, Cassidy leaned forward, out from under the edge of the musty canvas sheet. She tried to peer out between the forest of horses' legs and long whiskery horse muzzles that surrounded her; but she could see nothing in the darkness outside. The violent part of the storm was finally over. Now the only sound was the steady drone of the rain falling on the rocks and wet leaves outside the cave. That, and the slightly gritty sound the horses' hooves made on the rock floor of the cavern as they restlessly shifted their weight, and the deep mutter of their breath as they—

And then Cassidy knew what was missing.

"Wake up!" Cassidy shouted, swinging around to take a hearty whack at the tarp-shrouded lump nearest to her. "Quick—get up!"

The horses pulled back, snorting in alarm. The sleeping person she'd hit—Raphael, as luck would have it; he already thought she was nuts—jerked upright with surprising speed.

"What the hell?" he growled, glancing furiously around.

"Get up!" Cassidy repeated, struggling to kick her stiff legs free of the confinement of the ground cover. "We've got to get out of here—*now*!"

Yolanda and Kevin sat up, the looks on their faces simple variations of Raphael's expression of confused irritation. "It's the middle of the night," Yolanda pointed out in exasperation.

Cassidy was already on her knees, clumsily trying to get her legs clear of the tarp in which she had been so blissfully wrapped. As she struggled, she bumped into an object at the edge of the fire and sent the small metal pot clattering across the rocks. "We have to get out of here right now!" she panted, finally lurching to her feet.

Yolanda traded a quick glance with Raphael and Kevin. Despite its brevity, the look was eloquent enough. It was obvious they thought Cassidy'd been having another one of her "fits." Filled with twin surges of frustration and panic, Cassidy would have cheerfully banged all three of their heads together—if there had been time.

"Listen!" she shouted at them, waving toward the darkness beyond the mouth of the cave. "The water's stopped!" At their continuing expressions of blank-faced incomprehension, she elaborated, "The waterfall—can't you hear? It's *stopped*!"

Still sitting swaddled in his ground cover, Raphael yawned and obstinately locked his arms around his tented knees. "So what?" he said irately.

"All I hear is the rain," Kevin offered, blinking sleepily.

But understanding had finally come to Yolanda. Looking from Cassidy's agitated face to the dark sheets of water still falling beyond the barrier of the four horses' rumps, the older woman held up her hand in a command for attention. With her head cocked, a strangely intent expression came over her face. "Shit—she's right!" she suddenly exclaimed.

Even though Yolanda scrambled to her feet, Raphael and Kevin still looked confused and annoyed. "What the—" Raphael started. But Yolanda cut him off, making a furious gesture. In the last faint ruddy glow from the fire's embers, her face was weirdly awash in pale light.

"Quick, get the stuff together! We've got to get the hell out of here!"

His obedience to Yolanda was ingrained, but Raphael's habit of protestation was almost as automatic. He sprang agilely to his feet, but still complained, "I don't see why we—"

"There's no time to pack all that stuff," Cassidy insisted, already wedging her way between the big, damply steaming bodies of her gray and Raphael's mare. Ignoring the sharp ache of her cramped muscles, she scrambled up onto the gray's back with surprising efficiency. It was amazing, she thought peripherally as her knees gripped the horse's broad sides, what a little adrenaline could do for your reflexes. The mare snorted nervously, her hooves grinding dully on the wet rock of the cave mouth.

"But—" Kevin tried to ask, uselessly.

"It's the creek," Yolanda explained hastily, abandoning her ground cover and the rest of the little camp's gear. "Listen: There's no water coming over the falls anymore." Even as she spoke, she reached out and took Kevin's arm, jerking him unceremoniously to his feet and ruthlessly propelling him toward his chestnut mare. "The creek must have dammed up with debris from the storm!"

To the boys' credit, Yolanda didn't have to point out to them the obvious conclusion to that; the two of them immediately grasped the logical outcome. If—when—the crude dam on the top of the cliff broke up, the valley would suddenly become a lake, and their cave would be under water.

"Shit!" Raphael reiterated, his big eyes widening in his dark face. Yolanda didn't have to suggest that they mount up. Cassidy had never seen the two boys leap onto the chestnut mares with more alacrity. The instant all four of them were astride their horses, they abandoned the cave, their mounts eagerly wheeling around and plunging out with a clatter of loose stones into the rainy night.

Cassidy didn't even want to think about what might have happened if she had ignored the sense of foreboding she had felt when she had awakened, if she had just rolled over and gone back to sleep. The past couple of days had given her, if nothing else, a lot of practice in discerning things that were missing. In this case, recognizing the absence of something that should have been there might very well have proven to be a matter of life and death.

The rain was still coming down heavily enough that Cassidy quickly found herself completely soaked again. The gray mare's back was slick, and the horse scrambled and slid over the wet rocks and dodged around brush and fallen branches in the numbing darkness. Cassidy could barely make out the forms of the other horses and their riders in the sheeting gloom. She shivered in the unwelcomed chill of the icy shower.

They were on the far side of the creekbed, almost to the steep shaley hill that led back up to the trail, when Cassidy heard the deep grumbling sound. The grating rumble seemed to vibrate up from the ground, through the mare's legs, right to Cassidy's forked thighs. She looked back toward the cliff, the rain stinging her upturned face, just in time to see the tumbling forms of dozens of large and irregularly shaped objects catapulting over the edge of the rim. The gray whinnied sharply and surged forward, her hooves slipping on the slick rock. But Cassidy didn't need to look any longer to recognize what it was she had seen shooting over the falls and landing with such clattering and splashing in the pools below. The debris that had trapped the creek's waters was breaking up; the dam was coming down.

They had been riding in their usual order, Raphael and Kevin in the lead, with Yolanda and Cassidy following. For a split second, Cassidy ungraciously wished that she hadn't taken the time to argue with them, that she had just taken off when she had realized what was wrong. But before she even had time to work up a sense of guilt over that selfishly pragmatic thought, the little valley echoed with a low roaring sound, like the labored breath of a winded horse but magnified a thousand times.

''Damn it!'' Cassidy cursed, as she looked back helplessly in the blackness of the falling curtain of cold rain. As before, she could see almost nothing; but once again she knew even without seeing it just what she was hearing. She leaned over the gray mare's neck and dug her fingers deeply into the thick, wet mane. Then she buried her face between her forearms and just hung on.

The howling wall of water hit her like a full body blow, ripping her legs from the gray's barrel in an icy deluge of churning foam. For a few agonizing seconds, Cassidy hung beneath the mare's neck, her painfully wrenched arms shaking with the effort of trying to maintain her grip on the horse's mane. But the plunging movements of the horse's forelegs as the mare desperately treaded water jolted Cassidy, and the surging flood tore at her own ineffectually kicking legs. Within moments Cassidy felt the coarse strands of mane hair being ripped out from between her clawing fingers. As they slipped free, she made one last frantic lunge for the mare's neck. But the swollen tide snatched her away, and her hands closed upon nothing but the dark and roiling water.

Set adrift, Cassidy tumbled through the cold, fathomless cataract. *I know how to swim!* she reminded herself desperately. Then something big and solid tumbled past her in the churning water and impacted bruisingly with her chest. Cassidy clutched hold of the floating log and tried to pull her head up out of the water. But as she clung to the barrel of the chunk of fallen tree, the free end of it pivoted around and she soundly cracked the back of her head against another log. *Great—not again!* she thought, as pain bloomed again through her still-tender skull. Then her head was slipping beneath the surface, and the debris-clogged rampage of water wrapped her in its deadly embrace.

That was no log!

The incredulous declaration still echoed at the very fringes of Cassidy's consciousness. She was dimly aware of something huge and dark in the water beside her; it was a living thing, a swimming thing, powerful and sinuous. Her lungs were burning and she wanted to inhale. She knew that once she did, whatever the water creature was going to do to her would no longer matter. What the hell—she was abandoned in the strange world with no idea why and no hope of rescue; why not drown? There didn't seem to be much reason *not* to inhale.

But, as usual, while Cassidy was still thinking about it something else entirely happened. She felt the huge swimming thing bump into her shoulder, tentatively, almost gently. Then she felt an incredible ripping pain at the back of her head, as if her hair were being pulled out by its roots.

Cassidy knew the water creature had taken her in its jaws. So she just went limp and let the icy darkness close over her.

Chapter 6 ◀▥

"I think she's starting to come around."

The voice hovered somewhere above Cassidy, shrouded in the red-tinged fog that swam behind her closed lids; and although the words were distinct they seemed strangely hollow, as if they were being stretched out from across some great distance.

"Better tell Allen."

Cassidy felt a sudden hope—wildly surging but cruelly short-lived—that she might somehow be awakening from whatever weird nightmare had befallen her; that she might just open her eyes and not only find herself in a familiar place surrounded by familiar people, but also remember just who the hell she was. But the hope bloomed and then died in her mind, all within a matter of seconds. Even without opening her eyes, she knew that things were still dismally wrong. Although she could remember in excruciating detail what had happened from the time she had first found herself there, racing through the woods on the gray mare, to the last moment before she had lost consciousness in the icy flood, she still could remember nothing else: not who she was, not where she had come from, not how she had come to be there or why.

"Shit!" Cassidy murmured, with heartfelt sentiment. She tried to winch open her eyelids, which felt exactly as if they'd been permanently sealed shut with some of the same sort of heavy grit that seemed to be occupying most of the space inside her skull, where her brain had once resided.

"Shh," someone said soothingly. It was not the same someone who had spoken earlier, even if this second voice sounded equally hollow and remote.

A light hand, warm and dry, gently brushed at her forehead. "Can you open your eyes?" the second voice asked her.

"I don't know," Cassidy said; or rather, that was what she tried to say. What actually came out of her mouth was more like a hoarse croak, harsh and inarticulate.

"Shh. Don't try to talk," the gentle voice counseled her.

"Here, drink this," another voice suggested, and Cassidy recognized it as that of the first person who had spoken. The smooth metal rim of some kind of container was pressed against her lips. Cassidy took a deep, sloppy mouthful of the liquid it contained and swallowed it. Then her eyes flew open wide as, with a barking cough, she sprayed her benefactors with half of the drink she'd just taken.

"What the hell is that?" she croaked indignantly, straining and blinking against the brilliant daylight and the sudden flood of tears that overflowed her bleary eyes. She tried to sit up, still coughing; a strong hand on her forearm assisted her. But the abrupt return to an upright position only made her vision blur more spectacularly, and she felt her stomach roil with vertigo.

"It's okay," the second voice reassured her, as she was softly thumped on the back. "It's just tea—are you going to puke?"

"No—of course not!" Cassidy retorted, her irritation giving some badly needed tenor to her voice. She blinked furiously and her vision reluctantly cleared. With it, her sense of equilibrium improved and the vague feeling of nausea slowly receded. The swallow of hot liquid had burned its way down to her stomach and then leapt immediately, apparently without the need for any other intermediary, directly to her head. She swayed slightly, but doggedly kept her balance sitting upright, as she peered owlishly at her surroundings.

Cassidy was sitting on some kind of rolled-up blanket or bedroll, still clad in her own damp and filthy clothing, in a small clearing in the trees. It was fully daylight, and high sunlight filtered down between the green boughs of the old-growth forest around them. The brush trembled busily with the activity of birds. The grass and leaves were dry, but the air still held that invigorating fresh-scrubbed smell of the aftermath of a storm. Two people shared the little glen with her.

The woman who still held Cassidy by the forearm, the same woman who had gently touched her forehead and had patted her on the back when she had been choking, wavered into focus. She was younger than Cassidy, barely an adult, with the slim, small-breasted body of an athlete. Her delicate-looking, sympathetic face was framed by a corona of dark blond braids. She was dressed in a simple tuniclike shirt and loosely cut pants of some kind of coarsely woven tan fabric.

The other person, the one who still held the tin mug of hot tea and was eyeing Cassidy with genuine concern, was a young man. She hadn't been able to tell that from his voice, which was a soft soprano; and she was only able to tell it on sight by blinking and squinting directly at him. He was as slim and fine-boned as the young woman, whom he vaguely resembled, and in the loosely fitting clothing he wore his body was nearly androgynous. His long hair, the sere color of dead grass and held back by a thin leather thong tied around his forehead, was soft and fine enough to have been a woman's; but he had an adolescent boy's protruding Adam's apple, and there was nothing feminine about the prominent shape of his brow above his pale blue eyes.

"How do you feel?" the young woman asked Cassidy.

But all thought of her own condition had suddenly fled Cassidy's mind, along with any feeling of curiosity she may have been developing about her rescuers. Other concerns—sharp, discrete, and stinging, like the attack of hostile insects—jolted her. She reached for the blond woman's arm, her fingers closing over the coarse fabric of her tunic sleeve with an almost frantic grip. "What happened to the others?" she blurted out. "Yolanda, Kevin, Raphael—the people who were with me?"

The blond woman's soft brown eyes fell; the young man actually looked away for a moment. To her surprise, Cassidy thought that she could see tears in his eyes.

Despite Cassidy's deathlike grip on her sleeve, the girl with the braided hair kept her own hand lightly on Cassidy's forearm. "I'm sorry," she said quietly. "I don't know about the other two; we didn't find any trace of them. But the woman who was with you—Yolanda?—is gone."

Cassidy stared at her for a moment in stunned silence. Somewhere nearby a bird trilled loudly, pouring out its liquid call from the brush, a wordless dirge. When Cassidy spoke, her voice had once again been reduced to a hoarse croak and she felt her throat constrict painfully. "G-gone?" she said numbly.

The loss of Yolanda affected Cassidy more than she would have believed possible. Hell, right along she'd been convinced that she hadn't even *liked* the woman. But to discover that she was dead was an unexpected shock.

Interpreting the look on Cassidy's face, the young man with the long hair held out the metal cup again, offering it to her with a shy deference. When Cassidy shook her head in rejection, he offered gently, "For a while there we thought you were going to be a goner, too. You would have been, if it hadn't been for your horse."

"My horse!" Cassidy exclaimed, her head jerking around with a swiftness that made her vision suddenly blur again, and turned the trees into a fuzzy wall of green. "Where is she? Is she . . . ?"

"Easy, easy," the young woman soothed her, squeezing Cassidy's arm. "Your horse is fine. She's with our horses, down in the meadow."

"Is she all right?" Cassidy repeated, more insistently.

The young man spread his hands in an appeasing gesture. "She's fine, honest," he said. "She just got a few little nicks and dings from all the junk that was floating in the flood, but Aaron took care of her. It's nothing serious."

Exhaling loudly, Cassidy suddenly glanced from one young and expectant face to the other. "You said I would have died if it hadn't been for my horse," she said. "Why? What did she do?"

The two youths exchanged glances; they both looked surprised that Cassidy didn't seem to remember what had happened. "She pulled you out of the water," the blond girl said.

"Yeah," the boy elaborated, "she grabbed you by the hair when you were going under." He illustrated by seizing a hank of his own long hair at the nape of his neck. "She dragged you right up out of the water."

Automatically Cassidy's hand went to the back of her head, gingerly kneading her sore scalp. "So that's what happened," she murmured, relieved and vaguely embarrassed. "I thought it was a—" *A what?* she asked herself. *A water monster?* Grimacing, she shook away the thought. Then her expression sharpened as something else occurred to her.

"How did you find me?" she asked the two. "What were you doing out there in the middle of the night?"

Something in her question seemed to bemuse both the blond girl and the long-haired boy. "We could ask you the same thing," the boy pointed out wryly.

Cassidy felt a little stab of irritation, probably the harbinger of worse aggravations yet to come in dealing with these strangers. Why was everyone there so obtuse? But before Cassidy could make some annoyed retort to his comment, the girl spoke up.

"We knew you were following us," she told Cassidy. "That's

why Allen told Aaron to take the horses and keep on going, while the rest of us split off from the trail. We were hoping you'd split off, too, and go after us, since there were only three of us.'' She shrugged with a good-natured smile. ''When we saw that we'd figured wrong, we circled back around and came up the trail behind you.''

Cassidy felt an incriminating little twinge of guilt at the girl's matter-of-fact explanation, for it forcibly reminded her that she had been riding with a trio of people whose intentions toward the blonde and her companions had been dubious at best. Did they blame Cassidy for being part of that dogged pursuit? she wondered.

At that point the blue-eyed boy took up the narrative. ''When the thunderstorm got too bad, we had to hole up, too. We were downstream a ways from the falls, under a cutback. But when the water stopped coming down the creek, we got out of there quick.''

The girl with the crown of braids had become more subdued as the narration grew closer to the events that had ultimately led to the death of at least one of Cassidy's companions. When the boy hesitated, she stepped in, her voice measured and quiet. ''We heard the horses whinnying—that's how we knew you'd gotten caught in the flood. By the time we reached the place where you'd been trapped, you were the only one left.''

Cassidy looked past their concerned and sympathetic faces for a moment, staring sightlessly off into the green haze of the surrounding trees and bushes. When she felt that she could speak without there being an obvious catch in her voice, she asked, ''You didn't see Kevin or Raphael then?''

They both promptly shook their heads. ''Just you,'' the boy said, ''and her—the other woman.''

Biting down hard with her upper teeth on her lower lip, Cassidy managed to keep the tears from beginning. Then another thought suddenly came to her. ''What about Yolanda's horse?'' she asked them. ''A big bay gelding; did you see him?''

Again they shook their heads in unison. ''But he could have been swept pretty far downstream,'' the pale-haired boy offered. ''Your horse is the only one we saw, and that was only because she swam against the current to get to you.''

For some reason, although it held no logic, that fact strangely cheered Cassidy. If the bay gelding had survived, then perhaps so had the two chestnut mares—and so, by extension, had Kevin and Raphael. But if they were alive, then where the hell were they, and why hadn't they stayed to look for her? As Cassidy's temporarily elevated spirits quickly plummeted again, she regarded her two young rescuers with a certain morose fatalism. What difference did it make if Kevin and Raphael were still alive? They had never been of much help to her anyway.

"So, who are you two?" she asked the two glumly. "Riders?"

The blond girl seemed relieved to leave behind the unhappy recitation of what had happened at the flooded creek, but she made a wry face at Cassidy's comment. "Is that what the Horsemen call us?" she asked, although her tone was without rancor. "No, we're Villagers. I'm Meggie and this is Steven."

Realizing only belatedly that the term Riders was apparently taken to be derogatory, she stumbled for a response. "I'm Cassidy," she said quickly, only further depressed by how easily the assumed name came to her lips now. Would there come a time when she didn't even remember that she had once had another name? With a resigned sense of the inevitable outcome, she still felt compelled to ask Meggie "Can you tell me where we are?"

"Right now?" Meggie said. She made a small inclusive gesture with one hand, seemingly indicating the immediate vicinity. "This is Hector's Territory, but we have permission to cross it. We're about a day's ride out of our own territory."

Misinterpreting both Cassidy's stunned silence and the glassy look on her face, Steven quickly continued to further clarify Meggie's answer. "If you're wondering why we're moving horses through Hector's Territory so late in the season, it's because we've been having so many problems lately with the Horsemen—" He broke off abruptly, actually blushing, as he remembered who he was addressing. "I mean, uh, problems with—"

But Cassidy had not even noticed his presumed gaffe; she interrupted him, her mind racing, hope and excitement tripping all over one another. "You said 'our' territory," she said sharply, unable to keep the note of eagerness out of her voice. "Who are 'we'? What is this place called?" *And how did I get here?* she added in silent fervence. *Better yet, how the hell do I get back?*

Clearly puzzled, both Meggie and Steven stared at her as if they were totally bewildered by what she had just asked. "This is Hector's Territory," Meggie repeated helpfully, slowly enunciating every syllable. "And our territory is William's Territory."

Despair forced Cassidy's tone to flatten, her voice rapidly

losing all inflection. "And before this?" she asked dully. "Before Hector's Territory? What was the name of the place we crossed? What is the whole damned place called?"

A spark of something kindled in Meggie's gentle brown eyes, the beginning of comprehension. She leaned closer to Cassidy, her fingers still resting on her bare forearm. "Cassidy, how long were you riding with those other Horsemen?" she asked quietly.

"I don't know—two days," Cassidy responded, caught between the horns of a nameless anger and some formless pain.

Meggie threw Steven a quick glance; then she went on. "And before then?"

"I don't know!" Cassidy exploded, snatching her arm back from Meggie's touch. "*I don't know*, okay?"

Steven blinked in surprise. "You just got here," he said.

Yeah, no shit—you're a regular genius, Steven! Cassidy thought fiercely, crossing her bare arms over her chest. She glared at both of them, filled with a poorly realized but newly energized sense of savage frustration. "Yeah, I just got here," she snapped, "and I don't mind telling you, I'd just as soon be anywhere else!"

But Cassidy's biting sarcasm seemed to go right over their heads, and she saw only honest concern for her on their faces.

"Wow," Steven said. "How can you have just gotten here and still be a Horseman?"

His honest incredulity begged a civil reply. "I don't know," Cassidy admitted. "I didn't even know I *was* a Horseman until I got here."

"I'm sorry," Meggie said. "We knew you sounded a little confused, but we thought it was just from . . . what happened. We didn't know you were still adjusting."

Adjusting? An interesting choice of words, Cassidy thought.

"Don't worry," Meggie continued, her voice sympathetic and soothing, "you'll be all right once you've been here for a while. When people first get here they sometimes—"

Cassidy seized upon the implication of Meggie's words with an almost ferocious desperation. "What do you mean, when people first get here?" she demanded. "How many of the people here have come from somewhere else?"

Meggie and Steven exchanged a glance, their expressions openly confused but patently guileless. "I don't know," Meggie admitted.

Cassidy's hands darted out, grabbing hold of the coarse fabric of the front of Meggie's loose-fitting shirt. "What about *you*?"

she persisted, staring intently into the younger woman's surprised face. "Did *you* come from somewhere else?"

Meggie made no move to try to free herself from Cassidy's rude grasp; the only change of expression on her face was a slight and thoughtful frown of concentration. "They tell me that I did," she replied after a moment's hesitation, "but I don't remember it."

"I don't remember, either," Steven chimed in.

But Cassidy ignored him and concentrated on Meggie's deep brown eyes. "How long have you been here?" she asked quickly. "And when you first got here, did anyone else know where you'd come from?"

"I don't know," Meggie said, a thin edge of uneasiness evident in her voice. But Cassidy wasn't sure to which of the questions she was replying.

Cassidy abruptly dropped her hands from Meggie's shirtfront, gritting her teeth in frustration. The warning stab of a headache lanced behind her eyes and radiated down her jaw. If only she could ask the right questions, of the right people; *someone* there must know the answers! She drew in a long, deep breath and let it out with deliberate slowness. She realized she was on the verge of loud belligerence, a reaction that would hardly help endear her to these people who had, after all, probably saved her life. She had to sharply remind herself that her position was precarious at best, and that antagonizing them would serve only to accentuate the enmity that seemed to lay between them and the Horsemen. Her mind was already spinning, trying to find another more productive tack to take, when a fourth person arrived in the clearing.

Cassidy's first thought when the Rider came through the trees and into the little glen was automatic and filled with testy aggravation: *Oh, great—another nigger!* For the man mounted on the strawberry roan mare was a black. But before Cassidy could work herself up into a real fit of pique over that fact, she recognized something else—something that temporarily banished all other thoughts of self-pity, irritation, and anger from her mind. She gaped at the horse and its rider as if she were seeing something totally amazing; and in a way she was, for she had just found another one of the *missing* things: The roan mare was wearing a saddle and bridle.

Cassidy's initial sense of astonishment quickly gave way to a series of other conflicting emotions. She was excited and pleased to have discovered another familiar thing, a thing that *should* have been there. But then hard on the heels of that elation, she was filled with the frightening realization that from the beginning she hadn't even known that something so basic and elementary as riding tack had been missing from her experiences there. And if something so intrinsic to horsemanship had already been erased from her memory, what other simple facts might yet elude her as time went on?

"Shit!" she muttered, her hands knotting into frustrated fists.

She doubted that the black man had heard her. He reined in his horse a few yards from where she sat and surveyed the three of them in one quick, appraising glance. When he spoke, he addressed Meggie.

"Allen wants to know if she can ride," he said.

Both Steven and Meggie looked to Cassidy for the answer to that question. But for a moment Cassidy wasn't even aware of their inquiring looks; she was too busy studying the Rider and his horse. She had deduced that this must be Aaron, the man who had kept to the trail last night while his companions had split off, and the man who had tended to the gray mare's wounds. It was hard to judge the height of a man mounted on a horse, but from her perspective on the ground he still looked to be fairly short and unimpressively built. He was also a lot older than either Steven or Meggie; his broad, dark face was creased with wrinkles and his short wiry hair was shot through with gray. His roan was a fine-boned mare, at least two hands shorter than Cassidy's gray, with white socks on both rear legs. And the tack the horse wore was a bizarre pastiche of riding styles: a western-type hackamore bridle, a running martingale, and what appeared to be a modified, hornless stock saddle.

That she could so easily recognize and categorize the types of gear should have cheered Cassidy, she supposed; but instead this belated knowledge only served to make her feel increasingly depressed. Why hadn't she realized it before? For two days she had been riding all over the countryside without a single scrap of tack or equipment—how the hell could she have failed to notice that? She and Yolanda and the boys had been guiding their horses through some of the damnedest maneuvers that a horse and rider could make; and it had somehow just slipped her mind that they were doing all this without the aid of a single piece of gear to guide or control their horses? Things had been crazy enough before, but this was worse than crazy; this was scary, too. Was she losing more of her memory even in the two days she had ridden with the Horsemen? She wondered if she had first seen a saddle and bridle a week hence, would it even have registered as peculiar to her that the Riders used tack and the Horsemen did not? Considering that, Cassidy didn't know whether she was on the edge of bursting into tears or into hysterical laughter.

Finally she became aware that Meggie, Steven, and Aaron were all regarding her with looks of cautious expectation. Had someone asked her a question? Or did she just look as close to sliding off the edge as she felt?

"Cassidy," Meggie said gently, the brown eyes warm and calm, "are you okay? Do you think you can ride?"

Aaron's roan shifted restlessly, tossing her head. The buckles on her headstall jingled, a sound so right, so *normal*, that it almost brought helpless tears to Cassidy's eyes. The black man glanced from her to Meggie and said pointedly, "Allen really wants to get going; we've already lost half the morning."

Somehow gathering up the mass of emotions roiling inside her, Cassidy ruthlessly compressed and swallowed them down somewhere deep inside. She sensed that she had already pressed her inconsiderable luck to the limit with the questions she had already asked; the rest would have to wait if she didn't want to risk alienating these people. While she seriously suspected that they and the Horsemen with whom she had fallen in were old enemies, thus far they had treated her with fairness and compassion. And right then they were all that she had. There was no way she could have hoped to travel on alone, without even so much as food or a bedroll.

Abruptly pushing herself to her feet, she swayed unsteadily, almost tripping and bumping into Meggie. Steven quickly took her by the arm, steadying her and keeping her from falling. She gave him a small smile. "I'm okay," she said. "I can ride."

Meggie eyed her dubiously. "Are you sure?" she asked.

"Yeah," Cassidy lied, immediately convinced from the look of relief on Aaron's face that she had done the right thing—even if the thought of crawling back up on a horse again was about the least appealing idea she could conceive of right about then.

It took Steven only a moment to gather up the blanket and other bits of gear they had used in the clearing. Then the three of them walked along behind Aaron's roan, following as he led the way between the trees and through the brush, up a shallow slope, and over the grassy crest of a broad hill. Below them the terrain was meadowland, dotted with only a few scattered oaks and small clumps of dogwood. Spread out across the grass in a loose group were about twenty horses, tended by a man mounted on a tall, stoutly built piebald horse. One of the grazing horses was the gray mare; but she was not the first thing that drew Cassidy's attention, nor was the fourth Rider. The surprising thing that first caught her interest was the fact that nearly all of the other horses were pregnant mares.

As they came down the brushy slope toward the little herd, Cassidy stared in frank surprise at the condition of the majority of the horses. She quickly noticed that only a few of them weren't big-bellied: her own gray mare; two geldings, which probably were Meggie's and Steven's mounts; and a fat dun gelding harnessed with a heavily laden pack frame. All of the rest of the horses, which comprised a wide variety of colors, sizes, and physical types, were well along with foal. Was that the reason Yolanda and her apprentices had been so eager to catch up with the Riders? Raphael had been so adamant about the importance of not showing up at the Warden's without horses, and with these people were horses in fecund abundance. But given the obvious mutual antipathy between the Horsemen and the Riders, Cassidy had grown increasingly convinced with an uneasy certainty that her previous companions had not been horse traders.

Aaron rode down the hill ahead of them. His roan mare whinnied loudly as she approached her herd mates, and several of the grazing horses lifted their heads to answer her. The gray mare appeared comfortably entrenched amid the assortment of strange horses and was ripping up mouthfuls of grass with a methodical enthusiasm.

Cassidy realized later that she didn't even consciously consider what she did; it was just an automatic, almost casual thing, like a reflex. She just Called the gray. And promptly—although no word had been shouted, no signal had been given—the mare's head lifted and she nickered at Cassidy. Then she broke into a trot, approaching Cassidy. The Riders' reaction was not exactly one of surprise; obviously they knew enough about the infamous Horsemen that Calling was not an unexpected phenomenon.

Cassidy also had not realized how she would feel, how profoundly moved she would be by the sight of her horse. The gray was the one thing she had left from wherever she had come from, and the horse had saved her life. She fought back tears as the mare halted before her. The horse had a few small scrapes and a slight swelling across the bridge of her nose; but otherwise, as Steven had assured her, the mare was unharmed.

As the mare bumped her long head against the front of Cassidy's shirt, wiping her grassy mouth on her jeans, the expression on Meggie's and Steven's faces was one of pleased admiration. Aaron's expression was a little more reserved, but Cassidy could still tell that the black man approved of her close relationship with her horse. The only person who seemed in the least ambivalent was the fourth Rider, who now approached them on his muscular spotted horse.

"This is Allen," Meggie said needlessly, gesturing at him. "Allen, her name is Cassidy and she's only been here two days."

This got a reaction from Aaron as well as Allen. Cassidy saw the graying black man's dark eyes narrow perceptibly, and his roan horse shifted restlessly as his body automatically straightened in the saddle. The man called Allen leaned forward on the stout pie's back, his keen sand-colored eyes regarding her shrewdly from beneath bushy reddish-brown brows.

"You were riding with Horsemen," he said, his deep voice gruff but not accusatory. "That means you must have come here as a Horseman."

It was not exactly a question, but as she looked up at Allen, Cassidy found herself nodding anyway.

Even mounted on horseback, he was plainly a big man. Other than the gray mare, his piebald was the biggest horse in their group, and there was a reason the gelding was Allen's mount. Cassidy doubted that there was a bit of fat on the man; he was just solid and broad-shouldered. He had a full beard and mustache, both a shade lighter and ruddier than his sorrel-colored, shoulder-length hair. He wore the same coarsely woven, bland-hued clothing as the other Riders, yet on his frame it didn't appear quite so loose fitting. His piebald gelding, like Aaron's roan mare, wore a mismatch of riding tack: a hoop-ringed snaffle bit bridle with a scarred and square-skirted western saddle. But despite Allen's impressive size and his apparent position of leadership, Cassidy didn't feel exactly intimidated by him. If anything, Allen somehow struck her as oddly sympathetic.

Belatedly Cassidy realized that Allen was still studying her and the gray mare, even as she had been staring at him and his horse. Then he made a small economical gesture with the free ends of his reins. "You brought the horse with you?" he asked her.

Cassidy's hand slipped up the side of the gray's head, her fingers gently rubbing the base of one delicate ear. "Yeah, it seems that I did," she said simply.

Allen's appraising gaze held Cassidy a moment longer; then

he suddenly shrugged those broad shoulders, casually and almost indifferently. "Good," he said. "Then you didn't learn your skills from those bastards you were riding with." He gave his reins another little flip. "There may be hope for you yet." But for some reason that assessment did little to alleviate Cassidy's uneasiness about her position there.

Then Allen's eyes cut away from Cassidy, his attention swinging back to Meggie and Steven. "Come on, you two, get saddled up," he told them briskly. "We've got to get moving; we've got a lot of territory to cover today."

As the big, bearded man pivoted his horse around and started back across the meadow, for a long moment Cassidy just gazed after him. He was obviously important among the Riders, and yet he had elected to help her despite her dubious association with the Horsemen. That concession and the motivation behind it puzzled Cassidy. But from the moment she had first seen him, she had realized one thing about Allen: Whether or not he would reveal them, he *knew* things. And that was going to make him either a particularly welcomed friend—or a most formidable enemy.

If Cassidy had entertained any hopes of getting more information out of Meggie and Steven while they rode, she was quickly disabused of that notion. Although she didn't feel as spectacularly stiff and sore as she'd feared she would, initially she was more concerned with just working out the kinks from her joints and regaining her sense of balance on the gray's broad back than she was in interrogating her companions. Moving the band of pregnant mares through the rough and hilly terrain required a concerted effort on the part of all four Riders, and there was little opportunity for riding side by side or for conversation. Allen took the lead, with Meggie and Steven at the flanks of the herd, and Aaron in the rear. Cassidy found herself left to follow at the rear, as well. Obviously they weren't worried about her wandering off; more likely, she thought depreciatingly, they just wanted to keep her out of the way.

At least trailing along at the rear of the little herd gave Cassidy ample opportunity to study the horses. In type and physical characteristics, the mares were a mixed bunch, but all of them looked healthy and sound. Several of them also looked very close to term. One mare in particular, a dainty little dark chestnut the rusty color of dried blood, with a star on her forehead and one white forefoot, was already showing definite signs of impending foaling. Cassidy noticed that the mare had streaks of dried milk staining the insides of her rear legs, and the ligaments on either side of her tailhead had already dropped, leaving sunken grooves along her rump. As she watched the blood-colored mare pick her way down another steep and brushy slope after the rest of the herd, Cassidy found herself wondering why the Riders were moving the chestnut such a distance so late in her pregnancy. She had become certain that Yolanda and the boys had intended to try to steal the horses; only the intervention of the storm and the flood had prevented it. Still, given that added danger, it seemed especially foolish to be driving the little band of mares anywhere, much less through desolate terrain. It was just one more question in the puzzle, a puzzle that thus far seemed to be composed almost entirely of blank areas.

Cassidy figured it had been nearly high noon by the time they had started out, so she didn't expect the Riders to stop again for lunch. She didn't really feel hungry, but as the bright summer sun gradually began to slide lower in the western sky, her bladder gave her another, equally compelling reason to hope for a chance to stop. In late afternoon they crossed a small stream, a broad creek that usually was probably barely ankle-deep this time of the year but that was now still swollen from the storm. They slowed to let the horses water, but Allen didn't signal a halt, and no one made a move to dismount.

On the other side of the creek, the hills became lower, and the trees thinned out. They rode along a fairly well traveled looking track that wound its way through brush-dotted grassland and climbed up and down gentle slopes. Finally, when she couldn't stand it any longer, Cassidy dropped the gray mare back and let the herd go on ahead without her. As soon as the horses were out of sight over the crest of a low hill, she slid down off the mare's back and hustled into a clump of alders.

When she came back out of the bushes, still fastening the stud on the fly of her jeans, Cassidy looked up to see a single Rider on the skyline of the hill, his reins dropped to his horse's neck and the horse happily grazing. It was Aaron and the strawberry roan.

Cassidy vaulted back up onto her mare's back and sent her trotting up the slope to catch up. She was not embarrassed at having had to stop to relieve herself, but she didn't want any of these people to think she was inconsiderate enough to have slowed them down. "You didn't have to wait," she said to Aaron as she came abreast of his horse.

Smoothly gathering the horse's reins, the aging black man urged his roan forward again. "No problem," he said evenly, without so much as a sidelong glance at her. "But it's a good idea to stick together around here."

That would normally have been an opening worth pursuing; yet Cassidy didn't feel entirely comfortable beginning to fire questions at that man, especially given his seeming casual indifference, without first getting a little better acquainted with him. Her hand strayed down to straighten an errant swag of the gray's mane. Then she realized that the horse herself gave her the perfect opening.

"Steven told me that you were the one who took care of my horse for me, after she dragged me out of the river," Cassidy said, glancing sideways at Aaron's placid profile. "I didn't get a chance to thank you for that."

Aaron reined his horse over, reassuming his position at the rear of the herd. Cassidy let her gray follow, momentarily uncertain if she would get a response from him. "No big thing," Aaron said after a bit. "Wasn't much that needed tending."

Cassidy bent automatically to stroke the mare's sleek neck. "Well, thanks anyway," she said, "because she means a lot to me."

That made the black man look over at her. On his roan, he sat a good head shorter than Cassidy; yet his gaze seemed to meet hers quite levelly. "She's a good horse," he said. Then his dark eyes narrowed slightly and he added, "Course the Horsemen always seem to have the best."

"You don't think much of Horsemen, do you?" Cassidy said.

Aaron spat, forcefully and so unexpectedly that even the gray mare started a bit. "Thieves and cheats," he pronounced bluntly.

Before Cassidy could respond to that indictment, the wiry black man touched his heels to his horse's sides and the roan bounded forward to urge a straggling mare closer to the herd.

End of conversation, Cassidy thought dourly, letting the gray lope to catch up again.

In the end, however, it was the tough little black man—not Allen, not the more sympathetic Meggie or Steven—who provided Cassidy with more answers to her questions.

Chapter 7 ◀▥

Unlike Yolanda and her apprentices, her new companions did not seem determined to travel until darkness finally made it impossible. If nothing else, they were probably reluctant to push the pregnant mares too hard. As soon as the sun began to set, Allen signaled a halt and they bunched the little band of mares closer together. Once the herd was gathered, Aaron cut the cobby dun packhorse out of the group and snagged his halter rope.

"There's a creek down in the bottom of this valley," Allen said, gesturing toward the long sweep of meadow that lay before them, where the last of the sunlight still painted the waving knee-high grass a washed-out gold color. "Meggie and Steve and I'll run them down there to water, while you set up camp here."

By process of exclusion, Cassidy figured she was expected to stay with Aaron. The frizzy-haired black man had already turned his horse toward a nearby stand of oak, the dun packhorse plodding obediently after him. Scanning the terrain in the growing twilight as the gray mare followed them, Cassidy wondered why they were setting up camp there, in the copse of trees, instead of farther down the valley where there was water. But then again, she was afraid that once she started to question the sense of things in that place, she'd find she wouldn't know where to stop.

"I'll gather firewood," Cassidy volunteered immediately, earning herself a sharp look of surprise from Aaron. She slid off her mare's back and gave the horse a friendly slap to send her off after the rest of the herd to water. It was obvious that Aaron couldn't just give his roan and the packhorse the same freedom, but he was stripping off their gear as Cassidy started into the copse of trees.

As she bent to pick up sticks and struggled with the fallen

branches to break them into usable pieces, Cassidy thought about her sudden change of circumstances. The biggest immediate problem that she could see was that she couldn't be sure if she was any better off with the Riders than she'd been with the Horsemen. At least Yolanda had been willing—eager, in fact—to take her to the Warden. And if the dark-haired woman had been telling her the truth, then Cassidy's best chance of finding her way back home again seemed to lay with the Warden. Now she found herself dependent on the goodwill of the Riders, people who may have seemed at least superficially more civil than Yolanda and the boys, and certainly more forthcoming with information, but who also were antagonistic toward the Horsemen, and therefore probably toward their Warden, as well. It made Cassidy uncertain if she would find anyone willing to take her to him. If only there was some way she could convince the Riders it would be to their advantage to take her . . . Not real likely, she thought glumly, snapping a dry branch over her bent knee, since she knew almost nothing about the Warden that she could use as leverage—about as little as she knew about herself.

By the time she'd returned to the campsite, Aaron had the dun's pack frame emptied and was laying out cooking utensils and sacks of supplies. Around him on the leaf-strewn ground, bedrolls and other gear lay neatly arranged.

"Here, I'll take that," he said, reaching for the armload of wood she carried.

"I'll get some more," Cassidy offered, starting to turn away. But the strange look on Aaron's face stopped her.

"This is plenty," he said, dumping the stack of wood to the ground. "Hell, you could make two cookfires with this much wood."

Cassidy was confused and, what was even more perplexing, for a moment she wasn't even able to pinpoint the reason for that confusion. Then the cause of her uncertainty came to her, more as an image than as an actual concept: Kevin, his odd-colored eyes wide with fear, huddled in the storm-torn dimness at the rear of the cave.

Cassidy stared at the pile of wood; then, almost reluctantly, her eyes lifted to Aaron's weathered face. "Don't you, uh, aren't you going to make—watch fires?"

At first, seeing Aaron's brow furrow sharply, Cassidy was afraid she was going to have to explain what a watch fire was—a good trick, since no one had ever bothered to explain the damned things to her. But then, much to her surprise, Aaron actually grinned.

"Watch fires?" he echoed, shaking his head. "Guess you hung around with those Horsemen just long enough to get a little squirrely, woman!" He began to arrange the dry sticks, chuckling a little under his breath as he worked. Glancing up again, he fixed her with a perceptive but amused stare. "Next thing you know, you'll be tellin' me you believe in monsters."

Too startled to recognize if the comment was meant to be a joke, Cassidy just gaped dumbly at him. A vivid image leapt into her mind, a vision of the weird hallucination she'd had that first night down by the river. Was that creature what Aaron was referring to when he spoke of "monsters"? But before she could make a fool out of herself by blurting out some stupid question, she could see that the black man had not been serious. Still shaking his head, Aaron said, "Fetch me that canvas bag, huh? That one there, the one with the pots in it."

While Cassidy brought the bag, Aaron finished stacking his fire. He fished into the tubular sack and rummaged around until he'd found what he wanted. As Cassidy sat back on her heels beside him, he popped the lid on a flat tin box and pulled out something that caused her eyes to widen again. The little object that Aaron held in his stained and callused hand was a wooden stick match.

"Y-you've got matches!" Cassidy said, stupidly and needlessly, still gaping at him.

Aaron didn't even glance up at her as he struck the match's head on the horny edge of his blunt thumbnail; the tip of the match flared into life. "Yeah, I've got matches," he said in a certain tone of bemused tolerance, as he touched the flame to the tinder he'd placed beneath the wood.

"But—but where did you get them?" she asked incredulously.

Aaron looked up then, her completely unshuttered expression of shock probably visibly reminding him that Cassidy's ignorance was genuine and unaffected. "From the Tinkers," he told her. He snapped the metal box shut again, shrugging lightly. "Matches are one of the things they make for trade."

Aaron misinterpreted Cassidy's stunned silence for disbelief. He had no way of realizing just how startled she was by that simple divulging of information, or how his casual explanation had sent Cassidy's mind helplessly racing. He eyed her curiously for a moment, debating just what part of his declaration she had found unbelievable. Then he simply shrugged again and offered, "Most of our pots and pans come from the Tinkers, too. And things like tools and metal and leather goods. They'll trade for almost anything."

As Aaron turned toward the cooking utensils piled behind him, Cassidy suddenly blurted out, "Have you ever—do you have a cigarette lighter, too?"

"Cigarette lighter?" Aaron repeated, his brows canting. Once again Cassidy was nearly convinced that she was going to be forced to explain the inexplicable. But the black man just shook his head with another rueful grin. "What is that, some kind of found thing? One of your Horsemen buddies must've been a Finder, huh?"

Cassidy's head swam; for a few seconds she was actually dizzy. There was a sharp pressure pulsing behind her eyeballs, making her skull suddenly feel like it was two sizes too small for her brain. She fumbled frantically for the appropriate response, for the right question; but the best she could come up with was "A Finder? What's a Finder?"

Sighing almost delicately, Aaron plunked his bony rump down onto the dirt beside the newly crackling fire. "Woman, you really are *new*, ain't you," he said tolerantly. He rubbed one hand thoughtfully over his stubbled chin. "Finder's a guy who finds things."

Stung by what she thought was a flip answer, Cassidy said in frustration, "What do you mean, 'finds' things? Things that were lost?"

Shaking his head, Aaron patiently backtracked. "No, it's not stuff that's lost. It's like—" He paused, visibly searching for a way to clarify his explanation. He held out his hands, making a vague and yet strangely evocative gesture. "—Like things that ain't here otherwise. You know—*found* things."

Things like sunglasses, and cigarette lighters. In some weird way she could not have explained, Cassidy somehow understood Aaron's definition. What troubled her was that the very explanation itself should have raised some more pertinent questions; and yet she couldn't for the life of her get past the simple overwhelming fact that she had immediately recognized a cigarette lighter for what it had been—and yet Aaron didn't seem to know what she had been talking about. If they all came from the same place, why did she realize what a lighter was and Aaron didn't?

Another disturbing association occurred to Cassidy even as

she hastily grappled with the concept of "found things." If Kevin had been what Aaron referred to as a Finder, and if the things he had found did indeed come from the same place as Cassidy had, was there some other link between herself and the odd-eyed boy? And could that link explain why they had apparently shared the same sort of hallucinations? As she flailed around for the right thing to ask next, Cassidy was unexpectedly assisted by Aaron himself, who had apparently taken her silence for at least an elementary sort of understanding.

"Ain't many Finders," he remarked, reaching again for his cache of pots and pans, "which is a damned shame." He snagged a small cloth sack, and from it he poured something dry and rattling into one of the pots. Then he glanced over at her again. "Horsemen do seem to have more than their share of 'em."

"You don't seem to think much of Horsemen," Cassidy ventured with deliberate ingenuousness.

Aaron made a rude snorting sound. "Thieves and cheats," he reiterated gruffly.

"But you saved my life," Cassidy persisted, "took me in, even knowing that I was a Horseman."

Aaron paused, eyeing her up and down for a moment, his appraisal candid and plain. "Yeah, but you came here as a Horseman, so I guess we can't hold that against you," he said. "And I figure you weren't with that bunch long enough to be much of a thief or a cheat, yet."

"Who's a thief and a cheat?"

The voice right behind them made Cassidy jump; she had been so engrossed that she hadn't even heard Steven ride up. The boy dismounted from his sorrel gelding, swinging a bulging canvas water bag by its dripping strap. In the ruddy glow of the firelight, his boyish face was open and ingenuous, framed by the sweep of his long, hay-colored hair. "Who's a thief and a cheat?" he repeated, looking curiously from Cassidy to Aaron.

"That's not what I said, pretty boy," the grizzled black man teased Steven, making a grab for the water bag. "I said it'll be a *relief* to get something to *eat!*"

"Yeah?" Steven retorted, equally playfully. "Well, then you'd better get cooking, old man. Allen and Meggie are bringing the herd back up from the creek right now."

Aaron glanced up from pouring water from the canvas bag into one of the pots. "Then what are you doing around here, shirking work?" he demanded with unconvincing sternness.

"I came to get your horses to take them down to water," Steven explained, with a toss of his hair. "If you can spare them, that is," he added with exaggerated politeness.

Aaron waved Steven away with a big wooden spoon. "Get out of here then, if you intend to be of some use, you worthless rascal," he told the boy, with an affection his mock severity could not conceal.

Their bantering exchange made Cassidy smile, and she felt an almost inexplicable sense of pleasure, even if Steven's arrival had interrupted her conversation with Aaron. The two of them evidently were good friends, despite the disparity in age, and they obviously cared about one another. All of the Riders, in fact, seemed to get along very well with one another, and to be concerned about each other's welfare. Cassidy had seen evidence of that all day, from the moment she had regained consciousness after her near drowning. She had just been too preoccupied with her own circumstances to think about how these people had related to one another. Thinking back even further, she had to admit that there had been a genuine if slightly more rough-edged camaraderie between Yolanda and the boys, despite Yolanda's loud disagreements with Raphael. With a sudden stab of melancholy, Cassidy realized that she was the only one who did not have any kind of past with these people.

As Steven disappeared back into the gathering gloom with Aaron's roan mare and the dun packhorse, two more mounted figures loomed out of the darkness. The light from the cookfire sent huge, elongated shadows from Allen and Meggie and their horses quivering and skittering over the black trunks of the surrounding oaks. Allen's gelding shook his head, and his snaffle rings rang like soft chimes.

"You ready for supper?" Aaron asked them, waving his spoon.

"Just get us something quick for now, huh?" Allen requested. "Steve and me will take the first watch."

"Something quick?" Aaron complained, looking up from his kettles. "Only thing I've got that's quick is cold. You might take the time to eat a decent meal," he added peevishly.

"Why Steven?" Meggie interjected, derailing Aaron's complaint. "I can take first watch, Allen."

But the burly man shook his big bearded head at both of them. "We're keeping double watch tonight, with Gabriella so close. I just hope that horse holds out until we get home," he added firmly. To Meggie he said, "And I want you on second watch with Aaron, because if she foals it'll likely be after midnight, and you two both know more about foaling mares than either me or Steven.''

"I can help," Cassidy said quietly, so softly that at first she wasn't sure if they had heard her, since their initial response to her offer was total silence.

"You?" Allen finally asked, his tone more genuinely surprised than skeptical.

"I can take second watch with Meggie," Cassidy elaborated. "My mare is a quiet horse, and I've tended foalings before."

From where he squatted by the fire, Aaron's kinky eyebrows tented slightly. "That way we could take three watches instead of two," he pointed out to Allen. "You and me could take the third one before dawn."

Allen thought for a moment. "Okay," he told Cassidy, "get yourself fed and get some sleep. You and Meggie can spell us toward midnight."

Strangely pleased by this left-handed sort of acceptance from Allen, Cassidy watched as Meggie dismounted from her seal-brown gelding and began systematically to strip off his tack. It was only then, as Aaron grumblingly hunted up a cold meal for Allen and Steven, that Cassidy even stopped to think if what she had just assured them was true. Obviously Gabriella was the little rust-colored mare who was so close to term. Cassidy realized that she had known that the mare was nearly due, and that she had recognized all the signs. That must have meant something, mustn't it? But had she ever actually seen a mare foal? Settling back beside the fire with a small sigh, Cassidy found herself fervently hoping so.

Rolling out of the snug cocoon of her blankets beside the banked embers of the fading fire, Cassidy stretched stiffly and stepped carefully around Aaron's still-sleeping form. Steven and Allen were nothing more than dark silhouettes in the pale and waning moonlight as they silently unsaddled their horses.

"Everything's quiet," Allen said softly, while Meggie yawned and hefted her saddle up onto her gelding's back. She had unwound her braids from the top of her head; they snaked down her back like two fat gold ropes.

Cassidy had Called the gray mare. It was still a purely automatic reflex, and she saw muted surprise straighten Meggie's and Steven's postures when the big ghostly horse suddenly appeared of its own volition at the edge of the campsite in the grove of trees.

"How's Gabriella?" Cassidy asked, stroking the gray's lowered head.

"Quiet," Allen reiterated. "With any luck she'll hold out a few more nights."

A few minutes later Cassidy was following Meggie out of the grove of oaks and back down the long gradual incline of moon-burnished meadow to the bedding ground where the little herd grazed and dozed. The horses were all just dark shapes in the darkness. A few of them lifted their heads as Cassidy and Meggie approached; one mare nickered. But there was no sense of alarm, and an atmosphere of sleepy calm soon returned to the grassy slope.

At first Cassidy and Meggie rode around the perimeter of the band of horses, familiarizing themselves with the lay of the land and individually accounting for each horse. The night air was cool but calm, and Cassidy felt warm enough in just her shirt sleeves. Gabriella, the bloodred chestnut, was standing placidly hip-shot on the edge of a group of several of the other mares who were all well advanced in their pregnancies. In the faint and silvery moonlight, their big bellies looked weirdly distorted, the mares like some strange new variation on the equine species.

"She looks as innocent as can be, doesn't she?" Meggie said with a little snort of amusement, as they rode by the chestnut mare. "But she can be sneaky as hell when she wants to be. Last time she foaled, she got out of the mare lot and dropped her colt in the middle of the woods."

Surprise was evident in Cassidy's voice. "Last time? You mean she's your horse?"

Guiding her gelding around a low clump of shadowy box alder, Meggie corrected, "No, not mine personally. We don't have our own horses the way Horsemen do. All these mares belong to everyone in the village. But I know Gabriella real well, because my job is working with the horses."

Staring sightlessly out across the peaceful midnight meadow, Cassidy's mind raced to compose her thoughts. In the muzzy aftermath of sleep, she had almost forgotten that she was no longer riding with the Horsemen, and that Meggie, like Aaron, might actually be willing and able to answer some of her questions. All she had to do was *think*, and figure out what to ask the blond girl. The possibilities almost rendered Cassidy temporarily witless.

The gray mare blew softly through her nostrils, and the totally mundane sound served to jolt Cassidy out of her temporary silence. Patting the horse's sleek neck, she asked, "Meggie, some of these mares are so close to foaling—why are you moving them now? And where did you bring them from?"

Meggie had been studying the dark forms of a pair of the motionless mares. She glanced over at Cassidy and replied, "They're our broodstock. They were off to stud at Silverstone." Her slender shoulders shrugged, a subtle move in the near darkness. "They should have been moved a lot sooner, but we weren't sure before this that all of them were in foal."

"Then why couldn't you have left some of them, the really pregnant ones, there at Silverstone until they foaled?" Cassidy suggested, still puzzled.

But Meggie was shaking her head. "Allen didn't think it would be safe."

"Seems safer than moving mares that are this close to foaling," Cassidy noted. And the gray mare snorted again, as if in agreement.

By that time they had concluded their initial circuit of the herd, and Meggie reined in. She was shaking her head again, but there was no trace of hesitation in her voice as she promptly pointed out, "It's not safer to leave them when there're Horsemen around."

Temporarily stymied not only by the obstacle of her own ignorance, but also by the sensitive matter of her guilt by association, for a moment Cassidy could think of no response. When she was able to frame another question, she spoke again. "Meggie, Aaron said that the Horsemen are thieves, but if you're worried about them stealing these mares, wouldn't it be a lot safer to leave them in one place?"

Meggie tossed her head in a negating movement, her loose braids flapping around her shoulders like twin whips. "Horsemen don't steal the mares," she said, as if she was reminding Cassidy of something that the confused woman had momentarily overlooked. "They steal the newborn foals."

Cassidy was sure her mouth was gaping open; she knew she had felt her jaw actually drop. "B-but how could they do that?" she stammered. "How can they take foals that young without taking the mares, too?"

Cassidy's automatic reaction—*That wouldn't make any*

sense!—almost tumbled out her lips before she could remind herself that sense was not exactly a big priority in this place.

Meggie eyed Cassidy for a moment. Cassidy could not see the blond girl's precise expression, even in the moonlight; but from the set of her shoulders, Cassidy could tell that Meggie was wavering between forced patience and plain exasperation. "They don't *take* the foals," she explained with precision, "I said they *steal* them."

Too confused to try to couch her ignorance in terms of careful questioning, Cassidy just took the line of least resistance and admitted, "I don't understand, Meggie; how the hell do you steal a horse without taking it anywhere?"

"They don't actually take the horse with them—they steal its *spirit*, so they can come back and Call it whenever they want." Blinking, her pale lashes frosted with moonlight, Meggie stared fixedly at Cassidy's bewildered expression. Then the blond girl's delicate face dissolved into a gentle smile. "I'm sorry, Cassidy," she said. "I keep forgetting that you haven't been here very long yet. Because you *are* a Horseman, it's hard to remember that you're still a little . . . addle-headed . . . " Her voice trailed off as she studied Cassidy intently again for a moment. "It's just that you—well, you Called your horse and everything. It just seems that you . . . "

That I should know these things, Cassidy finished to herself for Meggie. No one could have wished that was true more than Cassidy herself. Shaking off the temptation to yield to further self-pity, Cassidy pushed forward with another question while she still had both Meggie's attention and her sympathy.

"I don't understand why the Horsemen have to steal the foals from your mares, though. Why don't they just breed their own horses?"

In the darkness Meggie stroked the long slope of her gelding's shoulder. "Some of them do," she said, with a touch of what sounded like reluctance in her voice. "Those aren't the ones we have trouble with." She hesitated a moment before she continued. "They say that at one time, years ago, the Horsemen bred almost all of the horses in the Territories and traded off their surplus. But then something happened, some kind of problem with their broodmares, and most of them went barren. That's when they started to steal foals. And maybe some of them decided that was a lot easier than raising them, because a lot of them still like to do it."

Cassidy considered that for a moment. The reasons for the

enmity between these people and the Horsemen were becoming clearer, but the dynamics of the situation still puzzled her. "But why do you let the Horsemen get away with stealing?" she asked. "Doesn't anyone try to stop them?"

"The mayors of the villages try to," Meggie replied. "And we always guard our broodmares, but it's pretty hard to always outmaneuver people who can ride like the Horsemen can."

Having ridden with them, Cassidy couldn't argue with that assessment. "But there must be some honest Horsemen," she persisted. "You said that some of them still breed their own horses; can't they—"

As the blond girl interrupted her question, for the first time Cassidy heard a note of curtness in Meggie's voice. "It'd help a lot if their own damned Warden would crack down on them and enforce his own laws," she said. "He has a stud farm, and he's supposedly banned the stealing, but we still don't get any restitution from him." Cassidy half expected the girl to spit on the ground in her contempt. "Sometimes I think he's the biggest thief of them all."

Cassidy winced silently at the harsh appraisal. Was that the kind of man she was hoping to rely on for help in regaining her memory and her home? But before Cassidy could speak again, Meggie had nudged her brown gelding forward, beginning another circle of the herd of mares. Cassidy didn't have to signal her horse in any way; the gray simply followed the gelding.

Cassidy was deeply immersed in thought, preoccupied with trying to thrash out some sense from everything that Meggie had just told her. The whole idea of Horsemen stealing a horse's spirit sounded like a bad joke, or at the very least like a silly superstition. But such brazen thievery would certainly explain a lot about the adversarial relationship between the Horsemen and the people they had called the Riders. Meggie's explanation had also made Cassidy freshly aware of just how precarious her own position might be. She realized that while they may have saved her life out of nothing more than common decency, their continued tolerance of her was based on their belief that she was too recent an arrival to have been corrupted by her fellow Horsemen. And with their obvious antipathy toward the Horsemen's Warden, Cassidy's chances of being guided by them to him were looking increasingly slim. Perhaps she could—

"Oh, *shit*!"

Meggie's soft curse cut into Cassidy's musings, and her head jerked up. Glancing hastily around, she didn't immediately see anything alarming in the quiet, moon-limned meadow, but then she followed Meggie's line of sight to where the group of grossly pregnant mares had been dozing. The horses still stood placidly and quiescent, but there was one notable change: The blood-chestnut mare was gone.

Swiftly scanning the rest of the little herd, Meggie muttered under her breath, "Damn that mare! She's snuck off on us!"

"She won't go far," Cassidy reassured Meggie, urging her horse forward. "If she's about to drop that foal, she just wants to find a more private place."

"The little shit!" Meggie reiterated, reining her gelding over behind Cassidy's gray.

"All we have to do is find where she's hunkered down, keep an eye on her, and then after she foals we can move her back in with the others," Cassidy said. She leaned back slightly, letting the gray mare pick her own direction. Foaling mares craved privacy, but she knew her horse could find Gabriella. Then it would just be a matter of a little discreet surveillance.

"Maybe we should wake Allen," Meggie said, following Cassidy as the gray cut off diagonally through a few low clumps of brush.

"If you want to," Cassidy responded, scanning the moonlit meadow before them. "But as soon as we find her, one of us can go back and watch the herd while the other stays with her."

Meggie thought for a moment, obviously ambivalent about splitting up. "Well, I kind of hate to get him up if there really isn't any trouble . . ." she said.

"She'll probably already have foaled by the time we find her anyway," Cassidy said. "You know how quickly it goes once they find a place and go into labor."

"Yeah," Meggie agreed, a hint of wry amusement edging out the indecision in her voice. "Last time her foal was all dry before we even caught up with her!"

Cassidy didn't say anything, but she sincerely hoped that they would have better luck with the wayward little mare. It would have been merely inconvenient to have had to chase some horse out in the local woodlot when she took the notion to drop her foal. But despite her bland assurances to Meggie, somehow Cassidy felt that their circumstances were quite different. For one thing, she thought grimly, Allen wouldn't have insisted on a double guard that night if he'd judged it safe to leave either the main herd or the foaling mare alone.

Cassidy's eyes tracked steadily across the sweep of darkened prairie, acutely aware of every shift of the gray mare's body and the searching swivel of her scimitar-shaped ears. Involuntarily Cassidy shivered, even though she wasn't cold. Night here was a different thing somehow, filled with all the aching emptiness of the *missing* things. And it wasn't just the implied threat of marauding, spirit-stealing Horsemen that was making her anxious. Aaron could scoff all he wanted about superstitions and watch fires and monsters; that night, more than ever before, Cassidy felt that she understood poor Kevin's nameless fears.

"There—I see her," Meggie whispered loudly, startling Cassidy out of her thoughts. The blond girl pulled in her gelding and pointed. "See her? Down there in that patch of feather-grass."

Peering into the near darkness, Cassidy's line of sight followed Meggie's pointing hand. After a few seconds of studying the paler color of the stand of tall tufted grass, she was able to pick out a darker, amorphous form. Then the shape moved slightly, confirming its identity.

"I think she's getting ready," Meggie whispered more softly.

They were too far away and it was too dark to really be certain, but from the vague movements they could see, Cassidy had to agree with Meggie's assessment. The horse shape shifted, head low, circling in the belly-high grass.

"One of us should go back to the herd," Meggie reminded Cassidy. She hesitated a moment and, when Cassidy did not respond to that, went on. "Gabriella knows me; I think she'll let me get up to her if I go on foot."

Still strangely apprehensive, Cassidy glanced overhead. The waning moon was sinking lower in the western sky; its argent light was growing thin and useless. And though she could see no cause for alarm when she scanned the surrounding prairie, Cassidy still felt the hairs stiffen on the nape of her neck and her arms pimple with gooseflesh. Was there something out there in the darkness? Or was she hallucinating again, her fervid imagination creating "monsters" out of the wavering surface of the moon-frosted summer grassland? But the adrenaline squirting into Cassidy's veins was genuine enough. There was danger there, as real as the sudden trip-hammering of her pulse and the sweat that crept along her hairline.

"No," Cassidy said, her voice low and urgent.

Meggie's eyes widened. "But we can't leave the herd any longer," she said. "And I—"

"Go back to camp," Cassidy interrupted, making an emphatic gesture. "Get Allen—get everyone."

Meggie's eyes had gone round with surprise. "Why? I thought that we—"

"Meggie, just *go*!" The gray mare jumped forward a step, startling Meggie's gelding. "Go get them," Cassidy repeated, a bit more calmly. "I'll watch Gabriella, but you have to go get them—*now*."

Meggie hesitated a moment longer, indecision plain in the taut lines of her slender body. Then she eased her hold on the brown gelding's reins and urged him forward, back toward the herd and the camp.

As horse and rider bounded away, Cassidy wondered if she'd done the right thing. *If I'm wrong, I'll just look like an idiot,* she consoled herself, slipping down off the gray's back. *And they already think I'm that.*

On the ground, Cassidy felt unnervingly exposed, vulnerable in a way that she had not been on the mare's back. She began to walk across the darkened grassland. Glancing back, she saw that her horse had immediately begun to graze, and she almost snorted aloud in self-deprecation. Just how dangerous could it be if her horse was just standing there eating?

Still, the pervasive feeling that something was wrong, that something was . . . waiting, continued to plague Cassidy as she carefully made her way to the patch of feathergrass. What was it Kevin had said about bears? Shivering again, Cassidy quickly glanced around in a complete 360-degree circle. Bears didn't range around out in open meadowland, did they? At night? She had to admit that she didn't really remember as much about the damned creatures as she would have wished—if she had ever known that much to begin with.

Cassidy was nearly up to the edge of the stand of feathergrass when she saw the dark silhouette of the chestnut mare suddenly drop. The mare was going down; the birth would be imminent. Cassidy immediately forgot all about bears and even her troubling premonition of danger. Once a foaling mare went down, her delivery usually followed very rapidly. If Cassidy wanted to be close enough to be of any use if there was a problem, she had to hurry.

Gabriella's star-faced head jerked up when she saw Cassidy approaching; but when Cassidy stopped several yards away, the mare's head dropped back down again with a deep groan. The reaction embodied in that sound was either annoyance or resignation, or some combination of the two. But when Cassidy held her place, the mare didn't try to get up.

The fading moon had slid down so far onto the western horizon that it's light was almost completely gone. Rather than try to rely on moonlight, Cassidy found that her own night vision could be sharpened by continually and minutely shifting the depth of her focus. In the same way that most predators, animal or human, could better detect motion than detail, constantly altering her focal point seemed to accentuate the very subtle contrast between the crushed feathergrass and the recumbent mare. Soon she could even see that Gabriella's tail and haunches were already soaked from the breaking of her waters. If everything went normally, the birth would proceed quickly.

The little rusty-colored chestnut was nearly silent. Even when Cassidy could see her sides bellow out and her abdominal muscles knot tightly with the effort of her contractions, the only sound the mare made was a long, low sigh. Gliding a few steps closer through the tufted, waist-high grass, Cassidy intently studied the horse's low, dark form. The reflective properties of wet surfaces highlighted the foal's emergence. Glistening in the faint moonlight, the slick, caul-covered projectile of its two pointing forefeet momentarily stood out against the dark mound of the mare's hindquarters.

Fresh gooseflesh prickled across Cassidy's back and arms as she stood quietly in the still grass. More excited than apprehensive then, she peered into the dimness. Even moving closer wouldn't have disrupted the birth at that point, but as long as everything was going well, Cassidy had no desire to disturb the little mare. The chestnut rested a few moments, her slender head bobbing slightly in time with her breathing. Then with several more strong, essentially continuous contractions, the bulk of the foal's body slipped from hers.

Gleaming with caul and mucus, the little body temporarily was clearly delineated from its bed of dark feathergrass. Although the mare was no longer pushing, she could not pause to rest. Her supple neck arched around and her muzzle found the warm and steaming form of her wetly shrouded baby. Daintily but without hesitation, she bit through the thick membrane that covered the foal and began to vigorously lick the slick and squirming body beneath it.

Cassidy couldn't yet determine the sex of the foal, since its rear quarters were still lying inside the birth canal. She couldn't even be sure of the foal's color, because in the dark all wet horses

looked more or less the same color. But she could see that Gabriella's baby shared at least one of its mother's features, a finely
shaped head with a white star in the center of its forehead. Gabriella nickered softly, her licking becoming a little less furious
and a little more gently maternal. And the little foal, struggling
almost impatiently to be completely free of her body, answered
Gabriella with a high-pitched and squeaky little nicker of its
own.

I really have seen this before! Cassidy thought in wonderment, still marveling anew at the intensity and immediacy of
the bonding between mare and foal. The baby was so alert, so
instantly cognizant, and yet it was also so completely vulnerable
and dependent. No wonder the Riders believed that Horsemen
could steal a foal's spirit, Cassidy thought; for at the moment of
its birth, the vital essence of the foal did indeed seem to be so
close to the surface that it could actually be touched and taken.

Cassidy's moment of philosophical reflection was shattered
by a loud whinny. Not Gabriella, she realized immediately, although the sound seemed close enough to have come from the
chestnut mare. The whinny had come from the gray mare. The
call had been urgent and warning, and she was rapidly approaching them across the night-cloaked prairie.

Cassidy spun around, just as the gray's pale shape emerged
out of the darkness of the shadowy meadow. Gabriella nickered
again at her foal, but this time the sound was deep and anxious.
Cassidy hoped the mare would not get to her feet yet; the um-
bilical cord was still attached, and if it was torn prematurely,
both the mare and foal could hemorrhage. The chestnut's head
hung protectively over her baby, her ears flicking around like
leaves caught in a high wind.

Cassidy caught the gray's neck in the circle of her arms. "What
is it, girl?" she murmured as the big mare whinnied again.
Cassidy felt her heart kicking in her chest; anxiously she peered
out into the cloaking darkness of the night. Yet despite Cassidy's
fear, the gray didn't exactly seem frightened, just excited. And
while Gabriella was obviously agitated, even her posture seemed
more defensive than fearful. Then Cassidy heard the distinctive
sound of hoofbeats drumming over the sod.

It couldn't be Meggie and the other Riders, Cassidy realized
immediately; the direction from which the sound came was
wrong, and it wasn't three or four horses, it was more like—

The gray mare whinnied again, loudly and almost directly in
Cassidy's ear. The indistinct silhouettes of two mounted figures,

black against near black, loomed against the skyline. Then a voice that Cassidy had not expected ever to hear again hissed loudly at her from the back of one of the horses.

"Shh! Keep her quiet, damn it!"

Cassidy was too shocked to come up with any quick repartee; and before she could speak, the rider who had addressed her had sprung agilely from his horse. As he scurried forward in the dimness, his gold earring winking faintly, Raphael commanded her irately, "Come on—get out of the way!"

Doing anything but getting out of his way, Cassidy deliberately stepped in front of the black boy, knocking into him and nearly sending him sprawling in the deep grass.

"What the hell are you doing here?" she demanded.

Righting himself with an indignant jerk of his broad shoulders, Raphael shot back at her, "Look who's talking! What the hell are *you* doing traveling with a bunch of Riders?"

Punching him in the center of his chest—an action designed to be more a gesture of outrage than one of actual deterrence—Cassidy said, "They saved my life—when *you* two left me to drown!"

"Rafe!" an equally familiar voice interrupted them.

Cassidy's glare shifted to the remaining mounted figure, dimly outlined in the darkness. "Kevin!" she barked at him. "What do you think you're doing?"

Another shrill little nicker from the foal on the ground instantly answered Cassidy's question for her. Her eyes shot from Kevin's silhouetted form, to Gabriella and her foal, and then back to Raphael. "Oh, no!" she exclaimed, making a grab for the boy's arm. "You're not—"

Raphael easily sidestepped her, but Cassidy lunged after him, her fingers closing on the thin fabric of his tank top. As he spun around to try to shake her free, Cassidy fell to her knees, pulling him down almost on top of her. "No!" she grunted furiously, only tightening her grip.

Cassidy didn't realize that Kevin had hopped down off his blaze-faced mare until she felt his hands grappling with her shoulders, his fingers digging into her flesh as he entreated, "Cassidy, let him go!"

"No!" she reiterated emphatically, glowering up into that familiar face with its odd-colored eyes framed by a slightly disheveled mane of silky hair. "You can't steal this foal!"

"Oh, yeah?" Raphael retorted, finally wrenching himself free of her grasp. He scuttled out of the reach of her flailing arms, nearly bumping into Gabriella's recumbent body. The little mare arched her neck protectively over her foal, nickering nervously at the scuffle.

"Cassidy, we *have* to!" Kevin pleaded, still gripping her tightly enough by the shoulder that she could neither reach Raphael nor twist around and disengage herself from Kevin's hold. Panting, she glared at Kevin as the ponytailed boy concluded, "We have to go to the Warden alone now; this might be our only chance to—!"

"No!" Cassidy shouted again, fiercely attempting to throw herself forward as she saw Raphael moving toward the newborn foal. "Raphael, don't you dare! If you touch that foal, I swear I'll—"

But at that moment, words failed her. She'd do—what? What if anything could she hope to threaten Raphael with in that place? The bizarre irony of it almost made Cassidy burst out laughing. After all, whom was she trying to protect—the Riders or the Horsemen? If she really wanted to reach the Warden, if she really wanted to find out where she was and how the hell to get back to where she'd come from, then she probably would be better off with Kevin and Raphael. The Riders were likely to be nothing but a dead end; did she really owe them anything? Hell, let Rafe "steal" the foal—what difference would it make? If anything, she probably should offer to help him, to expedite things so that all three of them could hurry up and ride out of there before they got caught.

In the few seconds it took for all of those conflicting impulses to swirl through her mind, Raphael had reached the damp little star-faced foal. Cassidy watched in mute fascination as he bent over the baby horse and spread his hands in a weblike net of fingers on either side of the delicate head. Leaning forward, while Gabriella nickered anxiously, Raphael lowered his face to the tiny bewhiskered muzzle. And then, although Cassidy could not see precisely what happened, she suddenly knew exactly what Raphael was doing. She knew because she had done it herself once, under other circumstances, in a lifetime frustratingly remote from the one in which she now found herself . . .

She had been there when the gray mare was born. She had been such a tiny filly, twin to a stillborn colt, and when she had slid from her exhausted dam's body, at first she had just lain there, limp and motionless. And Cassidy had pulled up that slender head, mucus streaming from the thin, elliptical nostrils, and had put her mouth over the little muzzle. Then, with all of her strength, she had breathed air into the lanky, lifeless form. And after a moment or two, the slippery rib cage had heaved and the tiny filly had coughed, spraying her with phlegm; and then she had begun to breathe for herself.

Within a heartbeat, Raphael had finished, his breath mingled with that of Gabriella's foal, its spirit stolen by him so that no matter who raised this horse or where it went, some day, when Raphael Called it, it would be his.

Kevin's viselike grip on Cassidy's shoulders had slackened; she hadn't even noticed because at some point she had ceased to struggle to free herself from it. She just slumped bonelessly to her knees, watching wordlessly as Raphael rose to his feet and slowly turned to face them.

When the sound came, it seemed to issue from some great distance, a place so far from them that by the time it reached Cassidy's ears, it no longer had any real meaning. It took the boys' stunned reactions, Raphael's gape-mouthed look of total astonishment and Kevin's frantic leap of pure fear, to jolt Cassidy back to her current reality.

The sound had been a gunshot.

Chapter 8 ◀▥

For one weirdly frozen moment no one moved, not even the startled horses. Then a curse of angry frustration bellowed out across the stretch of dark prairie behind them; Cassidy recognized the voice as Allen's. And then everyone moved.

Raphael and Kevin leapt like frightened deer, reaching their chestnut mares in about two strides and mounting so swiftly that Cassidy thought they were going to overshoot the horses' backs. Gabriella whinnied shrilly and lurched to her feet, rudely spilling her still-wet foal out onto its side. And Cassidy herself spun around to face the direction of Allen's voice, wildly but only briefly considering the merits of sprinting toward the gray mare and making a run for it, following Raphael and Kevin.

The one thing that kept Cassidy from fleeing was no longer a question of loyalty, or even the priority of survival. She stayed because the sound of the gunshot had already sent her mind racing, and she could never have turned away from the promise of something for which she had spent the last two days searching. She could not turn away from one of the *missing* things.

So rather than run, Cassidy went quickly to Gabriella, catching the nervous little mare by the mane and gently but firmly holding her near her foal. The baby whinnied squeakily, floundering across the grass in a tangle of legs, trying unsuccessfully to gain its feet. Its frantic attempts distracted the rust-colored mare and recaptured her attention. In a moment she was no longer concerned about Cassidy's presence, but was nickering supportively at the thrashing foal.

Cassidy flinched in the harsh light of an oil lantern as the glare struck her face. Allen held out the lamp in one hand; the long shape of a gun barrel rested in the crook of his other arm. Temporarily blinded by the light, Cassidy could not clearly see the big man's face, but she could imagine his expression. At least he wasn't shooting at her, too, she thought grimly.

Meggie's brown gelding nickered at Gabriella; the blond girl had to keep him reined in to prevent him from going right up to the chestnut mare. Cassidy thought that Meggie was about to dismount, but a command from Allen prevented her.

"Go back to the herd and help Steven," the big man told Meggie. "And tell Aaron to pack up; we'll leave at first light."

Meggie's long braids were disheveled and fraying; the glow of the lantern caught in the individual hairs, gilding them in a halo of light. She hesitated, glancing from Allen to where Cassidy still stood with Gabriella. "What—what about the foal?" she asked him, her voice colored with both defensiveness and uncertainty.

Cassidy still couldn't clearly see Allen's face, and the sudden vehemence of his response startled her, even though she was all too aware of his anger. "Damn the foal!" he exclaimed, the long barrel of the gun bobbing sharply. "We might just as well kill the damned thing outright!"

"Allen, no!" Meggie protested, ready to leap from her gelding's back to defend the baby.

The lantern, Cassidy realized then, was hooded so that its light was directed outward; all she could see of Allen was the bulky outline of his mounted figure and the jutting shaft of the gun's barrel. But she didn't need to be able to see his face to recognize the frustration and fury he was feeling. He shook his bearded head and made a restraining motion toward Meggie with the hand in which he held the lantern. The wash of stark yellow light swung wildly, painting not only Cassidy and Gabriella but also Meggie, her horse, and the foal in its coarse brilliance.

"Get back to the herd, Meggie," Allen said more quietly, almost wearily, Cassidy thought. His tone was more one of resignation than indignation then. "I won't hurt the foal—hell," he added sardonically, "who knows? Maybe we'll get lucky; maybe that bastard'll die before this horse gets grown and Called."

Meggie managed a small smile, but it never quite reached her eyes. With one last quick look at Gabriella's foal—a colt, Cassidy could see then, as the wobbly little creature lurched clumsily around within the glow of Allen's lantern—Meggie reluctantly reined her gelding around. Touching her heels to his sides, she headed him back toward the herd at a lope.

For a few moments Cassidy was unsure what to do next. The fact that Allen hadn't just summarily shot her didn't mean she had been exonerated, or that she would escape his wrath. As her colt made a particularly spectacular effort to rise to his feet and tumbled flat out into the feathergrass in a tangle of unwieldy legs, Gabriella nickered loudly and pulled away from Cassidy's grasp. She let the mare go. Slowly she looked up into the bleak glare of the lantern at the towering shape of the man on the horse.

"Call your horse," Allen said to her.

Cassidy hesitated, her eyes helplessly drawn to the long dark shaft of the gun, which was then pointed almost casually downward. In the light from the lantern, the metal of the barrel appeared oddly dull and unreflective. Jerkily, her head pounding, Cassidy stumbled through the haze of mental images she could call to mind. A rifle? But something about the stock didn't look right for that . . . if only she could *remember*.

Misinterpreting both her hesitation and her particular stricken look, Allen repeated, "Go ahead, Call her." He deliberately ducked the barrel of the gun lower, resting its muzzle against his booted foot as if to reassure Cassidy that he didn't intend to harm her.

But Cassidy couldn't take her eyes from the gun. It was right and yet not right. If it was a rifle, then it seemed a somehow crudely drawn representation of one, as if it had been made by someone who'd had a less-than-perfect grasp of firearms. And that made it significantly different from the rest of the *missing* things she had found there, for things like Yolanda's sunglasses and the cigarette lighter had seemed perfectly regular in appearance. Why then, if those things had been normal enough, was the gun somehow imperfect?

Her skull aching, Cassidy forced her mind out of that unproductive rut and looked up suddenly into the yellow ring of light, directly into Allen's shadowy face. "I wasn't with them, you know," she told him quietly. "I tried to stop them."

Allen was silent for a moment, but Cassidy could almost hear him frowning. Then he said, "Yeah, I know. We could hear you yelling." He shrugged, the big shoulders hitching. "I figure if you'd wanted to steal the foal, you would have done it before they ever got here—and you sure as hell would have been a lot quieter." He paused again, studying her in the darkness, and when he resumed speaking, his already gruff voice was pitched even lower. "Luckily for you, out here we're the only ones you'd have to convince of that." He made another gesture with the lantern, causing the light to splash crazily again. "Now go. I'll stay here with these two until they can make it back to the herd."

Staring up a moment longer at the big outline of his mounted figure, Cassidy turned and Called the gray.

Clearly dismissed, and apparently excluded from even helping Meggic and Steven with the herd, Cassidy rode back to the campsite. It was still dark, but the darkness no longer seemed so absolute or frightening, and she knew the dawn was slowly approaching. Aaron had stoked the fire and was bent over his kettles when she rode into the oak grove. He barely glanced up at her as Cassidy hunkered down on her abandoned bedroll and sat cross-legged, her knees pulled up under her chin.

After a time, he grunted, "Colt, huh?"

Eager for the warmth and acceptance implicit in human conversation, Cassidy quickly responded, "He looks like he'll be chestnut like Gabriella; he even has her star on his forehead."

Aaron made a snorting sound. "All her foals have that," he said, balancing the coffeepot on the edge of the coals.

"How many foals has she had?" Cassidy asked him, honestly curious as well as trying to prolong the exchange.

Briskly stirring something in a pot, Aaron answered without looking up. "Four so far." There was a period of silence, stretching out just far enough that Cassidy almost felt compelled to jump into it with some inane comment. Then the black man shot her a brief but pointed look and added, "Four if you count this one, that is—and I guess I don't see much call to, since the damned thing's been stolen right out from under us."

Feeling her face heat in spite of herself, Cassidy stared down into the low flames of the cook fire. "I tried to stop them," she reiterated, increasingly aware of just how unconvincing that statement probably sounded to these people.

But to her surprise, Aaron just shrugged. "Those bastards can be quicker than a greased snake when they want to be." He eyed her thoughtfully. "And I hear they had to go right over you to get to that foal." He spat on the ground. "Too bad that horseshit gun of Allen's misfired."

Her recollection of what happened out on the prairie rapidly replayed in Cassidy's head, and something suddenly fell into place. "The gun," she said slowly. The gun had misfired; that's why no one had been hurt. Abruptly she looked directly into Aaron's dark and weathered face. "Aaron, where did Allen get that gun?"

The instant the words were out of her mouth, Cassidy was already mentally answering her own question: *Yeah, I know, probably where these people get everything that doesn't fit—he "found" it,* she thought morosely. But to her great surprise, Aaron had a different explanation.

"Got it off a dead Trooper," the black man replied, barely glancing up from his cook fire. He spat again, that time into the fire, creating a brisk sizzle on the coals. "Damned thing don't work worth a shit most of the time anyway," he concluded dryly. "A good slingshot'd be worth a hell of a lot more."

Cassidy's mind was racing again, a flat-out contest between her desperation to know and the warning strobe of her headache. She tried not only to register what Aaron had just said, but also to integrate that information with what she had seen out on the prairie, and—most difficult of all—with the vague and maddeningly elusive fragments of memory she could apply to the simple concept of firearms. The gun was not a found thing then; could that be why it seemed to be somehow imperfectly made? And Aaron had said the gun belonged to a Trooper—a *dead* Trooper, Cassidy reminded herself. Troopers were some kind of Horsemen, Horsemen who were connected to the Warden. Cassidy was distressed to realize that the whole origin of the gun had only given her added evidence that a serious rift existed between her companions and her goal, the Horsemen's leader.

Temporarily abandoning that depressing line of thought, Cassidy reconsidered what had happened out on the prairie. Even if the gun had misfired, the moment she had heard the shot, she had recognized the sound. Once she had seen the gun, she knew what it was, and yet there was something odd about it. Unfortunately, whatever it was that was wrong was something too esoteric for her fragmentary knowledge or memory of guns. But more important, the instant she had heard the gunshot she had known for certain that she had found another one of the *missing* things: The gun was something that she should have expected to have found there, and yet she hadn't even realized that until she had actually seen it.

Cassidy didn't even realize that Aaron had spoken until the wiry man repeated his request, patiently but more loudly than should have been necessary. "I said," he said again, finally catching her attention, "if you're just going to sit around here chattering, how about running down to the creek and fillin' my water sack again?" As he spoke, he waved aloft the canvas bag on its leather strap.

Embarrassed by her inattention, Cassidy took the sack with a rueful smile. As she got stiffly to her feet and started away from the fire, Aaron called after her.

"Might as well get cleaned up, too, while you still can. Once it's daylight and that colt is about, Allen'll want to get moving again."

As Cassidy negotiated the path between the thick trunks of the oak trees, she was surprised to find that it was already light enough to see the terrain quite clearly. The eastern sky was streaked with streamers of pink and mauve. Across the long slope of grassland that lay beyond the grove of oaks, the dark shapes of the horse herd were silhouetted against the lighter color of the prairie. Cassidy counted two mounted figures, Meggie and Steven, moving around the periphery of the herd; but from that distance she couldn't tell if Gabriella was one of the horses, and she didn't see the new colt. Since she didn't see a third mounted figure, she also assumed Allen still hadn't returned.

Following the trail of trampled grass along the gradual incline toward the stream that cut through the center of the valley, Cassidy felt a whole litany of depressingly familiar aches and pains. Her legs and buttocks were still sore from all the riding; her knees stung from her rude landing when she'd been knocked off the gray mare; and she felt a burning hitch in her shoulders from the way Kevin had dragged her off Raphael. On top of all that, her head still hurt—not sharply or massively, but chronically, with the annoying kind of nagging throb that seemed to have become a perfect metaphor for all the frustrating aggravations of that whole place. *The hell with it!* she thought emphatically, swinging the empty water bag at a hapless clump of meadow daisies. She even took a certain grim satisfaction in having bluntly decapitated several of the pale, harmless flowers by the pointlessly violent act.

The small creek was lined by thick clumps of river willow, but in the hoofprint-pocked dirt was a clear indication of the path where the horse herd had gone down to the water's edge to drink the night before. Winding her way around the tall green whips of the willow sprouts, Cassidy studied the tracks in the damp sandy earth. She lifted the canvas water bag again, using it as a flail to hit the willow branches and spook up a couple of redwing blackbirds from the bushes. Watching the birds fly away, croaking their indignation at being so summarily disturbed,

Cassidy nearly walked right into the broad rump of Allen's big piebald gelding.

The horse was standing quietly hip-shot near the creek's edge. If he was surprised by her sudden appearance, he didn't act like it. Of course, Cassidy hadn't exactly been trying to sneak up on anyone; she'd been making enough noise to alert a deaf man, much less the average horse. The pie's long, strangely thoughtful-looking face turned toward her, his jaws slowly grinding and green whiskers of willow twigs sticking out from either side of his mouth.

Slung parallel to the horse's body, across the saddle's heavy skirts, the long barrel of Allen's gun hung hooded in its scabbard. Cassidy couldn't see much more of the weapon than its dark wooden stock, and that looked nicked and scarred. Previously the weapon must have been carried along with the rest of the gear on the packhorse, because Cassidy was certain the rifle and scabbard had not been on Allen's saddle when she had first seen him. Unwilling to touch the rifle, she merely stared at it for a moment. Then, reaching out to gently pat the piebald on his haunch, she slipped past him. Once she'd cleared his shoulder, Cassidy saw the reason the gelding was there.

The creek was a shallow and rapidly running stream, its low banks choked with thick clumps of sedge grass and arrowroot. A couple of yards out from the bank, Allen stood calf deep in the clear water. He was barefoot and his pants legs were rolled up, but he was generously splashing water onto his arms and chest, heedless of how wet he was getting his shirt. He had his back to Cassidy, and seemed so absorbed in his bathing that she didn't think he'd even noticed her, until she began to slowly back away from the creek bank. Then he swung around, water droplets spraying from his beard, and stopped her with a single look.

"I, uh, Aaron asked me to get water," she began to explain, holding the canvas sack aloft, as if in self-defense. "But I can just—"

Then Cassidy broke off; not because Allen had interrupted her, since he had yet to say a word, but because she could then see why the big man had come down to the creek to wash up. The front of Allen's coarsely woven shirt was blackened and there was a large shredded rent over his right breast, where it looked as if the fabric itself had somehow been torn apart. Beneath the tattered material, the skin of Allen's chest appeared stained or discolored with something dark and gritty.

Finally realizing that she was gaping, and that Allen hadn't even spoken to her, Cassidy just blurted out, "W-what happened to you? Are you all right?"

The ends of his sorrel-colored mustache lifted in an ironic little grimace. In the first light of morning, Allen's hair and beard were the same color as the sunlight. He made a gesture toward where the piebald horse stood placidly behind Cassidy. "Aw, it was just that damn gun," he said. He shook his head, water flying from his hair, and then took a few sloshing steps closer, right to the edge of the bank. "It's more trouble than it's worth most times." He brushed absently at the wet fabric of his torn shirt. "Misfired and nearly plugged *me* instead of that damn thief."

Automatically and without thinking, Cassidy stepped forward and reached out toward Allen. Her fingers tugged gently at the blackened material of his shirt; some of the fabric actually seemed to be stuck to his skin.

As Allen sucked in his breath with a hiss, his hands came up and he grasped her wrists. "Ow!" he protested.

"That's a powder burn," Cassidy objected. "If you don't get all the junk cleaned out of it, it could get infected."

Barely an arm's length from him, Cassidy stared directly up into Allen's face. As his eyes widened slightly with a mixture of surprise and skepticism, she could clearly see that they were not just sand-colored, they were almost the same reddish-gold color as his hair, and his pupils were black abysses.

"How would you know about things like that?" he asked her.

"Because I—" Cassidy's response, which had started off with a burst of automatic spontaneity, then sputtered out in the face of a lack of any continuing factual support. "I—I don't know," Cassidy was forced to admit, but she still boldly met Allen's eyes. "But it's true," she added.

To her surprise, Allen suddenly chuckled. "I don't doubt that," he said, dropping his hands from her wrists. "Well, let me get this shirt off and I'll wash it up, then."

Slightly flustered, for reasons that for once had little to do with her chronic lack of recall, Cassidy just nodded. She waited while Allen tugged the bottom of the shirt out from the waistband of his pants and wriggled his torso to pull the slip-on–style garment off over his head.

"Shit," he muttered once, his face buried behind the fabric as the tattered shirt pulled free of the powder burn on his chest.

Cassidy leaned forward again, lightly circumscribing the margins of the blackened area on his chest with her fingertips. The skin wasn't broken, but it definitely had been burned, and in that area the sprinkling of fine chestnut-colored chest hairs had been literally seared away.

"Well? What do you think?" Allen asked, making her jump involuntarily.

She glanced up into his face for just a moment, her heart thumping. Then she took the damaged shirt from his hand and replied, "I think if we wash it up good and you can keep it clean, it'll heal up all right."

"Hey!" Allen protested, as Cassidy grasped the edges of the rent in his shirt and pulled, ripping the coarse fabric with a tearing sound. "That shirt could have been fixed!"

"It's easier to just get a new one," Cassidy blithely assured him, as she tossed the remainder of the garment up onto the creek bank and swiftly bent to wet the smaller swatch of material she'd torn off from it. She was too preoccupied to realize she had just made a supposition that was completely unsupported by the immediately available facts; and she was too distracted to notice Allen's expression of puzzled irritation at her apparently unwarranted assumption. Cassidy soaked the piece of cloth in the cold clear water of the creek and wrung it out slightly. Studiously, her lips pursed in concentration, she touched the makeshift washcloth to the margin of Allen's burn.

"Ow!" he said, his breath once again hissing between his teeth.

So much for him being the stoic type, Cassidy thought absently, gently rubbing at his scorched skin. To her relief, the blackened coating and charred hairs began to dissolve and wash away with only a minimum of pressure. She bent again and dipped the soiled scrap of cloth into the creek, creating a small cloud of turbulent debris in the otherwise pristine water.

The second time Cassidy touched Allen's chest, the big man said nothing—although she doubted that it hurt any less. In a way she was uneasy about that silence, for within the cushion of its implicit consent she was allowed to realize that the situation was beginning to affect her in a way that she could neither anticipate nor understand. Carefully swabbing the raw, shiny red skin beneath the coating of burned gunpowder, she was both puzzled and disturbed by the strange stir of emotion she was feeling. She had been willing to touch Allen; she had, in fact, wanted to do it. Yet at the same time she felt a certain wary reluctance at the contact, and she wasn't sure where the conflict was coming from.

Bending a third time, rinsing the cloth scrap, Cassidy actually felt the skin on her face tighten with the prickling beginnings of a flush. The reaction was inexplicable to her; Allen certainly hadn't done anything to embarrass her—he hadn't complained again and he was being completely cooperative. She kept her eyes lowered, fixed upon the task at hand as she resumed her ministrations, but even that didn't seem to help. She tried to concentrate only on the reddened skin of his chest, to be absolutely thorough in removing all traces of charred matter. But his scent, a mixture of smoke and sweat and horses, teased her nostrils. The musculature across his chest and abdomen was flat and cleanly defined; her first impression of his lack of fat had been correct. In the undamaged areas of skin the hair on his chest appeared wiry, like coppery shavings, yet it was surprisingly silky beneath her fingertips. And his nipples—dusky-colored circles with a diameter greater than the span of her thumb—had grown stiffly erect in the chill of—

"Hey, Allen—what happened to your shirt?"

The sound of Meggie's voice made Cassidy jump; she nearly dropped the washcloth. Taking an involuntary step backward, she spun around to see the blond girl reining her little seal-brown gelding through the willows, around Allen's piebald and down toward the water's edge.

Allen, of course, had been able to see Meggie coming. His voice was entirely nonchalant as he stepped up away from the creek and replied, "Got blasted when my gun misfired, when I shot at that bastard." Shrugging as he picked up the garment's crumpled remains, he added, "Look what it did to my chest."

While Meggie leaned forward in her stirrups to peer at Allen's injury, Cassidy took a few more steps away from him, the wet cloth still dangling from her fingers. She still felt the strange heat glowing across her cheeks, and she knew that she must be blushing. Confused and inexplicably irritated, she struggled to understand what had just happened. Oblivious to Meggie and Allen's casual conversation only a few feet away from her, she flashed back to what she had been feeling right before the young woman had interrupted. She had been touching Allen's chest, washing off the gritty residue of the powder burn. . . She remembered the firm warmth of his skin, taut over the muscles, and the way the sunlight caught on his curly hairs, and the faint smell of—

And then, with a dizzying lurch, she remembered exactly what she had been thinking. She had known to just where that whorllike line of golden hair that trailed across Allen's belly led, after it disappeared into the well-worn waistband of his pants; and she knew exactly what she had wanted to do with him, as startling and astonishing as that act might seem to her.

Head thudding, blood pulsing hot in her ears, Cassidy suddenly looked up with the baffled realization that Meggie had asked her something, and she had missed it entirely. The blond girl's expression was friendly but expectant; and seeing Cassidy's slightly dazed look, she patiently repeated herself.

"After you take back Aaron's water bag, can you help me bring the herd down here to water?" Meggie asked Cassidy. "With Gabriella and the colt, it's going to take the three of us to manage them."

Glancing over at Allen, Cassidy saw that he had already walked over to his gelding and was casually adjusting the horse's cinch. "Uh, sure," she said to Meggie. "Just let me get this water back to Aaron, and I'll be right back."

Meggie's horse had drunk his fill. As she gathered the reins, he lifted his dripping muzzle and swung obediently around. Cassidy watched as Meggie guided him past Allen's gelding and back toward the meadow.

Weak-kneed, Cassidy squatted down by the creek's bank and hastily pushed the canvas bag under the surface of the stream. The water felt soothingly cool on her fingers, and for a few moments she just crouched there, staring down into the crystal clear liquid. Without volition, she found her thoughts returning to that astonishing vivid mental image of Kevin stepping nude from the river by the Horsemen's camp. The memory caused the same surge of uneasy excitement that she had just felt with Allen. But what was that feeling? And why had neither of the two men seemed to have been affected by it?

When she straightened up again and pulled the soaking wet bag out of the creek, she felt her shoulders burn in protest. Turning, she jerked back in surprise. Allen had been standing right behind her.

Cassidy looked up wordlessly at him, water from the canvas bag dribbling down her arms and dripping onto her boots. His eyes were not just sun-colored, she decided, they were actually bi-colored, gold in the center of his irises with a darker amber ring around the outer rim.

"Thanks for helping me," he said, making a small gesture with one palm toward his bare and reddened chest. His upper lip twitched slightly, something that was nearly a smile. "Guess if I grease this up with some of Aaron's horse salve and put on a clean shirt, I'll live, eh?"

Cassidy had to fumble for words. "Uh, yeah," she agreed, trying not to stare at him. She was still so stunned at the incredible thing she had found herself wanting to do with him, she felt that every detail of the proposed act must have been painted across her face, obvious for him to see. But even though his attention to her seemed somehow heightened, Cassidy did not sense that that unbelievable deed was what Allen was thinking about as he continued to gaze at her. She suspected that renegade desire and all of the giddy ambivalence that attended it were like her dreams and hallucinations and the elusive echoes of her memories: something she had carried with her that the other people in that place did not share.

Finally, after a few moments of uncomfortable silence, he said, "Meggie and Steven tell me that you think you came here from somewhere else."

"I *know* I came here from somewhere else," Cassidy told him, as calmly as she could.

"Do you remember anything about it?" he said.

Perhaps the moment called for a strategic lie—Cassidy wasn't certain anymore. It was becoming harder and harder to tell who the good guys were, to whom it was safe or propitious to tell the truth and with whom she would be better served by a little creative dissembling. But that time she was simply honest. "A little," she admitted. "Just bits and pieces—useless stuff mostly."

The big bearded man just calmly studied her for a bit longer, his scrutiny blunt but inoffensive. She didn't have the sense that he was assessing the veracity of what she had said; rather, he seemed to be considering his own response to it. "We should get back to the village by midday tomorrow," he said, "even with slowing down some for the colt." His big shaggy head cocked slightly, and again Cassidy was struck by the canny intelligence behind those gold-ringed eyes. "People there don't trust Horsemen, but I think they'll make allowances for you having just gotten here. They'll understand if you're still a little . . . confused." His eyes narrowed slightly but meaningfully. "But they won't understand you claiming to remember things from somewhere else. We've already got one woman there like that, and she's gotten herself in enough trouble with her crazy ideas. So just be careful what you say."

That said, Allen started to turn away, to go back to his horse.

Cassidy's arm shot out so quickly to stop him that she dropped the water bag.

"Wait!"

He paused, turning back to her. Cassidy's heart was hammering in her chest, victim of an excitement that was alarmingly similar to the one she had felt earlier at the creek. "This woman," she said, so hastily and urgently that she literally ran out of breath and had to pause before she could go on. "Has she—does she have the Memories?"

Allen eyed her curiously; Cassidy wasn't sure if his quizzical expression was in response to her question in general or to the term in particular. "I don't know," he said simply. "But she's like you; she thinks she came from the Slow World."

This time Allen had barely begun to move, had hardly begun to shift his weight to turn away from her, when Cassidy's hand closed over his powerful forearm. "Wait!" she entreated him, still breathless. "What do you mean, the 'Slow World'? Is that what you call where I came from? If this other woman came from there, too, then someone must—"

"I don't know," Allen repeated. "I don't know if the Slow World even exists, but there are people who think so."

"Doesn't *anyone* know?" Cassidy persisted. "If this other woman came from somewhere else, too, then—"

"That's just what some people think," Allen interrupted.

Frustrated, Cassidy forgot her customary respectful caution with him. "What do *you* think?" she demanded.

Allen shrugged, gently but eloquently. "Maybe we all came from somewhere else," he said, "but what does that matter? We're all here now."

Yeah, Cassidy thought, deliberately dropping Allen's arm, *we're all here now—but that doesn't mean that they can make me stay here.*

The view from the hill overlooking the long valley was nothing short of spectacular; it was easily the largest stretch of land that Cassidy had been able to see at one time since she had arrived in that strange world. All morning the terrain had hinted at what was to come. The sharply hilly country with its upland meadows, forested ravines, and little creeks as quick and cold as ice had gradually evened out into vast sweeps of green hills, cloaked in trees, with long easy approaches. Even the trail they had been following had changed from a faint and grassy path to a broad dirt track, liberally pockmarked with hoofprints and incised with long ribbonlike depressions.

That final hill looked down on an almost inestimable reach of land. The floor of the valley was at least an hour's ride away, so far away that the details of the landscape blurred into the distance. Cassidy let the gray mare come to a halt, and from her vantage point at the rear of the small herd of horses, she gazed out across the great hollow.

Allen and Meggie were riding point as they moved the band of mares along what, Cassidy finally realized then, could only be called a road. Aaron and Steven rode flank, keeping the horses from straying too far off to the sides in their natural search for forage. Cassidy rode her usual position of drag, trailing at the heels of the others. She didn't mind. In the day and a half since the incident with Gabriella's foal, she had been atypically subdued, just grateful that these people hadn't banned her from their camp. She never would have found their village on her own, and Allen had given her a compelling reason to want to go there.

Cassidy had mostly avoided contact with the big man since the previous morning. That wasn't too difficult to do, since she would have had to go out of her way to ride with Allen or to speak more than the most basic rudiments of campfire conversation with him. He was preoccupied with safely moving the horses. He seemed to have lost all interest in the things they had discussed down at the creek after she had treated his burned chest. And as for the other thing—the alarmingly graphic notion that Cassidy had had when she had touched him—well, it seemed that Allen had never shared that particular urge anyway, so there was not much likelihood of him pursuing it if Cassidy didn't.

Even I'm not too sure just what the hell that was all about, Cassidy mused, automatically brushing a fly off the gray mare's shoulder, *but I know that it's something important—something I was supposed to forget.* Just over the crest of the hill she could see Allen on his big piebald gelding, methodically scanning the road ahead of them while Meggie veered aside to guide back one overly adventurous bay mare. The incident under consideration had left Cassidy feeling more frustrated than disturbed. It continued to suggest to her that she had been tantalizingly close to discovering something more not only about that place, but also about the place from which she'd come. But no matter how many times she went back over it—what had happened, what she had thought, how she had felt about it—she could not get past the initial feeling of surprise. The rest of it, what it *meant*, was still lost to her.

Maybe when I get to this village, she told herself determinedly, urging the gray forward again. *Maybe when I meet this woman Allen told me about . . .*

That thought was still lingering comfortingly on her mind when Cassidy first saw the building. She wasn't sure if she had somehow signaled the gray mare to stop, or if the horse had just been as surprised as Cassidy had been. Either way, she felt her crotch impact painfully with the point of the mare's withers at the sudden halt. After that, she was too amazed to think about such trivial matters.

It wasn't even a house, she thought. Houses? *This is the first constructed thing I've seen here!* The building, whatever it was, was still a good distance off, ensconced in simple harmony with the land on a shallow slope, surrounded by tall trees. It couldn't be a house; it didn't have enough windows for that, and the only doors were big full-height things, hung on rails instead of hinges.

Like a barn—or a shed of some kind, maybe, for storage or—

Or what? Cassidy's mind reeled, racing after implications. But the flood of images that assaulted her proved to contain more questions than answers. But it was a building, an actual structure, something that had been made. And a village would have a lot of buildings, a lot of—

Of what? Grimacing in concentration as her head began to pound, Cassidy's whole body went taut with the effort of trying to conjure up the rest of the pieces of the maddening puzzle.

"Hey, are you okay, Cassidy?"

Steven's voice made Cassidy jump; in her struggle to remember she hadn't even noticed him ride up alongside her. Trying to smile, even though her head then felt as if her upper teeth were being hammered out of her skull from the inside, she pointed toward the long rectangle of the structure that lay ahead of them. "I just saw that building," she said with forced nonchalance, "and I was wondering what it was used for."

The long-haired boy politely looked in the direction Cassidy had pointed. "It's just a machine shed," Steven said, his pale brows tenting slightly at her interest in what must have seemed to him to have been an exceedingly mundane thing. Trying to be helpful, he added, "Lots of stuff is kept out here near the fields, instead of having to haul it back and forth all the time. There's probably not too much stored in it this time of the year."

Before Cassidy could digest that and try to formulate some

more useful questions, Aaron called out from the other flank of the herd. "Hey, you two, save the chat for later," he shouted. "You've got two stragglers over there."

As Steven urged his horse forward, Cassidy nudged the gray to follow. Still frustrated by her inability to extrapolate further from what she had seen—what kind of "stuff" would be in that shed?—she exerted a little more zeal than was strictly necessary in closing up the rear of the horse herd. After that, she no longer had time to fret over the machine shed.

It actually took Cassidy a few moments to realize that what she was looking at was a fence. That was because, looking back, she could see that the fence had been running parallel alongside the road for some time, although it was set back a bit, and also because the fence, made of woven wire and wooden posts, was such a simple and ordinary-looking thing that it literally seemed to be part of the natural terrain, and not man-made. And when she realized what lay beyond the fence, those dizzying and formless margins of the abyss that lay within her memory began to drop away frighteningly from beneath her.

They were cows—the kind of cows raised to eat, she knew automatically, not the kind raised for milk. Stout and blocky, their reddish hides trimmed in white, they were spread out in a casual swath along the edge of the well-grazed field that was enclosed by the wire fence. A few of them raised their heads as the Riders drove the horse herd past, but most were not even disturbed from their foraging.

Cows: They were one of the *missing* things. Cassidy's thoughts tumbled, a stampede of images, and for a moment the pain in her head grew so intense that she thought she was going to pass out. Then the furious pounding eased for just a moment, and she even had the name of the cattle's breed: Hereford.

At the head of the band of mares, Allen and Meggie had stepped up the pace. The horses, no doubt sharing their riders' eagerness to return home, were quite willing to cooperate. Even the herd had become more focused, funneling down the broad dirt road at a brisk jog trot. From her position at the rear, Cassidy was forced to view everything through a veil of dust. But even that hanging curtain could not conceal from her the onslaught of images that was yet to come.

Cassidy had barely been able to tear her eyes away from the cattle, even when they had ridden well past them. Beneath her, the gray mare jittered restlessly, picking up on and amplifying Cassidy's sense of upheaval. Cassidy looked ahead to either flank of the mare band, looking for Aaron and Steven; but both of the men were occupied with channeling the horses forward, and neither seemed to notice her growing excitement. Then the dirt road breasted a small crest and dropped gently lower, suddenly presenting Cassidy with such a panorama of sights that she could not hope to assimilate them all at once.

Fields—there were fields on either side of the road, cleared land distinctly separated by color and content, and filled with things that Cassidy realized with some amazement that she recognized: wheat, breeze-whipped and nearly ripe; corn, waist-high and neatly aligned in brilliantly green rows; and what? alfalfa? She was sure of it. And some things that were low and darker green, planted in rows, like beets or carrots.

They're farming!

And in the fields there were other people, lots of people, bent over hoes and adzes; and even a team of horses in harness, pulling a cultivator through the rows of fluttering corn. And on the road, coming up the long slope toward them, was a wagon with wooden sideboards and wide metal-rimmed wheels, pulled by a pair of—*I don't believe this!*—mules. There were more people in the wagon, like the people in the fields and like the Riders, all garbed in simple coarsely made clothes and all looking up and waving, excited to see that their mares were back, and—

What the hell's that noise?

Looking down to see why the gray mare's hooves were clattering as if she were crossing a rocky streambed, Cassidy saw that the road was paved here, with a solid seamless surface that looked like gritty, grayish asphalt. Then she heard the sound of barking. There were two dogs racing alongside the horse-drawn wagon, yapping playfully at either the approaching herd or at the—

Cassidy's head boomed, making her vision swim, and even the familiar bulk of the gray mare's body between her knees suddenly felt watery and insubstantial.

There were children, a half dozen or so boys and girls who rode in the back of the wagon, smiling shyly and waving. They were the last thing Cassidy saw, sepiaed in the fine powder of the suspended dust, before she felt the gray mare hesitate and she found herself sliding, gracelessly and inexorably, down to meet the road's dusty pavement as a relieving blankness rescued her overloaded mind.

PART TWO ◀▥

Chapter 9 ◀▥

"Is she prone to the fits?" someone said.

"I don't know. She'll be all right, though; she's coming around now."

The first voice was feminine but not familiar; the second voice was Meggie's.

Cassidy, her eyes still tightly screwed shut against the thunderous throb of a tremendous headache, slowly sorted through her vast inventory of aches and pains, seeing what had been added to the stockpile. She was somewhere dim and cool, laying on a firm surface with the subdued murmur of many voices in the background. Inside a building, she thought, from the artificial way the voices rebounded. She could smell smoke and the faint residue of old cooking odors.

"Where did you find her?" It was not the first voice, but another woman's.

Meggie again: "A couple of days out." Her gentle hand brushed the hair back from Cassidy's forehead. "She'd nearly drowned in a flash flood on Turtle Creek."

"Allen said she was riding with Horsemen." A third woman's voice—or was it the first woman again? Cassidy felt too woozy to be certain.

"She *is* a Horseman." That was Steven, and the statement was made with a certain simple pride. He added, apparently to Meggie, "Is she okay?"

"I'm okay," Cassidy croaked, and she felt her dry lips crack painfully with the effort. She cranked open her lids and squinted up into the blurry circle of faces that floated above her. Fixing on Steven's familiar face, she forced out, "My horse?"

Steven smiled, an expression that lit up his ingenuous face with unfailing brilliance. "She's fine," he assured Cassidy, reaching down and stroking her bare arm the way he would calm a nervous horse. "She's with the mare herd."

Trying to focus, Cassidy looked beyond Steven and Meggie and the immediate little circle of people who were bent over her recumbent form and scanned her surroundings. She was indeed inside of a building; but the automatic lurch that her mind made in trying to recognize, categorize, and extrapolate beyond that simple fact made her eyes ache and her stomach wobble with nausea. "W-where am I?" she asked shakily.

"Double Creek—our village," Steven said helpfully.

But Meggie gave him a little poke with her elbow. "She knows that," she chastised him. "She means where is she *now*." To Cassidy, Meggie offered, "You're inside the field house. We brought you here after you—" Meggie hesitated. "—after you fell off your horse."

Cautiously Cassidy glanced around herself again. The field house? Nothing about the term registered with her, and only her puzzlement at that odd fact kept her from becoming light-headed again.

She was in some kind of very large room, high-ceilinged, with exposed wooden beamwork and white plastered walls that were festooned with hanging cooking utensils and shelves of dishes. There was a long wooden counter along one side of the room and numerous tables and chairs. A surprising number of people surrounded her, all of them dressed in the drab garb of the Riders. The clothing, however, was their only common denominator; there were men and women of all ages and sizes, even a few blacks. Most of them looked quite concerned about her. All of them looked curious.

Seeing the bewildered expression on Cassidy's face, Meggie tried to explain. "A field house is, you know, where you can get food and drinks and stuff."

A restaurant, Cassidy's mind fuzzily supplied; or, given the place's rustic appearance, an inn or pub or tavern.

A gray-haired woman with twig-thin arms and shrewd bird-like eyes said to Cassidy, "Can you sit up? Here, drink this."

Cassidy recognized the woman by her voice as the one who had spoken first, when Cassidy had first regained consciousness. She peered suspiciously at the proffered mug. "What is it?"

"Oh, just a bit of brew," the old woman said, pushing the earthenware mug closer to Cassidy's face.

Cassidy grimaced as she caught a whiff of the eye-watering

fumes; but she was thirsty and her head was still pounding from trying to think. *Oh, what the hell,* she capitulated, accepting the mug. The "brew" was obviously a local effort and tasted similar to the strong beverage Steven had urged upon her when she had been recovering from her near drowning. The herbal taste was so strong and bitter that the stuff seemed nearly intoxicating. Coughing as the hot drink burned its way down her throat, Cassidy found herself wondering vaguely if the brew could be dangerous. But peering over the tilted rim of the heavy mug, she thought she saw approval in the gray-haired woman's bird-bright eyes.

It was the last thing she was aware of for some time.

Cassidy woke to the sound of dogs barking. Jerked into consciousness, a gush of adrenaline sending her heart thudding helplessly against her ribs, she sat up and sent some of the blankets that covered her slithering off the bed.

Oh, shit—what a lousy idea! she realized belatedly, as her head responded to the abrupt change in position with a tremendous surge of pressure that made her vision dance. She flopped back down onto the pillow, groaning as she clamped her eyes shut again. *What the hell was in that drink they gave me?*

The nearby sound of yapping went on unabated, but Cassidy chose to ignore it for the time being. Eyes still closed, she tried to remember exactly what had happened to her since she had regained consciousness in the field house. She quickly replayed the jumble of images and abbreviated conversation. She couldn't remember anything after she'd taken that drink from the old twiggy-limbed woman. But she didn't need to open her eyes again to know that she was lying in a bed—a real bed, even a clean one, from the feel and smell of it. And she was wearing . . . what? Nothing. Swell!

Cautiously cranking her lids open a fraction, Cassidy squinted in the room's dim light. There were several other beds there, similar to hers but all empty. The room's walls were the same rough white plaster as those of the field house, but completely unadorned, and the bare floor was made of broad boards of smooth unstained wood. The only furniture other than the beds was a pair of large wooden dressers. The single window was heavily shaded with drapes, but something in the nature and angle of what little light leaked through made Cassidy think that it was morning outside.

Slowly, her eyes still half closed, Cassidy pushed herself up into a sitting position again. Arms crossed over her bare breasts, she was glancing around the room looking for her clothing when the door swung open and a woman entered.

"Hey, you're awake—good!"

Cassidy blinked, partially in surprise and partially just in an effort to clear her gummy eyes. She stared stupidly at the woman who had just come into the room. She was about Cassidy's age, but a little shorter and decidedly plumper, with touseled brown hair and impishly wide hazel eyes.

"Where the hell am I?" Cassidy asked her.

The buxom woman grinned. She had a broad, agreeable-looking face with the kind of generous mobile mouth that seemed specifically designed for that very expression. "Wow, I forgot," she said, coming the rest of the way across the room to Cassidy's bedside. "You were totally out of it when Allen brought you in here last night."

"Wait a minute," Cassidy interrupted, feeling a sharp but nonspecific sort of pain stab through her skull at even the simple effort of trying to think. "Last night? You mean I came here *yesterday*?"

The woman's tone was sympathetic but incurably enthusiastic. "Yeah, yesterday afternoon." She peered at Cassidy for a moment. "Do you remember that part?" she prompted.

Automatically reaching to massage her throbbing temples, Cassidy threw the woman a quick and rueful look. "I don't remember anything after they gave me that damned drink!"

The brunette woman laughed, a sound so spontaneous and unaffected that Cassidy instantly felt the beginnings of a genuine rapport with her. "That was Ruth Ann and her infamous brew," she said wryly. "I guess they figured it'd either kill you or cure you."

"Yeah? Well, which one was it?" Cassidy muttered.

Unlike the drably clad Riders, the plump woman was dressed similarly to Cassidy in a T-shirt and jeans. Of course, her blue T-shirt was considerably more faded and was stretched across a far more impressive bosom, and her jeans, weathered almost to the point of colorlessness, seemed close to threadbare across her ample thighs. The woman casually rested one well-padded hip on the foot of the bed and said, "I guess you've still got a headache, huh?"

I've had a damned headache ever since I got here! Cassidy thought, but what she said was "What happened to all my clothes?"

"I took them last night to wash them," the woman explained. She made a small, vague but perfectly evocative gesture. "They reeked! Your jeans looked like they could have walked out and rode a horse all by themselves! Your stuff's all ready to wear again now, though."

"Thanks," Cassidy said automatically. Then she hesitated, realizing she didn't even know the brunette woman's name. "I'm sorry," she said, "I guess I don't even remember who you are."

"Oh, yeah!" The woman slapped her own forehead in a theatrical gesture of self-deprecation. "I should have known." She thrust out one hand. "Rowena. Allen told me you're called Cassidy," she added, as Cassidy shook her hand.

"Where is Allen?" Cassidy asked. "And what happened to my horse?"

"Allen's probably where he usually is—out working," Rowena said. "And you don't have to worry about your horse; they take better care of the horses than the people around here."

Before Cassidy could comment on that, the more or less continuous background noise of the barking dogs outside suddenly rose into a chorus of yips and then abruptly ceased. A loud voice roared, "Rowena? Are you in there?"

"Oh, great!" Rowena sighed, hefting her rump up off the bed and tipping her head in resignation toward the window. "That's the mayor; she's here to talk to you."

Cassidy's mind still felt dishearteningly fuzzy. "Mayor?" she echoed dumbly, glancing down at her own naked torso. "She wants to talk to *me*?" Her previous conversation with Meggie about Horsemen stealing foals came back to Cassidy in a rush; hadn't the blond girl told her that the mayors were the ones who had attempted to thwart the thievery? What had Allen and the others told the people of the village about the incident out on the prairie with Rafe and Kevin and Gabriella's foal?

"Don't worry, I can stall her for a while," Rowena said. "Come on, up you go." She beckoned to Cassidy with a rapidly fluttering motion of one hand. "I put your clothes in the bathroom, so you can wash up a little before you get dressed."

As she swung her bare legs over the side of the bed, Cassidy realized that she wasn't even wearing panties. Awkwardly but determinedly, she pulled one of the blankets off of the bed and wrapped it around herself as she rose to her feet. Rowena was pointing through the open bedroom door, to where another door opened off a short hallway. Dragging the long tail of the blanket behind her, Cassidy scooted across the smooth wooden floor.

"Go ahead and take your time," Rowena called after her. "I'll just tell her you're taking a leak!"

Sweeping into the smaller room, Cassidy found her hand automatically lifting to touch the wall beside the door frame. Temporarily baffled by the reflex, she turned a slow 180 degrees, her eyes wide with surprise. It really was a bathroom: two sinks, a shower stall, even an honest-to-goodness toilet. Soft light filtered through a translucent skylight in the ceiling, although there was also an unlit oil lamp set into a sconce on the wall. Wooden shelving held supplies like soap and stacks of towels, and there was even a braided rag rug on the floor. In some ways the room seemed actually homier than had the bedroom. In the broad and only slightly wavery mirror that spanned the wall over the double set of metal basins, Cassidy stared in glum fascination at the reflection of the tangle-haired, grubby-faced, blanket-swathed woman who used to be herself.

I really look like shit! she thought dispiritedly, poking with one finger at the ratted frenzy of her hair. For a moment she looked longingly at the shower; but she doubted there would be time. Dropping the blanket to the floor with a sigh, she reached out tentatively for the spigots on the nearest sink. Her head still spun woozily with the disorienting rush of the veritable deluge of the *missing* things. Ever since she had arrived in the village, she had been suffering from a form of sensory overload. She couldn't believe that it was the typical reaction of the other people who had come there, no matter how much allowance was made for new arrivals' "adjustment." Was she supposed to have forgotten all of the things that she was just then rediscovering— or was she just not supposed to realize that she had ever forgotten them in the first place? As she stared at her disheveled image in the mirror, Cassidy knew that everything she had thus far found in the house should have been there; yet in the back of her mind remained the tormenting tickle that there somehow should be even more.

Cassidy turned the faucets and water poured into the basin. The water was even warm. Using a washcloth and a bar of lumpy but sweet-smelling soap, Cassidy hastily scrubbed off the worst of the grime. There wasn't any way she could have washed her hair, so she had to settle for just plowing her wet fingers through it until most of the snarls were broken up. There were several combs, and even a collection of toothbrushes, on the apron that surrounded the basins; but Cassidy didn't feel bold enough to borrow any of them. She eyed the toilet with a mixture of awe and skepticism; but it was necessity that decided for her. She was inordinately pleased to find that the device flushed with satisfying vigor when she flipped the handle.

Just thinking about everything she saw there had goaded her throbbing headache to new heights. But it was impossible not to think about it. The whole little room was a marvel to her, a gift of remembrance. She was astonished anew at how much she'd forgotten already. *Even toilets!* she thought with despair. *For crying out loud, how the hell do you forget something like toilets?*

It was not any innate value of the fixture that so distressed Cassidy, it was the realization that if she could have been made to forget something so elementary, so basic, then whoever had brought her to this world had fully intended to erase all of her previous memory. And with that realization came the reminder of the disturbing possibility that perhaps she would continue to lose what memory she had retained, rather than be able to regain more.

As Rowena had promised, Cassidy's clothes were neatly folded and stacked on one of the shelves. They were slightly wrinkled, but they were dry and considerably cleaner than they'd been since her whole ordeal had begun. The rents in the jeans' knees had even been repaired, sewn with neat stitches. Cassidy quickly dressed, trying to let the ongoing sense of overwhelming confusion just slide over her, the specifics to be left for some later rumination. By the time she was pulling on her boots, she could hear the sound of voices from the outer part of the house: voices raised in a loud argument.

The house seemed too large to just be Rowena's home. The number of beds in the bedroom and the facilities in the bathroom all suggested to Cassidy some kind of communal housing. As she went out the bathroom door and followed the rising sound of the two voices, she noticed that there were several other doorways opening off from the short hall. At the end of the corridor she crossed a small lobby, then hesitated on the threshhold of what appeared to be some kind of large but well-worn parlor.

"Well, I don't see what the problem is then," Rowena was saying as Cassidy poked her head through the doorway. "It isn't like she—"

Rowena had her back to the doorway, but she broke off then, able to deduce from the expression on her antagonist's face that Cassidy had come into sight. Turning, Rowena beamed encouragingly at Cassidy. "See? Here she is now," she announced with impish vigor.

Cassidy edged into the big room, glancing around at the minimal furnishings. There was a long, shapelessly overstuffed couch and several similarly upholstered chairs. A large braided rug covered most of the floor, but the plastered walls were nearly bare, except for the sconces for the oil lamps. The only thing more surprising than the severity of the room was the mayor herself.

The woman who sat perched on the edge of one of the upholstered chairs was tall, gaunt, and sour-faced, her silvery-gray hair done up in a spiky nest of little braids. From the sharp planes of her weathered face she appeared to be almost pathologically thin, especially compared to Rowena; but the loose cut of her coarse-weave clothing effectively concealed most of the angles of her storklike body. Only the woman's hands, reddened and wrinkled, with sinewy fingers as lean as claws, betrayed her lack of flesh.

The old woman got to her feet as Cassidy entered the room. "Ah, you are Cassidy," she said in a voice that was unexpectedly smooth and mellow. She extended one bony hand. "I'm Misty, the village mayor."

What the hell kind of name is Misty? Cassidy thought immediately. She hesitated just long enough in offering her own hand to make the pause seem obvious and awkward. *Then again,* she conceded silently as she shook the strong dry fingers, *what the hell kind of name is Cassidy?*

The mayor threw Rowena a sharp glance. "I'm sure you'd like to get to your duties now, Rowena," she said pointedly.

"Oh, there's no hurry," Rowena replied, smiling conspiratorily at Cassidy.

Misty scowled, a truly effective expression on that already grimly honed face. "Cassidy and I have things to discuss," Misty said.

For a moment Cassidy wasn't sure if Rowena was trying to protect her from something—or if the sunny young woman really was so dense that she didn't get the hint. Could Rowena be trying to warn Cassidy about the mayor? With a sidelong and guarded glance at the old crone, Cassidy said to Rowena, "It's okay; I wouldn't want to keep you from anything."

Making a startlingly childish face of disapproval—she actually stuck out her tongue at Misty—Rowena shrugged good-naturedly

and gave Cassidy a little wave. "Okay, see you later," she said
as she left the room.

Alone with the skeletal gray-haired mayor, Cassidy felt a sudden flush of nervous apprehension. Misty was regarding her
with an almost predatory calculation. The woman's expression
made Cassidy again wonder just what Allen and the others had
told the Villagers about her. If they had told anyone about Raphael successfully stealing Gabriella's foal, even if they had totally
exonerated Cassidy, she seriously doubted that she would have
been treated so generously up to that point. But Allen must have
given the old crone some kind of explanation for why he had
brought Cassidy back with them. The question then was what
in that explanation had made Cassidy seem important enough
to warrant a private audience with the village mayor?

Shifting uncomfortably, Cassidy cautiously eyed the old
woman. When she had been with the Horsemen, Yolanda had
been keenly interested in anything Cassidy might have remembered—what Yolanda had called the Memories. If Allen had told
the mayor anything about Cassidy's conviction that she had come
from somewhere else, could it be that Misty wanted the same
thing of her that Yolanda had? And if that was so, would Misty's
desire work to Cassidy's advantage or would it spell her doom?
Allen had warned her about revealing her "crazy ideas" about
the place he had called the Slow World. Was this exclusive interview further evidence of his caution?

In that moment, eyeing the mayor with skittish caution, Cassidy made an important decision: She would lie to Misty if she
had to. She would do anything necessary to protect her chances
of getting out of that place again.

"Let's sit," Misty suggested, again surprising Cassidy with
the incongruous softness of her voice.

The old woman sank back down onto her chair and Cassidy
took another one a few yards away—about as far away as she
could conceivably sit and still be polite. The room was silent
and waiting, the overstuffed furniture as stolid as dozing beasts.
Cassidy glanced across to Misty and saw the mayor still watching her with an unnervingly singular stare. The silence stretched
out nearly to the point where Cassidy felt compelled to speak,
just to break it. Then Misty finally spoke.

"You say you've only been here a few days, yet Allen tells
me you're a Horseman," she said.

So much for small talk! Cassidy thought. She tried to avoid
giving the appearance of hesitating over her answer, although

her brain was churning furiously over what she was about to say. "Yeah, I guess I am," she said calmly, "if that's what you call it here."

Ignoring Cassidy's qualifying remark, Misty leaned a little closer, her deep-set eyes bright and unblinking. "You were a member of a band of Troopers when you got caught in the flood."

Once again it was not precisely a question; but it practically begged Cassidy to treat it as one, especially since her first and compelling reaction was to deny the charge. Only a deliberate pause—this time she didn't care if the old woman caught her temporizing—kept Cassidy from making a quick retort. Instead she quietly considered the mayor's statement and then responded to it.

"First of all, I wasn't a member of their band, even if I am a Horseman," she said. "They just happened to be the ones who found me when I first got here." She didn't explain exactly how Yolanda and the boys had happened to greet her sudden appearance; no need to give away anything extra to that predatory old crone. "And second, they weren't Troopers." *Not yet, anyway,* she added silently, again unwilling to reveal anything more than necessary.

Seemingly unperturbed, Misty shifted slightly on the edge of the upholstered chair. Her legs were crossed at the ankles; Cassidy was amused to notice that for all her gauntness, the woman's booted feet were huge, even bigger than Allen's.

"Where were the Horsemen coming from when they found you?" Misty asked.

Cassidy shrugged, not needing to feign ignorance on that count. "I don't know."

Misty's mouth thinned. "What direction then?"

"I don't know," Cassidy repeated.

The thin face sharpened critically. "You don't know? They were the first people you saw here, and you didn't even notice where they came from?"

"I was a little disoriented," Cassidy said.

For a few moments the mayor was silent, as if she were considering what Cassidy had just told her—or had just not told her. But Cassidy was not intimidated by that cool, steady stare. If anything, the exchange thus far had served only to stiffen her resolve not to cooperate with the woman.

"How many were in your group?" Misty asked.

"There were three of them," Cassidy replied, "but they weren't my group; they were just the people who found me."

"What Troop did they come from?"

Cassidy bit back the automatic urge to snap at the unpleasant old woman. "They weren't part of any Troop; they weren't even Troopers."

"Where were they going to?"

Cassidy had to remember to hold back for a moment and not to make her lie too obvious by just blurting it out immediately. "I don't know that, either," she said.

Misty's voice remained infuriatingly soft and calm. "What direction did you travel in while you were with them?"

Careful, Cassidy cautioned herself. If she contradicted the information Misty had gotten from Allen, the woman would realize Cassidy had been lying about much of the rest, as well. Pretending that it was an effort to recall—a pretense that was not too difficult to maintain, considering that her head still ached like sixteen sore teeth—Cassidy frowned convincingly and offered, "East, I think; east by southeast."

Apparently satisfied, Misty grunted softly. "And then you intersected the tracks of Allen's group."

Cassidy nodded her assent. Seeing no reason not to, she added as an additional bonus, "They followed the tracks because they wanted to steal the horses."

The old woman's thin mouth twisted in a nasty grimace. "Yes, I know full well what a Horseman's natural impulse is," she said sharply, and Cassidy had no doubt that she was included in that indictment. Then she fired off another question. "Did you see any other Troopers while you traveled with those three?"

Slowly and patiently Cassidy responded, "They weren't Troopers and no, we didn't see anyone else—Troopers or otherwise—until we found Allen and the others."

Cassidy couldn't tell if that satisfied Misty or not; her expression seemed to be perpetually frozen in a frown of disapproval. "Did they mention the movements of other Troopers, either in that area or anywhere else?"

Assuming an expression of befuddlement was no reach for Cassidy; she honestly could not figure out just where the old woman was trying to lead with her questions. "No, they never talked about stuff like that," she said honestly. "All they ever talked about was catching up with the Riders and stealing their horses."

Misty made a disparaging snorting sound. "Don't use that

term here," she said. "We're Villagers, not Riders. Your Horse-men friends only call us that to insult us—as if their skill with horses somehow excuses their crimes against us. They're noth-ing but thieves and cheats," she concluded, echoing what was obviously a popular sentiment among her people.

"What about my horse?" Cassidy asked. "I'd like to be able to check on her."

"You don't have to worry about your horse," Misty replied, in a tone that clearly implied that there were plenty of other things Cassidy should be worrying about instead. "She's safe with the rest of our horses."

Cassidy was about to protest when the mayor abruptly stood. She looked Cassidy up and down, bluntly and critically. "Allen has assured me that even though you are a Horseman, you're trustworthy and can be of use to us." Her pinched expression made it plain that she was skeptical of that evaluation. "He also told me that he thinks you're still a little too addle-headed to be assigned a job. We'll just see about that." She gestured briskly toward the doorway. "Go over to the field house; Ruth Ann will feed you some breakfast."

Too surprised by the sudden end of the interview even to rise out of her chair, Cassidy stared after Misty as the tall thin woman stalked across the room. At the doorway Misty stopped, swing-ing around again.

"You think about what I've asked you," she instructed Cas-sidy in that strangely wispy voice. "I'm sure you can remember more."

Then she was gone.

Alone in the bleakly furnished room, Cassidy realized, *She never even asked me about the Memories!* But far from being cheered by that surprising omission, Cassidy was left with an even more ominous feeling. Much as she wanted to protect the unique resource of her ability to recall and the fragile link with her past that it represented, her conversation with the village's mayor had left her in an even more precarious position.

If that isn't what she's interested in me for, Cassidy thought, then what the hell is?

Chapter 10 ◄▥▥▥

Misty's instructions concerning breakfast had been spoken more like a command than an offer, but once the unpleasant old woman had left the house, Cassidy found herself pretty much on her own. It would have been the perfect opportunity to explore the building further, but since her stomach was rumbling she decided to heed the mayor's directive and look for breakfast.

The main door that led out of the Spartan parlor opened directly onto a long covered porch that wrapped around the front of the house. Beyond the porch steps lay a neat strip of shorn lawn, and, beyond the grass, dappled by the fluttering shadows cast by the spreading limbs of several huge maple trees, lay the broad sunwashed expanse of a paved street. Stepping down a brick sidewalk and out onto the street's gritty surface, Cassidy turned back and took in the exterior of the large house from which she'd just come.

The two-story building was constructed in a simple style, with a steeply pitched shingled roof and plain weathered clapboard walls. The big porch was about the only thing that could have been called an adornment. Glancing up and down the street, Cassidy discovered that the nearby houses were almost identical to that one, and to each other. Their architecture was somehow familiar looking, and yet vaguely wrong. As with Allen's rifle, Cassidy could not quite figure out what it was about the buildings that seemed incorrect.

While she was studying the houses, Cassidy also noticed how utterly quiet the area was. The precise rectangles of lawn, the brick sidewalks, the smooth dusty street—all were nearly deserted. The only sign of life Cassidy saw was a pair of nondescript-looking dogs trotting rapidly down the street away from her. She almost called after them, just to keep from being left there alone.

Looking again at the big wooden house, Cassidy frowned, lost in thought. Her head still ached. If she could find the field house again, she would welcome anything they might feed her.

"Well, I see the old witch didn't bite your head off."

Cassidy jumped at the sound of Rowena's voice, which seemed to come from right over her shoulder. She spun around to find the buxom woman cutting across the lawn of the house next door. At Rowena's heels ambled the ugliest-looking dog Cassidy had ever—no, that was no dog: it was a goat!

"You scared the shit out of me," Cassidy said.

"Sorry," Rowena replied with a grin. "I would've thought our illustrious mayor would've done that already by now."

"No," Cassidy said, eyeing the animal beside Rowena, "she just asked me a bunch of questions that I didn't know the answers to—what the hell *is* that thing?"

Laughing, Rowena quickly and affectionately caressed the creature's long drooping ears. "He's a goat!"

The goat made a sound deep in his throat and rubbed his domed and hornless head against Rowena's well-padded thigh. He was nearly the size of a weanling colt and so his shoulders almost came up to her waist. His slick coat was a bizarre patchwork of colors—red and gray and tan and white. He had big round eyes the color of ripe wheat, with pupils that were horizontal ovals, and a pronounced roman nose that gave him an almost humorously solemn and wistful expression. He regarded Cassidy with friendly interest.

"What the hell are you doing with a goat?" Cassidy persisted, smiling in spite of herself as the big animal gently explored her hand with his nose.

"I'm a goatherd," Rowena said. "That's my job here." She grinned again, making an exaggerated sweeping motion that encompassed the whole of the street and the houses that lined it. "After all, we all live to serve the common good, right?"

Cassidy found herself grinning, as well. "The hell with the common good—you herd *goats*?" *I can imagine what Misty has in mind for me!*

Rowena's hand cupped the big goat's bony skull, lightly shaking it. "Hey, it's a living," she said. "Besides, I kind of like it now." She gave the goat a playful shove. "Sure beats pigs!"

Cassidy studied the goat with renewed interest. "I didn't think that goats were that big," she said.

"Most of them aren't," Rowena explained. "Billy's so big because he's been castrated; he's kind of like my guard dog."

Also her pet, Cassidy thought, noting the obvious affection shared by the plump woman and the big spotted animal. "Why don't you just use a real dog?" she asked.

Rowena laughed again; it was a hearty, infectious sound. "You don't know much about goats, do you?" she said. She slapped Billy's neck. "Goats like to shove dogs around; so if you use a dog around goats, you end up with a dog that either likes to bite goats or one who's scared stiff of them!" She tugged lightly on one of the goat's long dangling ears. "Billy works out much better."

Watching the big woman play with the goat, Cassidy felt the inquisitive part of her brain kick in again. With it she also felt the warning amplification of her headache. "Rowena," she said with a deliberate casualness, "why did they give you this job? Did you know something about goats before?"

Rowena looked up from petting Billy. Her broad and pleasant face had sobered slightly. "Before what?" she asked.

Oh, swell—I should have known. "Before you, uh, came here," Cassidy elaborated.

Rowena's expression brightened again, as if she then understood the question. "Naw, I didn't know a thing about goats," she said. "But they found out the hard way that in spite of this well-stuffed shape, I wasn't much of a cook. And I understand that my disastrous efforts as a seamstress are still legendary down at the clothing factory!" Rowena laughed loudly. "Guess they figured goats were one thing I couldn't screw up too badly," she concluded. She shifted topics as effortlessly as she drew her next breath. "You hungry?" she asked.

Slightly bemused by the sudden switch of subject, Cassidy hesitated for a moment. "Uh, Misty told me I should go to the field house and—"

"And let old Ruthless Ann poison you with that greasy junk she dishes out?" Rowena interrupted, "Yech—she's a worse cook than I am, and that's saying a lot! Come on." She reached for Cassidy's arm, literally tugging her along. "I've got plenty of food in my backpack in the goat barn. Why don't you come along with me today—before they think of something worse for you to do."

It was hard to resist Rowena's particular form of enthusiasm, especially when the course she offered Cassidy seemed infinitely preferable to the alternatives. Billy pirouetted on his hind feet and shot forward, cavorting ahead of them down the street. Laughing, Cassidy willingly surrendered to Rowena's lead.

They cut across a strip of lawn between two of the houses, quickly leaving the residential area of the village behind. From the rear of the buildings, Cassidy could see that the street was relatively short and that there were only a few dozen of the frame houses lining it. Far more impressive to her was the farm lot at the edge of the village. The structures there were far bigger, and even more elaborate. Cassidy was pleased to find that she could easily determine the purpose of the farm buildings by their shape and arrangement: huge, lofted horse and cattle barns; hay barns with louvered insets in the walls; long, low sheep sheds; a pig shed with a stone-walled lot; and several intricately constructed coops for poultry. Most of the architecture was close-framed, with walls of vertical rough-planed boards and steeply pitched wooden shingled roofs.

Studying the animal shelters, Cassidy once again thought about the gray mare. She missed the horse and wanted to go find her, but after Misty's curt comment, Cassidy was reluctant to risk drawing any unwanted attention to the gray. In some intangible way, Cassidy sensed that the mare was nearby and seemed content. Cassidy decided that so far her mare was likely to be more satisfied with life in the village than she was.

The goat barn stood at the edge of the vast complex of animal buildings, a relatively modest single-story structure made with fieldstone footings. As Rowena led her through the door, Cassidy took one last glance around the farmyard, which except for a few free-ranging chickens appeared deserted.

"Where is everyone?" Cassidy asked, following Rowena into the barn.

"Out working." Rowena paused to relatch the lower half of the dutch door behind them. "The cowherds've got the milking cattle out already, and the shepherds are out with the sheep." She grinned at Cassidy. "I told you everybody's got a job around here!"

The interior of the goat barn was pleasantly bright, naturally illuminated by long rows of square windows. The floor space was a warren of small stalls, each with its own hay manger and water cup, but the stalls were empty. The herd of goats was bunched in a larger pen at the rear of the buildings. It took Cassidy a moment to realize that these were milk goats and that Rowena must have already milked all of them earlier that morning, while Cassidy had still slept.

"Do you take care of all these goats by yourself?" she asked, a little overwhelmed by the sheer scope of the job.

"Mostly," the buxom woman replied, scooping up a tan canvas backpack from its perch on a stack of hay bales as they continued down the aisle. Billy charged ahead of them, bleating self-importantly at the penned female goats. Rowena rooted in the backpack as she walked. "I don't have to shovel the shit, though." She had pulled a paper-wrapped parcel from the pack and waved it at the rows of neat little stalls. "We have the muckers to do that."

Probably the exact job Misty will give me! Cassidy thought.

"Here, try this," Rowena said, offering Cassidy the parcel. "Better than anything you'd get at the field house."

The parcel contained several thick slabs of chewy bread, generously plastered with butter and jam. The food immediately improved Cassidy's mood, and she dug into a piece of the bread eagerly.

"Hey, girls, ready to go?" Rowena called out to the goats.

There were about forty or fifty female goats in the holding pen. None of them struck Cassidy as representative of any particular breed, or at least not any breed that she could recognize. *Then again, what the hell do I know about goats?* Cassidy reminded herself. Actually, on closer inspection, she saw that no two of those goats even resembled each other, much less some breed standard. They were an amazingly diverse lot, with colors that ran the gamut from white to black and every shade and combination in between. Some were small, almost pigmy size compared to Billy; others were big and rangy, nearly as tall as Rowena's pet. But most of the does were intermediate size, their backs coming up to about the middle of Cassidy's thigh. As Rowena freed them and they bounded out of the opened barn door, they bucked and frolicked across the cropped grass like frisky horses.

Munching on the chewy jam and bread as the two of them walked along behind the herd of milk goats, Cassidy was surprised to find out just how hungry she was; then she realized she couldn't even remember when she'd last had a regular meal. As soon as the thick slabs of bread had disappeared, Rowena reached into her backpack again and produced a canvas-covered bottle and offered it to Cassidy. Uncapping and tilting the container, Cassidy discovered the liquid it contained wasn't the expected water, it was goats' milk—thick, sweet, and cold.

Rowena laughed at Cassidy's expression of startled pleasure.

"After the evening milking, I float a bottle overnight in the well," she explained, taking a swig from the bottle herself. "It stays cold most of the day."

Several questions had automatically insinuated themselves into Cassidy's mind, not the least of which was why did the Villagers have milk goats there if they also had milk cows? But along with the questions came the inevitable prickling promise of another full-blown headache, and the nagging throb that had plagued her all morning had just finally begun to subside once she had eaten something. Bringing back that painful pressure behind her skull simply didn't seem worth it at that time, especially not over something as prosaic as milk goats. So Cassidy held off her questions and instead concentrated on taking in the truly beautiful scenery everywhere around them.

The cluster of barns and animal shelters sat on one end of the long low valley that formed the base of the village. Behind the buildings the land rose slowly in a gentle undulating sweep of meadow. Off to their right, Cassidy could see the distant gridwork of fences that formed a series of paddocks and small pastures. The larger fenced fields she had seen the previous afternoon as they had ridden into the village must have been even farther out from the barnyard. To their left, far enough away that the individual crops were indistinguishable, spread the vast patchwork of cultivated fields. But the stretch of pastureland across which they were following the goat herd was neither fenced in nor tilled. They had to hike a little farther before Cassidy began to see why.

The sun was high enough in the sky to be pleasantly warm on Cassidy's shoulders and bare arms, but there was enough of a breeze on the long hill that she didn't think the day would become uncomfortably hot. The goats had slowed their pace slightly, but they still were traveling without pausing to graze. Cassidy was puzzled by that. The grass they were walking through was a bit seedy, but it still looked lush and certainly palatable enough to tempt an animal that had been stabled overnight. Yet the goats, even Billy, showed very little interest in eating it.

"How far are they going to go?" Cassidy finally asked.

Rowena turned, gesturing expansively with one hand. "What do you mean, how far? They keep on going all day!"

"Don't they ever stop and eat?"

Rowena had snapped off a green stalk of goldenrod and was waving it aloft like a baton. "Oh, they'll eat all right," she said, "once they find what they like. But I'll warn you right now, they don't do much stopping."

Repressing the rest of her questions, Cassidy instead renewed her casual survey of the surrounding countryside. Toward the top of the slow rise of land she could see the thick green foliage of a stand of trees. The goats quickened their pace, some of them nearly trotting, and several bleating eagerly. Puzzled, Cassidy increased her own speed to keep up with Rowena and the herd of goats.

As they drew closer to the top of the slope, Cassidy could see that the trees marked the beginning of a series of rocky, deeply eroded gullies that were lined with a thick growth of brush and secondary trees. It was very typical of much of the land she'd ridden through in the days previous: stretches of rich meadowland interrupted by forested moraines and steep ravines. In a few moments the reason for the goats' haste became obvious. The entire herd dove into the dense bushes, eagerly ripping at the leaves and terminal twigs.

"They're eating the trees!" Cassidy blurted out in surprise.

Rowena laughed heartily at Cassidy's incredulity. "Sure they are—what did you think they ate? Goats are browsers, not grazers."

Suddenly Cassidy found many of her questions being answered—and with considerably less painful consequences than if she'd had to think of ways to phrase them all. "Then that's why you have to take them way out here to eat," she said, more to herself than to Rowena, "and why you can't just fence them in." She gazed down the steep incline of the brushy ravine, where the last of the herd was rapidly disappearing into the undergrowth. "Who the hell could fence this in anyway?" she noted.

Rowena rewarded her with an approving nod. "Goats are real scavengers," she said, gesturing with her sprig of goldenrod. "They'll eat all this woody junk that none of the other animals will touch—in fact they prefer it to pasture." She laughed again. "And that's probably just as well, because it's almost impossible to fence goats in. You ever see the way these stinkers can jump and climb? That's why I bring them out here to eat."

Rowena started down the steep slope after the herd. After hesitating only a second, Cassidy quickly followed. The incline was rocky and choked with brush and tree roots, and she had to hold up both forearms like a shield to part the dense branches. She didn't catch up with Rowena until they'd reached the bottom of the ravine. From there, Cassidy could see many of the goats again, all of them happily munching, their little wedge-shape tails flipping contentedly.

"This is where Billy really comes in handy," Rowena said, wriggling out of the straps of her backpack. "He kind of keeps an eye on all of them, and he usually raises a real fuss if any of them get too far away from the herd." She hooked the pack's strap over the stub of a tree branch and tossed her head to dispell a few opportunistic gnats that had been stirred up by their passage through the bushes. "They'll fill up here for a while, so we can take a little breather—at least until they take in their knotty little heads to move again."

A bit discouraged to find out how relieved she felt at the idea of a rest stop, Cassidy reverted back to the ways of the Horsemen and simply sank down, cross-legged, onto the stony ground.

Leaning her back against the trunk of a tree opposite Cassidy, Rowena looked down on her with some amusement. "You've been spending too much time riding and not enough time walking," she said. After reaching into the backpack for her bottle of milk, Rowena uncapped and upended it, taking a deep swallow. Then she passed it to Cassidy.

Forcing herself not to gulp, Cassidy sipped judiciously from the bottle. The cold milk tasted perfect; she viewed the greedily foraging goats with new appreciation.

Cassidy wasn't sure just how long they rested there, but it was long enough for her sweaty T-shirt to dry across her shoulder blades and for the nagging ache to ease out from the backs of her calves. Rowena remained uncharacteristically silent; it made Cassidy realize just how loquacious the woman usually was. But Cassidy didn't mind Rowena's chatter; in fact, she realized almost wistfully, after the grinding terseness of the Horsemen and the laconic utility of the other Villagers, Rowena's nearly nonstop talking was a welcomed change. Rowena was a continuing source of information even when Cassidy wasn't asking her anything! Allen's warning about bringing up her unconventional ideas still made Cassidy cautious, but it was hard to believe that the cheerful goatherd would present any threat to her safety. Cassidy just wished she could think at all, without the crippling pain of the pressure building inside her head.

Their rest at the bottom of the rocky ravine turned out to be a relatively short one, and Cassidy soon understood the meaning of Rowena's earlier comment about the goats not doing much stopping. As soon as their initial hunger was sated the herd was on the move again, searching the brushy hills for new morsels of greenery. Somehow Cassidy had had the vague notion that a goatherd's job consisted of mostly a little walking around and a lot of just sitting around watching the animals eat. She'd had no idea just how energetic the goats would prove to be and just how much physical stamina it took merely to keep up with them. After a morning of hiking up and down the steep slopes, climbing over rocks and roots and ducking branches, Cassidy began to understand what Rowena's daily life must be like.

Although the herding was a fairly strenuous job, it was strangely relaxing for Cassidy. Even with Rowena close by most of the time, there was little opportunity to talk, so Cassidy had a lot of time just to study the countryside and the goats. She found the activity engaging without being enervating, and it was refreshing to be able to spend time with someone without the attendant feeling that she always had to keep her guard up. What she had discovered about the Villagers' antipathy for the Horsemen in general, and the threat implicit in many of Misty's comments in particular, had combined to make Cassidy reluctant to push too blindly for answers to all of her questions. She realized that if she wanted to find out more about that place and what happened to bring her there, she would have to be circumspect about it. But that was what made being with Rowena so pleasant; as much as Cassidy wanted to be able to question her, it was nice to have some time when she didn't have to push herself to think. In fact, as the morning progressed, Cassidy's headache gradually receded to more manageable proportions.

When the sun was directly overhead, Rowena motioned for Cassidy to catch up with her. They had been following the herd diagonally across the brushy face of a rock-strewn moraine and Cassidy increased her pace only with caution, pushing aside the thick bushes and sidestepping over the loose, gravelly shale.

Little beads of perspiration stood out like dewdrops on Rowena's brow; she wiped her forehead with one plump freckled forearm. "I'm starved," she said. "Let's stop for lunch." She pointed. "See that big deadfall over there? There's a creek at the bottom of that gully. If we can get them headed that way, they'll probably stay put for a while, and then we can eat."

Rowena whistled sharply and moments later Billy bounded into view, long fronds of green branches hanging like whiskers from his mouth. "Let's go to water, Billy," Rowena called to him, swinging her arm toward the gully. "Water, Billy!"

The big lop-eared goat sprang off again, bleating loudly as he headed unerringly in the direction Rowena had pointed.

"Does he actually understand what you said?" Cassidy asked skeptically.

Rowena seemed surprised that Cassidy would even question that fact. "Sure," she said.

Obviously the spotted goat at least knew what "water" meant, even if he didn't appreciate the reasoning behind the command. As he ran toward the creek, bleating enthusiastically, the rest of the goat herd looked up and began to follow him.

A short time later both Cassidy and Rowena were plunked down in the shade, straddling the fallen trunk of a huge downed tree, while the herd of goats splashed in the clear shallow water of the rocky creek. Despite the antics of the animals, the ravine seemed a particularly peaceful place to Cassidy. For the first time in the days since she'd found herself in that world, her fatigue merely invited her to rest; there was no sense of danger or urgency. She found it oddly pleasant to just sit, legs dangling off the log, while a light breeze ruffled her hair and she and Rowena shared a meal of cold sliced meat sandwiched between thick slices of chewy bread.

After a brief flirtation with the creek, including a few playful butting matches and a lot of splashing, most of the goats seemed content to stay in the immediate area. There wasn't much in the way of marsh vegetation or sedge grasses along the creek banks, probably due to the rocky nature of the bottom of the gully, but the goats found plenty of other things to occupy them. Cassidy was impressed by the range of things they would eat, including wild grape vine, spikey hawthorne branches, and even the algae off the stones in the creekbed. Billy was the most indiscriminate of all, scrambling around to sample anything he saw any of the does nibbling at. It was only when several irate females in a row roughly butted him away from their particular finds that the big lop-eared creature sought solace with Rowena.

"Scram, you big glutton!" Rowena scolded him, pushing his shoulder with her foot as Billy edged up to the deadfall log and rubbed hopefully against her leg.

Cassidy tore off a strip of bread crust and dangled it in front of Billy's roman-nosed face. He gave an excited little bleat and the morsel immediately disappeared.

"You'll be sorry," Rowena warned Cassidy.

Cassidy didn't even have to ask the brunette why; within moments the big spotted goat was eagerly bumping against her dangling leg, and she found herself looking down into those disconcertingly human-looking wheat-colored eyes.

"He's a real begger," Rowena teased. "Now you'll have a friend for life."

But Cassidy merely tore off another strip of bread. This time she tossed it far enough away from where they sat that Billy had to bound off to hunt for it in the thick undergrowth beneath the big log.

"You better watch out," Rowena continued in the same tone of mock-caution. "If Misty finds out you're this popular with the goats, you'll end up stuck out here with me, Horseman or not."

The mention of the mayor's name brought an automatic frown to Cassidy's face. She knew the distasteful old crone had been trying to intimidate her and she hadn't bothered to conceal her disgust at housing a Horseman in her village. Yet even given that, Cassidy had found the unexpected nature of Misty's interrogation puzzling. Taking a nibble from the edge of her sandwich, she said, "I know she's not real happy to have me here. When she talked to me this morning, the only thing she asked me about was the Horsemen." Pausing to chew, she added, "I'm afraid I wasn't able to tell her very much."

Rowena had been taking a swig from the canvas-covered milk bottle. Swallowing deeply, she lowered the container and then grinned a milk-mustached grin. "Don't let that bother you; I don't think she really knows very much about them, either."

Just enough to know she doesn't like them, Cassidy thought. But what she said was "Don't they ever come here?"

Rowena flashed a crooked grin. "Not if the sheriff can help it," she replied, offering Cassidy the milk. "The last ones he caught were hanged."

Cassidy had just begun to drink, and she nearly choked on the milk. Clutching the bottle, she coughed until helpless tears welled up in her eyes and her throat burned. Rowena regarded her with a mixture of bemusement and concern, probably wondering if life-saving measures would be necessary.

When she was able to speak, Cassidy croaked, *"Hanged?* Why?"

Rowena shrugged again, as if the answer to that should be self-evident. "For stealing horses," she said simply.

Billy had returned from his hunt for the bread crust and was again nudging Cassidy's ankle, but she barely noticed him. She recalled Misty's scathing remark about the Horsemen's proclivity toward thievery; suddenly the depths of the woman's contempt seemed chillingly logical. Meggie had told her that the mayors tried to control the Horsemen's stealing, and Cassidy could understand that the horses were important to the Villagers' way of life, but it had just never occurred to her that the penalty for the crime would be so high.

What seemed even far less clear to her was just why Allen risked the old woman's wrath—and possibly Cassidy's own safety—by bringing her back to the village with him. Why were Misty and the other Villagers allowing her to stay, and could it possibly have something to do with whatever reason she'd been kidnapped and stripped of her memory in the first place? *Who could have wanted me that badly?* she wondered. She could not shake the pervasive feeling that the mayor wanted something from her, and that her fate was resting uncomfortably on the gaunt woman's ulterior motives.

Below them, Billy bunted harder against Cassidy's leg. Almost absently, she dropped the rind of her sandwich down to him. She looked across the log to where Rowena sat, her expression still mildly expectant. Forcing a casualness she did not feel into her voice, Cassidy said, "I didn't even know the village had a sheriff."

Rowena blinked owlishly. "You're kidding, right?" she said. "He's the one who brought you here!"

Suddenly Cassidy felt as if the sturdy log upon which she was sitting had abruptly fallen away from beneath her, and that all that seemed to be keeping her suspended above the ground was the steady eye contact that she still maintained with the goatherd. Rowena's comment had sent a numbing jolt through her, and in the resulting wave of near vertigo Cassidy had to deliberately concentrate on slowly setting down the milk bottle on the rough surface of the log in front of her.

"Uh, *Allen* is the sheriff?" Cassidy asked, her voice an uneven croak.

"Sure," Rowena said, "didn't he tell you?"

Cassidy realized that she was staring rather stupidly at Rowena. "No—no, he didn't," she replied, adding inanely, "I thought he was just in charge of the village's horses."

Billy had returned once more, his bony head butting hopefully against Cassidy's dangling leg. Rowena noticed his assault, even if Cassidy didn't seem to, and swung her foot at the goat, admonishing him "Scram, Billy!" Then to Cassidy she said, "He is in charge of the horses.'' She cocked her head quizzically. ''What else do you think a sheriff does?''

What else indeed? The renewed nudging pressure of the headache had begun to throb inside Cassidy's skull, much like the initial polite bumping of Billy's head against her ankle. It made Cassidy realize that the familiar dull pain had been gone from her head just long enough that she had not yet consciously noticed its absence. And now, just like Billy's persistent battering, she also realized that the headache was only going to get worse again, as long as she continued to feed its cause. The problem was that she didn't know how to stop the questions that kept forming inside of her mind.

Rowena leaned slightly forward, her brows drawn up in a little arch. ''Are you okay?'' she asked.

Cassidy waved down her incipient concern. ''Yeah, I'm okay; I was just thinking . . .'' She hesitated, debating the wisdom of trying to question Rowena.

Then again, what choice do I have? Unless I want to spend the rest of my life here, herding goats. . .

''Rowena,'' she said slowly, trying to be casual, ''what did Allen tell everyone about me when he brought me here?''

Rowena made a funny little gesture, a combination of tossing her head and hitching up her shoulders, that was both simple and yet eloquent. ''He said that you'd been with some Horsemen that had been following him and the mare herd, but you'd gotten caught in a flash flood and nearly drowned. He said that you were a Horseman, too, but that you were different from the rest of them.'' She paused. ''He said that you were a little confused yet.'' She added a gesture, a spiraling hand-to-head maneuver that had universal meaning. ''I think he tried to give everyone the idea that you were a few bales short of a load, if you know what I mean! I think maybe he wanted to keep people like Misty off your back.''

Almost involuntarily Cassidy felt herself relax fractionally. She returned Rowena's smile with a briefer, more cautious version. ''I don't think he was exaggerating,'' she said.

But Rowena laughed. ''Don't worry,'' she said, ''I think you're the most normal person I've met since I've been here—although that might not be saying much.''

Cassidy's headache was inching upward in intensity then, slowly but inexorably. *You could stop it if you really wanted to,* a cruel little voice inside Cassidy's head told her, *if you really tried*. But that was a flimsy, ineffectual kind of resolution, useless in the face of the questions that blossomed in her mind.

Cassidy dropped her gaze for a few moments, deliberately refraining from rubbing her temples and instead picking with a false nonchalance at the rough bark of the old log between her thighs. "Rowena, how long have you been here anyway?" she asked casually.

Billy had switched his attentions from Cassidy to Rowena. But rather than persisting in shooing him away, the brunette rubbed the side of his sinewy neck with her foot. The goat's expression was almost beatific with pleasure. "You mean here in the village?" Rowena asked, as Billy leaned blissfully into her caress. "Not real long; not even a full change of seasons, or however the heck you want to measure time."

Cassidy's pulse had begun to thud, each beat only accentuating the growing pressure inside her skull. Determinedly rejecting the small stirrings of a formless excitement she felt rising within her, she struggled to keep her voice low and calm. "Do you remember where you were before then? Before you came here?"

"Sure," Rowena said immediately, her foot lightly and rhythmically stroking the arched bridge of Billy's roman nose, "how could I forget Green Lake?" She grinned at Cassidy. "That was the scene of my legendary fiasco down at the clothing factory. I'm sure they still talk about me in Green Lake!"

Despite her advance effort to damp down her hopes, Cassidy still felt disappointment at the predictably typical answer. *We're all here now*, Allen had said to her. That seemed to be the limit of the outlook of these people—the inhabitants of this land of the *missing* things, the people of a world without dreams. Stricken with frustration, Cassidy did not even respond to Rowena's cheerfully self-depreciating confession. She just stared over the edge of the big deadfall at the green and brown patterns of vegetation and rocks below, which blurred into shapelessness as she squeezed shut her eyes. *Damn it, there has to be a way!* she thought, digging her fingernails into the huge log's rough bark. So intent was her resolve that she almost didn't hear Rowena when she went on.

"Or do you mean before Green Lake? Because I really don't remember that part anymore."

Cassidy's head jerked up, so abruptly that her brain seemed to rebound within her pounding skull, sending her into a momentary spasm of dizziness. "What did you say?" she asked sharply.

Rowena threw Cassidy a quizzical look. "I said I don't remember where I was before Green Lake," she repeated patiently. "I guess I might have known once, but I don't remember it anymore."

Cassidy's mouth was suddenly as dry as sand; her tongue felt numb and unwieldy. She had to make a distinct effort to get her words out clearly. "Rowena, are you saying that before you were here—before you came to Green Lake—that you came from . . . somewhere else?" she asked carefully.

"Sure," Rowena said. She made a vague but perfectly inclusive little gesture with one hand. "I think you did, too. I just don't remember anymore where it was."

Cassidy was nonplussed to find that her pulse rate had remained more or less steady; it was just that the force of each heartbeat seemed amplified, echoing thunderously through an aching skull that felt as sensitive as an exposed nerve, as fragile as an eggshell. She struggled with Rowena's words, trying to convince herself that she had heard her correctly.

"Rowena, are you saying that when you were in Green Lake, you knew that you had come from somewhere else?"

Rowena gave her a funny look, exasperation vying with patience. "Yeah—isn't that what I just said?"

Almost giddy with hope, Cassidy blurted out, "Then you must be the one Allen told me about!" At Rowena's blank look, she quickly went on to explain. "When we were out on the trail, he told me there was a woman in his village who was like me— a woman who knew that she had come from somewhere else."

Rowena's full mouth quirked wryly. "Yeah? Did he also tell you I don't remember where?"

Leaning forward, Cassidy startled Billy by spontaneously clasping one of Rowena's forearms. "Rowena, don't you see?" she said. "You're the only other person I've met in this place who once knew they came from somewhere else! Maybe you don't remember it anymore, but at least you *realize* that you don't remember."

Making an amused little snorting sound, Rowena gave Cassidy a lopsided grin. "Doesn't seem like much of a help," she said.

But Cassidy's enthusiasm was insistent. "But maybe it will be," she said, her fingers squeezing Rowena's arm encouragingly. "Maybe you can remember it again." She leaned even closer to the brunette woman across the big log. "Listen, when

I first found myself here, all I had to go on was some vague feeling—a feeling that I *belonged* somewhere else." Cassidy hesitated a moment, her voice automatically falling lower. "But in the days that I've been here, I've started to remember things, Rowena, things from before. And I've started to see that there are things *missing* here—things that should be here but aren't."

Cassidy paused helplessly, her eyes begging Rowena to understand her desperate explanation. And Rowena didn't try to pull back from her, but for a few long moments she was unsettlingly silent. It was only when the goatherd spoke that Cassidy could be certain that her trust and her plea had not been misplaced.

"I wish that I could remember," Rowena said, her voice slow, her inflection uncharacteristically flattened. "I know what you mean about feeling that things here are, well, *weird*." She paused, lightly biting at her full lower lip. "But I'm not even sure that I have that feeling anymore, Cassidy; I don't think that I've really had it since I left Green Lake."

Cassidy's other hand went out, swiftly and automatically, to grip Rowena's other arm. She gave the larger woman a gentle but emphatic shake. "You do still have that feeling—you have it right now, don't you? Rowena, you know what it means to *remember*."

The expression on Rowena's face flickered, mercurial as firelight, rapidly transforming itself from uncertainty to surprise and then to a tentative kind of recognition. "No," she corrected Cassidy with another one of her crooked grins, "I know what it means to *forget* to remember!"

So exhilarated by that first rare burst of success in her struggle to regain the truth, Cassidy tossed her head in mock exasperation, almost laughing aloud. "Rowena, you and I both came from somewhere else, even if we don't remember where it was. I think a lot of these people here did—maybe even all of them—even if they think they've always been here. And I'm going to find out just where that somewhere else is."

Rowena's pupils dilated, her eyes bright with an excitement that was more delight than shock. "How?" she asked.

"Somebody here must know—maybe even Misty." Cassidy's chin lifted in defiant determination. "Somebody must know why we were brought here, and how. And that means somebody must know how we can get back again."

Rowena shivered; Cassidy could feel the fine tremble run through the pale, freckled skin beneath her fingers. But Rowena was not only excited; Cassidy could also tell that she was suddenly frightened. "You're going to try to go back?" she asked in wonder.

Dropping her hands from Rowena's arms, Cassidy nodded resolutely. "Home, the Slow World—whatever the hell they want to call it, I'm going back."

Rowena actually jumped. She glanced hastily around the wooded ravine and when she spoke again, her voice had been automatically reduced to an unnecessary near whisper. "Where did you hear that term?" she demanded.

Surprised at the severity of the brunette's reaction, Cassidy said, "Allen used it."

Rowena glanced around them again, and as she did so, her voice became somewhat more normal in volume. "Well, maybe he can get away with it, but I wouldn't let anyone else around this place hear you mention the Slow World—unless you're looking for real trouble."

Cassidy felt a mixture of interest, apprehension, and annoyance at Rowena's behavior. "What are you talking about?" she asked.

Rowena exhaled softly. "When I was in Green Lake, there was a guy there named Jeff who was sort of like you. I mean, not a Horseman or anything, but he had this nutty idea he'd come from somewhere else, and he was always asking questions and talking about strange stuff." She rolled her eyes evocatively. "At first, everyone there just said he was having trouble adjusting, but Jeff seemed to be getting more and more upset when no one could answer his questions. Then one night he disappeared."

Cassidy realized she'd been holding her breath. "He ran away?" she asked.

But Rowena was shaking her head. "No, I don't think so," she said quietly. "Cassidy, I don't know what they did to him, but I think those Villagers got rid of Jeff somehow."

Disconcerted, Cassidy murmured softly, "Got rid of him . . . you mean you think they—"

Suddenly Rowena jumped, jerking alert on her perch on the deadfall. "Oh, shit!" she exclaimed, looking wildly around the little gully. "The goats—they're gone!"

Cassidy's head did a quick 360-degree scan, her gaze shooting over the rocky creekbed and the slopes of the brush ravine. There wasn't a goat in sight, not even Billy.

With more agility than Cassidy would have given her credit

for, Rowena sprang down from the log and began rapidly sweeping up the contents of her backpack. "Sneaky little shits!" she muttered loudly. She made a broad beckoning wave toward Cassidy. "Come on, we've got to hustle. If they get too far ahead of us, we'll be out here all night looking for them!"

Cassidy suspected that dire prediction was more hyperbole than fact, but she wasn't the goat expert. She quickly hopped down off the deadfall and started after Rowena. The goatherd was already scampering across the shallow creek, still muttering deprecations under her breath.

"How far could they have gotten?" Cassidy said as she followed.

But Rowena's expression remained grim. "Far enough," she said. "We'd better split up." She paused long enough to wave with one arm. "You go that way."

Cassidy didn't want to appear ungracious, but the rugged nature of the unfamiliar terrain did give her some pause. "What if I get lost?" she pointed out.

"You won't get lost. Over this hill's another ravine; at the bottom just hook left and follow the ravine until you meet up with me again. With any luck, by that time we'll have found the goats."

With any luck, I wouldn't even be here, Cassidy thought glumly. But she turned and gamely started up the brushy hill just the same.

Only minutes earlier it had seemed so pleasant just sitting there on the shady log in the gully. Cassidy had nearly forgotten the physical effort required to climb one of the steep hills. Loose shaley rock rolled beneath her boots and annoying clouds of gnats rose from the bushes as she forced the branches aside. By the time she was halfway up the slope her legs ached, her damp T-shirt stuck to her back, and her hair was plastered in strings to her perspiring neck and forehead. She silently cursed as a whiplike twig slipped through her fingers and snapped her smartly on the chest. And yet in spite of the aggravation of the goat herd's escape, Cassidy could not keep down the new surge of hope she felt: Rowena understood what she was talking about. Of course, Rowena had also reinforced Allen's warning to her about the dangers of such maverick notions; her revelation about the man she called Jeff had hardly been confidence inspiring. But Cassidy refused to be intimidated into giving up her search. And for the first time she had an ally.

Cassidy was thinking about what she had discussed with Rowena, rather than about where she was going, as she crested the top of the wooded hill. So regardless of all the experience she had gained in negotiating the rough country, she wasn't being careful enough. By the time she felt the toe of her booted foot catch on the half-buried tree root it was too late to try to regain her balance. The most she could hope to do was to roll as she fell, to minimize the damage.

As she tumbled over the crest of the hill and down the steep slope on the other side, the thick leafy branches of the heavy undergrowth slapped at Cassidy in a green blur. A wry thought—that she was glad she wasn't trying to sneak up on the goats—occurred fleetingly to her as various parts of her body connected jarringly with bushes, branches, roots, and the gravelly ground. Cassidy's final connection, nearly at the bottom of the hill, was made with the gnarled trunk of a hawthorne tree, bringing her to a wrenching halt.

The impact drove the air from her lungs, and for a few moments she was singularly unconcerned with anything not related to just being able to breathe again. The fact that she was bruised, scraped, and covered with filth seemed temporarily less urgent than filling her chest again. When she shook her head, a small avalanche of dirt and crushed dry leaves cascaded from her tousled hair.

It was then that the smell hit her. No, it was not just a smell, it was a *stench*, so overwhelming and cloying that for a moment she felt as if it were draped over her face in some physical form. Struggling to her hands and knees, Cassidy lifted her head. Then she forgot about breathing.

There was something—some *thing*—suspended from one of the thick twisted limbs of the hawthorne, almost directly above her. It was huge and black, and for a split second Cassidy thought that it was the burned and gutted carcass of a cow. But then she saw that it was neither a carcass nor a cow, even if it was that big and horrifically putrid. It was more like the giant body of a man, hung upside-down, with its torso weirdly everted. And as she looked up dizzily into that monstrous, stinking thing, she saw that within that prolapsed chest there pulsed something coiled and loathsome, glistening with strings of ropy slime that dripped like—

Cassidy had no awareness of having even turned or scrambled to her feet; she only realized that she had moved to flee when she felt the painful bite of a hawthorne branch's spurs raking the tender flesh of her upper arm as she hurtled herself over the rocky ground. Catapulted by a tremendous jolt of adrenaline, she ignored the minor pain of the thorn's gouge, just as she ignored her other aches and bruises. She literally did not even feel her feet touch the ground. She went through or right over the thick growth of brush as if it didn't even exist.

Cassidy didn't have the faintest idea how long she ran before she encountered the goats. It could have been thirty seconds, it could have been five minutes. As she crashed down the bottom of the ravine, her blood roaring in her veins and her limbs as light as wings, the small group of browsing goats leapt ahead of her with high-pitched bleats of alarm. As swiftly as Cassidy ran, the goats had the natural advantage; they stayed ahead of her as she crashed heedlessly through the tangled brush. By the time they encountered Rowena, Cassidy had the entire herd racing ahead of her, their eyes wide with panicked excitement.

Rowena halted Cassidy by literally tackling the smaller woman, catching her in a wild hug as Cassidy pounded past her.

"Whoa!" Rowena exclaimed, grunting as she swung Cassidy around. "Wait! What the hell are you doing?"

Jerking back so abruptly that she broke free of Rowena's arms and nearly fell, Cassidy stared at Rowena with a panting, wild-eyed incomprehension.

"Holy cow—Cassidy? Are you okay?" Rowena took a step closer, holding out her hand. "What happened to you?"

The adrenaline still burning in her veins, goading her in a seizure of hyperkinetic frenzy, it took an overwhelming effort of will for Cassidy to regain control. Within an instant, she realized that she not only needed to regain control, she also needed to come up with a credible alternative to the truth for Rowena. Because friend or not, there was no way in hell that Cassidy was going to risk the importance of her tentative relationship with Rowena over some crazy hallucination. She had already stepped out onto dangerous ground with the goatherd that afternoon when she had vowed to return to the Slow World; if she also confessed that she was seeing things—hideous things—how long would she still have Rowena's loyalty?

"Cassidy?" Rowena repeated, with slightly less alarm. She touched Cassidy's shoulder, gently brushing off a garland of shredded leaves. "Why are you all messed up? What happened?"

Shaking back her hair, Cassidy forced a little snort of irritation. "Oh, I tripped over a damned root," she said, emphatic about the truth as far as it went. "Some of the goats ran over me—I guess I scared them," she added apologetically.

"No shit," Rowena agreed, brushing again at Cassidy's dirt-smeared T-shirt.

"I'm sorry if I got them excited," Cassidy said, taking a half step backward, hoping to prevent Rowena from noticing the way her pulse still pounded and the fine trembling in her scratched and dirty hands. "I guess that isn't good for them, huh?"

Her concern successfully diverted from Cassidy to the goats, Rowena looked over her herd. "They'll probably all give cottage cheese tonight!" she said ruefully. "Come on, let's see if we can get them settled down and eating again."

Ignoring her bruised and abraded body, Cassidy quickly complied. It did not prove particularly difficult, as she was hardly aware of the bumps and scrapes she'd suffered. There was only one thing she was able to think about as she helped Rowena round up the goat herd again.

Am I really crazy? Cassidy wondered numbly, shaking more fragments of dried leaves out of her hair as she wound her way through the brushy ravine bottom. If not, why did she keep seeing things? Were the hallucinations some remnant of her previous life? Or—an even more disturbing thought—were they some kind of symptom caused by whatever imperfect process had been used on her to try to strip her of all memory?

There was still a third alternative, one that Cassidy stubbornly refused to consider but that kept nagging insidiously at her: What if the things she had seen were *real*?

But if that thing really was there, she asked herself reluctantly, *then what the hell was it?*

Chapter 11 ◄‖‖

The sun was hanging low in the western sky by the time Cassidy and Rowena made their way down the long slope behind the goat barn. The herd of does, their flighty excitement long since abated and their rapacious appetites temporarily sated, ambled docilely down the hill, their tight, elongated udders swaying rhythmically.

Disheveled and exhausted, Cassidy was particularly glad to see the barnyard again. Although she had managed to keep Rowena from detecting it, she was still badly shaken by what had happened out in the ravine. And while there certainly had been times out traveling on the trail when she'd felt worse than this, Cassidy had never felt quite so completely depleted by that enervating mixture of confusion and weariness.

Only Billy still seemed relatively fresh, bounding along the edge of the herd with his long scythe-shaped ears flopping. The herd funneled obediently in through the goat barn door, with hardly a backward glance and no more than a few halfhearted yummers of protest.

As Rowena shrugged the straps of her backpack off her shoulders, she gave Cassidy a critical look. "You look like hell," she said.

"Thanks a lot," Cassidy said, wiping one sweaty, briar-scratched wrist across her cheek.

"Hey, just remember you're still supposed to be too addle-headed to work!" Rowena said with a grin. Then her expression sobered with concern. "Why don't you go ahead and eat? I'll see you later."

Sorely tempted, Cassidy nevertheless hesitated. She waved at the last of the flag-tailed little rumps disappearing through the barn door. "What about the goats?" she asked dubiously.

Rowena just laughed. "The milkers help me. What, you think I milk all these goats by myself twice a day?"

Cassidy, who had in her ignorance presumed exactly that, just shrugged.

Rowena waved her off. "Go on; I'll be in before dark."

"Wait a minute," Cassidy protested. "Where am I going?" The thought of joining Misty and Ruth Ann and the rest of the Village's charming hags at the field house was not a particularly appealing idea, no matter how tired and hungry she was.

"Go to the herdsmen's house," Rowena said. She pointed toward the big high-roofed outline of the huge horse barn. "I always eat with them. Their kitchen is that long building, right on the other side of the horse barn."

Cassidy turned and walked a few paces before she hesitated again. "Wait a minute," she said again, swinging around. "Are they going to let me—"

"Go ahead," Rowena interrupted her, waving more emphatically. "All the horse people eat there. What's one more mouth?"

Muttering under her breath, Cassidy began walking again, her shoulders slightly hunched against the dull hitch she felt in her back. In the barnyard before her, the animal buildings and sheds lay spread like blocks of weathered darkness against a sky the color of cantaloupe. Cassidy could see some activity around the barns then, although the low oblique rays of the setting sun that glared off the buildings' windows and the darker bars of deep shadow made it difficult to recognize individuals from a distance. She heard cattle lowing and a few muffled thumps and clinks from the big L-shaped dairy. There were no chickens left out in the dusty strand between the barns, but a muted chorus of clucks and squawks filtered from the nearby coops. Looking across the dirt yard past the horse barn, she could see dark shapes moving in the maze of small paddocks.

Dragonfly. . .

The gray mare's presence had never been far from Cassidy's awareness all day, riding just below the surface of her consciousness like a subtle touch. The day had been, she realized then, the longest and the farthest she had been separated from the horse in all the time she'd been there. At the thought, Cassidy's throat tightened painfully. She hadn't realized how much she would miss the mare.

Then, without thinking, Cassidy Called the gray.

For a moment Cassidy felt nothing. She almost thought that

her memory of summoning the big horse before had been some kind of dream, a vague impression without any substance, just like so much of the information her mind had tried to process in the past few days.

Just like that thing in the woods—

But then Cassidy heard a whinny, full and throaty and deep, nearby and yet oddly muffled. She reached out with all of her strength through the bond that linked her to the gray mare, focusing all of her concentration on the image of the horse. Her chin lifting like a hound scenting the air, Cassidy turned toward the large blocky outline of the horse barn.

Dragonfly!

Several distinct thuds reverberated across the stillness of the evening barnyard. The mare whinnied again. Cassidy realized that the mare must be in the barn and probably confined to a stall, or she would have come by then. Cassidy quickened her steps, heading purposefully toward the nearest doorway to the massive wooden structure. But long before she had reached the doorway, it became obvious that the gray mare had found a way to circumvent her imprisonment.

A loud sharp sound, like the shearing screech of rending wood, cracked the air; then hooves clattered on pavement. There were other sounds as well by then, including shouts and curses, but they didn't concern Cassidy. The long shape of the gray's ghost-colored face and neck loomed in bold relief in the dim square opening above the closed bottom half of the barn's dutch door. The horse whinnied again. Then with a twist of her body that belied her size, and a surge that confirmed the agility and strength of her powerful haunches, the big mare launched herself out over the bottom half of the door and landed in the barnyard.

Cassidy held up her arms, forming a fragile circle of flesh to which the gray mare galloped as unerringly as she had heard and heeded Cassidy's Call. The cleanly planed head came over her shoulder and Cassidy buried her fingers in the thick tangle of the horse's silver-streaked mane, clinging tightly as tears of relief burned in her eyes.

"Where have you been, you big cow?" she murmured shakily, luxuriating in the rich horse-and-hay scent of the gray's smooth coat. "Lazing around, I'll bet, eating and—"

The words were snatched from Cassidy's mouth along with most of her breath as she felt herself suddenly being propelled backward by a furious yank on her hair. Before she could react, she was stumbling backward; she hit the dusty ground so hard with the seat of her pants that it made her teeth rattle. When she looked up she almost saw stars. What she saw instead was the looming form of a behemoth of a man, glaring down at her with outrage in his eyes.

"What the hell do you think you're doing?" he thundered at her.

Before she asked him the very same thing, Cassidy took a moment to rapidly assess the situation. From where she sat on the packed dirt of the barnyard, the man who towered over her appeared huge, even bigger than Allen. His scowling face was dirty and gleaming with perspiration, framed by a wild tangle of dark shoulder-length hair. From the smell of him and the look of the various stains on his well-worn clothing, he was a stableman. And from his demeanor he obviously had not appreciated the chaos the gray mare had caused in his barn.

The mare edged closer to Cassidy, nickering nervously. Cassidy held up a warding hand, as if to placate both man and mare.

"She's my horse," Cassidy quickly explained. "She just wanted to—"

"She's the village's horse!" the big man snapped back, glowering at the restlessly prancing gray mare as if he considered her mutiny a personal insult.

Cassidy was peripherally aware that they were beginning to attract an audience; perhaps "mob" would have been a more accurate term. Several other stablemen were starting to make their way across the yard, ropes and pitchforks in hand. Curious faces appeared in the doorways of the other buildings.

The dark-haired man peered down threateningly at Cassidy. His anger only made his size more impressive. "You're that Horseman Allen brought back here, aren't you," he said accusingly. "Well, don't go thinking you can pull those Horseman stunts around this barn."

Deciding that for the moment the ground was probably the safest place to be, Cassidy tried to appear entirely comfortable and nonchalant speaking from her seat in the dirt. "I'm sorry if I caused any trouble," she said. "I didn't realize my horse was in the barn. We share a link—a bond—and when she knew I was out here she—"

"She's not your horse, she's a village horse now," the burly man reiterated gruffly. "You aren't out running with those thieving Horsemen anymore." He was close enough that Cassidy could smell the rich odor of manure that clung to his boots and the sharper, muskier tang of his own stale perspiration.

Two of the approaching stablemen edged cautiously closer. Cassidy wasn't sure if their elaborate care was due to the gray mare's impressive escape, or to the big man's equally impressive display of temper. But there was one thing she was certain of, her one anchor there since her whole bizarre ordeal in that strange place had begun: The gray mare belonged to her. She wasn't about to let this big oaf or any of those other aggravating farmers take the horse away from her.

The gray mare had started to paw nervously, one big stone-colored forehoof cleaving a furrow in the hard-packed dirt of the barnyard. The horse's ears were half back, her white-rimmed eyes darting between Cassidy and the threatening stablemen.

"Mike?"

One of the stablemen, a halter and rope coiled in his hands, eyed the angry giant with a cautious air of expectation.

But Cassidy didn't wait for the big man to respond, or for the command she was certain would come with that response. With a hasty jerk that brought a sharp spasm of pain from the long muscles of her calves and thighs, she scrambled to her feet and sprang straight from the ground up onto the gray mare's broad back. The horse grunted, a sound that embodied both challenge and satisfaction, and beneath Cassidy's legs the powerful body bunched like a compressed spring. Cassidy gathered herself, everything in her poised for flight.

"*No!* Hold on—you stay right there, you hear me?"

Those words alone wouldn't have stopped Cassidy, even shouted as loudly, had they not come in a familiar voice.

Cassidy hesitated and the gray mare wheeled around nervously, her forefeet barely skimming the ground. Cassidy had to follow the direction in which the gathering of stablehands was looking to find from where the demand had come. Squinting into the low lemon-colored glare of the setting sun, she was just able to make out the bowlegged form of the wiry little black man as he hustled furiously across the yard from the horse barn.

"Then tell them to back off!" Cassidy shouted back at Aaron, while the big mare jittered anxiously beneath her. "Tell them to leave us alone!"

The hulking stableman glared balefully at Cassidy before swinging to confront Aaron. "I can take care of this," Mike warned, gesturing sharply at Cassidy. "She's trying to steal this horse."

Slightly out of breath from his hasty arrival, Aaron could at first only doggedly shake his head. "She thinks it's *her* horse, you dumb shit," he panted then.

To Cassidy, the insulting epithet seemed like an act of suicide on Aaron's part, given Mike's size and temperament. Then she realized that Aaron's tone was intended to make the term indulgently chastising, not antagonizing. At least Mike didn't seem to be taking personal offense; he just stood there staring somewhat stupidly at Cassidy.

Catching his breath, Aaron continued, "Remember what Allen said? She didn't steal the horse; it came here with her, already bonded to her. Why the hell do you think the mare broke out of the barn to get to her?"

Momentarily disarmed, Mike shot a sideways glance from Cassidy to Aaron and then back again. "She's not a Horseman here," he insisted. "She was trying to steal the horse." But the big man's voice had lost most of its previous bluster.

"She's not going to steal anything," Aaron said patiently, even as he beckoned emphatically to Cassidy with one hand. "She just didn't realize the horse was in the barn when she called her. Come on now, get down off of there," he added to Cassidy.

But Cassidy stayed put. The gray mare had stopped jigging around, but she was still wary, her curved ears flicking forward to point like semaphores at the suddenly motionless entourage of curious onlookers.

"Come on, we told you about this horse, Mike," Aaron repeated, thumping the huge stableman on one beefy shoulder. "Remember what Allen said about the girl and how she's bonded to the horse? Hell, it wasn't her fault the horse broke out of the barn."

Mike received all of that solemnly, with only the barest of glances toward Cassidy and the mare. With his shaggy head bent to hear the little man's words, the stableman looked considerably less threatening. Still, he looked even less threatening from the back of the gray mare than he had when Cassidy was sitting at his feet in the dirt.

The incident only added to Cassidy's serious doubts about coming to the village with Allen and the others. The fact that she still could see no alternative to what she had done did little to palliate her misgivings. And for a few moments the natural if irrational urge to just flee became so overwhelming that Cassidy could actually feel the gray mare beginning to gather herself beneath her, as if the horse only awaited the slightest signal from her to spring away. But before the rash thought became action, Aaron spoke again.

"Come on, get on down now," Aaron repeated to Cassidy, stepping closer to the snorting horse. "It's okay now." As he came alongside the sloping plane of the horse's sweat-speckled shoulder, he shot Cassidy a fierce if covert stare. "I said *down*!" he hissed under his breath. "Come on—before these assholes decide that their ropes would look a sight better around your neck than around this horse's!"

Cassidy's hands were still twined in the mare's thick mane, her fingers locked like armor over the horse's withers. "She's *my horse*!" she hissed back at Aaron. "She's not the damned village's horse—they're not going to take her away from me!"

Aaron temporized by stroking the gray's neck, his gnarled and stained hands slow and soothing. "I know that!" he whispered back harshly at Cassidy. "But don't push it now; just leave it lie, woman—or they'll take her anyway and Misty will see you hanged!"

The automatic words of threat, of protest, of rage died on Cassidy's lips as she looked down into the black man's face. Aaron's dark eyes were gleaming up at her, bright and hard, like water-scoured stones.

"Leave it go," he whispered again. "She'll still be right here."

Cassidy hesitated. When she pulled her eyes away from Aaron's and scanned the small crowd that had gathered in the dusty twilight of the barnyard, she realized that she saw no familiar faces there. Aaron was the closest thing to an advocate she had in that barnyard, and that realization almost made her more inclined to try to make a run for it than to do as he asked. But how would she have run? She had no food, no bedroll, no means to defend herself out on the rugged trails of the surrounding territories. And where would she have gone? From what she had been learning of the Horsemen and their Warden, she was no longer certain it was any safer among them than there with the Villagers. And so, in the end, she just breathed a small, low sigh of resignation and slowly slid down off the mare's back.

"Good girl," Aaron told her softly, gently thumping her on the back. Turning back to Mike and the others, he said more loudly, "Cassidy'll put the mare in one of the paddocks. And Mike, you leave that horse there, you hear me?"

Cassidy started to walk away across the yard, the gray trailing obediently behind her. Once the confrontation was over, she was surprised at how quickly the gathering of onlookers seemed to lose interest in her. None of them even followed her or watched to see if she actually did put the mare in the paddock.

Turning from latching the wide and cumbersome wooden gate behind the mare, and thinking even as she did so that the horse could easily jump the barrier if she needed to, Cassidy saw Aaron coming toward her in the deepening twilight.

For a long moment Aaron just looked out over the rails of the paddock to where the gray calmly stood, a ghost in the long shadow of the huge barn, her head lowered in casual indifference. He did not look at Cassidy, even when at length he spoke.

"She kicked down part of a stall door. Mike was just pissed off."

Both defiance and defensiveness rose in Cassidy, nearly inseparable in their heat. "I Called her," she retorted. "They can't keep her away from me."

Aaron's head turned then, his expression as mild as his voice. "Well, we won't remind them of that," he said. "Let Mike think she's just a fractious horse."

"But—"

"But nothing," Aaron cut her off, quietly but authoritatively. His intense eyes, bright as beads set in their netting of wrinkles, fixed Cassidy with a steely stare. "They won't hurt the damned horse. But you've got to leave it lie for now, or they'll take her away from you—or take you away from here."

"And hang me?" Cassidy retorted.

"Maybe," Aaron said calmly. "Right now, they're leaving you be because Allen brought you here and vouched for you, and they respect Allen. But you cause trouble over a horse, and there's nothing Allen could do to save your neck; he'd have to hang you himself."

Momentarily speechless, Cassidy just stared back at the bow-legged man. Dusk was falling so rapidly then that his face was fast becoming nothing more than a poorly defined silhouette against the dark backdrop of the horse barn's wall. She tried to think of a response, but she didn't know if she should thank Aaron for his warning or kick him in the shins.

"Get on up to the kitchen now," he said, breaking the deadlock. "If you're late, the rest of those pitchfork pushers will have eaten everything on the table." At her hesitation, he made a shooing gesture. "Go on, go!"

* * *

Cassidy didn't see Allen that night, or Meggie or Steven, even though she ate with the stablemen. Worse yet, Rowena didn't put in an appearance, either. When Cassidy had the chance to ask Aaron about it, he told her that Allen, Meggie, and Steven were "working" and that Rowena was eating with the shepherds that night.

Few of the diverse lot of men and women with whom she shared the low-ceilinged herdsmen's kitchen seemed the least bit curious about Cassidy, although that disinterest was hardly mutual. It seemed to her that few of them, even those she distinctly recognized from the altercation in the barnyard, gave her a second glance at their table. Aaron was the only one who even spoke to her, and then only in response to her questions. That bland indifference on the part of the Villagers, especially considering that some of them had only so recently seemed on the verge of lynching her, greatly puzzled Cassidy. In a way, they almost acted as if she were just a part of the group and had always been there. And yet, in another way, they acted as if she wasn't there at all.

Despite Aaron's warning, the communal meal was totally ample. It was fully dark outside by then, and the large dining hall was lit by the soft glow of wall oil lamps. The food was simple but filling, and Cassidy was sure it had all been grown right there in the village. After the meal the plainly clad men and women who had spent the day working around the barns and paddocks disappeared with alacrity. Cassidy wasn't sure where they all went so quickly, but there was a large house attached to the kitchen and none of them looked like a late-night crowd.

Cassidy was alone at one of the long wooden tables, sitting with the last dregs of some pretty good coffee and mulling ineffectually over everything that had happened that day, when Aaron sat down beside her.

"Misty's ready to assign you work," he said without preamble. "She figures if you can hike around all day after them damned goats, you're up to it, addle-headed or not." He paused for a moment, and when he continued his voice had taken on a certain wry twist. "She was going to put you on muckers' duty, but I convinced her it'd be a waste of talent, what with you being a Horseman. So you'll sleep here in the stablehands' house from now on and tomorrow you'll start working for me."

Cassidy tried to thank him, but even as she turned to speak Aaron waved her down. "First thing tomorrow," he said, "and you'll work hard."

* * *

Cassidy slept deeply that night, bone-tired and achingly sore, in one of the big communal bedrooms in the house where the stable workers lived. There, in a clean and simply appointed bed with the soft snores of the several other men and women in the room as accompaniment, she had a dream.

It was the first dream that Cassidy had had, or at least the first dream she could remember having had, since that night on the trail when she had alarmed the Horsemen with her nightmare. It was not precisely the same dream, but it was eerily similar. But this time at the end, at the part where she leaned down to embrace the gray mare's neck, the horse did not transform into the huge dark creature that Cassidy had seen in the river. Instead, she found herself embracing a huge human shape, black and gleaming, pulsing against her and filthy with slime.

She woke up sweating, her pulse pounding. For a long time she just lay rigidly in the narrow bed, staring up at the dim expanse of the bedroom ceiling with her throat closed achingly tight and her eyes filled with tears.

Why am I here? she thought, blinking into the darkness. *Who would do something like this to me—and how am I ever going to get back home?*

The buckskin colt stood nearly motionless, his weight poised neatly over his center of gravity. From the set of his sleek head and neck he appeared relaxed, but his ears were pricked sharply forward toward Cassidy. He looked as if he were waiting for something.

A few yards from him, Cassidy stood in the center of the circular breaking pen that had been constructed behind the horse barn. She, too, was motionless, her arms hanging easily at her sides. She watched the colt.

He was a two-year-old, small but wiry and fit, with a coat the bright pure gold color of ripe oats. He had striking black points—mane, tail, lower legs, and dorsal stripe. There was a place near the top of his neck, right at the base of his head, where one of the other young horses must have chewed on his mane, and for a short stretch it stood up in a dark tuft, giving him a cheerily rakish look. He was wary but smart, and Cassidy had been working with him for three days.

The first morning after the incident with Mike in the barnyard, Cassidy had been relieved to find that Aaron intended to keep his promise about having her work with the horses. He had personally taken her through the barn, introducing her to the other horse people and laying out equipment for her.

"You know how to break colts?" Aaron had asked her.

"Sure," Cassidy had said automatically, innately confident that she was not lying. She had not even needed to think about her response; she just knew that the gray mare was only one of many horses that she had trained.

"Good" was all that the weathered black man had grunted.

It turned out that Aaron had had good reason to rescue Cassidy from a career of forking manure or premature death by hanging. She had been surprised to find that the village had a formidable backlog of unbroken young horses. None of the current foal crop had been halter broken, and only a few of the yearlings and two-year-olds had received any handling. As she had followed Aaron from paddock to pasture, Cassidy had begun to wonder how the hell these people came to have any ridable horses at all. She had also been struck by a chillingly logical possibility: Could that be the reason she had been summarily kidnapped and brought there?

Following Aaron into the barn's tackroom, Cassidy had been shaken by the cold pragmatism of that thought. Still, even the sense of that purpose seemed oddly skewed by the facts. If she'd been brought there to train horses for a bunch of farmers, why hadn't she been brought directly to the village instead of being dumped out in the middle of nowhere, where she could be set upon by a pack of the Villagers' antagonists, the Horsemen? Unless she had been escaping . . .

"If there's anything else you need, we can either make it or get it for you," Aaron had been saying then.

"Who usually breaks your horses?" she had asked Aaron, glancing over the longe lines and bitting harnesses he had laid out for her, their buckles dull with tarnish and their leather mottled with mildew.

"There hasn't been anyone since old Burt left us," Aaron had said.

From the way he'd said it, Cassidy had assumed that "old Burt" had died. Hopefully not from injuries sustained while breaking horses, she had thought, dismissing the tangle of neglected tack with a wave of her hand.

"I won't need all this stuff," she had told Aaron. "I know a better way."

The old man's dark eyes had narrowed skeptically. He probably wondered if he had acted too hastily in rescuing Cassidy from the ranks of the muckers. But he was the first person in the stables to understand and approve of the training method Cassidy used on the green colts and fillies. In the eyes of the other stablehands, the progress she had made in just three days must have seemed nothing short of miraculous. She was working with horses that had barely even been halter-broken when she had started, and already she had most of them obeying basic commands at liberty. The Villagers may not have understood her methods, but they certainly understood her results.

Slowly and casually, Cassidy raised one arm and held out her hand to the buckskin colt. For a moment longer he stood frozen, his big brown eyes widening slightly as his nostrils ballooned in a nearly soundless snort.

Come on, she willed him, *you know what I want . . .*

And then, although Cassidy had not moved or said a word, the colt slowly stretched out his neck toward her. His ears pointed straight forward, his nostrils fluttering like valves. He had not yet moved a hoof and yet he appeared to be leaning forward on the tips of his toes, anticipating.

Come on . . .

Suddenly the buckskin's muscles fired, his joints and tendons unlocking as he stepped directly forward and came to a halt at the tips of Cassidy's outstretched fingers.

"Good boy," she said, softly but emphatically. She reached up and stroked him at the angle of his jaw, where his flat gold cheek blended into his throat. He pushed his head into the caress, his eyes half closed in contentment. "Good fella," she reiterated more loudly. "You're pretty smart for a green-ass colt, aren't you?"

"You aren't doing so bad yourself," a voice behind her said.

Cassidy was startled, but because she didn't want to spook the colt, she made a deliberate effort to not reflexively spin around at the sound of Aaron's voice. Instead she lightly slapped the buckskin on the neck and dismissed him by dropping her arm and walking away from him.

The black man stood on the other side of the high fence of the round breaking pen, his thin sinewy forearms resting on one of the upper rails. The first time Cassidy had seen him standing like that by the pen he had been watching her with ill-concealed dismay as she patiently and doggedly followed a big sorrel filly around and around the confines of the small corral. Her methods had left him totally baffled and more than a little scornful. How could you break horses without a longe line and a halter, without so much as a whip with which to signal them? He hadn't understood Cassidy's bizzare system, and she had been just smart enough to not try to explain it. She just let Aaron and the others watch. And what they had seen was that in less than a day she had even the biggest and wiliest of the unbroken horses standing to be approached and then touched by her; and that in another day or two even the most obstinate of those horses would willingly come to her. All that was done without the use of whips or ropes. Cassidy had not needed to think about what to do; the method came naturally to her and played upon a horse's most simple instincts. Training horses was obviously something she had done before. By the end of her first day as village horse trainer, that had become clearly apparent to everyone, and Cassidy had regained some small measure of security. She may not have felt particularly comfortable, but at least the threat of lynching no longer seemed imminent.

Cassidy glanced back over her shoulder at the buckskin colt as she approached Aaron. The horse was amusing himself by rubbing his chin along the top fence rail on the far side of the pen. He was a good one, this oat-colored horse, smart but tractable. Cassidy had the fleeting thought that if only the people in the village were as reasonable and as comprehensible as the horses, the answers and information she needed before making her escape would be a snap.

"You're doing a good job with him," Aaron told her. "With all of them."

Cassidy almost made some automatic retort, but at the last moment she stopped herself and just shrugged, accepting the compliment as she brushed back her tousled hair with the back of one hand.

Aaron eyed her for a bit before he spoke again. "Your buddy Rowena will be eating with us tonight." He held up a warning forefinger to forestall any comment Cassidy might make before he had finished. "You two stay out of trouble and the mayor doesn't have to know she's eating down here again."

Biting down on her lower lip, Cassidy stared at Aaron for a moment before nodding. In the three days she had lived and worked with the stablehands, she had not seen anything of her buxom friend. Since she seriously doubted that the separation was Rowena's choice, she had to assume that someone had intervened to keep them apart. She could think of only one reason why anyone would want to do that, which kind of narrowed down the choices of who the culprit might be. And so, even though Aaron obviously knew how much she wanted to see Rowena again, Cassidy tried to stifle her enthusiasm. The last thing she needed was more trouble.

After Aaron had gone back to work, Cassidy turned the buckskin colt out into one of the paddocks again. She brought another horse in to the breaking pen, a rangy liver-colored bay filly who needed more work on building up her confidence around people and more experience in being handled. While she worked with the filly, Cassidy thought about Rowena. She was surprised by how much she had missed the woman. The fact that Allen, Meggie, and Steven all were also still gone had only served to accentuate Cassidy's loneliness in the village. Although Aaron had remained pretty close-mouthed about their whereabouts, and there was no one else she dared ask, Cassidy suspected that the three of them were out moving horses again. And just as she could appreciate the value of horses for farming and transportation, she was also willing to concede that her status as a Horseman made it unlikely that anyone would confide in her concerning the details of any such moves.

Cassidy had had a lot of time to think in the last three days because training the horses, while constant and serious work, was also basically very simple and repetitive. Cassidy had been able to use the time to organize a lot of things in her head. Although she hadn't been able to remember anything more from her past, she was coming up with a lot more questions. And while she was fully cognizant of the danger of asking those questions, she still had one person in the village whom she felt she could trust.

That night when Rowena came into the herdsmen's kitchen, she slid into an empty chair across from Cassidy, about halfway down the long table. Her conspiratorial grin made Cassidy acutely aware of what a dour and colorless lot the people around her usually were. She hadn't really given it much thought, because by the time she'd come into the kitchen to eat at night she was too tired and hungry to complain about what lousy company the herdsmen and stablehands were. But Rowena's return dramatically pointed out the contrast that existed between the goatherd and the rest of the village people.

It wasn't that the Villagers were exactly unfriendly, Cassidy had to admit. Even Mike treated their new horse trainer with a casual civility, almost as if the incident in the barnyard had never happened. But perhaps that was what lay at the root of Cassidy's problem in understanding these people's reactions to things. If something didn't directly threaten the security of the village, they seemed largely unaffected by it. All they seemed to think about was their work. They weren't precisely unfriendly—they were just boring.

Rowena, on the other hand, was anything but boring. Cassidy hardly noticed what she was eating after the brunette woman sat down at the table. She just kept mechanically shoveling it in because she was hungry; but her attention was hopelessly drawn to Rowena, who only aggravated the situation by winking, grinning, and throwing surreptitious mocking looks at the people seated around them. Only Cassidy's determination to stay out of trouble, and an occasional warning glance from Aaron, seated at the head of their table, kept her from bursting into giddy laughter at several points.

The moment they had finished eating, Cassidy slipped through the throng of barn workers dispersing at the kitchen door and out into the warm dimness of the summer evening. She waited for Rowena in the shadow of the long building. When the brunette joined her, the two of them wordlessly walked along the edge of the cow barn and then out across the dark and quiet expanse of the milking yard.

It had been a hot day and the ground still seemed to retain some of that heat. The sparse and closely cropped grass of the milking yard was dusty and dewless; an occasional unpalatable weed was the only thing that stood more than ankle high in the whole field. Cassidy glanced back at the huge blocky forms of the barns as they walked. They did not stop until the black silhouettes had receded to miniature size and they were nearly to the pasture fence.

"Boy, am I glad to see you!" Rowena exclaimed then, enfolding Cassidy in a hearty, spontaneous hug. "After what happened the other night with your horse, I was afraid maybe they'd sent you away or something."

Stepping back, reluctant for a moment to leave the hold of Rowena's plump arms, Cassidy responded, "Me? Where the hell were *you* the last three days? I thought maybe they'd exiled you back to that clothing factory!"

Laughing, Rowena gave Cassidy's arms another quick squeeze before she let go. "Naw, they'd never send me back there, believe me!" She made a vague gesture, waving off toward the east where the neat confines of the milking yard bordered on the fenceline of one of the cattle pastures. "They sent me out with a bunch of the shepherds to Stony Breaks."

"Stony Breaks? What's there?"

"It's just some land way out in the middle of nowhere where they usually run flocks of sheep all summer." Rowena sobered, her mouth pursing thoughtfully. "It's funny, though, because we went out there to bring in all the sheep, and they usually don't do that until late in fall."

Cassidy sobered, as well. This had not been one of the things she had been planning on asking Rowena about, but her curiosity had been piqued. And anything out of the ordinary in the village routine might be a clue to whatever conspiracy had initially brought her there. "Then why do you think they brought all those sheep back in now?"

Rowena shrugged. Despite her queenly size, the way she performed the gesture always seemed casually graceful. "Damned if I know," she admitted. "But everyone's acting like there's something up."

"What do you mean, 'something up'?"

Rowena shrugged again, no less eloquently. "I don't know. Maybe they're worried about Horsemen," she offered.

Now Rowena had touched upon one of the things Cassidy had wanted to ask her about. She recalled the peculiar insistence of Misty's interrogation several days earlier. "I thought the Horsemen only stole horses," she said. "Why would the villagers be worried about the sheep?"

Rowena made another gesture, more expansive than a shrug. In the near darkness of the summer evening, Cassidy could not see details of her expression, only the curly outline of her rebellious hair and the occasional flash of her teeth. "Beats me," she said, "but everyone around here seems to think that whenever there are Horsemen around, strange stuff happens."

These people wouldn't know "strange" if it hit them over the head! Cassidy thought to herself. But Rowena's comment had struck a chord in her. Almost involuntarily, she thought back to the hallucinations she'd had, most particularly that stinking apparition she'd seen out in the ravine. And she realized that her palms had suddenly begun to sweat.

"What kind of stuff?" Cassidy asked carefully.

Rowena seemed a little perplexed by the gravity of Cassidy's tone and the importance she seemed to attach to what Rowena had told her. "Maybe it doesn't have anything to do with the Horsemen," she offered, not exactly answering Cassidy's question. "Stony Breaks is just a lot of overgrown hilly pastureland; maybe they were worried about predators." She grinned suddenly, the faint ambient light catching on the hard rim of her teeth. "Hell, maybe they just wanted to get me out of the village for a few days—before you and me plotted to overthrow the mayor!"

Cassidy laughed, mostly because Rowena expected and wanted her to. In fact, Rowena's joking comment may have come perilously close to the truth. Cassidy had become increasingly aware that both she and the goatherd could be imperiled by the temerity of Cassidy's probing. Yet she found that she couldn't—or wouldn't—let go of it. She knew there were a lot of ways she could have tried to ease into asking Rowena what she really wanted to know, but she liked to think that her friendship with Rowena made that type of maneuvering no longer necessary. In fact, complex machinations would have seemed almost insulting in dealing with this cheerfully forthright woman with whom Cassidy had made a solemn pact to find the truth.

"Rowena," Cassidy said, "have you ever heard people talk about monsters?"

"Monsters?" Rowena gave a little hoot of laughter. "Cassidy, you've been sitting around too many camp fires!"

Cassidy hesitated a moment, uncertain whether to continue to pursue the topic or simply to acquiesce by pretending that she had just been joking. She was, strangely enough, both relieved and disappointed to find that Rowena appeared to have only ridicule for the concept of monsters. As disheartening as it might be to confront the fact that she had been hallucinating, that still seemed preferable to the alternative. And yet, if such creatures did not exist, if they were merely some kind of hangover from the remnants of her own imperfectly erased memory, then why had there been others who had believed in them? Cassidy was almost certain that Kevin had had encounters similar to her own and that those encounters explained the odd-eyed boy's fears. Was there then some sort of connection between the hallucinatory creatures and the place from which she—and perhaps Kevin—had come?

"So," Cassidy said, "then you don't think they really exist?"

Rowena blinked, surprised to find that Cassidy was actually serious. "You gotta be kidding," she said. "There's no such thing as monsters; that's just a figment of these yahoos' imaginations."

"Rowena," Cassidy reminded her dryly, "these yahoos *have* no imaginations."

"Can't argue with that," Rowena agreed.

Even if Cassidy couldn't be sure about the monsters, she had already become convinced that she was right about the imagination part. She had to spend almost all of her time during the day working with the young horses, but she had been able to slip away for a time each evening after dinner to wander unobtrusively around the small village. And one of the baffling impressions she'd confirmed was that everything in the place, from the plain clothing, to the buildings, to the conversations over dinner, showed a remarkable lack of originality.

"I mean, just look at the houses," Cassidy continued, a tone of earnestness creeping into her voice. She made a frustrated gesture, her hands circumscribing a boxlike shape in the air. "Did you ever notice that every house in the village is essentially the *same* house? Most of them are even the same size. It's almost like someone had one idea of what a house should look like— and that's the only idea any of them ever had!"

Rowena frowned, an unaccustomed expression that cleaved a furrow in her usually smooth brow. "You're right," she admitted. "And it's not just the houses. Look at the clothes—and the food." She made a face. "Boy, they always serve the same things!"

Not unexpectedly, Cassidy felt the first niggling pressure of a headache begin to pulse behind her eyes. But she refused to stop. "Even the people themselves," she said. "I thought the Horsemen were single-minded, but the people here are even worse. They're all so—so—"

"*Boring,*" Rowena pronounced with an impudent grin. "You're so right, Cassidy!"

More confident now, partially because Rowena seemed to have drawn a distinction between "us" and "them," Cassidy stubbornly ignored her headache and forged on. "Rowena, do you remember how I said that things here seemed off the track somehow; that some things were missing?" When Rowena nodded, she continued, "Well, I'm not sure yet what all those missing things are; but I think I've started to figure out what some of the stuff is that doesn't seem right."

Rowena's demeanor had grown serious again. She quickly glanced around them, but aside from a chorus of crickets, they were quite alone in the warm darkness. "You mean like the houses?" she prompted.

"Like the blandness, the sameness of everything," Cassidy said. The headache was more insistent, a steady little strobing of pain that beat in time with her pulse. Working around it, she struggled to organize what she wanted to say. In the end it came out in a bit of a jumble, a rush of earnest and anxious observations that summarized her discoveries of all that did not fit in with her own innate sense of the way things should be.

Cassidy had a virtual litany of inconsistencies about the village. Primitive methods of agriculture coexisted with the relative sophistication of odd things like Allen's rifle. The village had nothing more than pedestrian and horse traffic and yet it had broad, paved streets. The houses were poorly lit with inefficient oil lamps, yet boasted such things as flush toilets, running water, and window glass of remarkable quality. The most frustrating thing for Cassidy was that she could see the incongruity, but she couldn't explain it—because she couldn't remember what was *missing*.

Spreading her hands in a helpless gesture of entreaty, Cassidy asked, "Rowena, do you ever find yourself walking through the doorway into a dark room and just automatically reaching out for something?"

Rowena frowned again. "Like what?"

"I don't know—something on the wall; something that isn't there."

Rowena shook her head. "No," she had to admit, "not really. But the other stuff," she hastened to add, "like the roads, I have thought about that and it does seem kind of stupid."

Still determined, Cassidy came at the problem from a slightly different angle. "Rowena," she said, "the first time I saw Allen's gun, I *knew* what it was; I would have known what it was used for, even if I hadn't seen him use it." She made a broad and nonspecific gesture that was more an expression of exasperation than it was an attempt at clarification. "Don't you see? I knew what a gun was because it's something that belongs to the place we've come from."

But although Rowena was sympathetic, she remained maddeningly unconvinced. "Cassidy, the first time I saw a goat I knew what it was, too—so did you, for that matter," she reminded her. "You can't tell me that the first time you saw a horse or a bird or even a mosquito that there was anything weird about the fact that you knew what it was."

Momentarily stymied, her head throbbing, Cassidy looked away across the dark expanse of pasture. "No, that's not what I mean," she muttered doggedly. "I could figure it out if I could just *remember*."

When Cassidy looked back, Rowena was regarding her with a certain gentle intensity. And in that moment Cassidy could glimpse the core of real strength that lay beyond the woman's glib exterior.

"You meant what you said the other afternoon, didn't you, Cassidy? About trying to go back home again?"

"Damn right I meant it!" Cassidy blurted out, heedless of being overheard.

Rowena reached out, her fingers closing around Cassidy's upper arm. "Good," she said emphatically, "because I want to go back with you."

Cassidy hesitated, almost unwilling to believe the gift of Rowena's complicity. "We've got to be very careful," she said.

But Rowena cut her off with a single motion, her hand slipping lower, grasping Cassidy by the wrist. "I'm not afraid," she said. "And I know we can do it—look at how much stuff you've figured out already." She looked solemnly into Cassidy's eyes, renewing the offer of her loyalty. "And I'm going to keep thinking about all the things you told me tonight. Maybe I'll start to remember something, too."

Between the blinding thumping of her headache and the sudden lump that had risen in her throat, Cassidy did not try to reply. She just clasped Rowena's plump hand and squeezed it, sealing the pact they had made three days earlier in the rocky ravine.

Chapter 12 ◀▥

The next day Cassidy was back in the breaking pen. As had become her habit, she was spending the morning working with the youngest and greenest horses first. She was standing in the center of the round pen with a liver chestnut filly, facing her patiently, just about to get the horse to stand for her for the first time, when a familiar voice hailed her from the other side of the fence.

Cassidy looked up in surprise. "Meggie," she said, genuinely happy to see the slender blond girl again. As Cassidy came over to the side of the pen, Meggie climbed up onto one of the lower rails and hung with her elbows over the top rail, smiling in greeting. "Where have you been?" Cassidy asked her. "I haven't seen you since—"

Meggie interrupted her with a vague wave. "Oh, Allen and Steven and I have been out near the border of our territory," she replied. "With all this trouble . . ." As her voice trailed off, she abruptly shifted topics. "But I've been hearing from everybody about the way you've been training the horses. I think it's great," she added warmly.

Unexpectedly gratified by Meggie's simple praise, Cassidy took a moment to look back across the pen to where the reddish-brown filly stood quietly watching them, her delicate ears tipped curiously in their direction. "It's really pretty basic stuff," she said modestly. "The only trick is to make the horses think they're doing exactly what *they* wanted to do. It just takes patience." She gave a little laugh. "That and time, which is something I've had plenty of."

Meggie smiled again, a sunny expression that seemed tailor-made for that fine-boned face. "Well, when you've finished with all the young stock I'm going to let you retrain that thick-headed little gelding of mine." She shifted her weight on the fence rail, the wood bouncing slightly beneath her booted feet. Although it had already become another hot day, Meggie appeared to be comfortable enough in her loosely-fitted clothing. As she leaned over the fence rail, her browned arms bare below the rolled-up sleeves of her tunic, she quickly got to the point. "Listen, Cassidy, the reason I'm here is that Allen sent me back to get some more help. The fence in one of the big pastures has a break in it, and a bunch of the yearlings are missing. Do you want to go?"

"Go?" Cassidy echoed stupidly. "You mean help find the horses?"

"Allen doesn't think they could have been out for too long because the trample marks are still fresh," Meggie went on. "But it looks like at least eight of them are gone, and even if they don't split up it'd take forever for just him and Steven and me to search the whole valley by ourselves. So he sent me back to get some more people to help."

"Sure, I'll go," Cassidy said immediately. But her eager and automatic assent was quickly tempered by the reality of doubt. Since Meggie had been absent from the village in recent days, Cassidy wondered if the blond girl appreciated the uneasy truce by which Cassidy had kept her position there. "That is, if you're sure it'd be okay for me to go," she said, "because I'm not sure I'm supposed to—"

Grinning, Meggie hopped down off the fence. "I already asked Aaron," she said, "and it's fine with him. And he can assign you wherever he wants to."

Relieved, Cassidy scrambled up over the rail fence of the breaking pen. "It'll just take a minute to get my mare," she assured Meggie.

"Don't worry," Meggie said, "I still have to find a few more people yet."

A sudden thought occurred to Cassidy. Impulsively she called out to Meggie as the young woman strode off across the barn yard.

"Meggie, did Allen tell you to ask me?"

The moment she asked, Cassidy realized how silly the question sounded. But Meggie just turned and grinned again. "Not exactly," she replied. "He just told me to be sure to get people who could ride well enough that they wouldn't be more of a hindrance than a help." She shrugged. "So I thought of you."

Somewhat chagrined, Cassidy hurried to the paddocks to get the gray mare.

Although she had managed to make some time every day to spend with her horse, grooming the mare and fussing over her, Cassidy had not been up on the gray's back since the evening of the incident in the barnyard with Mike. No one had precisely forbidden her to ride the horse, but Aaron had made it clear to her that it would be prudent to let things calm down a bit longer before risking anything so possessive and independent. She hadn't been able to just get out and go anywhere since the first day she'd spent herding goats with Rowena. One of the main reasons she'd jumped at the chance to go with Meggie and the others to look for the yearlings was that she had missed the feeling of freedom and power and silent communion she had found only on the big mare's back. It also would be nice to be able to get away from the methodical repetitiveness of work in the training pen, and good to see Meggie and Steven again. There was no other reason, she told herself firmly, refusing to admit what she might have been thinking when she had asked Meggie if Allen had specifically mentioned her.

Meggie had enlisted the help of three other Villagers. The two men were stablehands whom Cassidy recognized from her work around the barn, but she did not know them by name and was relieved when Meggie casually introduced them to her. Dirk was a tall, lanky brunet with a perpetually stubbled face, and Doug was a stouter, balding man with thick eyebrows and wispy strands of blond hair. The third volunteer was a muscular young woman named Clarice who worked as a cook in the herdsmen's kitchen. They all treated Cassidy with a polite sort of indifference, and seemed far more interested in selecting and tacking up their horses than in any needless chatter.

Although Cassidy was eager to renew her friendship with Meggie, she found it awkward to try to talk to her during the ride out to the yearling pasture. She hoped there would be more opportunity later, after their work was finished and before Cassidy had to return to her own job.

The yearling pasture was a huge enclosure, and Meggie explained that the break in the fence had occurred on the far side, in some of the rougher terrain out beyond the reach of any other fence lines. The five riders cut through hilly meadowland, partially wooded terrain that looked very little like pasture and more like some of the wilderness that Cassidy had ridden through during her travels with the Horsemen. The morning had begun with the same kind of clinging humid heat that had marked the past several days, but the wind had picked up a bit and the sky was slowly filling with clouds. The gray mare was eager, barely restraining herself to the jog-trot pace that Meggie set. On the horse's broad back, Cassidy felt happier and more comfortable than she had in days. There was a simple exhilaration to being astride the horse again, a satisfaction that had been only partially replaced by the long hours she had spent working with the village's horses. She found herself reaching down spontaneously and frequently to straighten the horse's errant mane and to stroke her sleek neck. Wherever she had come from, whoever she had been, Cassidy sensed that riding the gray mare was intrinsically where she belonged.

After they had ridden for nearly a half hour, cutting a long diagonal across the pasture, they finally intersected the fence line. The gray mare was still fresh and frisky, and was reluctant to drop down to a walk again.

"The break's just a little farther up the fence line," Meggie said, pulling in her little seal-brown gelding and turning him alongside the fence.

As they rode again in silence, Cassidy studied the woven wire fence. It was a sturdy barrier, stapled to thick wooden posts and convenient tree trunks. It didn't look like the kind of fence that most horses, even adventuresome yearlings, could easily have breached. Cassidy would have ventured this opinion to Meggie and the others if there had been any real opportunity for conversation; but the blond girl and the other three Villagers seemed to be all business. As they followed the serpentine course of the tautly stretched wire barrier, Cassidy was forced to consider the likelihood that the young horses' disappearance had not been merely an accident. And leading the list of possible causes for their disappearance, at least in the Villagers' minds, would have to have been the Horsemen. Everyone had been alluding to the unspecified and nettlesome "troubles," and there was no doubt in Cassidy's mind that the missing yearlings would fall squarely into that category. And if that was the case, and Horsemen had anything to do with it, Allen might have been something less than enthused to see that Meggie had enlisted Cassidy's help in the search.

Cassidy was riding right behind Meggie as they came over the crest of the last lightly wooded hill before the break in the fence. In the small hollow below them, Steven and Allen were waiting on their horses beside the ruptured section of wire. Both horses' coats were streaked with the stiff tracery of dried sweat, but they stood quietly and calmly in the fetlock-deep grass as Cassidy and the others approached down the gentle slope.

Steven stood up in his stirrups and gave a little wave. "Hey, Cassidy," he called out to her.

Cassidy found herself smiling, embarrassingly glad to see the young man again. Allen, on the other hand, merely gave Cassidy and the others a silent nod. His scabbard and gun were immediately evident, strapped to hang behind the right fender of his saddle. Beneath his shaggy hair and beard and the drooping sweep of his mustache, the big man's expression was gravely serious. It was not the kind of expression that invited a smile, even one given in greeting, so Cassidy just returned his nod and then carefully looked away from him.

"Have you figured out for sure how many of them are gone?" Meggie asked Allen, swinging her fidgeting gelding toward the fence line.

Allen made a broad gesture to indicate the rest of the huge pasture. The shifting of his body in the saddle made the leather creak and caused his stout piebald gelding to raise his head. "Steve and I checked the rest of this end of the field," Allen said, "and there's no sign of them, so it looks like all eight of them are gone."

"Shit," Dirk said. The lanky stablehand was mounted on a fat little mare who looked about two hands too short for someone his height, although Cassidy had noted that Dirk was a good rider. Cassidy wasn't sure if he was referring to the number of yearlings that were missing or to the magnitude of the break in the fence. "Look at that fence," Dirk said. "Allen, that wire wasn't just cut!"

Between the two trees that had served as fence posts, about fifteen feet of the woven wire was completely demolished. It looked as if it had been stretched out until it had been literally torn apart. What was left of the fencing, long glittering strands that were rawly stripped of all cross wires, lay in tangled coils amid the brush on the other side of the fence line.

Clarice urged her horse up close enough to the wreckage to be able to pluck one of the distressed wires from the bushes. She pulled the strand up and held it aloft where it slowly twisted in her hand like a dying snake. Her gaze shot to Allen. "No horse broke this thing down," she said needlessly.

Cassidy had been thinking much the same thing; even a team and wagon driven through the fence at full gallop couldn't have ruptured the wire mesh so spectacularly. And she couldn't imagine that anyone trying to steal the yearlings, Horsemen or not, would have been careless enough to have left such a large and obvious hole in the barrier. Considering that the ground and surrounding trees and brush were virtually unmarred, it was difficult to understand exactly how the destruction of the fence had been accomplished, much less by Horsemen. But Allen didn't seem to feel that there was any real need to address Dirk's and Clarice's observations, and Cassidy felt it would have been particularly impolitic for her to have offered an opinion when the group had already so obviously adopted a conclusion more adapted to their prejudices than to the facts.

Allen just tossed back his unruly sorrel hair and said, "The horses' tracks aren't more than a few hours old. Steve and I followed them for a ways, but they split up once they get into the rough country. We're going to have to split up, too, if we're going to find those horses before it gets dark."

Allen's gaze swung over the assembled group and he jabbed the air with one blunt forefinger. "Meg, you take Dirk with you and go west. Clarice, I want you and Doug to go with Steve and head straight toward the river." He gave Cassidy a brief sidelong glance. "Me and Cassidy will go east."

As the horses were shifted around to accommodate Allen's instructions, the big bearded man added sternly, "And stick together; don't split up any further, no matter what you find."

The horses carefully picked their way between the fallen strands of fence wire. On the other side of the ruined fence, Meggie said to Allen, "As soon as we find them, we can drive them back here. I brought the fencing tools, so we can fix the wire right away."

Riding beside Meggie, Dirk flashed her a wry, bucktoothed grin. "Let's worry about *finding* them first, Meg," he reminded the blonde.

Outside of the yearlings pasture the brush and growth of scrub trees was thick enough that the other two groups of riders quickly disappeared from sight. Allen hadn't even glanced back at Cassidy before he reined his piebald toward the east. She was perfectly willing to let Allen lead on. The gray mare followed in his gelding's tracks as the big barrel-chested horse blazed a trail through the worst of the undergrowth.

Although the sky was completely clouded over, it did not look like the kind of sky that threatened rain, and Cassidy found the overcast conditions a welcomed improvement over the sun's glaring heat. Sweating had become a way of life the past few days. Even Allen's coarsely woven tunic was darkened with dampened patches at back and armpits. Flailing through the thick scrub was arduous enough as it was. Beyond the heat and humidity, the constant slap and scratch of the branches and the continuous buzz of the gnats and other insects that they disturbed from the foliage were an annoying accompaniment.

Cassidy used the interlude of silent travel to appraise Allen—or Allen's back, since that was about as much of him as she could see. The burly man sat erect in his saddle, balancing his weight on the balls of his feet in his stirrups, his big head slowly swiveling as he methodically scanned the terrain ahead of them. Other than the accoutrements of tack and clothing, he could have been some kind of big shaggy animal, solemnly surveying its territory, alert for any danger.

It was difficult for Cassidy to keep from thinking about Allen in other ways, as well. For although she may have consciously rejected the idea, if she had been asked about it, she would have had to admit that finding out that Allen was the village sheriff had indelibly altered the way she viewed the big gruff man.

When she had first met him, despite a certain natural wariness, she had felt a puzzled gratitude for his willingness to take her into his group and then back to his village. But when she began to understand the depth of the enmity between his people and the Horsemen, Cassidy had grown uncomfortably baffled by why Allen had protected her. Had he brought her back to the village only because she had a skill that they needed—could he in fact have had something to do with the fact that she had been kidnapped in the first place? If that was the case, then the Villagers were thieves just as surely as the Horsemen they despised.

If she went past the bristling fortress of suspicion about Allen and his motives concerning her, and further examined her own feelings about him as simply a person, Cassidy would have also had to confess that the episode down by the river, when she had treated his burned chest, had had an equally profound effect on the way she subsequently reacted to him. She just didn't know what to do with those feelings.

But Cassidy found herself determined to get by without having to analyze them. There was just too much there that she didn't want to explore, or at least not yet. Even the suggestion of searching her feelings about him brought on the warning pressure of one of her hellacious headaches; and she was damned if she was going to trudge around out in that rough country with a throbbing headache to boot. So she willed herself to avoid any deeper speculation about her companion and just contented herself with watching Allen's back and keeping up with the pace he set.

The heavy brush gradually thinned out, largely because the ground had grown too poor and rocky to support the bigger bushes. The terrain had become very hilly, short-grass meadows dotted with low scrub and intersected by large scarlike slashes of exposed flaking shale. The only trees were a few wind-gnarled red cypresses. Cassidy couldn't imagine how Allen could find horse tracks or any kind of trail in that country, but he continued to watch the ground closely, so she assumed he was following something. So intent were both his progress and his demeanor that Cassidy was surprised and relieved when Allen's gelding suddenly came to a halt in front of her.

Even when the brush had thinned out and she could have ridden side by side with Allen, Cassidy had kept the gray mare single file behind the piebald. She told herself that it was because she didn't want to take a chance on interfering with Allen's tracking, but actually it was because she would have felt uncomfortable riding alongside him. He had shown no interest in casual conversation, and she didn't want to have to try to attempt it with him. It was far easier just to stay behind him and watch his back and not have to think about anything further. Still, Cassidy was grateful for the chance to stop. Despite the clouds, the back of her T-shirt had begun to stick to her skin, and her mare's sweat was slowly gluing the inseam of Cassidy's jeans to her inner thighs and butt. A chance to hop down off the gray and walk around for a bit would be welcomed indeed.

The mare stopped because Allen's gelding had stopped. It took Cassidy a long moment to realize that although Allen had reined the big horse in, he was showing no inclination to dismount. Instead he was staring straight ahead, looking down from his vantage point on the crest of the hill at something that Cassidy could not yet see. The bearded man's whole body was held motionless, poised in the saddle. In fact, for a period of time the only movement on the scrabbly little slope seemed to be the wide and soundless flutter of the gray mare's nostrils as she tested the air.

What the hell is going on? Cassidy wondered. Her head cocked quizzically and she automatically tightened her calves against the mare's broad sides. For just a second the gray horse hesitated; then, the thin skin of her nostrils working like bellows, she slipped silently up beside the piebald. From that position Cassidy could see over the top of the hill.

The hollow that stretched below them was similar to a dozen others that they had already traversed since they'd left behind the shrubby woodland. It was narrow and fairly deep, surrounded by the short-grass hills. The only cover was a few stunted pines. At the bottom of the hollow lay two of the village's missing yearlings, both quite dead. One was sprawled in the miserly grass, its neck obviously broken; the other had been disemboweled. And crouched before the second yearling's body, sitting up on its rump like an overgrown dog while it raked the horse's entrails across the blood-soaked turf, was a mountainous creature covered with heavy silver-streaked umber fur.

Oh, sweet heaven—that's a bear!

Allen's hand closed over Cassidy's forearm, almost causing her to faint from shock and surprise. She hadn't even seen him reach for her.

"Don't move," he said softly. "We're upwind from it—I don't think it even knows yet that we're here."

Wonderful! Cassidy thought, feeling giddily light-headed from adrenaline while her heart hammered uselessly in her chest. *Don't move?* "Then let's just get the hell out of here!" she whispered back at Allen.

Down in the little valley, the feeding bear had discovered some particularly succulent portion of the yearling's innards. It bent forward and rooted vigorously with its dark snout, making loud slurping noises that to Cassidy's disconcertment sounded remarkably like the way some of the stablehands ate soup. Appalled, she tore her gaze away long enough to shoot Allen an anxious look. "Let's go!" she hissed fiercely. "Before that son of a bitch comes looking for dessert!"

Allen had released Cassidy's arm, but he stolidly shook his head. "Uh-uh," he said quietly. "Once a bear gets a taste for horsemeat, it'll keep on killing horses."

Cassidy was tempted to point out what to her was the obvious fact: The bear may have been lunching on the dead yearlings, but it was extremely unlikely that it had either the ability or the incentive to kill two healthy young horses, especially so close together. She doubted that the creature had actually killed either horse; it was merely a scavenger, making the most of the carnage that someone or something else had left behind for him. But just as it had been patently pointless to try to suggest that perhaps something other than Horsemen had breached the yearlings' fence, Cassidy also understood that there would be no advantage in trying to contradict Allen's assumption about the bear. So all she said was "Yeah? Well, what if it gets a taste for *people*?"

But Cassidy thought she knew what the big burly man had in mind. She was certain of it when she saw Allen's hand slide down and unfasten the strap on his saddle scabbard. Slowly and painstakingly, his eyes never leaving the gorging bear, he slipped the long barrel of the rifle out from its leather sheath and brought it up across the pommel of his saddle. He let the dull gray metal cylinder lightly rest against the side of his gelding's neck; the horse never even twitched.

But Cassidy couldn't keep quiet. "What the—? You're going to *shoot* it?" she whispered incredulously. "What if the damned gun misfires again?"

"Shh!" Allen reprimanded her. "We may be upwind, but that bear's not *deaf*. You stay here. I'm going to move in a little closer."

"*Closer?*" Cassidy hissed in disbelief.

"Shhh!" Allen repeated more emphatically. "Yeah, closer; I'm not sure if I can hit it from here."

As he spoke, Allen slowly gathered his reins in one hand. "Just stay put," he told Cassidy. "If there's trouble, I want you to find Steve and the others and track down this horse-eating bastard."

"Track down the bear?" Cassidy sputtered. "If there's trouble, what about *you*?"

Allen looked at Cassidy then, just a quick sidelong glance, but it was enough for her to see the hard edge of his teeth flash beneath his upper lip and the ruddy-colored skirt of his thick mustache. "Cassidy," he said wryly, "if I have trouble with this bear, there won't be enough left of me to worry about."

Then Allen delicately touched his heels to the piebald gelding's sides and the big horse moved off, catlike and soundlessly, down the rocky slope.

To Cassidy's surprise and relief, the huge bear seemed to remain totally oblivious to their presence, even as Allen's horse cautiously edged down the hill toward it. The gluttonous creature just continued to sit there before the yearling's mutilated carcass, ferrying out bits of entrails with its dinner plate–size forefeet and occasionally rocking forward on its fat buttocks to use its snout to tear loose some morsel. The sounds it made were absolutely disgusting. Cassidy could hardly stand to watch or listen as the shaggy animal ate, especially knowing that the bloodied mass of flesh upon which it fed had so recently been a frolicsome yearling horse. Even the gray mare seemed repulsed as she stood frozen in place with her wide nostrils fluttering at the reek of death.

Allen moved in far closer than Cassidy could be comfortable with, far closer than she ever could have forced herself to go. She held her breath as the spotted gelding stopped and stood stolidly. With infinite care, Allen raised the rifle to his shoulder and laid the wooden stock against his hairy cheek. Only then did it occur to Cassidy to wonder how good a shot Allen was, even presuming that his crudely made weapon would work properly. Almost simultaneously, another question occurred to her.

I wonder how fast a bear can run, she thought as Allen sighted down the long barrel of the gun. *Then again, maybe just the noise that damned gun makes will—*

The boom of the gun firing reverberated with startling volume in the bowl-shaped valley. Seemingly concurrent with the sound, Cassidy saw the furry bulk of the great bear jerk upright, as if it were suddenly sitting at attention. The pointed head slowly swung around, its bloodied snout lifting to scent the air. The bear's expression—if bears had expressions—appeared to be a mixture of perplexment and mild annoyance at being disturbed at its meal.

Shit!—did Allen miss it? Cassidy thought frantically. On the piebald horse, Allen was rapidly fumbling with the breech of the rifle. It took Cassidy a moment to realize that he was trying to reload the weapon.

The bear's head stopped scanning and locked into position then. To her horror, Cassidy saw that it was looking directly at Allen and the spotted gelding. As the huge creature sat staring at the mounted man, Cassidy finally realized that not all of the blood on the beast's coat was from the dead horses. A bright splash of vivid crimson decorated the back of the bear's neck, obvious testimony to Allen's marksmanship. It just looked as if it were going to take more than one shot to stop the bear.

If she hadn't seen it herself, Cassidy never would have believed that an animal of the bear's size and bulk could have moved with such incredible speed and agility. Even as she watched it happen, it took several seconds before her mind was willing to accept what her eyes were telling her. In the space of a heartbeat the bear was on its feet and running with astonishing speed toward Allen and his horse. Cassidy's previous question about a bear's speed was being answered with a terrible and graphic emphasis, and so precipitously that she was helpless to intervene.

"Allen!" Cassidy screamed, frantic with the breathless kind of desperation usually reserved for nightmares. But this was no dream. The charging bear was as remorseless and deadly as a bolt of lightning; she was certain she was about to witness a slaughter.

As Allen continued to struggle to load the rifle, he gave the piebald his head and the horse wheeled around to flee. There was no way they could have hoped to outrun the bear, but at least they didn't have to provide it with the convenience of a stationary target. As the massive shaggy body slammed into the horse's rear quarters with an audible thump, the big piebald staggered sideways and then went down. Allen fell clear and rolled; the long-barreled gun flew from his grip.

The bear used both of its huge forefeet like bats, claws as long as carving knives slicing through the piebald's hide. The horse screamed, a sound of both outrage and agony, and tried to lurch free. The next blow from the bear's powerful paw caught the gelding full on the side of the head. To Cassidy's utter horror, the force of the impact nearly decapitated the horse. Blood—brilliant, red, and thick—shot in twin gouts from the severed arteries in the gelding's neck, and the horse's shrill scream was abruptly stifled. The bear, temporarily blinded by the hot spray of gore, sat back suddenly on its rump and roared in irritation at being interrupted in its attack. Then, rubbing its face against the thick fur of its upper forelegs to clear its vision—a gesture that Cassidy found unnervingly human—the bear lurched to its feet again.

The bear stumbled over the body of the spotted gelding while its victim's muscles were still reflexively twitching and jerking. Its massive head swung around and it seemed to have to squint to be able to locate its remaining objective. The beast's target was the same as the one Cassidy's eyes helplessly sought: Allen, sitting there dazed in the scrubby grass, his rifle lying useless a good twenty feet from his reach.

It had nothing to do with loyalty, and even less to do with courage. Not that Cassidy was incapable of either, but she had literally frozen with shock and fear. It was the gray mare that made her an unwitting hero.

When the big horse bounded forward beneath her, Cassidy nearly lost her balance and toppled backward off the mare. If it hadn't been that they were racing downhill, she might very well have fallen off. As it was, she was forced to cling desperately to the galloping horse. Then the gray made a sound that Cassidy had never heard before. It was not a whinny or a scream, but a *roar*, like a tremendous loud exhalation of air. In that weirdly elongated moment as they raced pell-mell down the steep and shaley slope toward what Cassidy thought must be a certain death, the gray's hooves pounding like thunder, she got her first real sense of just what this horse that she called Dragonfly could really be—what a Horseman's horse could really be, whether in that world or in her own. The horse was more than just an extension of Cassidy's body, she was an extension of her will. The gray was a war-horse; not fearless, perhaps, but fearsome, a creature of powerful and independent volition.

The gray's bellow and her charge had the desired effect. The bear's head swung around again as it temporarily forgot Allen to face this new antagonist. With a certain detached sharpness of vision, Cassidy was satisfied to note that the bear's wound was bleeding more profusely, obviously aggravated by the exertion of slaying Allen's horse. Still, Cassidy found herself hoping that her mare wasn't planning to take on the creature one on one.

The big gray roared again, a noise that made the hair on the back of Cassidy's neck literally stand on end. They swept past the bear with hardly six feet of clearance. Clearly perplexed, the huge shaggy form pivoted, its slitted eyes following the new threat. Doubtless the creature wasn't accustomed to being attacked by a horse, and the novelty bought them a little time. Cassidy really didn't have a plan—it hadn't been her idea to come tear-assing down into the hollow in the first place—but the notion of just scooping Allen up and then getting the hell out of there was starting to look pretty good. She tried not to remember the bear's astounding speed, or the fact that the mare would be carrying double weight.

The damned thing's been wounded—it's losing blood, she thought desperately. Maybe it's slower now . . .

Then the gray mare suddenly slid to a halt, her rump pulled so far under her that her rear hooves sliced sharp furrows in the thin sod. Cassidy was not well enough prepared to be able to keep her seat. She slipped over the mare's withers and slid down along her shoulder, landing gracelessly at the horse's forefeet— practically on top of Allen's gun.

"Cassidy!" Allen was shouting at her, before she could even

clear her head or get her bearings at suddenly finding herself unhorsed. "Get it—the gun!"

The gray mare wheeled around again and stood facing the bear. Her neck was arched like a stallion's, crowned with the wild disarray of her thick silver mane and her breath jetted loudly from her dilated nostrils.

Cassidy had to crawl on her hands and knees through the bristly grass to reach the gun. *Thanks for dumping me off, you ungrateful shit!* she thought as she groped for the weapon's wooden stock.

"Did it ever occur to either of you two assholes," she muttered under her breath as she hefted the surprisingly heavy rifle, "that maybe I don't know how to shoot this thing?"

From beside the piebald gelding's body, perhaps one hundred feet away, the bear stood up on its hind legs and gave a bawling cry of rage. Then it dropped back down onto all fours and began to lope toward Cassidy and the gray mare.

Okay—so I can learn!

Cassidy jerked the barrel of the gun up, pointing it without even trying to aim or sight. At the rate the bear was moving, she figured that by the time she got off a shot it was going to be near enough to present a very large target. Only belatedly did it occur to her to wonder if Allen had been able to finish reloading the weapon.

Dragonfly! Get the hell out of the way! was Cassidy's last thought before she squeezed the trigger.

At the last moment the gray mare sprang aside with another bellow of defiance. The horse's movement and the raw sound of her challenge was sufficient to distract the charging bear briefly. For a split second the giant creature hesitated, then veered, presenting Cassidy with a broadside target.

Both the kickback and the explosive noise were much greater than she had expected, and the discharge of the rifle knocked Cassidy over flat on her back. She lay there stunned, waiting to feel the brutal slash of claws or the fetid breath of the bear's bloody maw in her face.

But nothing like that happened.

Cassidy's ears were still ringing when Allen reached her. She had a monumental headache that for once had nothing to do with her trying to remember her past. As he tried to help her to her feet, she realized that there was no way in hell that she could keep her balance yet. So Allen ended up just lifting her, holding her up by the armpits like a sack of oats.

"You okay?" Allen asked gruffly. His voice echoed tinnily in Cassidy's ear. She felt cold and shaky, and for a brief moment she thought that she might vomit.

Cassidy stared down at her arms and the front of her shirt, which were liberally splattered with a spray of blood. When she looked up again she saw why. When the bear had fallen, it had somersaulted across the sod, the huge carcass coming to rest almost on top of her. Its pointed snout was dug into the dirt. And her desperate shot had blown away a good part of the top of its skull.

Chapter 13 ◀▥

"Geez, you'd think the least they could have done is given you the rest of the day off!"

Cassidy gave Rowena a crooked smile, even if the goatherd couldn't see it. "Well, they did let me knock off work when it started raining," she observed wryly.

The two women sat side by side on one of the huge wooden beams that formed the framing of the hay mow in the dairy barn, dangling their legs over the sweet, clover-scented darkness. Above them the rain, which had begun a short time before dusk, drummed softly on the barn roof. When the wet weather had made their walk in the milking yard impractical, Rowena had suggested climbing up into the vast sanctuary of the hayloft. Cassidy had readily agreed, particularly eager for her friend's company that night.

For all of her loquaciousness, Rowena had proven herself quite capable of thoughtful silence when that had seemed appropriate. The day's events had been traumatic enough for Cassidy but at least violence and danger were things she could understand. She had, in fact, come to understand them a hell of a lot better in the past week than she felt she ever had in all of her previous life. What she could not understand, and what she still found more deeply disturbing and profoundly unsettling than the viciousness of the bear's attack, was the way Allen and the other Villagers had reacted to what had happened. She had not exactly been surprised, but their response had only served to further emphasize what she considered a depressingly skewed set of values among the people there. Exactly what sort of worth did they attach to human life if they valued a few horses over Allen's life?

Meggie and Dirk had arrived minutes after Cassidy had shot the bear. They had headed in the direction of the valley as soon as they had heard Allen's first shot. Steven, Clarice, and Doug had arrived shortly after them. While everyone had expressed their relief that the bear had been killed, no one—even Allen—had seemed particularly impressed with the fact that he and Cassidy had just narrowly escaped death. Perhaps if either one of them had been seriously injured or killed, the response would have been different. And it wasn't that the Villagers' reaction to what had happened was completely without emotion; in fact, the loss of the three horses, especially Allen's piebald gelding, caused a great deal of regret and outrage. Allen couldn't even bring himself to touch the mutilated body of his horse. Steven and Dirk quietly salvaged his gear for him. And yet none of them, not even the usually perceptive and compassionate Meggie, seemed especially concerned with the possible psychological trauma that might have been caused by their nerve-racking ordeal. Once assured that Cassidy was physically unscathed, the blond girl joined the other stable workers in soberly planning the hunt for the remaining missing yearlings.

Cassidy had endured the ride back to the village in a sort of numb haze. Despite the accuracy of Rowena's deprecating comment, Cassidy did not even mind so much that she had been expected to go right back to work in the breaking pen when they had returned. And she certainly didn't want to go back out with Allen and the other riders to continue the search for the rest of the missing yearlings. The methodical routine of working with the young horses helped Cassidy distance herself from the aftereffects of what had happened out in that valley and gave her the rest of the afternoon to come to terms with its weirdly dispassionate aftermath.

Because she couldn't understand the reaction of Meggie and the others, Cassidy at least temporarily avoided trying to analyze it. While she patiently handled the green colts and fillies that had been given into her care, she instead thought about something else that the afternoon's events had kindled in her mind. Perhaps the Villagers were not given to emotional responses, but she was. And there had been a moment that afternoon out in that scrubby-grass little hollow, when she had found herself on the ground with Allen with an unfamiliar weapon in her hands and a wounded bear about to charge her, when Cassidy had realized that there were people and things worth caring about—even in that place.

"Hey, at least Hank the Dink gave you a decent-size piece of pie for dessert tonight,'' Rowena said, interrupting her thoughts. ''That must count for something, huh?''

Rowena's comment came after an interval of silence, and Cassidy had to scramble for a moment to put it into context. When she had, Cassidy smiled softly in the darkness. ''Just means that no one else seems to like gooseberry pie,'' she replied, giving Rowena a playful nudge with her elbow.

The news of the bear's attack and the death of the horses had spread quickly, at least around the barns, and by the time the rain had brought a halt to the day's work, and the various herdsmen and stablehands began to gather in the big kitchen for supper, most of the Villagers had heard at least some version of it. But again their reactions had been dishearteningly dispassionate. Cassidy still wasn't certain if the typically flat response was due to some previous and frequent exposure to the random brutality of their environment, or if it said something far more sinister about them. She couldn't help but wonder if whoever had brought them here, and by whatever process had so ruthlessly destroyed their memories, had also caused that almost epidemic sort of emotional opacity.

Cassidy hadn't expected cheers or toasts of congratulations at supper—or at least she told herself that she hadn't. But it wouldn't have seemed out of line to her for at least the people with whom she worked every day to have said ''Hey, we're glad you're still alive, Cassidy. Thanks for shooting that bear.'' But nothing even remotely that sentimental was said. Perhaps if Allen or Meggie or Steven had been there, something more friendly might have been said. As it was, the closest anyone came to even acknowledging Cassidy's action was when one of the cooks—a man Rowena always referred to as Hank the Dink, for reasons Cassidy did not need to have explained to her—remarked that since the mortal wound had been delivered to the bear's head, he and a couple of the boys could go out the next day and salvage the beasts's skin. If it hadn't been for Rowena sitting across the table from her and mugging shamelessly, Cassidy probably wouldn't even have had the appetite to eat that unusually large piece of gooseberry pie.

Below them in the darkened recesses of the cow barn, where the drowsy milk cows still sorted sleepily through their hay, one cow lowed softly. Cassidy swung her feet slowly, thinking again of the things she had been mulling over that afternoon in the breaking pen. She wasn't sure how to frame her questions about them to Rowena. It wasn't because she was reluctant to ask her friend about those things, or about anything, but because she wasn't sure if Rowena would understand what she was getting at unless she was extremely blunt about it. All Cassidy was certain of was that out of the day's traumatic events she had managed to salvage something, an insight into her own feelings that had been sparked by the incident in the valley. And she was certain that it was something of real significance to what was *missing* there.

"Rowena," Cassidy said with deliberate casualness, still swinging her feet, "why doesn't the village keep a stallion? Why do all the mares have to be sent off to be bred?"

Beside her on the loft beam, Rowena's broad shoulders shrugged. It was too dim in the barn for Cassidy to be able to see more than just the roughest outline of the brunette's body, but they sat close enough together that Cassidy could almost feel the movement of the gesture. "Too much trouble to handle one, I guess," Rowena said. "They don't even keep a buck—a male goat. I have to take all my does to Green Lake in late winter to get them bred."

"But they keep bulls for the milk cows and the beef cattle," Cassidy reminded her. "And they've got boar pigs and roosters and—"

"Hey, is this one of those *weird* things?" Rowena interrupted excitedly. "Is it kind of odd that they don't have a stud horse or a buck goat?"

The bigger woman had shifted sideways on the beam, turning eagerly toward Cassidy. Then it was Cassidy's turn to shrug. "Do you think it's odd?" she asked. Although that hadn't exactly been the point of her initial question, she was willing to listen to any opinion that Rowena might have.

But Rowena just gave a little snort. "Not necessarily," she pointed out. "Buck goats really stink, and you only need them once a year. Why feed a smelly goat all year for that? And maybe there isn't enough of a mixture of bloodlines in the village mares to make it worth using just one or two stallions of their own. They've got all kinds of stallions at Silverstone. Most of the mares from all the territories around here go there to be bred."

Cassidy couldn't think of a graceful segue from that, so she just leapfrogged right into her next question without one. "Rowena, the first day I came here I saw some kids. I think they were helping in the fields. But I haven't seen them since."

Without being able to see the big woman's face in the darkness, Cassidy was temporarily unable to judge Rowena's reaction to the remark, or the reason why she seemed to be hesitating before saying anything. Then suddenly Rowena began to chuckle loudly.

"Oh, you mean *children*," she said. "When you said 'kids,' I thought you meant, you know, *kids*—baby goats!" She gave a little hoot. "And I was wondering how the hell anyone had figured out a way to make the darn things work in the fields!"

Cassidy had to laugh, as well. "I forgot I was dealing with the village goatherd," she admitted. "But there *are* children here, right? I know I saw them that day."

Rowena made some vague gesture in the darkness. "Yeah, ten or eleven of them, I guess. They aren't allowed to hang around down here by the barns, which is probably why you haven't seen them again."

Cassidy paused for a moment, debating how to continue. She had stopped swinging her feet, even though she hadn't yet realized that she had. From somewhere below them in the dark mountains of hay, a kitten mewed plaintively.

"Rowena, do you know whose kids they are?" she finally asked.

"Paula takes care of them most of the time," Rowena said. "I don't think you've met her—a big fat woman with red hair? Sometimes Tom and Otto watch them, though, so that might be why you saw them in the field that day."

"No, that's not what I meant," she said quickly. "I meant who do they belong to? Whose children are they?"

Rowena's puzzlement came through clearly, even before she said a word. She hesitated a moment before answering and her big body canted just slightly closer to Cassidy's. "The village's, I guess," she said, perplexity plain in her voice.

Somewhere above them in the vast vaulted darkness of the half-filled haymow several pigeons conducted a sleepy shoving match. A single downy feather, floating downward unseen, brushed against Cassidy's bare arm and then was gone. Cassidy found that she had been holding her breath. Slowly letting it out, she said, "Rowena, where did the children come from?"

Rowena gave another little snort. "Hah!" she said. "Probably from wherever the rest of us came from—I thought that was what we were trying to find out!"

Backtracking for a moment, Cassidy tried a different tack. "All of the animals that they raise here have babies, right? Even if they don't keep the stud here, they have the mothers—horses, cows, goats, pigs, sheep, whatever—right?"

Rowena was nodding; Cassidy didn't have to be able to see it to know that. Cassidy paused a moment again and then delivered her closing argument.

"Then whose babies are the children, Rowena? Where are *their* mothers?"

For the first few seconds Rowena was absolutely motionless. When she did move, her big body jerked sideways on the beam, so abruptly and vigorously that for an instant Cassidy was afraid she was going to have to try to catch hold of her larger friend to keep Rowena from tumbling off into the haymow below them.

"Geez, Cassidy—you're right! Those children are baby *people*!"

Cassidy almost had to smile at the shocked emphasis in Rowena's exclamation. Perhaps the only reason she didn't was that the realization, which had come to her only that afternoon, had been equally incredible to Cassidy herself. In a moment of revelation every bit as startling to her as her realization that she had come from another place, Cassidy had discovered her first clue to one of that place's primary *missing* things.

Rowena's hands shot out in the darkness and clutched Cassidy's upper arms in an excited grip. "Wow—do you realize what this means?"

Cassidy certainly did. "I don't think those children belong here, Rowena; no more than you or I do," she said. "I think they were brought here, too. But doesn't it make you wonder: Why don't any of the women who are *here* have babies?"

Rowena began laughing then, loudly and almost a little hysterically. Her fingers bit into the bare skin of Cassidy's arms and her braying peals of laughter shook them both on the wooden beam. When she could finally speak, Rowena's voice was a half-choked gasp.

"I can tell you why none of the women here have babies: no stud service!" Rowena had to stop and catch her breath before she could go on. "None of these guys would know what to do, Cassidy. They all think that their thing is just something to piss through!"

Rowena's crude hilarity was contagious; Cassidy found herself laughing raucously, too. In fact, the two of them laughed until Cassidy's sides ached and the tears were streaming across her cheeks. If her bladder had been full enough, she probably would have wet her pants. Rowena finally had to let go of Cassidy's arms just to keep her balance on the beam. Cassidy wasn't sure if the boisterous outburst was appropriate, or even if it had been fueled by actual amusement or more by despair; but it was necessary.

Surprisingly, it was Rowena who first found her voice again. "Geez, Cassidy, you're right," she said. "I had completely forgotten about this, but . . . ." She paused and Cassidy knew that the brunette was staring at her in the darkness. When Rowena resumed, her voice had grown softer and lower. "When I was in Green Lake, when I first got there, there was this guy that I—that I *liked*, you know? But I didn't really understand what I expected from him, and he was—" Rowena made some kind of vague gesture in the darkness. "He was like all of these guys. He was nice to me," she added quickly. Then she chuckled ruefully. "But then again, he was nice to everyone—even the chipmunks he fed little tidbits to!" She shook her head. "He just didn't have a clue."

Quietly, gently, Cassidy said, "Then you know what I'm talking about, don't you? The way these people live—this isn't normal."

"Boy, I'll say," Rowena agreed heartily. "They don't have sex—they barely even have *gender*!"

Cassidy found Rowena's blunt comment eerily apt. All of her initial feelings of confusion and uneasiness about the way in which men and women interacted—or rather, failed to interact—in this place had finally come to a head out in the breaking pen that afternoon. For it had been there, while she had been trying to avoid thinking about one kind of puzzling behavior and had ended up thinking about puzzling behavior of a slightly different sort, that Cassidy had suddenly realized the basis for her feeling that again something was *missing*. Then all of it—from her reaction to Kevin's casual nudity, to the impulse she'd had when she'd touched Allen by the river, to the village's communal sleeping arrangements—all made instant if cockeyed sense. The way men and woman acted toward each other there felt strange to Cassidy because it *was* strange.

At first, her amazing rediscovery of sex had so tidalwaved Cassidy with the overwhelming sense of how pervasive that basic phenomenon *should* be that it took her a bit of time and effort to come back to the crux question: Why was human sexuality absent there? Incredible as it might have seemed, could these people also have *forgotten* sex? But sex wasn't just something learned or acquired, like a name or where you came from. Sex was an integral part of what you *were*. How on earth could anyone, any power, have made all of the people there simply forget something that should have been as much a part of their physical makeup as the will to eat, sleep, or preserve their own lives?

"Wow, this is so crazy," Rowena was saying. There was a tone of both disbelief and excitement in her voice as she sat facing Cassidy on the loft beam. "I mean, how can they keep breeding all these animals and not catch on?" Another little hoot of laughter escaped her. "Then again, can you see someone like Clarice having babies? She'd probably eat them!" Rowena gave another snort of laughter, more breathless again. "And geez, Cassidy—these guys! Is there even a guy here that you could imagine, you know, *doing it* with?"

That was a question which Cassidy chose to treat as rhetorical. Even then the memory of what she had been thinking when she had touched Allen down by the river the morning Gabriella's colt had been born was making her face feel hot, and she was grateful for the concealing darkness in the hay mow. She swiftly redirected the topic.

"Rowena, listen," she said seriously, "have you ever heard anyone here talk about being related to anyone else? A brother or sister, maybe; or parents?"

Rowena quickly sobered, as well. "Cassidy," she said quietly, "in all the time I've been here, this is the first time I've even heard anyone use those words."

Both of them were silent for a moment, pondering the enormity of what they had discovered. Cassidy found that she had mixed emotions about the revelation. On one hand she felt excited and vindicated, because it definitely was *not* a normal situation. Even Rowena could understand that and had confirmed her suspicions. But on the other hand that realization only made the whole fact of her existence there even more ominous and frightening. What kind of place had she been brought to where people didn't even know what sexual attraction was? Who or what could possibly be responsible for simply eliminating sexual activity between these men and women? That seemed to Cassidy to be a power far greater than whatever force had first created the human species and set it on its natural path. And the thought of being manipulated by such a power was truly terrifying.

Far below them, in the lower part of the dairy barn, a wooden door rumbled shut.

"We'd better get back," Cassidy said reluctantly, suddenly

feeling more vulnerable than ever, "before anyone notices we're spending so much time together."

Shifting slowly in the darkness, Rowena turned on the wooden beam and began to inch her way along on her butt, back toward the crosspiece and the wooden ladder that led down to the mow floor. Pausing at the beams' intersection, she looked back toward Cassidy. From the tone of her voice, Cassidy knew Rowena was shaking her head.

"This is so *weird*, Cassidy," she said. "I know there's a lot of strange stuff around here, but this has got to be the weirdest!"

Cassidy could have agreed with her, but she didn't. She was still afraid that maybe Rowena would yet be proven wrong.

When Rowena didn't show up for supper in the herdsmen's kitchen the next evening, Cassidy felt the slow roll of alarm deep in her belly. Had someone noticed that they'd gone up into the haymow? Could anyone have overheard even part of their conversation there? Cassidy's continuing sense of paranoia was like a bad toothache, nagging and impossible to ignore. When Rowena failed to appear for two evening meals in a row, Cassidy decided to break with precedent and ask about the goatherd's whereabouts.

Even though Cassidy had gotten to the point of carrying on simple conversations with several of the stablehands, she couldn't bring herself to ask any of them about Rowena's absence. Instead she caught up to Aaron as he was about to head out the kitchen door and pulled him out into the shadowy yard to question him.

Aaron had always been tolerant of Cassidy's friendship for Rowena, and he looked only mildly put out at being detained. "She's been out working with the shepherds again," he said. "She'll be back again tomorrow."

Cassidy caught herself before she asked Aaron if the shepherds had been to Stony Breaks again. She reminded herself that such things were not common topics of conversation in the village, and revealing what the goatherd had discussed with her might have been saying too much. Instead Cassidy had just thanked Aaron, and ended up following him back to the stablehands' quarters.

Later Cassidy lay in her bed in one of the big communal bedrooms, listening to the soft chorus of snores and nasal breathing, unable to fall asleep. She stared up at the pale plaster of the ceiling and tried to decide what to do next. There was no longer any doubt in her mind that she was going to have to do *something*.

Cassidy's mind seemed to have slipped into full run then; it was no longer so easy to just keep putting aside the things she kept thinking about. Part of it was Rowena's complicity, she was sure; knowing that there was even one other person in the village with her who didn't believe in that world-as-given was a powerful reinforcement to Cassidy's own doubts. Part of it was just momentum. Having discovered a discrepancy as large and glaring as the universal nonsexuality of the people there had started a process of investigative thought that just could not be put aside again, even for sleep. And part of it was fear. She could no longer ignore her suspicion that the persistence and return of her own memory would eventually put her into direct conflict with the reason for which she had been brought there.

Remarkably enough, the oppressive headaches that had plagued her earlier efforts to think or remember were gradually lessening in intensity. Sometimes if she concentrated too hard or for too long about one particular thing, the painful pressure in her skull returned. But Cassidy had found that she could ameliorate that discomfort by merely backing off and coming at the question from another angle. And the dread of a full-out pounding headache no longer kept her from doing everything she could to remember more.

Despite her initial insomnia, eventually Cassidy did fall asleep in the familiar dimness of the herdsmen's bedroom. And when she slept, she dreamed.

As was often the way of dreams, when she abruptly awoke from it, momentarily disoriented and tangled up in her bed covers, all she could clearly remember was the final part. And what she remembered made her flush with embarrassment and hastily glance around the still-dark room, filled with relief to assure herself that the occupants of the other beds still slept solidly. For it had not been the gray mare who had been clenched between her thighs in that dream, and the graphic physicality of the act in which she had been engaged still clung to her body with the sweet torpor of a thick syrup.

Briskly rearranging the covers, Cassidy tried to dismiss both the memory and the sensation of the dream. But there was one thing that reassured her as she drifted back into sleep. The imagined man with whom she had been coupling had not been Allen; his body had been far too lithe and slender for the burly sheriff. Her lover had been faceless, without identity—or perhaps rather, in the strange logic of dreams, he had merely been someone whose face and identity she could not then remember.

It began to rain again the next morning. Cassidy had to abandon her sessions in the breaking pen, but there was too much day left to just quit working entirely, so she brought some of the young horses into the barn, put them in box stalls, and spent the rainy afternoon fitting them with various pieces of tack. If there was one flaw in her unconventional method of training the colts and fillies, it was that the Villagers who would ultimately be using those horses did not have her Horseman's ability to handle or ride them without some artificial means of control. So Cassidy devoted some time to accustoming the horses to the various pieces of equipment, making sure that they would be trained in a more conventional manner, as well.

Cassidy honestly enjoyed her work with the young horses. It was the only thing that seemed to have earned her any respect at all with the Villagers—heaven knew her prowess as a bear hunter certainly hadn't—and she knew that it was an enduring link with the life she had led before she had been brought there. That combination made for a powerful incentive to do a good job; she often thought that Aaron must have realized that when he had urged Misty to let her work with the horses.

Near dusk, a transition that was made considerably murkier by the gloomy overcast skies of the afternoon, Cassidy stripped the last of the bridles, surcingles, and saddles from the young horses and turned them all out. Then she hauled the gear back to the barn's big tack room. It was not her duty to formally clean every piece of equipment that she used; there were other workers, stablehands, who did all of the heavy cleaning. But because she was a Horseman and because her respect for her equipment was something innate, Cassidy always wiped off the worst of the dirt and sweat before she put away any tack that she had used.

That evening as she sat alone in the cluttered tack room, the drumming of the rain on the roof and windows was rivaled only by the persistent grumbling of her empty stomach. She straddled one of the wooden saddler's benches, its seat polished smooth by dozens of rumps before hers, and laid out the bridles across her knees. Then she bent to grope in the small keg that held the rags and cast-off scraps of cloth that were used for cleaning.

She had already begun to pull the reins of the first bridle through the wadded-up folds of the dull, grayish cloth she had grabbed before she noticed that there was something different about that particular scrap of material. Pausing, she shook out the rag and spread it across her thigh. Then she stared at it thoughtfully for almost a full minute. Anyone watching her would probably not have noticed anything amiss. They would not have been able to feel the way her heart was racing or the sudden unexpected ballooning of the old familiar pressure inside her skull as she looked down at the tattered bit of cloth.

Cassidy slowly refolded the rag, forming a small square wad of fabric. Then she tucked the little packet into one of the rear pockets of her jeans and selected another cloth from the keg.

"We went out to Stony Breaks again," Rowena told her. "More sheep; I didn't think the village even *had* that many sheep!"

Cassidy and Rowena had slipped out again as soon as possible after the evening meal. It was still raining lightly, more of a mist than a shower, but they had not gone up into the dairy's haymow that time. Cassidy had become more cautious about frequenting any one spot for their meetings. Instead they stood in the narrow paved alleyway between the hog barn and the sheep barn, leaning back against the side of the hog building so that the overhang of the roof protected them from the worst of the wet. In the thin watery light of the oil lantern that Cassidy had taken from its hook inside the hog barn door, she could see that Rowena's expression was a mixture of exasperation and excitement.

"You don't think they're sending you out there because of us, do you?" Cassidy asked her quietly.

Rowena's brows arched. "Us? You mean because anyone's suspicious of all the time we spend together?" She shook her head, water droplets flying from her unruly hair. "Naw, they aren't smart enough to be suspicious. They're sending me out there because me and Billy can herd sheep!"

Flashing her a smile, Cassidy fussed with the lantern, trimming its wick as low as she could without dousing it. Filching the match had been harder than borrowing the lantern, but it was unlikely that anyone would miss either. Cassidy didn't want to take any unnecessary chances, but what she had to do that night could not be performed in the darkness.

"I'll tell you, Cassidy," Rowena went on—as she was wont to do if Cassidy didn't provide her with any interruptions—"now that I know about some of this stuff you've found out, nothing seems the same around here." She grinned raffishly. "It's really hard to keep a straight face around most of these guys, now that I remember about sex!''

"Well, I think I've found something else that's important,'' Cassidy told her, passing Rowena the dimmed lantern. She reached into her jeans pocket and pulled out the dingy scrap of cloth. Turning so that Rowena could see it in the muted glow of the lamp, she shook out the rag and held it up.

Rowena frowned, squinting as Cassidy unfurled the unimpressive little swatch. "What is it?'' she asked.

Holding the cloth stretched out between her hands, Cassidy said quietly, "What do you think it is?''

The rag was torn from a piece of old clothing. It appeared to be the front of a T-shirt, one very similar to the ones both Rowena and Cassidy wore. Only the scrap that Cassidy held up contained a single printed word: ADIDAS.

Rowena studied the fabric for a moment, much as Cassidy had studied it in the seclusion of the tackroom. "Adidas,'' Rowena said slowly—except that she pronounced it "addie-das,'' with the accent on the last syllable.

Once again Cassidy felt her heart racing in her chest. Her mouth felt as dry as lint and she was uncertain of her voice. Slowly, deliberately, she looked across into Rowena's face and asked her, "Do you know what it means?''

Rowena frowned more deeply, shook her head, and then shrugged. "Uhn-uh,'' she admitted.

But that scarcely mattered to Cassidy. Her heart still wildly thumping, almost light-headed with excitement, she hoped that Rowena wouldn't notice the way her hands were trembling as she revealed her most recent discovery.

"Rowena,'' she said, "you know how to read, don't you?''

Rowena looked sharply at her; the frown remained and her brow was furrowed with suspicion. For just an instant, Cassidy feared she had miscalculated by showing the rag to Rowena. Because if what Cassidy believed she had discovered was actually true, she may have gravely blundered by even bringing up the subject, unwittingly violating yet another of the weird, hidden proscriptions of that world. But then the brunette woman suddenly smiled, and Cassidy was able to resume breathing.

"Shit!'' Rowena said. "Cassidy, how did you—?''

Cassidy interrupted her, holding out the torn scrap of T-shirt like a flag as she spoke. "Have you ever seen anything here with writing on it? Pieces of cloth or paper—even a sign or a nameplate? Rowena, does anyone else here know how to read?''

"Shit," Rowena said again, more solemnly then, her broad face creased in thought. "No, there's nothing with writing on it here; or at least nothing I've ever seen." Her expression grew anxious, her hazel eyes bright in the wavering, rain-washed light of the lantern. "But I know how to read—right? Addie-das," she repeated, almost reverently.

"Adidas," Cassidy said, gently correcting her pronunciation.

"Adidas!" Rowena exclaimed. Grinning then, she triumphantly met Cassidy's eyes. "Cassidy, I can *read*!"

"Yeah, you sure can," Cassidy said, clapping Rowena on the back. "But no one else around here seems to be able to—or if they can, they're sure hiding it pretty well." Cassidy's voice dropped, revealing the depth of her own incredulity. "Rowena, what kind of a society is this? What kind of people can get along without a written language?"

A little snort of laughter escaped from Rowena's lips, a sound that even in her excitement she still tried to stifle. "The same kind of people who can get along without sex," she pointed out.

"You and I can read," Cassidy went on, her own excitement regenerated by that discovery. "We just never realized it because there wasn't anything here that was *written*. Rowena, we didn't forget *how* to read—we just forgot that we already *knew* how to read."

Rowena cocked a brow quizzically. "Cassidy, what are you saying? Do you think that all the other people here can read, too—but that they just don't read or write because it's—*slipped their minds*?"

"I don't know," Cassidy admitted. "But I still think that most of them—maybe all of them—came here from somewhere else; and that means that some of them must be like us."

But Rowena was shaking her head. "No, that means that some of them maybe *were* like us—before they forgot everything they ever knew."

"Forgetting everything is part of it," Cassidy said. "I'm sure of that. We all were supposed to forget everything."

"Then why do you still remember? And why do I know what you're talking about?"

"I don't know!" Cassidy repeated, more loudly than she had intended.

Both of them were silent for a few moments as the implications of what they had discussed sunk in. The only sound was the muted grunting of the pigs in the hog barn and the steady drip of water from the barn roof. It was Rowena who spoke first, all humor gone from her tone.

"You said before that there must be someone here who knows how we all got here—someone who might be able to tell us how to get back."

Weighted by caution, Cassidy nodded almost reluctantly. "When I was with the Horsemen, I overheard them talking about it." She hesitated momentarily before going on. "It has something to do with their Warden."

"The Warden of Horses? Oh, great!" Rowena said in dismay. "Cassidy, from what everyone says, he's some kind of thug!"

"Who says that—Misty?" Cassidy retorted. Then her voice dropped, lowering in determination. "Rowena, I don't care if he's a homicidal maniac who eats raw sheep for breakfast. If he knows anything about how we got here, he might be the only one who can help us get back."

The next morning Cassidy was working in the breaking pen when she heard Mike calling for her. She had just mounted up for the first time on a trim little rose-gray filly, a horse that four days ago had barely been halter broken, and Cassidy's first reaction to the big man's bellowing summons was bald annoyance. She had worked hard to win the filly's confidence, and she resented the interruption at such a critical phase in her training. But she could hardly just ignore the head stableman. She reined in the filly and slowly dismounted again.

"Cassidy?"

Mike was so tall that when he stood outside the round pen's high fence, his mop of unruly black hair stuck up over the top rail. Despite the fact that she had managed to develop and maintain a civil working relationship with the man, Cassidy still could not overcome her ingrained mistrust of him. He peered between the poles, his deep-set eyes narrowed.

"The mayor's looking for you," he said.

"What?" Cassidy said, even though she knew she had heard him correctly.

Mike knew it, too. "Go on," he told her, "I'll take care of the horse."

He moved around to the pen's gate where Cassidy met him, leading the gray filly by the reins. "She's up at the field house," he said.

As she strode across the barnyard toward the field house, Cassidy's mind churned. It was a beautiful morning, the kind of perfect temperate summer day that often followed a rain, but Cassidy suddenly lacked the ability to appreciate it. As she walked across the grassy verge and onto the broad paved street, she looked past the nearest house to the low slope of the village fields, where a scattering of blandly clothed men and women were wielding hoes amid rows of soybeans. But she looked at them without really seeing them. Rowena's flippant words from the night before kept coming back to haunt her: *These people aren't smart enough to be suspicious.*

No one's too dumb to be suspicious! Cassidy thought warily.

Cassidy hadn't been back to the field house since her first afternoon in the village. But she didn't have any problem finding it again on her own. The village just wasn't that big, and by process of elimination the field house wasn't too hard to pick out from the stultifying sameness of the surrounding houses. She even recognized Ruth Ann, the birdlike woman who had tried to poison her with her herbal brew. She was sitting on a bench on the field house's wrap-around porch, peeling potatoes into a big metal tub.

"Wipe your boots!" she cackled sharply at Cassidy, watching her pass with eyes that were as bright and black as a crow's.

Inside, the field house was dimly lit by ambient light and nearly deserted. Most of the tables and chairs had been pushed aside and stacked as if someone had been cleaning the floor. The large room smelled of stale smoke and sausage. Cassidy hesitated just inside the doorway, scanning across the gloomy expanse of empty tables until she saw three figures near the fireplace. Two of the people were Misty and Allen; the third was a man she didn't recognize. And although she hadn't heard a word spoken, Cassidy somehow had the impression that they had been arguing before she walked in the door.

"Come over here, Cassidy," the mayor said, beckoning.

Allen and the stranger were seated at one of the field house's wide wooden tables, but Misty was standing. She remained standing as Cassidy crossed the big room. "Sit down," she said. It was, as usual, neither a suggestion nor a mere pleasantry.

Cassidy glanced over at Allen as she slid onto one of the plain wooden chairs. It was the first time she'd seen him since the afternoon she had killed the bear, a period of absence about which she realized she felt a curiously ambivalent mixture of irritation and relief. But if she expected any overt reaction from Allen, she would have been disappointed. His expression did not change when she sat down; his face was solemn, his sandy-gold eyes unblinking beneath his bushy brows.

Neither Misty nor Allen moved to introduce the other man. Cassidy took him in with a quick, surreptitious look that soon became an outright stare. He was tall and lanky with thinning blond hair and a hairline that had receded far enough to lend prominence to his tanned forehead and pale blue eyes. He wore the same kind of coarsely woven tan clothing that was typical to the area; it took Cassidy a moment to discover why his particular attire seemed unusual. Then she realized that he was wearing something around his neck, a strip of patterned blue fabric that was knotted under the collar of his tunic. The man was wearing a necktie.

Surprise and amusement at the discovery occupied Cassidy so thoroughly that not only did she continue to frankly stare at him, she also failed to realize it when Misty asked her a question. It was only when she felt Allen's booted foot kick hers beneath the table that Cassidy's head jerked up.

"Excuse me—what did you say?" she asked Misty.

The gray-haired old woman was every bit as dour and thorny as Cassidy had remembered; and her voice, deceptively soft, still had the same power to chill. "I said," she repeated sharply, "now that you've had a chance to get settled in here, I expect you'll be better able to answer my questions."

Rather than apprehension, Cassidy felt a surprisingly strong resolve. Looking directly at the bony old crone, Cassidy thought acerbically, *I wouldn't count on that, you old bat!* But what she said, her jaw tightening even as she nodded, was "Ask whatever you want."

Misty took a step forward so that she stood in front of Cassidy, looking down at her. "When you rode with the Horsemen, what other people did you meet?"

The question was not what Cassidy had expected; for a long moment she couldn't even think of the truth, much less a satisfactory lie. "Uh, no one," she finally blurted out. "We never met anyone else—at least not until we started following Allen and the other Villagers."

This seemed to be the answer Misty expected. Whether or not she believed it was something Cassidy couldn't tell for certain. She was still too baffled by the direction of the woman's interrogation to be able to interpret Misty's reaction accurately. She had expected to be called out about her suspicious association with Rowena; instead Misty seemed to be returning to the subjects she had grilled Cassidy about when she had first come to the village.

Still gazing down at Cassidy, the mayor said, "You're telling me that in all the time you rode with the Horsemen, they didn't make contact with anyone else?"

The old woman's dark and remorseless eyes fixed Cassidy in an unshakable hold; she found it impossible to look away. "I was only with them for a couple of days," she reminded Misty. "We didn't see anyone else."

"They didn't mention any other people—someone they were going to meet, perhaps? Or someone they were looking for?"

Cassidy had to make a conscious effort not to squirm. It was ridiculous—she easily outweighed the bony old woman, and probably could have beaten the crap out of her in a fair fight. But this was not a fair fight, and Misty's soft smooth voice carried a world of menace.

"No," Cassidy lied. She was damned if she was going to mention the Warden to that old fart, especially since they seemed to hold him in such contempt. "All they wanted were horses; they were looking for people who had horses."

Out of the corner of her eye, Cassidy saw the lean blond man exchange a swift glance with Allen. The man's face was composed, his pale eyes cool. His tie no longer made him seem amusing; in fact, there was nothing about the stranger that seemed innocuous. She remembered the stiff and sudden silence in the field house's big room when she had first entered. She was certain that Misty and the two men had been arguing; had it been Cassidy's fate they had been debating?

Cassidy shot a brief and surreptitious glance at Allen, but the sheriff sat stolidly contemplating his own big hands, which rested before him on the surface of the table with the fingers loosely laced together. It was obvious she would not be able to count on him to defend her in any way. Well, the hell with him, then, she thought; she could handle Misty on her own. If the mayor's questions weren't about her and Rowena, or about the Memories, how bad could they be?

"They never spoke of anyone else?" Misty persisted in that incongruously modulated voice. "Maybe someone else who might be looking for horses, too?"

Cassidy shook her head for emphasis. "No," she reiterated, the lie strengthening with each repetition. "We didn't see anyone else, and they never talked about anyone else—at least not in front of me."

To Cassidy's surprise, Misty suddenly made an abrupt dismissive gesture at her and said, "That's all then; you can go back to work now."

Cassidy hesitated, startled by the unexpected dismissal. To keep from gaping at Misty, she quickly looked instead to Allen and the blond man. But both of them remained silent and expressionless.

"Go on now," Misty repeated, making a shooing motion with her sinewy hands.

Cassidy pushed back her chair and got to her feet. She was still confused, but that feeling was rapidly being replaced by a sense of relief and an eagerness to get away from the thoroughly unpleasant old woman. With a stiff little nod to the mayor and the two men, she turned and strode swiftly toward the field house door.

Outside on the porch, Ruth Ann looked up with a toothy but humorless grin as Cassidy hopped down the steps. The beady-eyed woman's cackling laugh followed Cassidy as she hiked furiously up the wide and sunny street.

Cassidy expected to feel relieved. After all, Misty hadn't even asked her about anything important, and she still hadn't given any indication that she even knew anything about Cassidy's discoveries, her subversive activities with Rowena, or the Memories. But the expected relief failed to remain rooted as Cassidy strode purposefully back toward the barns. Instead a vague and poorly-defined sense of dread nagged at her, and her thoughts kept returning to Misty's puzzling and obsessive questions. What was the old woman trying to get from her? Did she suspect anything of what Cassidy had discovered since she had been in the village? Cassidy didn't think so, because she could not believe the mayor would be so disinterested if she had suspected anything. But if that wasn't Misty's concern, then just what the hell was she so stubbornly searching for? The possibilities were almost enough to give Cassidy a headache.

By the time she had reached the edge of the barnyard, Cassidy slowed her manic pace and willed herself to relax before she tried to return to her work with the young horses. There was no way she could be calm with them when she still felt so much inner turmoil. In the shade of the towering wall of one side of the horse barn, she leaned for a moment against the smooth bark of a small linden tree and waited for her breathing to return to normal. She closed her eyes and pictured the man with the necktie, the blue-eyed stranger who had been arguing with Misty and Allen before she had entered the field house—the man who had then sat there and said nothing. Who was he? And what did he have to do with—

"Cassidy?"

Fortunately, Allen had spoken her name before his big hand had landed on her shoulder. Even at that, Cassidy nearly jumped out of her skin in surprise. She spun around to confront him. "Shit!" she exclaimed when she saw who it was, her reaction a mixture of shock, relief, and anger.

Allen actually took a step backward. His retreat was a reaction that would have been amusing given their relative sizes, had Cassidy not been so totally spooked by his sudden appearance behind her. She had been so deep in thought that she had never even heard him coming up after her.

Allen did not apologize for startling her. Cassidy had to grit her teeth and remind herself once again that she should not expect such a normal response from anyone there. Rather, he looked down soberly at her and said without preamble, "I wouldn't tell Misty anything but the truth if I were you. She can always tell when someone is lying."

Cassidy stared up at him, squarely and somewhat defiantly. "You think I'm lying to her?" she asked him.

But even as Allen had not felt contrite for having startled Cassidy by coming up behind her, he was not then baited by her show of antagonism. "I don't know if you are," he said. "I'm just telling you that she can always tell."

"Fine," Cassidy said. Pivoting sideways, she neatly stepped away from between Allen and the trunk of the linden tree. "I'll keep that in mind the next time she wants to interrogate me!"

Cassidy moved forward, starting to walk briskly away from Allen, propelled by a surge of anger she had not realized had been laying so close beneath the surface of her emotions. Was she angry at Allen, angry at Misty—or just angry at whatever hidden forces had brought her there in the first place, robbing her of her memory and her other life? For the moment it hardly mattered. Cassidy realized that in some perverse way she actually *enjoyed* the anger; it felt empowering, and it was long overdue.

Allen caught up with her in a few long strides, reaching out to grip Cassidy by the shoulder and forcing her either to stop or try to drag him. Cassidy spun around, ready to confront him with the full glory of her newfound anger. But when she was actually facing Allen again, the vehement words seemed suddenly frozen in her throat and he, too, looked down at her in uncertain silence.

Allen was tired, bone-weary and worn out. Cassidy was chagrined to discover that she had not even noticed it earlier when they had been in the field house. Looking up into his bearded face, she saw that his eyes were sunken with fatigue and rimmed with deep lines that had not been there before. Cassidy suddenly remembered where Allen had probably been for the last two days and what he had been trying to do.

"Are the—did you find the rest of the yearlings?" she asked him hesitantly.

Allen shook his shaggy head. Something in the simple motion spoke of an unutterable weariness that went far beyond the limits of mere physical fatigue. "We found two more dead ones yesterday," he said. "Ripped apart. But not the last four—not yet, anyway."

Cassidy found herself extremely aware of the touch of his big hand on her shoulder. Clumsily she stumbled to direct her thoughts toward some conclusion. "That's why Misty was asking me all those questions again, wasn't it? You don't think it was Horsemen."

Allen looked directly at her for a moment. He seemed reluctant to discuss the disappearance of the horses with her. But finally he shook his head again.

"Naw, I don't think it was. Horsemen are more careful about stealing horses, and they sure wouldn't have any reason to kill them." He paused again, studying her face with an intensity that quickly dispersed what little had been left of Cassidy's earlier anger. "Besides," he added then, "it's not just horses that've been disappearing."

Cassidy's mind raced. "The sheep at Stoney Breaks—" she began.

"Yeah, sheep," Allen confirmed. "Horses and sheep and cattle—even hogs. And we aren't the only ones with trouble."

"The man in the field house—?"

Allen shrugged, finally dropping his hand from her shoulder. "Rodney, the sheriff from Silverstone." He glanced away for a moment, his eyes panning the cloudless morning sky. Then he looked down at Cassidy again, shaking his head.

"I don't know," he said. "Maybe I never should have brought you here."

Anger, like fresh flame from smoldering ash, reignited in Cassidy. "You think I had something to do with this?" she demanded of him. "I told Misty and I'm telling you: The three Horsemen I rode with were the *only* people I saw here before you pulled me from that flooded creek—and they sure didn't go around killing horses! If you don't trust me, why the hell did you take me with you? Why did you bring me here? Why didn't you just leave me there to drown?"

During her tirade Cassidy had automatically stepped forward. She found herself standing practically under Allen's chin, but she was too angry to back off as she glared up at him, as if daring him to reply.

But Allen ran the strong blunt fingers of one hand back through the thick tangle of his hair and met her challenge with calm resignation. "I didn't mean because I didn't trust you, Cassidy, I just meant because you're different," he said. Again, it was not an apology, merely an explanation. "With all the troubles we've been having, these territories aren't a safe place for you. No one will understand that you're . . ." His voice trailed off, a lack of articulation born as much of weariness as of his inability to explain himself. "It might have been better for you," he said finally, "if I'd left you out there with the Horsemen."

It was the closest thing to honest concern that he had displayed for her since Cassidy had met him. Surprised and disarmed, she was rendered temporarily speechless.

Allen looked down silently at her. Every time she was away from the burly sheriff for a while, Cassidy forgot just how big he was. His shoulders looked twice as broad as hers and his big tanned hands, while scarred and stained, were curiously expressive when he used them to gesture.

"The other day in the valley," he said, "why did you go after that bear? I told you that if there was any trouble you should go get Meggie and the others."

In spite of herself, Cassidy was incredulous. "That bear would have killed you!" she exclaimed.

But Allen was unruffled. "It could have killed you, too," he reminded her. "Then the damned thing would have gotten away clean. You were supposed to go get the others, so the bear wouldn't get away."

Cassidy understood his pragmatic logic even if she didn't subscribe to it. Tamping down her irritation, she said evenly, "The others would have come anyway; they heard the shots."

Allen couldn't argue with that. Temporarily outmaneuvered, he considered her explanation in thoughtful silence.

Cassidy tried not to look up at him. Instead she fixed her gaze on a point somewhat lower, near the collar of his coarse tunic, where she was fascinated to note the rhythmic throbbing of his pulse beneath the surface of the tanned skin of his throat.

"Did it ever occur to you," she asked him, "that I thought it was important to save your life?"

Allen blinked. "That bear could have killed more horses," he said. "The horses are more important to the village than I am."

Once again Cassidy did not bother to point out the obvious: The bear had not been behind the loss of the yearlings. She feared that something far more ominous was, but she was not about to debate that point with Allen then. "Yeah?" she said. "Well, maybe you were more important to *me*."

Then she turned on her heel and walked away from him, around the side of the horse barn. This time Allen did not follow her. When she got back to the breaking pen and finally looked back, Cassidy could see Allen trudging across the barnyard, his head bent, his hair ruffled by the breeze.

That evening Rowena did not appear in the herdsmen's kitchen for supper. Allen wasn't there, either, but that wasn't unusual, and Cassidy told herself that she didn't particularly want to see him anyway. The vague sense of discontent and apprehension that had been dogging her all day was only exacerbated by Rowena's absence. Cassidy wondered if she had been wrong in thinking that Misty suspected nothing about the two of them.

After supper Cassidy was so deeply immersed in thought as she left the kitchen that she didn't even notice Rowena approaching her in the near darkness of the dirt lot between the dairy and the horse barn. When she looked up and saw the goatherd, her sense of relief and joy was so great that Cassidy found herself feeling embarrassingly grateful for Rowena's presence.

"Hey, save me any leftover pie?" Rowena teased her.

"Where the hell were you?" Cassidy demanded, trying unsuccessfully to conceal her relief.

Rowena shrugged, falling into step beside her. "Aw, one of my goats broke her leg. I had to wait after milking until Paula would come and set it."

Abashed by her own insensitivity, Cassidy quickly offered, "I'm sorry, Rowena—is she going to be okay?"

"Sure," Rowena said, "she's a goat, not a horse!"

They walked together in silence for a while. They both had become so familiar with the layout of the buildings, alleyways, pens, and paddocks that they could have navigated their way around the barnyard in total darkness. The night was not completely without light, but the two women knew exactly where they were going and slipped past the edge of the dairy as easily as two shadows gliding over the ground. When they reached the slope behind the sheep barn they climbed for a few minutes, until they reached a huge pile of fieldstones that had been dumped there by the village's farm workers.

When both of them had selected and straddled appropriate boulders, Rowena spoke into the darkness. "What's the matter, Cassidy?" she asked. "Did something happen today?"

Rowena's perceptiveness was such a radical departure from the typical nonchalance of the other Villagers, Cassidy didn't know whether she was going to laugh or cry. Reluctant to do either, she quickly said, "I got another grand summons from Misty."

Rowena shifted her rump on her rock. "What did the old crow want?"

"Same thing as last time: Answers I don't have to questions I can't figure out." Purposely skirting the details, Cassidy moved on to conclude, "Whatever's going on, she's convinced I've got something to do with it."

Rowena gave a little snort. "For all you know, maybe you do," she pointed out.

At her friend's quip, Cassidy felt her melancholy mood lift slightly, and she was doubly grateful for Rowena's friendship. There were a lot of things she had not yet shared with the goatherd. Sitting there on the fieldstones in the warm darkness of the summer evening, Cassidy suddenly felt impelled to risk changing that.

"Rowena," Cassidy said, "when you first got here, first got to Green Lake, did you ever . . . dream?"

Looking across at Rowena, Cassidy could just barely make out the dim outline of her body, like an exaggerated appendage of the pile of big stones. In the calm blackness of the sheep meadow, the only sound seemed to be the gritty chirping of the crickets. And in the sudden stillness, Cassidy wondered if she had made a mistake in asking the question.

"A dream," Cassidy began slowly, "is like a—"

Rowena's voice was so low and breathless that at first Cassidy could barely recognize it as that of her friend. "I *know* what a dream is," Rowena said. When the brunette suddenly leaned forward toward her, Cassidy could see that Rowena's hand had flown to her mouth in an automatic gesture of disbelief. "Geez, Cassidy—I know what a *dream* is!"

Cassidy realized that her heart had suddenly began kicking in her chest. She felt the shivery warmth of excitement flush through her limbs. "Rowena," she said, "did you—have you had any dreams since you've been here?"

Rowena hesitated, her hands pressed to her chest as if to control her own heartbeat, her fingers knotted under her breasts. "I'm not sure; I think maybe I did." She leaned closer to Cassidy again, her clothing carrying the faint smell of goats. Her voice had grown completely earnest.

"At first—when I was in Green Lake—I had some kind of fits. At least that's what they called them: fits."

"Dreams," Cassidy murmured. Then aloud, she told Rowena about her own experience among the Horsemen when she'd had the nightmares. She did not reveal the subject of the bad dream, but explained, "They don't know what dreaming is; they don't have any idea. So they call it 'fits.' "

"Have you had any more dreams since you've been here?" Rowena asked.

"Yeah," Cassidy said, not wanting to have to elaborate. "Not any more that scared the locals, though."

Rowena hesitated for a moment, then said, "I guess dreaming must be one of those things we were supposed to forget, huh?"

"I think so," Cassidy agreed. "But now that you remember what dreams are, maybe you'll start having them again. If you do, try to remember what they were about."

"Do they have to do with the Memories?"

"Not exactly," Cassidy said. Then, reluctantly, she gave Rowena the gist of her own latest dream.

Rowena chuckled appreciatively in the darkness. "Now that'd be the kind of 'fit' that'd really give these yahoos something to wonder about!" she said. "I'm starting to understand why they kicked me out of Green Lake."

"Yeah, me, too," Cassidy assured her. "You were too normal to fit in there."

Both of them were silent again for a moment. From down the long slope, Cassidy heard the distant creaking sound of someone working the big pump for the water cistern in the barnyard. Farther still, a solitary dog barked a few times. The village was shutting down for the night. Soon she and Rowena would have to return, each to her own house, and try to fit in to a place where neither really fit any longer. Cassidy felt a lump rise up in her throat; she swallowed hard to keep down the unwanted tears. But despite her resolve, she found herself asking Rowena about the very things she had sworn to herself did not matter to her.

"Rowena, what do you know about Allen?"

"He was the one who brought me here," Rowena replied disingenuously.

Puzzled, Cassidy asked, "You mean from Green Lake?"

Cassidy could not see the grin in the darkness, but she could hear it in Rowena's voice. "Yeah, when they kicked me out of Green Lake!" She paused a moment, and when she went on her tone had become more sober.

"Cassidy, they thought I was crazy. I didn't fit in there—they didn't want me. I don't know what would have happened to me if Allen hadn't stepped in and offered to bring me back here. Now I can see why I didn't fit in there; but at the time I was just scared and unhappy. Allen brought me back here and convinced them to try me with the goats. He really saved my ass."

Just like he saved mine, Cassidy thought automatically. But just as automatically, she had to wonder *Why?* The bearded sheriff must have seen that Rowena was "different," too. Could that be the key to why he had protected Cassidy, as well? Being unable to discern a motive for Allen's puzzling protection had been unnerving enough; suspecting that his interest had something to do with the abilities she and Rowena shared in common was more than unsettling, it was threatening.

But for whatever reason Allen had intervened on Rowena's behalf, Cassidy realized that since she had come to the village, she had been rapidly undermining his efforts. *And now I've made sure that you won't ever fit in again anywhere in this world,* she thought, suddenly morose. But what she said was "Rowena, do you . . . like Allen?"

Again the invisible grin was clearly evident in Rowena's inflection. "You mean 'like' like—or *really* like? Not that it makes much difference around here," she added. "I'm afraid he's just like the rest of the guys in that regard."

Cassidy's awkward silence told Rowena as much as any words could have. "Wow, Cassidy," she said into the uncomfortable span of silence, "you and—and *Allen*?"

Cassidy sighed, softly but purposefully. "No, not me and Allen," she corrected. "Not me and anybody—not in this place."

Later, as they made their way back down the rolling hill toward the sheep barn and the rest of the barnyard, Rowena consoled Cassidy with a determined piece of logic. "Look at it this way," the brunette said. "It's one more damned good reason for wanting to get back to where we came from!"

But Cassidy already had all the reasons she needed; she had more reasons than she had hope. Beyond the basic longing to find out who she was and where she had come from, she had more pressing reasons for wanting to return to her own world. For with each passing day, her safety grew more and more imperiled, and the need to find the answers might soon become a literal matter of life and death.

Chapter 14 ◀▥

Several days later, in the middle of a night that was slashed by a rambunctious thunderstorm, Cassidy again was deep in the throes of another dream.

In the dream, she was struggling in the embrace of someone's arms, grappling with him for control of a rifle that was interposed between their bodies. At first she thought it was Allen with whom she wrestled, for it was his gun they were fighting over. But her antagonist was not the sheriff; it was a shadow-man, his identity maddeningly obscured.

As the fruitless struggle continued, the rifle suddenly began to change form. Its dull metal barrel split open, unfurling like the petals of a flower, each separating prong then swelling and uncoiling like a roiling streamer of smoke that curled up around Cassidy and her phantom opponent until—

Cassidy was catapulted out of that fitful sleep by someone vigorously poking her in the side.

"Come on, get up! Cassidy!"

Groaning in protest, Cassidy rolled over in bed. A dim figure loomed over her. She recognized the distinctive aura of Marcia, the women who slept in the bed next to hers. Despite the village's impressive indoor plumbing, Marcia apparently never bathed. Before Cassidy could ask her what the hell was going on, she heard shouting from outside the house. The voices were loud enough that Cassidy didn't need any further explanation as to why she had been awakened.

"Fire! Everybody out—*fire!*"

Barely a minute later, Cassidy was stumbling out the doorway of the stablehands' house, hopping to pull on her second boot. Wind and a spray of rain hit her full in the face as she tripped down the front steps. Hastily orienting herself, her gaze swept the barnyard.

The stormy sky was like a black blotter, soaking up what little light spilled from the houses. People running across the wet grass were visible only in dull relief against a backdrop of thrashing rain the color of dark slate. The shouting seemed to come from everywhere.

"Meggie!" Cassidy cried, lunging forward to grasp the arm of the familiar blond girl as she dashed past. "What's happened? Where's the fire?"

Meggie swung around but kept on moving; Cassidy had to run alongside her to keep up. "They think it started in the little barn," Meggie shouted as a volley of thunder boomed overhead. "We're trying to keep it from spreading!"

The "little" barn was not exactly the most aptly named building. It was little only in relation to two of its closest companions, the huge dairy and the horse barn. It was an L-shaped two-story structure, bigger than the hog barn and nearly as large as the sheep barn, that was used mainly to store wagons and other farm implements. Its upper floor was used as a workshop for the making and repair of smaller hand tools.

As they approached the little barn, Cassidy still did not see any sign of fire. People were milling around in the rain, some of them carrying lanterns and buckets. There was a lot of shouting but no one seemed to be in charge. Then she and Meggie came around the far side of the building and the full force of the storm's wind hit them.

Acrid smoke, the same murky color as the wet night, streamed past them. Gasping, Cassidy choked on a breathful and began to cough. Her vision blurred as the smoke filled her eyes.

Meggie grabbed Cassidy's arms and dragged her farther, past the wind-torn billows of smoke and out into the fresher air of the lashing rain. She gestured emphatically. "We're getting water from the cistern and the dairy tank!" she shouted. "Help find all the people with buckets and get them over here!"

Cassidy hesitated a moment, trying to figure out how to avoid having to return through the stinging pall of smoke. Then she began to run around the far side of the building, keeping herself upwind from the fire. As she ran she couldn't help but consider the essential irony of the situation. The Villagers may have had running water and flush toilets in their houses, but they were appallingly poorly equipped to fight something like a barn fire. First of all, whoever had designed the layout of the barnyard had obviously never considered what would happen if one of the structures were to catch on fire. The barns, which all were not only almost totally made of wood but were also filled with flammable materials like hay and straw, were too close together to be isolated from the flames successfully. It may have been a convenient arrangement, but from a safety standpoint it was stupid. Most of the animal barns had running water inside, but there wasn't sufficient water pressure in the pipes to get water out to the walls or roofs of the buildings. The only sources of water outside of the barns were the watering tanks and the main cistern.

As Cassidy came around the edge of the little barn and saw the uncoordinated efforts of several of the herdsmen, who were clumsily trying to form a bucket brigade from the tank outside the milking yard, her only thought was *Hell, the rain is probably doing more good than they are!*

Cassidy heard a muffled crashing sound from inside the burning building; suddenly bright orange flames appeared at the roofline, lapping eagerly along under the eaves. After that, Cassidy had no more time to spend faulting the judgment of the village's founders. She grabbed a bucket right out of the hands of a confused mucker and raced back around to the other side of the barn.

Cassidy couldn't find Meggie again, but there was no problem recognizing what had to be done. A double line of bucket-passing workers stretched from the cistern to the doors of the besieged building. She took a place near the head of the line. By then her clothing was soaked through to her skin, but she was soon grateful for the driving rain. The heat from the fire was intense, and she could not imagine how the last people in the line, those who were furiously ferrying the water in through the doors, could bear it.

As she grappled with the slippery buckets, Cassidy realized she was not frightened by the fire. Even as the flames raged higher, they did not seem like a personal threat to her. Her response was machinelike, driven by some confusing blend of pragmatism and loyalty. Oddly enough, for the first time since she had come to the village, she felt as if she could understand something of the motivation behind the people's daily lives. She merely did what had to be done.

Cassidy was not sure how much time had passed since she'd been rousted out of bed—time had long since ceased to have much meaning—when she heard someone shouting her name.

Slinging back her dripping hair off her flushed and gleaming forehead, she looked up without even missing the next bucket that was being passed to her. A rain-soaked figure appeared alongside the line of bucket brigadiers, holding up a guttering lantern.

"Cassidy, come on!" Aaron shouted. "I need you!"

When Cassidy got closer to the wiry man, she could see that his hair and clothing were tarred with wet soot. There was a smell to him, too, a sharp and unpleasant stink that was more than just smoke.

"The fire's jumped to the hog barn," he explained grimly. "There's still some sows with piglets in there—we've got to get them out!"

Cassidy couldn't for the life of her imagine why Aaron was in charge of the pigs, but it didn't seem to be an opportune time to ask. She quickly followed him across the storm-washed barnyard, her soaked boots slipping in the freshly churned mud, her stringy hair plastered to her wet cheeks. Outside the long, low hog barn several of the swineherds milled in apparent confusion. One woman was carrying a mud-splattered shoat by its armpits, the young pig squealing in protest. Fat, sausagelike coils of smoke rolled out past the lamp-lit doorway and then were attenuated and snatched off into the darkness by the swirling wind.

"This is the only door left that isn't blocked yet by smoke!" Aaron shouted, gesturing with the lantern. The light leapt wildly over the wet side of the barn. "Steven is in there already, but it's gonna take at least the three of us. The damned sows keep trying to attack him, and then they double back!"

Cassidy's gaze jumped from the barn door, where the faint reflected flicker of flames was already dancing in the shadows, to the swineherds pacing uselessly in the rain, and then back to Aaron's weathered and dirty face. *I'm not going in there!* she thought. *What does he think I am—stupid?*

"What the hell about *them*?" she demanded, waving at the swineherds.

But Aaron just doggedly shook his soot-streaked head, repeating impatiently, "I need you; it's going to take all three of us!"

Not only stupid, but expendable! Cassidy thought glumly, eyeing the dim and smoke-filled interior of the hog barn. Aaron had only partially convinced her. But before she could further debate his command, she heard a sound that sent a chill down her spine and suddenly compelled her to obey him.

Trapped inside the burning building, the pigs were screaming. There was no other term for the dreadful sound they made. As she stumbled over the wooden threshhold and groped ahead of her for the first pen partition to guide her, Cassidy could hear the horribly shrill and unnervingly humanlike cries of the sows and the higher-pitched, ear-splitting shrieks of the terrified piglets. Danger or not, it was a sound she could not ignore.

Inside the building the smoke was almost unbearably thick. Cassidy's nostrils burned and her eyes began to tear so profusely that she could hardly keep them open. She cracked her shins on something hard—the metal edge of the two-wheeled feed cart from the feel of it—and nearly fell to her knees. Then she felt Aaron's sinewy fingers digging into her shoulder and heard the black man's voice rasping in her ear.

"Crawl!" he croaked at her. "Get down and stay close to the floor!"

Cassidy didn't have much choice. If she had breathed much more of the smoke, she would have passed out. Dropping down to the paved floor of the aisle, she felt the relatively cool stone beneath the palms of her hands. Her knees ached from crawling on the unyielding surface. From behind her, Aaron was pushing her forward. She could hear his hoarse breath coughing and gasping practically in her ear as she scuttled along.

The screaming of the pigs grew much louder, almost deafening, as they crept forward through the hellishly smoky barn. Cassidy could not believe that Steven had made it in that far; she kept expecting to bump into his unconscious body sprawled on the floor in the gloom. What she encountered instead as she scrabbled along the wet dirty floor was one very large, very agitated sow.

The big sow was milling about in the aisleway, screeching in fear and confusion as she tried to call all her piglets to her side. Behind her, forming a garish backdrop to her anxious pacing, the entire section of the exterior wall of the building was aflame. In the leaping, strobing light of the fire, Cassidy could see long dark forms, like scattered logs, strewn across the hog barn floor. It took her a few seconds to realize that they were all dead pigs. Beyond their bodies, huddled in fright against a pen partition, she saw three other sows with their litters. And beyond the sows, squirming on his belly with his clothing plastered with pig shit, was Steven.

"Get her!" Steven shouted, waving at the enormous sow in the aisle. "If she goes out, these ones will follow her!"

The slightly built young man looked like an apparition from hell. His hair was blackened and hung in greasy strings; his filthy clothing was torn and covered with manure. He gestured again at them, even more vehemently, his eyes like two vivid, clean splashes in his otherwise grimy face.

"Get her!" he insisted.

Aaron spurted past the sow, his hands and knees slipping in the pig manure that liberally splattered the aisle floor. Next to the fire-painted bulk of the huge pig, Cassidy thought he looked laughably insignificant. She figured that Aaron had about as much chance of chasing the sow out of there as the pig did of sprouting wings and flying out through the roof.

The big sow swung around, her tiny eyes squinting painfully at the intruder. Her babies were shrieking in terror, the sheer volume of their high-pitched cries making Cassidy's ears ring. Enraged and confused, the sow lunged for Aaron. With a deceptive agility, he scurried past her and tried to goad her into chasing him back up the aisle. But as he sprang by her, she shot forward, her front tusks raking his thigh. Aaron collapsed with a grunt.

There was no gray mare to supply her with impetus; Cassidy acted instinctively and totally of her own volition. When she saw Aaron go down in the hog barn aisle, she realized that one of several things was about to happen: The furious sow would stop to savage him, or she would just trample over him and take after Cassidy instead, or she would turn and run back deeper into the burning barn and wait for the roof to fall in on her and the rest of the hogs. Cassidy didn't like any of those choices. So she took the only action she could think of on such short notice.

Scrambling to her feet, Cassidy vaulted up over the huge sow's side and landed on her back, straddling her. The pig's body was as broad as a horse's, but more rounded and far bristlier. There also was nothing to hang on to. The ride was going to be a short one, so Cassidy wanted to make the most of it. She gave a loud whoop, a sound that was nearly as shrill and discordant as the pigs' screams, and slammed both booted heels into the sow's massive sides.

Probably more surprised than intimidated, the sow lurched forward down the aisle. All around her, Cassidy could hear the staccato popping of burning wooden shingles dropping down from the barn's roof, landing in the aisle and pens like little shooting stars. The heat had grown tremendous; Cassidy felt her eyebrows pucker. But as they raced toward the doorway, the relative coolness of the thunderstorm slapped her body like a cold shower. Just inside the doorway the sow suddenly dodged sideways to avoid the same feed cart that Cassidy had almost fallen over on her way in, and Cassidy went sailing off from her back. She landed on the stone floor, dazed and coughing, while a veritable stampede of squealing piglets thundered past her.

Cassidy had just gotten to her hands and knees and was reaching for the first pen partition to pull herself to her feet when the other three sows and their babies raced past her. Again she was knocked to the floor, a surface that by that time had become well greased with pig manure. Cursing, she looked back into the burning building. For a moment she could see nothing except a murk of smoke, spasmodically illuminated by flashes of light as flaming bits of wood dropped down from the roof. Then she saw two figures emerging from the inferno, the shorter one limping as the taller one half pulled, half carried him along.

As she reached out toward Steven, someone grabbed Cassidy around the shoulders from behind. Someone else lifted her legs and she was dragged, not quite carried, from the blazing hog barn. There was a certain indignity in being towed along on her heels across the muddy barnyard, but the finer aspects of her unceremonial transportation were somewhat lost on Cassidy. The rush of relief she felt at escaping the heat, noise, and choking smoke greatly ameliorated any sense of outrage she might have felt under better circumstances. As she was lowered to the ground, she tilted her head back and let the rain pelt against her flushed cheeks, heedless of its sting. She didn't even mind that she was sitting right in a puddle of water.

"You okay?"

It was Steven at her elbow, crouched in the mud, his long hair tangled like a snarl of wet grass around his filthy face.

Blinking the rain out of her eyes, Cassidy nodded. "It was hotter than hell in there," she rasped at him. "How could you stand it?"

Steven just grinned. In the dark turbulence of the storm-lashed yard, the white edge of his teeth glinted like pearls. "Pretty good trick with that sow," he told Cassidy, speaking practically into her ear to be heard above the sounds of the wind, fire, and shouting. "I think I'm gonna tell Allen to have you start breaking all of our pigs to ride, too!"

"Where's Aaron?" Cassidy asked, looking hastily around them. The yard was churning with scurrying stablehands and herdsmen, few of them seeming to be engaged in any organized activity. But she didn't see the gray-haired black man anywhere.

"He's okay," Steven said quickly. "Otto is taking him up to the house to clean up his leg."

Cassidy shook back her wet hair. "Steven, why were you . . . ?"

But she found herself trying to ask the question to empty space; Steven had disappeared again, back into the smoky gloom that blanketed the yard.

Cassidy rolled herself out of a sitting position and onto her hands and knees. The cold mud stung the fresh abrasions on her hands and her knees ached sharply. She knew she was going to have impressive bruises. Even the rain no longer felt refreshing. But as she quickly surveyed the chaos in the trampled barnyard, she realized she had to get moving again. The fire had already spread to the sheep barn; unless the wind suddenly shifted or abated, the huge dairy would be next. With a grunt of effort, she pushed herself to her feet. There were things that had to be done.

When Mike found her some time later, Cassidy was commanding the crew at the sheep tank. Shouting out instructions to the poorly organized shepherds, she had put together a bucket brigade. When the head stableman rode up, she was furiously working the handle of the pump.

Mike's horse splashed up to the sheep tank, his big hooves sending up a spray of slurried mud. Thunder crashed overhead. The stout horse—wet, he was the same color as the soaked earth that dirtied his legs and belly—pranced nervously, the metal shanks of his bit gleaming in the firelight.

"Cassidy, I need you!"

Cassidy's head jerked up. She clung to the pump handle, momentarily too breathless to speak.

Drenched by the storm, his dripping hair plastered to his oblong skull, Mike only vaguely resembled the shaggy-haired giant Cassidy was used to seeing around the horse barn. His face and clothing were grayed with a patina of wet ash, and Cassidy saw that the chunky knuckles of one of his meaty hands were scraped and bloody.

"What?" she panted up at him, annoyed and resentful at the interruption.

"I need you," he repeated gruffly. "Get your horse and come with me."

Too exhausted to mount an effective protest, Cassidy did not dispute Mike's curt summons. Besides, the chance to get up on the gray mare and leave the strenuous and largely useless monotony of the bucket brigade suddenly seemed like a very attractive alternative. She paused only long enough to reach out and grab the arm of the first man in line at the tank and drag him up to the pump to work the handle. Then she turned and hopped down into the mud.

Mike was gone, but Cassidy caught up with him by the paddocks. As she hobbled stiffly across the trampled barnyard, which had become a dark morass gluey with muck and littered with bits of charred wood and ash, she could see why the stableman had selected her to help him. He really hadn't had much choice.

When the fire had been discovered in the little barn, all of the horses in the adjacent horse barn had been turned out into the paddocks. As the fire had intensified and spread, the paddock gates had been opened, too, freeing the horses to flee out into the pastures beyond. Other than Mike's own frightened mount, there wasn't another riding horse in sight. And Cassidy suspected the horses out in the fields would be too spooked to be caught, even if Mike had tried to ride out after them. Ironically, he had to rely on Cassidy exactly because she was a Horseman.

As she sloshed across the muddy yard, Cassidy called the gray mare. It was an act as automatic as keeping her balance in the treacherous footing.

By the paddock fence Mike struggled to keep his prancing horse under control. He had to use both of his hands on the reins, and Cassidy could see the gleaming half-moons of the whites of the brown horse's eyes as he rolled them toward the burning buildings. The gelding's nostrils flared, fluttering in distaste and agitation in the smoky air.

"Wind's starting to shift," Mike said tersely as soon as Cassidy had reached him. "The broodmares were turned out into that little river-bottom pasture, but now they're gonna be right downwind from the fire." He gestured, a motion that further spooked his horse and made the big gelding almost drop out from beneath him. "We gotta get down there and turn them out through the back gate, before it gets any worse."

Away from the heat and stink of the burning sheep barn and the laborious exercise of working the pump handle, Cassidy felt the chill of the cold rain anew. She shivered so hard that her teeth rattled. Still, Mike's errand seemed infinitely preferable to the losing battle to quell the fires.

"How many mares are out there?" she asked him.

Mike hesitated a moment; his reluctance to reveal information to her was almost a reflex. To the Villagers—and to Mike most of all—Cassidy was still first and foremost a Horseman, and his instinct to guard the village horses from her was deeply ingrained. Then he realized why Cassidy was asking. If the two of them were going to have to cover that pasture alone in the dark and storm, she would need to know how many horses needed to be accounted for. "Fourteen," he said, still begrudgingly, "and nine of those with foals."

Mike's skittish earth-colored horse whinnied sharply. Like a ghost from out of the gloomy veil of smoke that blurred the darkened paddock, the gray mare appeared, gliding like a wraith over the short wet grass. Without even slowing she tucked up her forelegs and neatly cleared the top rail of the closed gate, landing with a thump in the soft earth on the other side. Then she swung hard about and slid to a halt before Cassidy, her breath shooting out in twin gusts that sent the smoky mist scattering.

For a brief moment Cassidy ringed her arms around the big mare's neck, burying her cheek in the pungent-smelling mass of the horse's wet mane. The mare's slick coat was dark from the rain, and water ran in distinct runnels from her rump and barrel. But the heat from the big body was strong and comforting, and as Cassidy hopped up onto the broad back, she felt the welcomed warmth quickly seep through the chill of her clammy jeans.

It took Mike a minute to unlatch the gate. His fretful horse kept sidestepping away from the paddock fence, but the burly stableman was astute enough to realize that if he was to step down from the saddle, he might not be able to hold the headstrong gelding. Finally the gate swung free. As they rode together across the closely cropped ground, Mike had to struggle to keep his horse from bolting, so strong was the gelding's instinct to flee from the fires.

Although Cassidy's entire body ached exquisitely, she felt a strange charge of energy once she was up on the gray mare's back. There was more shared between her and the horse than just body heat; on the mare's back Cassidy felt whole. Lightly gripping the gray's sides with her calves and knees, Cassidy sat poised alertly, peering ahead into the stormy darkness. She was the first to reach the paddock's far gate. She leaned forward to unlatch it and let Mike's jittery brown gelding skitter through; then she refastened the gate behind them.

As they started down a lightly wooded slope in the serpentine river-bottom pasture, Mike was able to gather both reins in one hand again. The brown gelding was still anxious, but being able to move away from the fires was calming him. Other than the occasional and more distant flashes of lightning, the night was stultifyingly dark and the unfamiliar ground was dotted with brush and trees and rocks. The force of the storm seemed to be declining, but the shift in the wind was carrying a persistent pall of smoke out over the field, which, combined with the gloom, made visibility almost nonexistent. Cassidy rode lightly and trusted the gray mare.

They reached the river. Even in the dimness, its silvered surface rippled moltenly. Mike led the way along the narrow dirt track that had been worn by the horses' countless passages along the water's edge. Cassidy realized then that the rain was finally diminishing, too, reduced to a feathery drizzle. Water-filled hoofprints gleamed like little half-moons in the lightning's faint glow. She leaned forward and rubbed the gray mare's neck, her own neck and shoulders so stiff that her muscles stung in protest.

The river-bottom field was a fairly small pasture, usually used to contain the riding and work horses that were in need of a temporary lay-up. It was too rough and too far from the barn to be normally used for mares and foals. Even though the mares were unfamiliar with the field, Mike expected the smoke would drive them down along the river toward the far end of the long pasture. There a gate opened up into one of the sprawling, partially wooded meadows used to pasture the young stock. If luck was with them—admittedly luck had not been much in evidence so far that night—Cassidy and Mike could hope to not have to do anything more than just open up another gate and free the mares and foals to run into the larger pasture.

As Cassidy's eyes adjusted to the darkness, the terrain took on slightly more definition. The shapes of bushes and small trees, their leaves glistening with rain, slipped by. And the smoke, although less noxious at that distance, still slithered like an oily film through the damp night air.

The first thought that sprang into Cassidy's mind when she heard the muffled thud of hoofbeats from behind them was that she and Mike had made the wrong assumption: The mares and foals were not at the far end of the pasture near the gate after all; they were still behind them—and coming up fast. Then she realized, in that vague but very certain way particular to anyone who had spent their life working around horses, that it was not the band of mares and foals that she was hearing. The hoofbeats were too hard, too regular, too driven. The horses were carrying riders.

Mike had also heard the pounding hoofbeats. He began to pull in his excited gelding, using both hands on the reins again. Twisting in the saddle, he threw Cassidy a quick look.

"Sounds like Meggie and the others must've caught some of their horses," he said, trying to hold in his sidestepping brown gelding.

But Cassidy knew that Mike was wrong. Cocking her head, she listened intently as the distant drumming drew closer. No, not village horses, she thought, her fingers suddenly knotting in the gray mare's mane. There was something about the sound, some quality of gait or beat that was incompatible with the way the Villagers rode. And there was something else—something out there both alien and sinister, something that made the hair on Cassidy's arms and on the back of her neck stand up with an aching stiffness.

She stared uselessly into the misty gloom, the dark air a nearly impenetrable wall of smoky opalescence, as the cadence of galloping hooves grew louder. *Not village horses—*

Twisting around on the gray mare's back, Cassidy tried to signal Mike. She didn't want to have to shout with riders approaching, but even as she desperately gestured to the big stableman, she feared it was too late for evasion.

Beside Cassidy, Mike was trying to rein in his snorting gelding. Anxious and impatient, the dark horse swung around in a circle, nearly slamming into the gray mare. The thrumming of hoofbeats continued to grow closer. But that was not all. Then Mike suddenly froze in his saddle, and Cassidy was certain that he, too, sensed that they were being followed by more than Villagers.

The gray mare spun around, her forefeet leaving the ground as she pivoted sharply on her haunches, her muscles coiled like springs. But the mare was not frightened, she was excited. Cassidy had begun to believe that the gray mare did not know what fear was.

Cassidy on the other hand was intimately acquainted with that particular emotion, and she felt the familiar tingly flood of adrenaline spike along her veins as her wet legs gripped the mare's broad barrel. Something was coming—the awful something that lay out there in the clinging darkness, apart from the approaching riders. But it was too late to try to outrun it, if indeed that would ever have been possible. Other horses might be outrun, but this *thing* . . .

As she glanced frantically around for some kind of cover, Cassidy was dismayed to find that the brush along that stretch of the riverside trail was sparse and low—too low to conceal something the size of their horses, even in the near darkness. The edge of the riverbank, a rocky cutback that was only about knee-high, would have been even more useless.

At least we can get off the damned trail, so we don't just stand here and get run over, Cassidy thought with grim resignation. She called out to Mike as she urged the gray mare forward; but even as the horse responded, she saw that Mike would not be able to follow her.

As daringly acrobatic as any of Rowena's goats, the stout brown gelding shot straight up into the air and then flipped sideways, like a leaping sunfish. Mike was literally spun from the saddle. Cassidy heard the dull thud of the big stableman's body impacting with the wet ground. But before she could slip down from her horse's back to go to his aid, she saw something that kept her frozen on the gray's back.

For one weirdly logical moment, Cassidy thought it was smoke. That would have at least had the virtue of having made some sense; but the reality made no sense at all.

Something—or some *things* actually—were racing toward them over the dark, fog-shrouded ground. Even when the things were close enough to see, Cassidy had difficulty comprehending what she saw. So huge that she could make no true estimation of their seemingly endless length, the shadowy creatures were like tremendous undulating coils of greasy smoke, each easily the diameter of a horse's girth. And like the bizarre transmutation of the rifle barrel in her dream, each roiling shape assumed a separate life of its own.

Too stunned to move, Cassidy just cringed in horror as the filthy-looking serpentine forms silently flowed at her—over her, *through* her—at an incredible rate of speed. As they passed, despite their insubstantiality, they carried an odor that was gaggingly foul, a stinging miasma of burned and rotting flesh that filled Cassidy's nostrils like a clot of clinging slime. Instinctively she ducked her head, squeezing shut her eyes as something wet and cold pelted the side of her face.

The gray mare whinnied loudly, swinging around beneath

Cassidy. Cassidy opened her eyes just as the tall shadowy forms of several galloping horses burst from the murky darkness, headed directly toward her. Of the hideous smokelike creatures, no trace remained.

Their speed unchecked, the horses and riders bore down on Cassidy with surprising swiftness, the thunder of their hoofbeats filling the damp air. Four mounted figures passed by her so quickly that Cassidy, still reeling from what she had seen, didn't even get a good look at them. But she heard a harsh clanging sound ring out as the horses clattered over the rocky trail, and suddenly she recognized one of the reasons why their hoofbeats had sounded so different to her: The horses were shod.

Wheeling her mare around to watch the rapidly retreating riders as they slipped back into the darkness, Cassidy didn't even hear the next set of horses coming until they were almost on top of her. There was no time for evasion, even if there had been somewhere to hide.

Mike's gelding gave a shrill whinny, a sound of either excitement or challenge or both. Beneath her, the gray mare reared. Only her fingers, still tightly knotted in the long silvery mane, prevented Cassidy from sliding off the wet slickness of the mare's back. The gray's thin nostrils fluttered, ballooning her sides with the intake of breath. Three more horses and riders burst out of the mist, steam pouring like smoke from their sleek bodies.

The gray mare rose again, half rearing that time, an excited little squeal escaping her. But Cassidy loosed her hold on the horse's mane. Heedless of the danger these new riders might present, she slid over the mare's side and dropped down onto the muddy path. The only thing she was worried about at the moment was Mike.

After locating Mike's bulky body in the slippery grass, Cassidy crouched down beside him, calling his name. She would hardly have described the big stableman as her friend, but he had hit the ground hard, and he was not moving.

"He'll be all right. He just got the wind knocked out of him."

The voice from directly behind her was feminine, raspy but somehow soft.

Still crouching, Cassidy spun around, her boots slipping on the wet turf. She had not heard anyone behind her, yet the mounted woman was almost on top of her. Looking up from her position on the ground, the huge dark shape of the woman's horse loomed enormous. Stunned and speechless, all Cassidy was capable of was staring up at the horse and rider.

The night air was like sludge—cool, wet, and gray—and there was barely enough light by which to see. But the mounted woman was so close to Cassidy that she could see the fine network of distended veins beneath the wet silky hide of her fidgeting horse, as well as the distinctive cut and marking of the woman's clothing. Then her horse snorted and blew through its nostrils, sending the foggy air swirling, and the movement finally shook Cassidy from her nearly trancelike state.

"Who—who are you?" Cassidy demanded shakily, still crouched defensively beside Mike's motionless body.

In the dimness the woman's lips curved in a small smile. She was young, Cassidy's age at the most, and had an elegantly spare face with high lean cheekbones and dark deep-set eyes. Her hair was a riotous crown of short curls, undefeated by the dampness and held in nominal check by a braided band of leather that encircled her forehead. Her expression was openly curious.

"I think a better question would be, who are *you*?" the woman said.

The young woman's clothing owed nothing to the drab sort of homespun favored by the villagers. Her V-necked tunic and tight trousers appeared to be made of softly tanned leather, and were lavishly festooned with fringes that seemed more ornamental than functional. The surface of the leather clothing was elaborately incised and dyed with a darker pattern of fanciful design, particularly across the arms, chest, and lower legs. It was the first time since she had left Yolanda and the boys that Cassidy could remember having seen anyone wear something not only for its utility but for its decorative value.

The curly-haired woman's horse—a mare, Cassidy finally noted—snorted again, shaking her head impatiently. The mare was easily as tall as the gray and just as powerfully built, with a small white star on her forehead and a coat the crisp color of freshly brewed coffee. The horse was ornamented as well, with thin, dyed, leather strips and tiny feathers braided into the wavy masses of her mane and some kind of oblong pendant made of dark leather or wood suspended by a narrow thong at her chest. The mare sidestepped a half pace, making the pendant swing. It was only then that Cassidy realized the horse wore no tack.

Cassidy stared up at the horse and her rider, all of her perception reduced to the quick and anxious hammering of her heart. "You're a Trooper," she blurted out, surprised by the hoarseness of her voice.

"And you appear to be a Horseman," the woman said, her expression perplexed.

Hoofbeats drummed again over the wet turf. Two horse-size shadows reappeared out of the clinging gloom from farther up the trail. Cassidy had been so startled by the appearance of the woman before her that for a few moments she had entirely forgotten that the rider had not been alone—just as she had momentarily forgotten the very real danger she was in. Because as she had gazed up at the leather-clad woman who sat with such casual ease astride the star-faced mare, Cassidy had only been able to think of one thing: The woman was a Horseman—a real Horseman, and not the poor imitations that Yolanda and her would-be apprentices had been. She was one of those Troopers to which the others had aspired, possessing the full realization of the skills Cassidy herself was still only dimly aware of.

And if, as Yolanda had said, the Troopers served the Warden, then the woman just might be Cassidy's one hope to find a way out of that place.

"Valerie?"

The call, in a strong masculine voice, came from one of the other two riders who had halted their horses just beyond the range of Cassidy's vision in the near darkness. Cassidy knew the other two Horsemen were waiting there on their wet and sweat-slicked horses; she could hear the moist gusting as the animals exhaled forcefully and impatiently.

The woman on the brown mare glanced over toward her companions. "Coming, Walt," she said calmly.

Empowered by a sudden surge of desperation, Cassidy bolted to her feet. "Wait!" she cried out, her hands raised in entreaty. "Those—those *things* you're chasing . . . what *are* they?"

The brown mare had been sidestepping, impatient to get past the dark form of Mike's body where he still lay sprawled on the muddy ground. But the woman called Valerie restrained the horse, looking down at Cassidy with widened eyes.

"You saw them?" she asked, her throaty voice low and intense.

Cassidy nodded vigorously. "I've dreamed about them," she rasped, her voice a rough whisper.

Valerie's penetrating gaze traveled rapidly up and down Cassidy's wet and filthy form, her lips pursing thoughtfully at what she saw. "You're a Horseman and you dream," she murmured, almost to herself. "What are you doing among these farmers?"

"I don't belong here with them!" Cassidy said, her hands

still raised in supplication. "Please—I have to get to the Warden! Take me with you!"

"Valerie, let's go! They're getting away!"

Cassidy had not even noticed one of the other Troopers had ridden closer until the man had spoken. Her head turned helplessly in his direction, immediately prepared to plead her case with him, as well.

The man who had spoken, the man Valerie had called Walt, was not quite close enough to Cassidy for her to see him as clearly as she had been able to see the woman, but she could tell that his style of clothing and ornamentation were similar to hers. He was a tall, fair-skinned man with short dark hair and a neatly trimmed beard. And although he sat his horse, a white-stockinged chestnut, with a casual poise, Cassidy could tell that both he and the horse were impatient and eager to be off.

Valerie's mare shifted more anxiously, resisting the woman's restraint, eager to join her fellows in the chase. "What do you know of the Warden?" Valerie asked tersely.

"I know that he leads the Horsemen," Cassidy replied with a breathless urgency. "That he believes in the Memories."

The woman Trooper froze; even her restive horse suddenly ceased her nervous prancing. "You have the Memories?" Valerie asked.

"Yes!" Cassidy cried, "Please—take me with you!"

The coffee-colored mare swung around, momentarily concealing Valerie's face from Cassidy's view. The Trooper had to use the sheer force of her bond with the horse to keep her from just bolting. Valerie looked down at Cassidy, her expression a mixture of excitement and frustration. "We can't take you with us—not now," she said. "But you must go to the Warden."

Cassidy took a few steps toward Valerie, her waterlogged boots slipping on the muddy, trampled grass. "But *how*?" she asked. "I don't know where he is—I don't even know where the hell *I* am!"

Cassidy could see how badly Valerie was torn by her dilemma; but it was the Trooper's duty that ultimately won out. She reached down, stripping something from the brown mare's mane and tossing it toward Cassidy. "Go to the garrison," she called out as she finally let the horse spring forward again. "Give this to the guard, ask for me there!"

"Wait!" Cassidy shouted, her hands still raised impotently into the air. "Where is the garrison—how do I *get* there?"

But the big star-faced mare had already leapt away down the

boggy trail and was quickly swallowed by the same murky darkness that had so swiftly concealed her companions. Cassidy could only stand there helplessly, her boots sticking in the soft muck, as even the faint and muffled hoofbeats of the Troopers' horses faded from the dark, damp air.

When she could no longer hear the hoofbeats, she slowly bent and retrieved the small object Valerie had tossed her. It was one of the ornamental fetishes from the horse's mane, a whimsical device woven of horsehair, a tiny feather, and a few beads.

Cassidy might have stood there much longer, feeling utterly frustrated and abandoned, had not Mike given a deep groan. Spurred into action by the sound, Cassidy dropped down again beside the big man. She tried to help him sit up, but Mike just moaned and rolled away from her. In a moment she heard loud retching, and she found herself feeling a surprising sympathy for the burly stableman. The next time she tried to help him, Mike caught hold of her arms and pulled himself into a sitting position.

Shaking back his long muddy hair, Mike looked around in woozy confusion. Cassidy realized he must have struck his head when his horse had shied so violently.

"My horse?" he began hoarsely.

"He's right over there," Cassidy assured him. The brown gelding, considerably subdued, had not gone far. He stood with Cassidy's gray mare near the foggy riverbank, both horses matter-of-factly cropping off dripping twigs from the low brush that grew there.

"We've gotta—*damn*!" Mike swore, breaking off. He shook his head again, as if by doing so he could somehow shake off the solid ache in his skull.

"Maybe you better not try to move yet," Cassidy cautioned him. She was beginning to realize that Mike probably had not seen the creatures that had spooked his horse; or, if he had seen them, he did not remember it.

But Mike would have none of Cassidy's caution. "Our mares!" he exclaimed, struggling to get to his knees. "Damned Horsemen—our *mares*!"

"Okay, okay," Cassidy soothed, wincing as Mike's thick fingers dug into the flesh of her arms in an attempt to use her as a lever with which to attain his feet again. "Don't worry, we'll go after the mares."

"Damned thieves!" Mike spat, lurching up, propelled as much by his rage as by any physical capacity.

''We'll go after them,'' Cassidy repeated calmingly, stumbling after Mike as he staggered drunkenly across the slippery sod toward the horses.

Cassidy did not say it, but she knew that when they got to the end of the river-bottom pasture the far gate would be open and the mares and the foals would be gone. She also knew, although she would not have said that, either, that those mares and foals would be found somewhere out in the large fenced field beyond the gate, unharmed and safe from the smoke. She knew that the Troopers had not been there to steal horses, because from the moment she had laid eyes on Valerie she had known that they were not thieves. Cassidy knew with certainty what the Troopers were: They were *hunters*.

She didn't know what the foul creatures were that they were hunting, except that she was fairly positive that the hideous things were not hallucinations—they were *real*. They were real and the Warden was real, and Cassidy was going to find him, no matter what it took. The little feather fetish she had tucked in her pocket burned like a talisman, because Valerie's reaction had convinced Cassidy that the Warden of Horses was the key to the entire mystery that had brought and bound her to this strange world.

Chapter 15 ◀▥

As the first pearly-gray luminescence of false dawn touched the ragged remnants of the night's stormclouds, Cassidy stood with the gray mare beneath the softly fluttering leaves of the long row of beech trees that shaded the horse paddocks. Toward the east the rolling fields and wooded pastures looked freshly rinsed and serene under their light misting of morning fog. Even the birds were singing energetically, darting from dripping branch to drenched grass with all of their customary vigor. Only by looking west, back toward the barnyard, could the night's true devastation be seen.

By the time Mike and Cassidy had returned from the river-bottom pasture, all of the major fires had been extinguished. But even at dawn the remains of the hog and sheep barns still smoked and smoldered. The little barn, where it had all begun, had been reduced to nothing but a sunken pile of wet ash, punctuated by the skeletal fragments of a few blackened and fallen beams. There was a small pit in one corner of the dairy roof, as if the fire had tasted a sample of it and hadn't found the building to its liking. Miraculously the rest of the huge barn had remained untouched. Most of the murk that lingered in the gradually light-ening air was just mist then, not smoke; but the stink of burned wood and hay and the acrid odor of other scorched things still persisted. The barnyard was ankle-deep in mud, pocked with puddles that were still afloat with soggy ash.

Cold, dirty, and unbearably weary, Cassidy leaned closely against the gray mare's big solid shoulder, her stiff fingers slowly and carefully working through the snarls in the horse's damp mane. She felt a numbing sense of fatigue that went far beyond the bumps and bruises and aching muscles and yet her mind was surprisingly alert, energized by what had happened to her out along the river-bottom pasture.

Ever since the day Allen and the other Riders had brought her to the village, Cassidy had never given up hope that she could find out where she had come from, and how to get back there. Her alliance with Rowena and the amazing discoveries they had made together had only served to heighten her confidence that the mystery of this place could be solved. But the previous night marked the first time she had actually been given a specific goal.

Encountering the Troopers had been a watershed experience for Cassidy. For a time she had even doubted their existence. But then, ironically, by meeting Valerie and her Troop, Cassidy had not only confirmed their existence but also validated her own.

In the days she had spent in the village, Cassidy had often doubted her own sanity. What if she was wrong in her persistent belief about her past? What if there was no other place—no Slow World to return to? What if she was just . . . crazy?

But then the image of Valerie, looking down from the back of her mare with her eyes widening in recognition of Cassidy's knowledge, returned to sustain her belief. The Trooper knew what dreams were, what the Memories were, and her support had suddenly invested Cassidy with purpose.

Unwillingly, Cassidy's thoughts also returned to the horrific images of the roiling blackness she had seen along the riverbank: the creatures of the air that the Troopers had been pursuing. For the first time she had proof that the hideous things were not just hallucinations, they were real, and other people had seen them, as well.

In the puddle-dotted milking yard the dairy cows were lowing in the faint and hazy light. A small group of herdsmen, their soggy clothing still smudged with soot and mud, wrestled with the wooden bars of a makeshift gate. Pausing with her fingers hooked in the mare's mane, Cassidy let her gaze sweep slowly across the barnyard.

The Warden is the answer to all this, she thought. Even without Yolanda or her apprentices, Cassidy had no choice. She had to get to the Warden of Horses.

The sweep of Cassidy's gaze abruptly halted, caught by movement along the big dark, rectangular shadow of the side of the horse barn. Cassidy watched as a single figure made its rapid and stealthy way along the edge of the building to the paddocks.

By the time the figure had slipped through the gate and had started up the slope, she could see that it was Rowena.

The goatherd's clothing was wrinkled and spattered with filth; her usually exuberant hair lay flat and lank against her head. She moved across the wet ground with the cautious haste of someone reluctantly prodded into hurrying. As Rowena drew near enough, Cassidy could see that the tips of her dirty hair, as well as her eyebrows, had been lightly singed by last night's fire.

"Are you okay?" were Rowena's first words to Cassidy.

"Me? What about *you*?" Cassidy took a step away from the gray mare and toward Rowena. "You look like shit," she confided. "What the hell happened to your eyebrows?"

Grinning, her mouth a slash of clean in her otherwise grimy face, Rowena touched her fingertips to her brow. "Like 'em?" she said. "It's gonna be the new style around here, believe me!"

Cassidy's answering laugh owed more to her sense of relief at seeing Rowena again than it did to the proposed humor of her friend's quip. But even Rowena's grin didn't endure.

"Listen," Rowena said quietly, "Mike has some of the other stablehands looking for you. I don't think they know yet that you're out here."

Cassidy shrugged, distracted by her own plans. "He probably wants me to ride out with him and help gather up the horses," she said. The gray mare and Mike's gelding were the only two horses left in the village; the others were all still scattered in the far fields.

But Rowena was frowning. "I don't know, Cassidy. I think something is going on."

Cassidy looked intently at Rowena. For the first time in hours, she felt the oddly energizing tingle of adrenaline prickling at her nerves. Her voice automatically dropped as she asked, "What do you mean? What kind of something?"

Cassidy wasn't naive enough to believe that Misty was going to let her just ride off and leave the village, especially considering Cassidy's ultimate goal. She would have to slip away on her own, and the sooner the better. She had hoped to be able to say good-bye to Meggie, Steven, Aaron, and even Allen, but that wouldn't be very prudent. Riding out with Mike might be her best opportunity; Cassidy was certain the gray mare could easily outrun his gelding, and she would have a good head start before the rest of the Villagers caught their mounts. But Rowena's wary comment brought Cassidy to a state of instant apprehension.

Rowena took a quick, almost unwilling glance back over her shoulder at the shadowy barnyard that spread out below them in the faint light of dawn. Other than the herdsmen and the cows, the scene was eerily still. Rowena hesitated, licking her parched lips.

"Those Horsemen you and Mike met out by the river? People are saying that they had something to do with the fire. And Cassidy—I think they think that you had something to do with it, too."

Coming hard on the heels of Cassidy's newfound sense of purpose and direction, the idea seemed especially ludicrous. For a moment, Cassidy could only gape at her friend. "What?" she said. "I thought they said the fire was caused by lightning."

Cassidy had her own very serious doubts about that. She suspected those filthy smokelike creatures that had roiled along the river-bottom pasture had had something to do with the conflagration, a suspicion that had only been enforced by the Trooper's desperate pursuit of the greasy wraiths. But Cassidy never would have proposed anything so crazy to the Villagers.

But Rowena was shaking her head. "No, that's just what they thought at first. But the fire started inside the little barn—on the bottom floor, not on the roof. Cassidy, it was deliberately set."

"But—why?"

Rowena spread her hands helplessly. "They think the fire was just a diversion, something to keep us all busy and to get us to drive all the animals out away from the yard, so the Troopers could easily get at them."

Cassidy shook her head; not slowly, in negation, as Rowena had, but briskly, as if she were trying to clear it of something that defied understanding. "That doesn't make any sense," she protested. "Rowena, those Troopers didn't even steal any horses—and they could have had the whole lot of them! And as for me being in cahoots with them—well, if that was the case I sure wouldn't still be here anymore, would I?"

The look of sympathy and trust that Rowena gave her made Cassidy's face heat with shame; because recalling what had happened out there by the river made her suddenly remember that she had most definitely tried her best to go with the Troopers. And to her chagrin she also realized that if she had been given the opportunity to go with them, she would have done so immediately, without even thinking of Rowena and their promise to each other that they were going to find their way out of there together. But Rowena didn't seem to notice Cassidy's sudden discomfort; or if she did notice it, she mistakenly attributed it to Cassidy's indignation at having been falsely accused of collusion with the Horsemen.

"I know that, Cassidy," Rowena assured her. "But you know Misty; she's nuts about anything to do with Troopers. If Allen was here, he could probably talk some sense into her, but with—"

The brunette broke off, noticing the way Cassidy was again staring off in the direction of the barnyard. "Aaron," Cassidy said softly, her chin lifting slightly.

The lean figure of the wiry little black man was crossing the alley between the horse barn and the dairy. He was walking with a slight yet noticeable limp, but his pace was steady and purposeful. It was unlikely that he would draw any attention to himself in the nearly deserted barnyard. Cassidy was not surprised to see that he turned at the paddock fence and slipped through the gate.

"Uh-oh," Rowena murmured at Cassidy's side. "If anyone else saw him come out here, or follows him from the yard . . ."

But Cassidy just stood motionless, waiting silently as the grizzled man approached them.

As he came across the paddock, his bootheels sinking into the spongy hoof-pocked ground, Aaron's swiftly assessing gaze swept from Cassidy to Rowena and then back again. As he walked up to them Cassidy could see that his thigh had been quite expertly bandaged; the broad swath of white cloth around his legs was, in fact, the only clean thing on him. She also noticed that he had a large but shallow abrasion right above the thumb on his right wrist, undoubtedly another legacy of the incident in the hog barn. Aaron's eyes, bright as beads in the grimy stubble of his ash-colored face, were avid and shrewd, but his manner seemed totally ordinary, gruff but not unkindly.

"Misty's looking for you," he said. His tone was matter-of-fact, but there was an edge of warning in his expression.

Cassidy nodded shortly. "Yeah, so I've heard."

Aaron glanced sideways again, briefly taking in Rowena. Then he said, "She told me to go look for you." He paused, his eyes resting on Cassidy's dirty, weary face. "Of course, I told her I didn't know how long it might take to find you."

Cassidy took a quick, almost reflexive half-step forward toward the weathered little man, her hand flying up to grasp the front of his filthy tunic. "Aaron, I didn't do it—you know that, don't you?'' Cassidy's voice quavered and nearly broke. ''I didn't start the fire, and I didn't have anything to do with those Troopers!''

When she was standing that close to Aaron, Cassidy could see that there was a big patch on the shoulder of his tunic where the fabric had been so deeply scorched that its weave had lost all texture. The rough skin of his face was greasy with soot, and he still reeked of smoke and pig shit. Staring into his gleaming eyes, Cassidy suddenly realized just how little she really knew about him. She could not begin to fathom the depth of his strength and determination.

Aaron's expression barely changed; he seemed at the most to be mildly impatient with Cassidy. ''I know that,'' he said. His tone suggested that it was almost a reproach to his intelligence that Cassidy should even have to mention her innocence to him. ''But I don't run this village, and Misty's getting them worked up to a major set-to down there.'' His eyes narrowed. ''I know Allen had his reasons for bringing you here—but I don't think getting you hanged was one of 'em.''

''Hanged!'' Rowena exclaimed. ''After everything she did last night?''

But Cassidy just steadily met Aaron's gaze. ''Is Mike going to be okay?'' she asked, a little surprised to find that it really mattered to her, and feeling more than a little guilty that she hadn't asked after him sooner.

''Yeah, he's just wore out,'' Aaron said, ''just like the rest of us. So's that horse of his.'' Just the slightest edge of his white teeth showed under the curl of his dark upper lip as he added, ''In fact, wouldn't surprise me if that poor old horse just ain't up to much of a run right now.''

As obliquely as it was given, Aaron's implication was painfully clear. Cassidy was not the only one who realized she had to leave the village as quickly as possible.

Before Cassidy could respond to Aaron's comment, he was digging in his pants pocket. With his free hand, he caught hold of Cassidy's wrist and turned it palm up. Then his hand briefly covered hers, wrapping her fingers around the items he had transferred into it.

''Be careful out there, you crazy woman,'' Aaron said softly.

The intensity of her emotional reaction caught Cassidy by surprise; she felt her knees become as fluid as water. Her gratitude for Aaron's faith and complicity caused a lump to rise in her throat, making speech impossible. With sudden tears blurring her vision, Cassidy could only watch helplessly as Aaron turned and began to limp back across the paddock. Somehow she doubted that he would have allowed her to thank him, even had she been able to get the words out.

Cassidy swiftly shoved the articles that Aaron had given her— a couple of dozen sulfur-tipped matches and a folding knife— into her jeans pocket. As the old man passed out of earshot, she turned to Rowena and grasped her by her fleshy upper arms.

"Rowena, I've got to get out of here right now."

"No shit!" Rowena shot back. The guileless hazel eyes locked with Cassidy's. "And I'm coming with you."

Startled by Rowena's assertion, Cassidy had to fumble for words. "Rowena, you don't have to—they don't suspect you of anything. And I don't know how safe it's going to be where I'm going."

Rowena cut off Cassidy's earnest declaration with a no-nonsense shake of her head. "We're in this together, remember?" Rowena's voice thickened as she pushed on. "I want to go back home, too." Then she began to grin. "Anyway, Cassidy, you owe me: You made me remember *sex*! You don't think I'm gonna stay here now, do you?"

Cassidy was forced to grin back, but neither the expression nor the emotion lasted. "All right," she agreed, "but we've got to go *now*, while no one here is in any shape to come after us. With all this talk of hanging, I sure as hell don't want to still be around here once they finally start to catch their horses again!"

Or when Allen gets back, Cassidy couldn't help adding to herself, although the simple thought of the big bearded man was strangely painful, and she immediately pushed it aside again.

Turning to the gray mare, Cassidy quickly ran her hands down the sides of the horse's long supple neck. Lowering her head, the gray snorted softly into her tangled hair. Then, stepping back, Cassidy sprang up onto the horse's back. The motion was swift and automatic, but it set off a discouraging chorus of aches and pains in her exhausted body. For a fleeting moment as her cramped legs gripped to fit to the mare's sides, Cassidy's sense of purpose momentarily wavered. For all its faults, the village had become her home, her mundane little anchor in an alien land. To flee it so precipitously, stocked with nothing more than a handful of matches and a pocket knife . . .

Yeah, you could always stay here and get hanged, the acerbic little voice inside her head reminded her helpfully.

Good point, the rest of Cassidy's mind conceded. She shifted her buttocks slightly on the mare's spine, striving for the least uncomfortable position, and glanced down the slope toward the barnyard. Outside the dairy, Aaron was engaged in conversation with one of the herdsmen; the exchange did not look friendly.

Cassidy's gaze jumped to Rowena. "Let's go," she said with finality.

But a sudden stricken look had fallen over Rowena's normally puckish face. "Cassidy, wait—I have to get Billy!"

"*Billy?* Rowena, we can't take a goat with us."

But the brunette was adamant. "I can't leave him here, Cassidy; he's *mine*. I raised him from a kid!"

Cassidy looked down at Rowena from the gray mare's back, sympathy warring with impatience and fear. She shook her head with dogged insistence. "We can't take him, Rowena. He'd never be able to keep up; it wouldn't be fair to him."

Tears glistened on Rowena's soot-smudged cheeks. "I can't leave him here," she repeated desperately. "What if they *eat* him?"

Cassidy leaned forward over the mare's shoulder, reaching down for her friend's hand. "They won't eat him, Rowena," she reassured her. "They still need him." She squeezed the warm, dirty fingers in her own. "He's the only one who can keep the rest of those damned goats in line!"

Rowena gave a short, harsh little laugh, but it was largely reflexive and there was no conviction behind it.

Cassidy tugged firmly on her hand. "Besides, he's too tough to eat! Come on now, get up here behind me. We have to get out of here."

Her face still streaked with tears and grime, Rowena looked up dubiously at the tall plane of the gray mare's back. "I can't," she said.

"Sure you can," Cassidy said. "Here, I'll step her over to the fence so you've got something to climb up on."

"Cassidy, I can't—I don't know how to ride."

"You don't have to ride," said Cassidy blithely. "All you've got to do is sit and hang on."

At Cassidy's urging, the mare sidestepped over to the paddock fence. Awkwardly and with some further hesitation, Rowena climbed up onto the second rail and then lurched over onto the horse's broad back. Once she had scrambled astride, she clamped her legs around the mare's barrel and her arms around Cassidy's shoulders.

"Wait, not so tight!" Cassidy said with a grunt. "Grab me lower, around the waist. And you don't have to grip the horse so hard, or she'll start to buck!"

"I told you I don't know how to ride!" Rowena shot back through gritted teeth, but she complied with Cassidy's orders.

As the gray mare swung away from the paddock fence and stepped out from beneath the long row of beech trees, Cassidy looked back down the slope toward the barnyard. The sun was visible then, a brilliant sphere of ruddy gold light on the eastern horizon, slowly swimming its way up from the tattered remnants of the night's stormclouds. The long hill of the paddock was stubbled with green, each blade of grass hung with diamonds of dew. Farther below, in the milkyard, a visibly agitated group of field workers had gathered around Aaron, gesturing furiously while the little man merely kept shrugging and shaking his head.

Let him be safe, Cassidy prayed silently. *Don't let Misty blame him when she finds out I'm gone.*

They slipped through the back gate into the larger pasture, the mare's hooves nearly soundless on the wet turf. Cassidy felt the first real warmth of the sunlight on her bare and mudstreaked arms. The soft solidity of Rowena's body bumped gently, rhythmically against the back of Cassidy's as the gray horse started across the vast slope of the meadow.

Rowena's voice came nearly in Cassidy's ear, startling her. "You have any idea where the hell we're going?" she asked. It was not a complaint, but simple curiosity. Having resigned herself to leaving Billy, Rowena seemed to view their covert escape as something of an adventure.

Cassidy, on the other hand, understood some of the larger implications of the journey they were about to undertake. It was not an adventure, it was a mission.

"I don't know yet exactly how to find him," Cassidy admitted, urging the mare into a trot. Her voice was filled with determination. "But I do know that once we find this Warden of Horses, we'll find out how to get back home again."

And as the gray mare's ground-eating gait rapidly began to put the village far behind them, Cassidy could not allow herself to consider any other possibility.

The Slow World
will continue in
Book Two:
The Warden of Horses
from
Del Rey Books